THEOCRITUS

A SELECTION

IDYLLS

1, 3, 4, 6, 7, 10, 11 and 13

EDITED BY
RICHARD HUNTER

*Reader in Greek and Latin Literature in the University of Cambridge,
and Fellow of Pembroke College*

CAMBRIDGE
UNIVERSITY PRESS

PUBLISHED BY THE PRESS SYNDICATE OF THE UNIVERSITY OF CAMBRIDGE
The Pitt Building, Trumpington Street, Cambridge CB2 1RP, United Kingdom

CAMBRIDGE UNIVERSITY PRESS
The Edinburgh Building, Cambridge, CB2 2RU, United Kingdom
http://www.cup.cam.ac.uk
40 West 20th Street, New York, NY 10011-4211, USA   http://www.cup.org
10 Stamford Road, Oakleigh, Melbourne 3166, Australia

First published 1999

Printed in the United Kingdom at the University Press, Cambridge

Typeset in Baskerville and Greek New Hellenic 10/12 [AO]

A catalogue record for this book is available from the British Library

Library of Congress cataloguing in publication data

Theocritus.
[Idylls. Selections]
A selection / Theocritus; edited by Richard Hunter.
p.   cm. – (Cambridge Greek and Latin classics)
Poems in Greek; commentary in English.
Includes Idylls 1, 3, 4, 6, 7, 10, 11 and 13.
Includes bibliographical references and index.
ISBN 0 521 57416 1 (hardback) ISBN 0 521 57420 x (paperback)
1. City and town life – Egypt – Alexandria – Poetry.   2. Country life
– Mediterranean Region – Poetry.   3. Pastoral poetry, Greek.
1. Hunter, R. L. (Richard L.)   II. Title.   III. Series.
PA4442.A5H86   1998
884'.01 – dc21   98-12922 CIP

ISBN 0 521 57416 1 hardback
ISBN 0 521 57420 x paperback

CONTENTS

CONTENTS

PREFACE

The need for a new commentary on Theocritus, and particularly one with a literary bias, is, I hope, self-evident. How far the present volume goes towards filling that need is a matter for others, but I should say that I do not think that I was ever so deluded as to aim to 'replace Gow', and (like Sir Kenneth Dover before me) I hope that both my debt to Gow's monumental edition and our abiding dependence upon it are clear from every page of my own commentary. I regret, of course, that there are only eight poems in the present collection, but I would have regretted much more the inevitable silences which a larger corpus would impose, within the (admirable) parameters of Cambridge Greek and Latin Classics. Moreover, the longer I worked on this book, the more these eight poems seemed to hang together in ways that I had never suspected, and I hope that some sense of this emerges from the separate discussions.

Another regret is that there has been no space to pursue *Nachleben* at any length. I have, by means of the sign >, indicated where a verse of T. has been an important model for Virgil, but I am only too aware that such mechanical devices conceal more than they reveal. Doubtless I have missed some examples, but some apparent omissions may reflect a judgement about what constitutes 'an important model' rather than oversight or ignorance.

My debt to willing friends and critics is, as ever, very large. Pat Easterling, Marco Fantuzzi, Philip Hardie, Ted Kenney and Laura Rossi commented upon a draft typescript and saved me from much that I would not have wanted to see the light of day; where I have shamelessly adopted their suggestions, they will, I hope, recognise genuine gratitude. John Henderson helped me to believe that I understood something of Idyll 7 and Eclogue 9; as always, Neil Wright listened patiently and refused to settle for easy answers. Susan Moore's copy-editing taught me more than I care to confess.

An award under The British Academy Research Leave Scheme helped bring this project to completion.

CONVENTIONS AND
ABBREVIATIONS

1. Except where it is relevant to the argument, poems of the Theocritean corpus are all cited as though 'genuine'; thus, 1.7, 23.7, *not* 1.7, [23].7.
2. Translations are my own, unless the translator is identified.
3. The works of Homer (*Il.*, *Od.*), Apollonius (*Arg.*) and Virgil (*Ecl.*, *Georg.*, *Aen.*) are cited by title only.
4. (i) Unless otherwise specified, references to Callimachus are to the edition of R. Pfeiffer (Oxford 1953–9).
   (ii) *EA* = Bion, *Epitaphios Adonidos*.
   EB = [Moschus], *Epitaphios Bionis*.
5. Abbreviations for periodicals usually follow the system of *L'Année Philologique*.
6. In the spelling of Greek names, ease of recognition has been the principal aim. The names of authors are usually 'latinised', whereas other names may be transliterated.
7. The following editions of Theocritus are cited by author only:
   A. Fritzsche, 2nd ed., Leipzig 1870
   U. von Wilamowitz-Moellendorff, Oxford 1905
   K. Latte, Iserlohn 1948
   A. S. F. Gow, 2nd ed., Cambridge 1952
   K. J. Dover, London 1971
   C. Gallavotti, 3rd ed., Rome 1993
8. Modern works cited by author and date only are listed in the Bibliography.
9. Collections of texts and works of reference are abbreviated as follows:

CA	J. U. Powell (ed.), *Collectanea Alexandrina* (Oxford 1925)
CEG	P. A. Hansen (ed.), *Carmina epigraphica Graeca* (Berlin / New York 1983, 1989)
CGFPR	C. F. L. Austin (ed.), *Comicorum Graecorum fragmenta in papyris reperta* (Berlin / New York 1973)

Chantraine	P. Chantraine, *Grammaire homérique* (Paris 1948–53)
CPG	E. L. Leutsch and F. Schneidewin, *Corpus paroemiographorum Graecorum* (Göttingen 1839–51)
Davies–Kathirithamby	M. Davies and J. Kathirithamby, *Greek insects* (London 1986)
Denniston	J. D. Denniston, *The Greek particles* (ed. 2, Oxford 1954)
FGrHist	F. Jacoby (ed.), *Die Fragmente der griechischen Historiker* (Berlin 1923–30, Leiden 1940–58)
GG	*Grammatici Graeci recogniti et apparatu critico instructi* (Leipzig 1867–1910)
Goodwin	W. W. Goodwin, *Syntax of the moods and tenses of the Greek verb* (ed. 2, London 1889)
GP	A. S. F. Gow and D. L. Page (eds.), *The Garland of Philip and some contemporary epigrams* (Cambridge 1968)
HE	A. S. F. Gow and D. L. Page (eds.), *The Greek anthology: Hellenistic epigrams* (Cambridge 1965)
K–B	R. Kühner and F. Blass, *Ausführliche Grammatik der griechischen Sprache. Erster Teil: Elementar- und Formenlehre* (3rd ed., Hanover 1890–2)
K–G	R. Kühner and B. Gerth, *Ausführliche Grammatik der griechischen Sprache. Zweiter Teil: Satzlehre* (3rd ed., Hanover / Leipzig 1898–1904)
KRS	G. S. Kirk, J. Raven and M. Schofield, *The Presocratic philosophers* (2nd ed., Cambridge 1983)
Lampe	G. W. H. Lampe, *A patristic Greek lexicon* (Oxford 1961)
LGPN	P. M. Fraser and E. Matthews (eds.), *A lexicon of Greek personal names* (Oxford 1987–)
Long–Sedley	A. A. Long and D. N. Sedley, *The Hellenistic philosophers* (Cambridge 1987)
LSJ	*A Greek–English lexicon*, eds. H. G. Liddell, R. Scott, H. Stuart Jones, R. Mackenzie (9th ed., Oxford 1968)

LfgrE	*Lexikon des frühgriechischen Epos*, eds. B. Snell *et al.* (Göttingen 1979–)
LIMC	*Lexicon iconographicum mythologiae classicae* (Zurich / Munich 1981–97)
Molinos Tejada	T. Molinos Tejada, *Los dorismos del Corpus Bucolicorum* (Amsterdam 1990)
Otto	A. Otto, *Die Sprichwörter und sprichwörtlichen Redensarten der Römer* (Leipzig 1890)
PGM	K. Preisendanz (ed.), *Papyri Graecae magicae* (2nd ed., Stuttgart 1973–4)
PMG	D. L. Page (ed.), *Poetae melici Graeci* (Oxford 1962)
PMGF	M. Davies (ed.), *Poetarum melicorum Graecorum fragmenta* i (Oxford 1991)
Polunin– Huxley	O. Polunin and A. Huxley, *Flowers of the Mediterranean* (London 1965)
Preisigke	Fr. Preisigke, *Wörterbuch der griechischen Papyrusurkunden* (Berlin 1925–7)
RE	*Paulys Real-Encyclopädie der classischen Altertumswissenschaft* (Stuttgart 1893–)
Roscher	W. H. Roscher (ed.), *Ausführliches Lexikon der griechischen und römischen Mythologie* (Leipzig 1884–1937)
Schwyzer	E. Schwyzer, *Griechische Grammatik* (Munich 1939–53)
SEG	*Supplementum epigraphicum Graecum* (Leiden 1923–)
SH	H. Lloyd-Jones and P. Parsons (eds.), *Supplementum hellenisticum* (Berlin / New York 1983)
SLG	D. L. Page (ed.), *Supplementum lyricis Graecis* (Oxford 1974)
SPG	R. Foerster, *Scriptores physiognomonici Graeci et Latini* (Leipzig 1893)
Stephens– Winkler	S. A. Stephens and J. J. Winkler (eds.), *Ancient Greek novels. The fragments* (Princeton 1995)
SVF	J. von Arnim (ed.), *Stoicorum veterum fragmenta* (Leipzig 1905–24)

Thompson, *Birds*	D. W. Thompson, *A glossary of Greek birds* (2nd ed., London 1966)
Thompson, *Fishes*	D. W. Thompson, *A glossary of Greek fishes* (London 1957)
TrGF	B. Snell, R. Kannicht and S. Radt (eds.), *Tragicorum Graecorum fragmenta* (Göttingen 1971–)

INTRODUCTION

1. THEOCRITUS

The only ancient text about T. which may be quite close in time to the poet himself is an anonymous epigram:

ἄλλος ὁ Χῖος, ἐγὼ δὲ Θεόκριτος ὃς τάδ' ἔγραψα
εἷς ἀπὸ τῶν πολλῶν εἰμὶ Συρακοσίων,
υἱὸς Πραξαγόραο περικλειτᾶς τε Φιλίννας·
Μοῦσαν δ' ὀθνείαν οὔτιν' ἐφελκυσάμαν.

(Anth. Pal. 9.434 = Epigram [xxvii] Gow)

The Chian is another, but I, Theocritus, the author of these works, am a Syracusan, one among many, the son of Praxagoras and renowned Philinna, and I have taken to myself no alien muse.

This is plausibly interpreted as an opening 'advertisement' for an early (third-century) collection of T.'s poetry; it distinguishes T. from a homonymous Chian writer and politician of the late fourth century.[1] That T. came from Syracuse (or at least Sicily) may reasonably be deduced from his own poetry (cf. 11.7, 28.16) and was the almost unanimous opinion of antiquity;[2] the importance of Sicilian literary traditions in his own work is very clear, and 'bucolic poetry' was, for subsequent poets, 'Sicilian' or 'Syracusan' because of him (cf. *Ecl.* 6.1, 10.51). Explicit internal reference dates Idylls 14, 15 and 17 to the reign of Ptolemy Philadelphos (*c.* 283–246) and the latter two poems to the period of his marriage to Arsinoe (*c.* 278–268); Idyll 16 for Hieron of Syracuse is perhaps to be dated *c.* 275.[3] T.'s

---

[1] Cf. Cameron (1995) 422–5, Gutzwiller (1996) 133–7, Hunter (1996a) 92.

[2] So already explicitly *EB* 93. The *Suda* Life records an alternative view that T. was a Coan who moved to Syracuse; this is most probably an inference from Idyll 7, though it is noteworthy that although both 'Praxagoras' and 'Philinna' are common enough names throughout the Aegean, both are well established on Cos, cf. *LGPN* s.vv. That T. had close connections with that island is, of course, all but certain, cf. Intro. to Idyll 7 below.

[3] Cf. Hunter (1996a) 82–7.

career thus probably began in the late 280s and extended into the middle of the century.

The identifiable settings for T.'s poems are Sicily and South Italy (?1, 4, 5, 6), Cos (7) and Alexandria (15, 17, ?24). Many indications point to the flourishing intellectual and poetic culture of the Eastern Aegean: T.'s friendship with the doctor and poet Nikias of Miletos (cf. Idyll 11, Intro.) and the allusions in Idyll 7 by 'Simichidas' to Asclepiades of Samos and Philitas of Cos place T. at the heart of a remarkable period for Greek poetry. There is, however, no sign that he also wrote scholarly prose works, as did many of the leading 'Alexandrian' poets.[4] The corpus broadly divides into 'western' and 'eastern' poems, with the two major poems for patrons looking to Syracuse (Idyll 16) and Alexandria (Idyll 17). It is tempting to think of an 'early' Sicilian period, followed by a later career in the East, but any rigid schematism would be unwarranted; Idyll 11 deals with a Sicilian myth and is addressed to a Milesian.[5] In a study of the flora of T.'s poems Alice Lindsell demonstrated that this belongs very largely to Greece and the Aegean, not to Sicily, even when the poems are set in the West.[6] Literary inferences from this about the 'realism' of the natural world in T.'s 'western' poems are safer than biographical ones.

The composition of relatively short hexameter poems, marked by sophisticated allusiveness and linguistic novelty, many of which elevate sub-literary or 'low' forms to a new status, clearly places T. within élite third-century poetic production. Echoes of Philitas and Asclepiades are more than probable, however hard to identify, and there seem to be clear allusions to Aratus;[7] Callimachus and T. may

---

[4] The notice in *Hypoth.* Idyll 11 (p. 240 Wendel) γέγονε δὲ [sc. ὁ Νικίας] συμφοιτητὴς Ἐρασιστράτου κτλ. is sometimes (e.g. Lindsell (1937) 79) understood as 'Nikias was a fellow student with T. of Erasistratos', but the natural meaning is rather 'Nikias was a fellow student with Erasistratos ...' There is no assertion that T. studied medicine.

[5] If Idyll 24 is to be as early as 285/4 (cf. Griffiths (1979) 91–8, Cameron (1995) 54–5), then this would be clear evidence against discrete Sicilian, Coan and Alexandrian periods.

[6] Lindsell (1937).

[7] Cf. Idyll 6, Intro.

each allude to the other in different poems,[8] and another poet working at Alexandria, Posidippus, seems to allude to T.'s poems on the Cyclops.[9] Most striking of all is the fact that Idylls 13 (*Hylas*) and 22 (*The Dioscuri*) handle two stories which occur on either side of the division between Books 1 and 2 of Apollonius' *Argonautica*, and close textual similarities rule out the possibility of chance. Apollonius was probably a somewhat younger contemporary of T.,[10] but there are strong literary arguments in favour of Apollonius' priority in these Argonautic episodes.[11] Versions of *Arg.* 1–2 may have been composed relatively early in Apollonius' career, perhaps many years before Books 3–4; such a hypothesis is at least not out of keeping with the fact that all the surviving verses of the so-called *proekdosis* ('pre-edition') of *Arg.* come from Book 1.

Of the thirty poems (or Idylls)[12] collected in standard editions of T., some twenty-two are generally accepted as the work of T. himself;[13] there is also no reason to doubt the authenticity of some at least of the twenty-five epigrams ascribed to T. in the *Anthology*. In addition, scraps of another paederastic poem in Aeolic dialect sur-

---

[8] Call. *Epigr.* 46 very likely refers to Idyll 11 (below, p. 222–3), and *Epigr.* 22 may allude to Idyll 1 (cf. P. Bing, *A&A* 41 (1995) 129–30, Stanzel (1995) 61–4, J. Larson, *CP* 92 (1997) 131–7); Idyll 17 and Call. *h.* 4 have an obvious intertextual link, but this has been very variously interpreted; of other alleged echoes 26.30 – Call. *h.* 4.98 (cf. Cairns (1992) 19–20) and 22.116 – Call. *h.* 3.186 are among the most plausible. Cf. in general G. Schlatter, *Theokrit und Kallimachos* (diss. Zurich 1941). The views of 7.47–51 may be in sympathy with Callimachean aesthetics, but there is no obvious or necessary allusion to Callimachus in those verses, cf. nn. ad loc.

[9] Cf. 11.60, 6.7nn.

[10] His poetic career may (like Callimachus') have continued into the reign of Euergetes, cf. Hunter (1995) 24–5.

[11] Cf. below, p. 264–5, Hunter (1996a) 59–63. It goes without saying that many scholars have taken the opposite view.

[12] The origin of the term εἰδύλλια, which the scholia apply to all of T.'s poems (not just 'the bucolics'), is unclear; Pliny uses it of his own hendecasyllables without any bucolic reference (*Epist.* 4.14.9, cf. *CIL* viii 5530), but in Greek the term seems exclusively attached to T. 'Little types' is a plausible book title, particularly given the variety of T.'s poetry, but no date can firmly be attached to it, cf. Gutzwiller (1996) 129–33.

[13] Idylls 8, 9, 19, 20, 21, 23, 25 and 27 are commonly regarded as spurious.

vive on a papyrus (Idyll 31), and Athenaeus preserves a passage from a poem called *Berenike* of which there is no other trace in the tradition (fr. 3 Gow); how much of T.'s poetry has disappeared without such traces we cannot tell.[14] Within the extant corpus, broad groupings by language, metre,[15] form and subject are possible. Idylls 1, 2, 3, 4, 5, 10, 14 and 15 are 'mimes', that is, 'playlets' set either in the town or the countryside with more than one character, though Idylls 2 and 3 have only one speaker.[16] In Idyll 6, however, a rustic 'mime' is surrounded by an authorial frame and the poem has an addressee; Idyll 11 may be seen as an expanded version of this latter form − an authorial opening and address are extended to 18 verses, but the song of the Cyclops which follows has obvious affinities with the 'mime' of Idyll 3. Idyll 7 clearly has something in common with these poems, but in form, as in every other respect, it occupies a unique place in the corpus, and indeed in the history of Greek literature. A first-person narrative frames a song-exchange between the narrator and another character, Lykidas 'the goatherd'. Idyll 13, the other poem in this volume, offers an addressee a mythological exemplum to illustrate a universal truth about *eros*, rather like an expanded version of a passage of early sympotic elegy; as such, it stands close to traditional poetic modes.[17] Nevertheless, this poem on Hylas, in which the exemplum is related in third-person narrative and the only direct speech is a single verse spoken by 'a sailor' within a simile, has much in common with Idyll 11, also addressed to Nikias on the theme of *eros*, in which the bulk of the exemplum is devoted to the first-person song of the Cyclops. This is a good illustration of the

---

[14] The *Suda* reports 'Some ascribe to Theocritus also the following: *Proitides, Elpides, Hymns, Heroines, Epikedeia, Lyric Poems, Elegies* and *Iambi, Epigrams.*' This is a very mixed lot of doubtful authority. One striking omission from what survives is erotic epigram.

[15] Cf. below, Section 4.

[16] Idyll 2 has a second 'speaker', but Delphis' words are reported by Simaitha.

[17] So, Idylls 17, 22, and 26, for all their novelties, belong recognisably to traditional hymnic patterns, 18 has clear links with the lyric tradition and 24 is a short epic narrative. Idyll 16, however, is in formal terms a remarkable surprise.

dangers of rigid classification. The Theocritean corpus is in fact peculiarly resistant to scholastic and formalist approaches to 'genre': no poem is quite like any other, but the impression is rather of the constant rearrangement and fresh patterning of elements drawn from a repertoire which seems familiar, but is in fact being created before our eyes. Constant difference within the unchangingly familiar was to remain a feature of the bucolic/pastoral tradition. So too, each poem is shot through with humour, but the tone ranges from the irony of incongruity to the uncertain edges of burlesque.

It is in the poems set in the countryside, whatever their differences in structure and form, that T. created something almost wholly new. The third century saw many poetic 'inventions', one-off 'sports' which were to have no subsequent resonance. T.'s creation of a stylised rural world of external peace and emotional turmoil was to have an extraordinary influence upon the western literary tradition.

2. BUCOLIC POETRY

The earliest collections of T.'s poetry of which we know were called Βουκολικά (below, p. 27), and this is the title which Virgil adopted for his 'pastoral' poems; the 'bucolic terminology' and the poems in which it appeared (particularly Idyll 1, which headed all ancient collections)[18] were presumably felt to represent something distinctive in T.'s work. Moreover, the similarities between all the poems set in the countryside will have been as clear to ancient scholars as they are to us;[19] indeed, an interest in the poetic evocation of rural landscape appears throughout the corpus, not just in the 'bucolic' poems. What requires explanation is the 'bucolic terminology' itself. The scholia to T. are preceded by late antique or Byzantine versions of an essay which traces the origin of τὰ βουκολικά to certain cults of Artemis in Lakonia or Sicily. T.'s surviving poems clearly have nothing to do with such rituals, and this scholiastic account, which perhaps goes back at least to Theon (Augustan period), seems to

---

[18] Cf. Idyll 1, Intro.
[19] Cf., e.g., Lawall (1967), Van Sickle (1970), Segal (1981) 176–209.

have been modelled upon Peripatetic accounts of the origins of Attic drama.[20] Such a 'ritual' construction is in fact true to an important element in the literary history which T. constructs for his own poems,[21] but it tells us nothing about their designation or genesis.

In Idyll 5, Lakon challenges Komatas to a contest in singing (διαείσομαι 22) in which Komatas will 'bucolicise for the last time' (ὕστατα βουκολιαξῆι 44); when Lakon agrees to the location of the contest, he tells Komatas 'compete with me from there and bucolicise from there' (αὐτόθε μοι ποτέρισδε καὶ αὐτόθε βουκολιάσδευ 60). When they ask Morson to judge the contest, Lakon tells him that 'we are competing [to see] who is the better bucoliast' (ἄμμες γὰρ ἐρίσδομες ὅστις ἀρείων | βουκολιαστάς ἐστι 67–8). The contest itself takes the form of an 'amoebean' (i.e. alternating) exchange of couplets, in which the second singer must, to some extent, follow and try to cap the themes set by the first;[22] those themes are more or less exclusively rustic. The literal meaning of βουκολιάσδεσθαι should be something like 'play/behave like a *boukolos*', but in Idyll 5 'bucolicising' clearly means competing in an exchange of extemporised verses (which themselves are never described as 'bucolic'). Such competitions are well attested in many historical cultures,[23] and literary stylisation into a competition of pairs of hexameters does not disguise the essentially popular character of the form. Neither Lakon nor Komatas is a βουκόλος in the strict sense, so T. may be alluding to (or creating the illusion of) a familiar terminology which associates such song-competitions with the countryside. No other certainly genuine poem of T. presents an amoebean contest

---

[20] Cf. E. Cremonesi, 'Rapporti tra le origini della poesia bucolica e della poesia comica nella tradizione peripatetica' *Dioniso* 21 (1958) 109–22. For efforts to take these accounts seriously cf. R. Y. Hathorn, 'The ritual origin of pastoral' *TAPA* 92 (1961) 228–38, Trencsényi-Waldapfel (1966), G. J. Baudy, 'Hirtenmythos und Hirtenlied. Zu den rituellen Aspekten der bukolischen Dichtung' *Poetica* 25 (1993) 282–318. The *Hypotheses* found in our scholia of T. are modelled on the dramatic *Hypotheses* of Aristophanes of Byzantium (cf. Wendel (1920) 88–9).

[21] Cf. Idyll 1, Intro.

[22] Cf. Serrao (1971) 69–70.

[23] Cf. R. Merkelbach, 'ΒΟΥΚΟΛΙΑΣΤΑΙ (Der Wettgesang der Hirten)' *RhM* 99 (1956) 97–133 (= Effe (1986) 212–38).

of quite this kind, but 'exchange' is important, to varying degrees, to the structure of 1, 4, 6, 7 and 10, and it is tempting to believe that it was always suggested by 'bucolic' terminology.

In Idyll 7 Simichidas suggests to Lykidas that they should 'bucolicise together' (βουκολιασδώμεσθα 36), which suggests an exchange of song, for the context is Simichidas' declaration of their musical and poetic powers through which 'each of us may benefit the other' (36). Lykidas' response concludes (49–51):

ἀλλ' ἄγε βουκολικᾶς ταχέως ἀρξώμεθ' ἀοιδᾶς,
Σιμιχίδα· κἠγὼ μέν – ὅρη, φίλος, εἴ τοι ἀρέσκει
τοῦθ' ὅτι πρᾶν ἐν ὄρει τὸ μελύδριον ἐξεπόνασα.

Come, Simichidas, let us straightaway begin the bucolic singing [or 'song']. And I – see, my friend, whether you like this little song which I recently worked out on the mountain.

From this it is clear that in Idyll 7 'bucolicising' involves an exchange of songs, though not the extemporised and amoebean performance of Idyll 5; one of the participants is (or looks like) a goatherd (13–14), and there is good reason to think that Simichidas proposes 'bucolicising' precisely because he is in the countryside and confronted with a master poet of the countryside, and because 'bucolicising' is associated with herdsmen. The song which Simichidas subsequently performs picks up some of the themes of Lykidas' song, and Simichidas presents himself as learning his songs 'while a *boukolos* on the mountains' (92), as though the status of 'real' *boukolos* was necessary for 'bucolicising' (cf. n. *ad loc.*). Such ironic literalness is manifested also in the matter of his song (goats, Pan etc.), whereas Lykidas sings a complex *propemptikon* for a beloved boy which includes the myths of two legendary herdsmen-poets, Daphnis the oxherd and Komatas the goatherd. Thus βουκολικὰ ἀοιδά in Idyll 7 is most probably to be understood as 'bucolic singing' or 'bucolic [exchange of] song', and there is no clear sign that the individual songs of Lykidas and Simichidas could themselves be called 'bucolic'.

In Idyll 1 a goatherd urges Thyrsis to entertain him with a song, 'for you sing the sufferings of Daphnis and have reached mastery in the bucolic Muse' (19–20). The song which Thyrsis proceeds to sing about Daphnis ὁ βουκόλος is punctuated by addresses to the Muses, asking them to begin, continue and conclude βουκολικὰ ἀοιδά. Here 'bucolic' can apparently describe a single song, as commonly in later poetry (e.g., *Epigr.* 2.1–2 'Daphnis who played bucolic hymns on his lovely syrinx', almost certainly post-Theocritean). Nevertheless, in asking Thyrsis to sing his masterpiece, the goatherd recalls a time when Thyrsis sang in competition with 'Chromis of Libya' (23–4), and the most natural inference is that on that occasion Thyrsis sang 'the sufferings of Daphnis'; to 'reach mastery in the bucolic Muse' itself evokes an agonistic setting, as the opening verses too suggest a series of contests against Pan and the Muses. Thyrsis' song thus derives from a context of competitive exchange, and Idyll 1 itself presents a series of such exchanges: the 'competition of compliments' with which the poem opens (cf. 1.1–11n.), the exchange of an *ekphrasis* of a marvellous cup for the song about Daphnis etc. In Idyll 1, therefore, the 'bucolic' terminology is not to be explained solely in terms of Daphnis ὁ βουκόλος, the legendary subject and inventor of bucolic song (cf. Idyll 1, Intro.)

Of the poems in which 'bucolic' terminology does not appear, Idyll 6 has a competitive and Idyll 10 a non-competitive song-exchange, in one case possibly and in the other certainly not between two herdsmen.[24] There is at least no positive internal reason to believe that the solo performances of 3, 11 and 12, let alone the 'urban mimes' in 2, 14 and 15, were for T. himself βουκολικά.

With the exception of Daphnis himself (Idylls 1, 6) and Damoitas (6.1–2n.), T.'s musical herdsmen are not oxherds (βουκόλοι); why then is the singing of Idylls 1, 5 and 7 βουκολικά, rather than, say, αἰπολικά, a possibility in fact raised in Idyll 7 by the juxtaposition of Komatas the goatherd to Daphnis the oxherd (and cf. 1.56)?[25] βουκολεῖν and related words are found from an early date used of animals other than cattle,[26] but this is hardly an adequate explana-

---

[24] On the possible implications of the name Boukaios, however, cf. 10.1n.

[25] Late antiquity found an answer in the 'bucolic hierarchy', cf. Σ *Proleg.* c Wendel, 1.8on. Of some interest in this connection is Euripides' description of Apollo working as a herdsman, βοσκήμασι ... συρίζων | ποιμνίτας ὑμεναίους (*Alc.* 576–7).

[26] Thus, for example, Homer's Boukolion is a shepherd (*Il.* 6.21–5) and cf. *Il.* 20.221 ἵπποι ... βουκολέοντο, Eupolis fr. 19 K–A etc.

tion. Later sources make Daphnis ὁ βουκόλος the 'inventor' and/or principal subject of τὰ βουκολικὰ μέλη,[27] but we have seen reasons for thinking that this does not even account for the terminology of Idyll 1. In the course, however, of an account of types of song, Athenaeus (14 619a–b) reports: 'There was a song for people leading flocks, the so-called βουκολιασμός. Diomos was a Sicilian oxherd, and he invented this type; Epicharmus mentions him in the *Alkyon* [fr. 4 Kaibel] and the *Shipwrecked Odysseus* [fr. 105 Kaibel].'[28] Here is another Sicilian tradition of 'bucolic' singing, but one not tied to the particular legend of Daphnis nor, to judge from Athenaeus, restricted to oxherds. Whether or not Epicharmus said anything about Diomos, other than merely mentioning his name, we do not know; it is, of course, possible that the term βουκολιασμός does not pre-date the Hellenistic scholarship which made Diomos an 'inventor', but it is at least as likely that the term is in fact older. It can only be a guess that some βουκολιασμός at least was (or was believed to be) antiphonal or amoebean, but it does not seem too rash a guess. If this is right, then T.'s 'bucolic' terminology will result from a creative reworking of traditions of Sicilian song-making, which may themselves have been to some extent scholarly constructions.[29] Even if, however, the literary history inscribed in T.'s poetry may be largely his own, it can hardly be doubted that there was a history. To judge from the parody at Ar. *Plutus* 290–315, it seems very likely that Philoxenus had already exploited Sicilian traditions of 'bucolic song' for his famous *Cyclops or Galateia*,[30] and Euripides' *Cyclops*, set on Sicily, contains a very 'Theocritean' song (41–62), which may similarly exploit the audience's belief in such a Sicilian tradition.[31]

---

[27] The sources for the myth of Daphnis are gathered in Intro. to Idyll 1.

[28] Cf. Hesychius β 906. At 14 618c Athenaeus, on the authority of Tryphon (late first cent. BC), lists βουκολισμός (*sic*) as a type of αὔλησις.

[29] Nauta (1990) offers a helpful account of some of these matters, though I cannot share his wish to introduce a uniform and reductive sense for 'bucolic' terminology in the genuine T.

[30] Cf. Idyll 11, Intro.

[31] Cf. Seaford on vv. 41–81. Seaford notes Sophocles' *Inachos*, in which Argos sang (apparently) while guarding Io (fr. 281a Radt, R. Pfeiffer, *SB München* 1938, 2, 28–9); no testimony, however, applies the term βουκολικόν to this song.

Epicharmus wrote comedies at Syracuse in the first half of the fifth century.[32] Mythological burlesque was very prominent, with Odysseus and Heracles as important characters; the *Cyclops* (frr. 81–3 Kaibel) presumably dramatised the events of *Od.* 9, and the *Amycus* (frr. 6–8 Kaibel) presented the story which T. treated in the first part of Idyll 22. As a famous figure of Sicilian literary history, Epicharmus will in any case have been important for T.; Epigram 18 describes a Syracusan statue of the comic poet. The presence of 'bucolic' material in Epicharmus must remain speculative, though some of the myths he treated are clearly suggestive, and the title Ἀγρωστῖνος 'Bumpkin' (frr. 1–3 Kaibel) is a further hint. It is at least tantalising that the *Suda* (ε 2766) gives Tityros (cf. 3.2, 7.72) as one of the names of his father (another name is Χίμαρος (Kid)!); these names may have had their origin in an Epicharmean joke, but even such a joke might have been important for T. as he constructed links between his poetry and the great figures of the Sicilian past.[33]

Direct borrowings by T. from the mimes of Sophron of Syracuse (fifth century) are attested by the scholia only for the 'urban mimes', Idylls 2 and 15.[34] Sophron's playlets, written, at least in part, in a kind of rhythmical prose, were divided into those with male and those with female characters. Among the former were 'The Fisherman and the Countryman' (frr. 43–5 Kaibel)[35] and 'The Tunny-Fisherman' (frr. 46–9 Kaibel).[36] Idyll 3 certainly evokes related traditions of quasi-dramatic solo performances,[37] though ones not specifically linked to Sicily. Like most things about him, the scope and length of Sophron's mimes is uncertain, but he enjoyed a particular reputation for the depiction of character (ἠθοποιία), and stories of Plato's

---

[32] Cf. esp. G. Kaibel, *RE* vi 34–41, Pickard-Cambridge (1962) 230–88.

[33] Radt speculates that apparent Dorisms in the satyric *Diktyoulkoi* of Aeschylus (frr. 46a–47c Radt) mark a debt to the *Diktyes* of Epicharmus; certainly the chorus of Aeschylus' play, 'all farmers, vine-diggers, shepherds' (fr. 46a 18–19) are 'bucolic' enough.

[34] Cf. Hunter (1996a) 116–23.

[35] Kaibel is probably correct to include here a reference (fr. 45) just to 'The Countryman'.

[36] Cf. 3.25–7n.

[37] Cf. Idyll 3, Intro.

admiration for his work probably pre-date T.[38] Aristotle adduces 'the mimes of Sophron and [his son] Xenarchus and Socratic dialogues' as examples of mimetic prose to which no generic name has been assigned, whereas, he complains, it is regular to class as 'poetry' everything which is written in verse, regardless of whether it is mimetic or not (*Poet.* 1447a28–47b16). For Aristotle, Sophron's mimes were mimetic representations and hence, in the most important sense, poetic, but in clothing mimes in the grandest of metres, T. turns the Aristotelian question on its head; is this mimetic verse 'poetry'?[39] As a model for T., Sophron is thus important also for the kind of literary issue his poetry was thought to embody.

That the *Idylls* were designed to be read is suggested both by the prevailing conditions of literary reception in the third century and by the pictorial care with which setting and action are detailed.[40] Recitation or even 'performance' by more than one actor is certainly not an implausible complement to reception through reading, and Virgil's *Eclogues* were indeed performed.[41] Aelian's pejorative description of T. as ὁ τῶν νομευτικῶν παιγνίων συνθέτης (*NA* 15.19) perhaps suggests that he thought of the *Idylls* as 'playlets'.[42]

In the centuries which followed T., 'bucolic' turned into 'pastoral' by a process which both narrowed its focus to certain elements of T.'s 'bucolics', notably love and the relations between man and nature and between present and mythical past, and expanded the range of such song by giving primacy to the metaphor of the poet as herdsman. What in T. were 'generic possibilities' became 'generic

---

[38] Cf. Douris, *FGrHist* 76 F72. The evidence is gathered by A. S. Riginos, *Platonica. The anecdotes concerning the life and writings of Plato* (Leiden 1976) 174–6.

[39] Relevant here also is Aristotle's reported observation (Diog. Laert. 3.37 = fr. 73 Rose) that Plato's dialogues are halfway between poetry and prose (τὴν τῶν λόγων ἰδέαν αὐτοῦ μεταξὺ ποιήματος εἶναι καὶ πεζοῦ λόγου).

[40] Cf. Hunter (1993b) 40–3, where, however, 'solely' (p. 40) overstates the case.

[41] Cf. N. Horsfall, *A companion to the study of Virgil* (Leiden 1995) 249–50.

[42] Cf. Gnesippos ὁ παιγνιαγράφος, below p. 108. παίγνιον itself, of course, could refer to a non-dramatic text.

expectations'.[43] Neither this process nor the clear differences between the manner of post-Theocritean 'bucolic' and Virgil's *Eclogues* can be traced in any detail here,[44] though bucolic irony deserves a brief note. Idylls 7, 10 and 11, at least, self-consciously exploit their scripted rusticity, and to some extent this is an ironic mode which subsequent 'Theocritean' poets never sought fully to recapture.[45] In T. the 'generic possibilities' have not yet hardened into a familiar code agreed between poet and reader, so the bucolic metaphor itself is still a major poetic concern. Harry Berger has usefully described part of this concern as, in the terminology of Harold Bloom, a distinction between 'strong' and 'weak' pastoral. For Berger Idyll 7 is 'strong pastoral or metapastoral ... which ... presents itself in the act of (mis)representing the pastoral that fathered it ... [It] constructs within itself an image of its generic traditions in order to criticize them and, in the process, performs a critique on the limits of its own enterprise even as it ironically displays its delight in the activity it criticizes ... [and] traditionally fashions as its target a generalized image of weak pastoral.'[46] None of T. is, however, 'weak pastoral' in the purest sense: 5 perhaps comes closest, whereas 4, 7 and 10 fit the 'strong' model particularly well. Here, as in so many respects, the subsequent pastoral tradition found in T. a range of linked possibilities, not a readymade template.

3. THE *LOCUS AMOENUS*

Greek literature did not suddenly discover the countryside in the Hellenistic period.[47] Both nature and those who work with it are present in the *Iliad* (the similes, the Shield etc.)[48] and even more obvi-

---

[43] The happy formulation of F. Muecke, *AUMLA* 44 (1975) 170–1.

[44] Among helpful contributions are Arland (1937), L. E. Rossi, 'Mondo pastorale e poesia bucolica di maniera: l'idillio ottavo del corpus teocriteo' *SIFC* 43 (1971) 5–25, Van Sickle (1976), Halperin (1983a), Effe (1989), Alpers (1996), Reed (1997), Fantuzzi (1998a).

[45] This is how I would reformulate the picture in Effe (1989) of an 'ironic' T. ranged against the 'sentimentality' of subsequent bucolic.

[46] Berger (1984) 2–3.

[47] The fullest treatment of this subject is Elliger (1975).

[48] Cf. Griffin (1992).

ously the *Odyssey* (the Cyclops, 'Goat Island' (9.116–151), Eumaeus); Sappho wrote one of the most evocative of natural descriptions (fr. 2 Voigt), and Aristophanes' *Peace* offers many images of the country-side in harmony. Virtually all landscape description in literature is more or less 'typical', i.e. its particularity lies in the place-names attached to it and its function within the text, rather than with 'unique' natural features.[49] T. stands out by the range and detail of the flora which fill his landscape, not because he looks at the coun-tryside in a quite new way; what *is* new perhaps is his exploitation of such typicality to reflect upon his own poetic practices (7.135–47n.).

It is nevertheless true that Hellenistic art and literature seem to show a greater interest in the countryside and its people than is obvious earlier.[50] Explanations in terms of a 'weariness' with life in increasingly large cities and a nostalgia for a past of constructed simplicity are easy enough to offer, but very hard to control. The phenomenon cannot be considered in isolation from other artistic, intellectual and social developments: Epicureanism and Cynicism, 'realism' in Hellenistic art, the increasingly narrow concentration of political and economic power, and so on. At one level T. can be seen as part of a general literary trend. In the probably rather earlier epigrams of Anyte from Arcadian Tegea we find dedications to Pan and the nymphs and 'inscriptions' which invite weary travellers to rest and cool themselves,[51] and the roughly contemporary epigrams of Leonidas of Tarentum offer a whole series of rustic dedications, including one to Hermes and Pan in a setting of stylised natural beauty, such as is conventionally called a *locus amoenus*.[52] What is lacking from these poems, however, is any sense of the bucolic exchange, the emotional suffering and the interplay between man

---

[49] To some extent, of course, this relation between the particular and the general is a function of how we order experience and express that experience in familiar language, but landscape is an area of ancient literary expression in which this 'typicality' is particularly marked.

[50] Cf., e.g., Himmelmann (1980), Bernsdorff (1996).

[51] For Anyte cf. *HE* I 35–41, II 89–104, D. Geoghegan, *Anyte. The Epigrams* (Rome 1979), K. J. Gutzwiller, 'Anyte's epigram book' *Syllecta Classica* 4 (1993) 71–89, Bernsdorff (1996) 90–186.

[52] *Anth. Pal.* 6.334 (= *HE* 1966–71), cf. 1.1, 7.135–47nn.

and nature which characterise T.'s poetry; this is not merely a difference between the epigram and the mime, but an indication of how T. uses this stylised countryside to illuminate literary experience.

Plato's *Phaedrus* occupies a special place in the history of the literary presentation of landscape.[53] The urban Socrates, for once out of his 'natural habitat', specifically draws attention to the (typical) beauties of nature – cool water, the shade of a plane tree, statues of the Nymphs, cicada song – and marks them as aesthetic pleasures inimical to intellectual progress (230b–d, cf. 1.1n.). The *Phaedrus* establishes such pleasures as a privileged *locus* not just for τὰ ἐρωτικά, but specifically for the exchange of competing views of *eros*. Moreover, Socrates tells a myth of the origin of cicadas from men who were so besotted with the new pleasure of song that they neglected to eat and drink (258e6–9d8); *inter alia*, this is an aetiological myth for the *mousike* which distinguishes men from sheep. For Socrates, the highest form of *mousike* is philosophy, but in the world of Theocritean bucolic, song is more often than not the result of emotional distress, precisely that distress which animals do not feel. Plato's cicada-men have successfully made the transition: they have escaped human desires[54] and been rewarded with the undiluted pleasure of song and divine privilege after death. For a Daphnis, however, and those who seek to imitate him, there is no such freedom from disturbance.

At the very heart of Idylls 1, 3, 6, 7, 10, 11 and 13 lies *eros*, whose irruption into the bucolic world destroys the hoped-for ἀσυχία ('quietness'). In Idyll 1 the young men depicted on the cup, 'long hollow-eyed with love', are set off against the child in the vineyard absorbed in his own play. Like the cicada-men, the child has no concern for food nor yet feels the weight of *eros*; he is the only character of the bucolic poems who is 'self-sufficient and at peace'

---

[53] Murley (1940) is the standard reference, but that does little more than gather a mixed bag of evidence, cf. also Pearce (1988) 297–300, Gutzwiller (1991) 73–9. For the *Phaedrus* and Idyll 7 cf. below, p. 145–6. For the *Phaedrus* and later pastoral cf. Hunter (1997).

[54] The common view that cicadas were 'born from the earth' (Davies–Kathirithamby 124–6) suggests their asexuality; the Anacreontic poet calls the cicada ἀπαθής (34.17), and this will cover, *inter alia*, sexual desire. For the 'realities' of cicada sex cf. Arist. *HA* 5 556a25–b20.

(αὐτάρκης καὶ ἀτάρακτος). The Cyclops of Idyll 6 claims a similar contentment, but his triumph is at best qualified and uncertain. At the other extreme from the child, the Daphnis of Idyll 1 offers a model of self-inflicted pain, of the refusal to take what is on offer. Daphnis is an aetiological figure for all subsequent herdsmen both because of his music and because it is *eros* which is his undoing; it is *eros* (1.130) which puts an end to herding, syrinx-playing and (in Idyll 10) reaping. Song is both a product of *eros* and an activity that may bring temporary alleviation (10.21–3, Idyll 11), but it really only serves to highlight human distress, a distress not felt by the animals that the herdsmen guard (1.151–2, 3.2–5 etc.). It is, as Priapos makes clear in Idyll 1, the very proximity of the animals with their uncomplicated mating habits which throws the emotional suffering of the herdsmen into pathetic relief; the fantasies and rôle-playing in which the herdsmen indulge function as an assertion of humanity – in the poet's construction, sheep and goats do not cause each other such pain.[55]

This paradoxical conflict – the desire both to imitate the animals in escaping from desire (11.75, 1.85–6n.), as Plato's cicadas did, and to 'pursue the one who flees' as a marker of difference from them – is expressed in the figure of Pan, the god of herdsmen and their poetry.[56] Half-human and half-goat, Pan's duality embodies both straightforward animal sexuality and the emotional obsessiveness we associate with human beings, and particularly T.'s herdsmen. The familiar stories of Pan's unhappy love for Syrinx and Echo display the transformation of one into the other: an animal lustfulness becomes an obsessed longing for what is now beyond reach as the god kills the object of his desire. Something of Pan's doubleness also infects the tone of T.'s poems: just as the god may inspire terror or laughter (cf. *h. Pan* 36–47), so too can the sight and plight of the unhappy satyr-like lovers of Idylls 3 and 11.

The delusion and disturbance which *eros* brings has obvious points of contact with philosophic accounts of desire, and Thomas Rosenmeyer sought to draw a close link between the Theocritean pursuit

---

[55] This is another area in which post-Theocritean pastoral developed what are merely suggestive hints in T. (cf. 10.31–2).

[56] Cf. Idyll 1, Intro.

of freedom from disturbance and Epicurean ideals of *ataraxia*.[57] For Epicurus[58] *eros* arose, roughly speaking, from a combination of heightened desire and false opinion. Both Epicurus and Lucretius, in his famous account in *DRN* 4, recognise sexual desire as something which *may* safely and easily be satisfied, but which is dangerous because it so easily turns into something deleterious to our happiness; it is a pleasure we may give ourselves, but we are lucky if we avoid the harmful entrapment which results when desire passes into *eros*, with its obsessive focus upon the loved individual. Lucretius saw the way of avoiding the worst excesses of *amor* as not thinking about (or being with) the beloved (cf. Epicurus, *SV* 18) and taking care to empty your seed *in corpora quaeque* (4.1065).[59] In Idylls 1, 3 (cf. 3.1–2n.) and 11 (cf. 11.75) the cure is available, and Priapos' account of Daphnis' behaviour (1.82–91) seems to fit the pattern – Rosenmeyer ((1969) 81) calls the phallic god a 'good Epicurean' – but this is not enough to allow the conclusion that T. explicitly evokes Epicurean ideas.

Poetic and philosophical traditions use very similar language to describe *eros*, and illustrative material might as well be drawn from Plato as from Epicurus.[60] It is indeed part of philosophy's rhetoric to describe 'morbid desire' in the language of poetry and myth, since it is in these realms, not in the world of reason, that such desire belongs. This is *philosophy's satire*: thus Lucretius' famous 'diatribe' (4.1171–91) on the *exclusus amator* must be seen as an elaborate version of a traditional weapon in the armoury of philosophy. This similarity in the language of poetry and philosophy makes assertions of philosophic influence in T. particularly hazardous, however tempting it may be to see 'doctrine' placed wittily in the mouth of a Priapos or a (?) deluded Cyclops (6.28n). This would be *poetry's satire*: not the philosopher caught out in hypocrisy nor the malicious misrepresentation of doctrine – Epicurus never lacked for that kind of

---

[57] Rosenmeyer (1969) *passim*. 'Freedom from disturbance' is not of course exclusively an Epicurean ideal, cf. 7.126–7n.

[58] Cf. Brown (1987) 101–22, Nussbaum (1994) 140–91.

[59] This too is a traditional attitude, cf. Antisthenes at Xen. *Symp.* 4.38.

[60] Cf. 13.64–71n.

detractor[61] − but doctrine manifested in the deluded fantasies of satyr-like rustics and exemplified against a background of simple carnality. At what point easy guesses about what goes on inside a goatherd's mind cross paths with philosophical reflection upon the nature of *eros* is an insistent question towards which these poems nudge us.

4. METRE

The great majority of T.'s poetry, and all the poems included in this book, are written in dactylic hexameters which, along with elegiac couplets, are the dominant metre of all Hellenistic élite poetry.[62] The basic pattern is:[63]

$$\overset{1}{-\cup\cup}\,|\,\overset{2}{-\cup\cup}\,|\,\overset{3}{-\cup\cup}\,|\,\overset{4}{-\cup\cup}\,|\,\overset{5}{-\cup\cup}\,|\,-\cup$$

By the third century, the hexameter was the standard metrical form for a very wide range of poetic subjects and tones, but no writer of hexameters could escape the Homeric heritage, which had shaped, indeed created, the whole tradition of *epos*, the word which is as close as the Greeks came to a 'generic' term for poetry written in hexameters. Any writing of hexameters was a conscious or unconscious engagement with Homer; in T.'s case, it was very conscious.[64] Moreover, the choice of the hexameter for the 'bucolic mimes' was not merely the result of the general poetic and performative trends of the time. T. married 'low' subject matter, resonant of a tradition of prosaic mime and/or popular song, to a metre, significantly called τὸ ἡρωικόν,[65] which theorists regarded as the most 'poetic' measure and the one most removed from the rhythms of ordinary

---

[61] Cf. Diog. Laert. 10.6−8, D. Sedley, *Cahiers de Philologie* I (1976) 121−59.

[62] For these developments cf. Hunter (1996a) 4−6, Cameron (1995) *passim*.

[63] This section assumes a working knowledge of the basic patterns and prosody of the hexameter. Those without such knowledge will find helpful guidance on pp. xxii−xxvii of Dover's edition, and cf. also M. L. West, *Introduction to Greek Metre* (Oxford 1987) 19−23.

[64] The fullest treatment of T.'s engagement with the Homeric heritage is Halperin (1983a).

[65] Cf. Demetrius, *On style* 5 'The hexameter is called "heroic verse" because of its length and appropriateness for heroes.'

speech, cf. Arist. *Poetics* 1449a27–8, 1459b34–7 'the hexameter is the stateliest and weightiest (στασιμώτατον καὶ ὀγκωδέστατον) of the metres; for this reason it is the most receptive to rare words (γλῶτται) and metaphors'.[66] In using in his hexameters words drawn not from the inherited poetic language, but the pastoral world of herdsmen or the chatter of Alexandrian housewives, T. issued a challenge to received notions of poetic appropriateness, τὸ πρέπον; elevated metre was supposed to be accompanied by elevated style and subject matter.[67] Of the poems in the present collection, it is Idylls 3 and 4 where the productive clash between metre and verbal style is most sharply felt.

Three related aspects of the Theocritean hexameter deserve special attention here.[68]

1. *Dactyls and spondees.*[69] The élite hexameter poetry of the third century is, in general, more dactylic than Homer and tended to reduce the number of verse-schemes which were used at all commonly. Thus Callimachus, for example, has a very clear preference for a hexameter with only one spondee, the favoured place for which is in the second foot.[70] Broadly speaking, the 'epic' poems of T., including Idyll 13,[71] conform to this general tendency, as also do

---

[66] Cf. *Rhet.* 3.1404a34–5, 1408b32–3, Demetrius, *On style* 42 'the heroic verse is solemn and not suited to prose, being resounding (σεμνὸς καὶ οὐ λογικός, ἀλλ' ἠχώδης)'. γλῶσσαι in this context are largely archaisms, often from Homer, which were often no longer fully understood, cf. below, p. 21.

[67] Some of the most familiar theoretical statements in this field are, of course, later than T. (e.g. 'Longinus' 30.2), but it is hardly to be doubted that there is an academic, as well as a poetic, background to T.'s practice.

[68] What follows is heavily indebted to Kunst (1887), Legrand (1898) 314–42, Brioso Sánchez (1976) and (1977), West (1982) 152–7 and Fantuzzi (1995a). My account aims to be as descriptive as possible; the detailed statistics supporting that description may be found in the works listed. Unsurprisingly, there are differences between the statistics of different scholars, but I hope that the general picture is not in doubt.

[69] The commentary uses a combination of *d* (dactyl) and *s* (spondee) to indicate the pattern of the first five feet of a hexameter, e.g., *dssdd*.

[70] There are helpful tables in W. H. Mineur, *Callimachus, Hymn to Delos* (Leiden 1984) 35–6, and see also B. A. Van Groningen, *La poésie verbale grecque* (Amsterdam 1953) 33–4.

[71] On the special metrical characteristics of Idyll 11 cf. the Introduction to that poem.

Idylls 3 and 7,[72] whereas Idylls 1, 2, 4, 5 and 6 are markedly more spondaic than the third-century norm. It is the first half of the verse which carries the bulk of this spondaic weight; two successive spondees in this part of the verse are very common, and three are not rare. Spondaic rhythm may still be used to enhance meaning (cf., e.g., 1.71–2), but the general effect of verse-weight in recitation and reading must have been rather more striking than it may appear to us today. Doric dialect and a vocabulary marked by many words which had never appeared in hexameter poetry before obviously play an important rôle here,[73] but as these are 'mimes', it is tempting also to see an attempt to produce a less smooth, more 'mimetic' hexameter. If so, this would not be because the spondee is, in Greek eyes, closer to speech than the dactyl (quite the reverse, in fact), but because the very deviation from contemporary poetic tendencies would effect distance from the artifices of 'literature'.

Some Hellenistic poets favoured verses, and often successive pairs of verses, with spondaic fifth feet, so-called σπονδειάζοντες. Whereas some 5% of Homeric verse and 6% of Hesiod show this feature, the figure for Callimachus is some 7% (though there are wide variations between different poems) and for the *Argonautica* 9%, whereas Aratus and Euphorion show in the region of 15%. Once again, there are marked distinctions within the Theocritean corpus. Whereas the 'epic' poems are statistically close to the figures for Callimachus and Apollonius, σπονδειάζοντες are extremely rare in the bucolic mimes (1.3%): there are none in Idylls 3, 4 and 6, one in 5, three in 7 and four in 1. Idyll 2 also has only one example, thus again following the 'bucolics' metrically, whereas Idyll 15 has eleven (7%). From a rhythmical point of view, this avoidance of the fifth-foot spondee to some extent compensates for the increased spondaic weight of the first half of the verse, and must be seen in conjunction with the treatment of the fourth foot, to which we now turn.

2. *'Bucolic diaeresis'*. From Homer onwards, there was a clear preference for word-division after the fourth foot (some 60% of Homeric verses), and an even stronger preference for the fourth foot to be

---

[72] Idyll 7 also has verbal features in common with the 'epic' poems. Cf. below, p. 23.

[73] Cf. Fantuzzi (1995a) 251–3.

dactylic when it was followed by word division (i.e. $\underline{4} \cup \cup \|$, the so-called 'bucolic diaeresis'). In Callimachus, there are virtually no examples of $\underline{4} - \|$; the avoidance of such a break is known as 'Naeke's Law'.[74] Again, there are important differences within the Theocritean corpus. Taken together, some 85% of verses in Idylls 1–7 have a dactylic fourth foot (against 73% in the 'epic' poems) and some 80% of all verses in those poems show the pattern $\underline{4} \cup \cup \|$, and there are at most three examples of $\underline{4} - \|$; considered individually, the figures for 'bucolic diaeresis' range from 74% for Idyll 7 to 90% for Idyll 5. It is again noteworthy that the behaviour of Idyll 2 is close to that of the bucolics, whereas Idyll 10 has only 58% 'bucolic diaeresis' and two breaches of Naeke's Law, Idyll 14 has 67% and one breach, and the figure for the rest of the corpus is around 50%. Idyll 11 is again entirely remote in style from the bucolic mimes.[75]

3. *'Callimachean rules'*. Callimachus' metrical practice forms a useful point of reference for all third-century poets, for his hexameter is subject to a sophisticated series of 'rules' governing the positions in the line occupied by words of a certain shape and the positions at which word-division may occur, and these 'rules' offer a useful guide to the 'conservatism' or 'modernity' of other poets.[76] Thus, 'Naeke's Law' described above is one such rule, 'Hilberg's Law' forbidding $\underline{2} - \|$ another, and 'Hermann's Bridge' forbidding $\underline{4} \cup \| \cup$ another.[77] These 'rules' are, for the most part, standardisations of universal tendencies within the Greek hexameter of all periods, and any closeness between Callimachus and T. need not imply direct influence. An analysis by Marco Fantuzzi[78] has confirmed that it is, again, Idylls 1, 3, 4, 5, 6 and 7 which cohere most closely in their observance of the 'Callimachean' rules; Idyll 2 is somewhat more lax, but remains close to the 'bucolics', whereas Idylls 10 and 15 are ranged with the 'epic' poems (including Idyll 13) in a much looser respect for

[74] Cf. 1.130n.

[75] Cf. the Introduction to that poem.

[76] Helpful accounts of the Callimachean 'rules' may be found in Hopkinson (1984) 51–5 and A. S. Hollis, *Callimachus, Hecale* (Oxford 1990) 15–23.

[77] Cf. 10.26–7n.

[78] Fantuzzi (1995a); the basic point is made already in Di Benedetto (1956) 56–8. E. Magnelli, *MD* 35 (1995) 135–64, presents some modifications of Fantuzzi's results concerning the treatment of the second foot.

these norms; Idyll 11 is again idiosyncratic in its remarkable freedom. Broadly speaking, therefore, the 'new' bucolic mimes are marked by a close approximation to the 'new' metrics of Callimachus, whereas the 'epic' poems remain closer to inherited patterns of generic practice.

5. LANGUAGE

Homer bequeathed a linguistic style to all hexameter poets, whatever their native dialect and theme; the language of Homer, predominantly Ionic, characterised by a multiplicity of alternative forms and littered with words whose meaning had, by the third century, long been uncertain, is the basis of most surviving hexameter and elegiac poetry. Even purely local, 'non-literary', poetry shows the clear influence of the epic tradition. The poems included in the present volume differ, however, from the inherited conglomerate in three broad and related ways.

1. *Vocabulary.* We saw above that, just as the hexameter was regarded as a high and serious rhythm removed from ordinary speech, so it was most receptive to rare and archaic words, which in practice often meant words inherited from Homer. Despite their sophisticated density of Homeric allusion, however, the language of the bucolic mimes is relatively free of such arcane vocabulary; a tension exists between the associations of the metre and the language in which that metre is expressed. Moreover, the rich botanical and pastoral vocabulary may function as a kind of ironic alternative to the traditional lexicon: such words are constructed as further removed from the experience of T.'s intended audience than Homeric glosses would be. Be that as it may, T.'s sophisticated use of a 'technical' vocabulary, and one probably indebted to the botanical scholarship of Theophrastus as well as to his own observation,[79] marks this as an élite discourse. By a familiar literary paradox, the appearance of careful detail works as much against as with both 'realism' and *enargeia*.

2. *Morphology.* Hand-in-hand with vocabulary goes the familiar Homeric/Ionic morphology: genitives in -οιο, datives in -οισι and -αισι, verbal *diektasis* (4.57n.) etc. Such features are, for the most

---

[79] Cf. Lindsell (1937), Lembach (1970).

part, metrically guaranteed, and so their place within the poems can be securely plotted. Di Benedetto (1956) showed that the quantity of such features differs strikingly from poem to poem. Idylls 10 and 11 have very few such features, whereas there is a fair sprinkling in Idylls 1–7, with Idyll 7 having more than any other; Idyll 13, which Di Benedetto did not consider, seems to stand close to Idyll 7, and is, in any case, not straightforwardly 'epicising'.[80] Three points may be made about these results. The mere fact that the relative scarcity of such features allows them to be used as a diagnostic tool shows how far T.'s language has come from the traditional language of the hexameter. Secondly, just as there is a productive tension between metre and vocabulary, so the interplay between humble words and poeticising morphology is a central stylistic feature to which readers must always be alert;[81] such interplay is a major constitutive feature of a poetic self-consciousness which openly displays, rather than seeks to conceal, literariness. Thirdly, in the bucolic poems language and metre seem to move in parallel: the more 'Callimachean' poems also seem to be the most 'Homerising', and thus the ones which most obviously display their 'poetic' character.

3. *Dialect.* The predominant dialectal colour of all the poems in this volume is Doric; T. came from Dorian Syracuse and his poetry draws its most obvious inspiration from Sicilian poetic traditions (above, Section 2). Moreover, Idyll 1 tells a Sicilian myth and may be set there, Idyll 4, like 5, is set in Dorian South Italy, Idyll 7 is set on Dorian Cos, and Idylls 6 and 11 tell the story of the Sicilian Cyclops; Idylls 3 and 10 have no explicit setting that we can now recover. It is also now very hard to recover the 'resonance' of such Doric hexameters. Later theory, almost inevitably, saw a *mimesis* of the language of rustics, a rough equivalent of the mock 'West country' accent given to 'countryfolk' in some branches of English comedy.[82] There

---

[80] Cf. Hunter (1996a) 44–5.

[81] Cf. Fabiano (1971).

[82] Cf. Σ *Proleg.* p. 7, 8–10 Wendel; 'Probus' on Virg. *Ecl.* pp. 326–7 Thilo–Hagen, *Bucolica Theocritus facilius uidetur fecisse, quoniam Graecis sermo sic uidetur diuisus, ut Doris dialectos, qua ille scripsit, rustica habeatur*; Di Benedetto (1956) 49–50; Halperin (1983a) 148–52. A much more subtle Byzantine interpretation is found at Σ *Proleg.* p. 12, 4–25 Wendel.

is, however, no contemporary evidence that Doric would be the inevitable choice for such a *mimesis*, and this view leaves far too much unexplained about the use of Doric throughout the corpus and in other poets of the third century. We should also be wary of assuming a single explanation or a single flavour for all poems. It may be that there *is* an element of *mimesis* in the Doric of, say, Idyll 10, which is absent from the conspicuously different mode of Idyll 7, whereas elsewhere the language may evoke the high Doric lyric tradition of Stesichorus. We, like ancient scholars, read Theocritus in 'collected editions', but if we force ourselves to think rather in terms of the individual poem, then it will be variety rather than sameness which strikes us with greatest force.

The Doric character of the poems reveals itself partly in the use of a few specifically Doric words (e.g. λῆν 'to be willing'), but much more importantly in the phonology and morphology of words common to all dialects. 'Doric' is in fact a very broad designation covering sub-dialects spoken from the western to the eastern edges of the Greek world; a 'Doric' poet often had a variety of metrically equivalent and equally 'dialectal' forms from which to choose. Local differences persisted for some time in the face both of something like a Doric *koine* and what was to prove the much more potent threat of the Atticising *koine* which gradually took over the Greek world. It seems clear that, as well as using 'epic' features in his 'Doric' poems, T. combined within single poems 'Doric' features which were never found together in any real speech community. In this he would have been following the practice of literary poetry from Homer onwards: virtually all high Greek poetry, particularly the three great traditions of epic, lyric and tragedy, is composed in a composite, 'artificial' language which functions, in part, as a marker of distance from ordinary discourse. This view of the language of the 'bucolics' has indeed been challenged. C. J. Ruijgh (1984) argued that their language is essentially that of an expatriate Cyrenean élite living in Alexandria, modified by a number of forms influenced by the Attic *koine*. Ruijgh's case cannot be considered proven,[83] either on linguistic grounds or on the basis of what little we can reconstruct of T.'s poetic career, but the dialectal chaos which reigns in both papyri

[83] Cf. Hunter (1996a) 37.

and manuscripts means that we are too often unsure of what T. actually wrote to allow clear judgements about why he wrote what he did.

A catalogue of some features of T.'s Doric is appended; Homeric and *koine* alternatives which also occur are not listed. This list has no claims to exhaustiveness, and other phenomena are noted in the Commentary as they arise.[84]

I Phonology

(i) Long *alpha* is retained, and may also appear in so-called 'hyper-dorisms' in place of an original long *e*, cf. 1.44n., 1.109–10n.

(ii) Medial -ζ- may appear as -σδ- (though the earliest papyrus consistently presents the former spelling). This is a standard feature of ancient texts of Sappho and Alcaeus, where it seems to be a conventional spelling to mark 'the preservation of the pronunciation [zd] in Lesbian after it had changed to [z(z)] elsewhere' (W. S. Allen, *Vox Graeca*, 3rd ed. (Cambridge 1987) 59). It occurs also in ancient texts of Alcman, and if indeed T. used this convention, he may have considered it a feature of Laconian Doric. For discussion see Arena (1956), W. B. Stanford, *PRIA* 67 (1968/9) c.1–8, Gallavotti (1984) 5–6, Ruijgh (1984) 76–80, Molinos Tejada 120–31.

II Nouns

First declension

(i) Masculine genitive in -α (<αο), cf. 4.1 Φιλώνδα, 7.75n.

(ii) Acc. pl. -ἄς, as well as *koine* -ᾱς, cf. 1.82–3n.

(iii) Gen. pl. -ᾶν.

Second declension

(i) Gen. sing. -ω (<οο), cf. 1.6 χιμάρω, 1.29 τῶ (= τοῦ).

(ii) Acc. pl. -ως (<ονς), cf. 1.92 τώς (= τούς), 1.121 ταύρως, *or* -ος, cf. 1.90 τὰς παρθένος, cf. 1.82–3n.

---

[84] The Commentary makes no attempt to deal systematically with T.'s poetic dialect; I have in the main followed Gow and/or Gallavotti.

III Pronouns

First person

Nom. sing. ἐγών cf. 3.24n.

Dat. sing. ἐμίν

*Nom. pl. ἁμές, ἄμμες

*Acc. pl. ἁμέ, ἄμμε

*Dat. pl. ἁμίν, ἁμῖν, ἄμμι(ν)

Second person

Nom. sing. τύ

Acc. sing. τέ (1.5), enclitic τυ (1.60 etc.), τίν (cf. 11.39n.)

Gen. sing. τεῦς, τευς, τεοῦς (11.25–7n.); for τεῦ and τευ cf. 10.36–7n.

Dat. sing. τίν (with long iota) or τοι

*Nom. pl. ὑμές, ὔμμες

*Acc. pl. ὑμέ, ὔμμε

*Dat. pl. ὑμίν, ὑμῖν, ὔμμι(ν)

* The status of these forms in T. is particularly uncertain, cf. Gow II 300 n. 1, Molinos Tejada 142–9.

Third person

T. seems to have used both Doric νιν and Ionic μιν, and choice is often very difficult. The pronominal adjective is τῆνος, rather than (ἐ)κεῖνος, cf. 7.104n.

IV Verbs

1. Infinitives

(i) Thematic infinitives in -εν, as well as -ειν/-ην, cf. 1.14n.

(ii) Athematic infinitives in -μεν, 7.28 ἦμεν etc.

2. Personal endings

(i) 2nd pers. sing. pres. act. -ες, as well as -εις, cf. 1.1–3n.

(ii) 1st pers. pl. act. -μες, ἦμες 'we were', 7.2 εἵρπομες etc.

(iii) -τι rather than -σι is regular, hence 3.48 τίθητι, and 3rd pers. pl. act. -οντι, -αντι, 1.38 μοχθίζοντι, 43 ὠιδήκαντι.

3. Contracted verbs

(i) εο > ευ, 1.107 βομβεῦντι etc.

(ii) Apparent interchange between -άω and -έω verbs, cf. 3.18–20n., 7.51 ἐξεπόνασα.

(iii) Athematic declension of contracted verbs, 7.40 νίκημι, 1.36n.

4. Verb 'to be'

3rd pers. pl. pres. ἐντί; for singular ἐντί cf. 3.37–9n.
3rd pers. sing. impf. ἦς.

5. Tense formation

(i) Futures in -σέω with subsequent contraction, 1.14 νομευσῶ, 7.71 αὐλησεῦντι.

(ii) Verbs in -ζω (-σδω) form futures and aorists with -ξ-, 1.12 καθίξας, 1.97 λυγιξεῖν.

(iii) Perfects with present endings, 1.102 δεδύκειν (infinitive), 11.1 πεφύκει (with n. ad loc.).

6. Feminine participles

In -οισα, rather than -ουσα or -ωσα (so also Μοῖσα). Inscriptions attest such forms for Aeolian Lesbos and Dorian Cyrene, and they occur also in high lyric and Syracusan texts. T. may have taken such forms from the lyric tradition, but their origin and status in his poetry remain a matter of dispute, cf. Braun (1932) 181–93, Ruijgh (1984), Gallavotti (1984) 37–41, Molinos Tejada 151–8, Hunter (1996a) 37 n. 142.

V Miscellaneous

(i) Apocope of prepositions is regular, 1.74 πὰρ ποσσί, 10.22 ἀμβάλευ, 11.1n.

(ii) T. uses both Doric κα and Ionic κε, cf. 7.53–4n.

(iii) ἔγωγα, τύγα, though γε seems standard in the bucolics.

(iv) ἦνθον rather than ἦλθον etc.

6. TRANSMISSION

The early history of the circulation of T.'s poems is a fascinating and frustrating subject which cannot be pursued at any length

here.[85] Individual poems were presumably at first recited and circulated separately; some of the transmitted titles may perhaps go back
to the age of the poet himself, but the majority will have crystallised
in the subsequent tradition. Whether T. ever produced a 'collected
edition' of some of his poems we cannot say, and it would be rash to
assume that the strong sense of generic form which marks his poems
was given concrete expression in a 'poetry book'; their stylistic dis-
tinctiveness makes tempting the idea that T. produced a book of 'the
bucolics', but it must be admitted that there is no external evidence
to support the hypothesis. That Athenaeus (7 284a) can cite from a
poem, the *Berenike*, of which there is no other trace in our ancient
and medieval texts, suggests that this poem at least travelled separately. In the *Eclogues* Virgil echoes the spurious Idylls 8 and 9 and
'non-bucolic' poems such as Idylls 2 and 17,[86] and it is not unlikely[87]
that he used an edition prepared by the grammarian Artemidorus of
Tarsus in the first half of the first century BC. The *Anthology* preserves an epigram of Artemidorus with the heading 'For the gathering together of the bucolic poems':

Βουκολικαὶ Μοῖσαι σποράδες ποκά, νῦν δ' ἅμα πᾶσαι
ἐντὶ μιᾶς μάνδρας, ἐντὶ μιᾶς ἀγέλας.

(Anth. Pal. 9.205 = Epigram [xxvi] Gow)

The Bucolic Muses were once scattered, but are now all united
in one fold, in one flock.

Such a collection, presumably with the title Βουκολικά, will have
begun with the strictly 'bucolic' poems, but may have included other
poems as well, and also the work of other poets. Be that as it may,
the fact that in the probably early ἄλλος ὁ Χῖος epigram (above,
Section 1) T. is not yet presented as a 'bucolic' poet is surely significant. The primacy given to T.'s 'bucolic' poems by the subsequent
tradition will be a result of the development of a 'genre', attested by

---

[85] The main arguments and bibliography for what follows can be traced
through Wilamowitz (1906), Gow i lix–lxii, Gutzwiller (1996).

[86] Cf., e.g., I. M. Le M. DuQuesnay, 'Vergil's fourth *Eclogue*' *PLLS* i (1976)
25–99.

[87] The implications of Servius' famous remark, *sane sciendum est septem eclogas
esse meras rusticas, quas Theocritus decem habet* (*Buc. Prooem.* 3.21), are at least
ambiguous; for an ambitious attempt to build upon it see Vaughn (1981).

the spurious poems and by Moschus and Bion, in the two centuries separating T. from Virgil.

Some 180 medieval and Renaissance manuscripts containing Theocritean poems are known.[88] Shared errors demonstrate that all our MSS ultimately go back to a common ancestor, which itself contained corrections, variant readings etc. An increasingly rich papyrus record (though not yet dating earlier than the first century AD) and the preserved scholia on Idylls 1–18 and 28–9, which may ultimately go back to the work of Artemidorus' son, Theon, confirm the presence of significant textual variation (and not just in matters of dialect) from an early date. The MSS fall into three broad families, though they may change their affiliations from poem to poem; the principal MSS used in this edition and the order in which they present the poems are as follows:[89]

> Ambrosian family (K) 1, 7, 3–6, 8–13, 2, 14, 15, 17, 16, 29, *Epigrams*
>
> Laurentian family (PQW) 1, 5, 6, 4, 7, 3, 8–13, 2, 14–16, 25
>
> Vatican family (AGLNU) 1–18.

Of these families, the Ambrosian tradition of K seems the most trustworthy, and the Vatican the least, but the papyri make it clear that no medieval family offers privileged access to ancient traditions, and the modern editor should assume that truth may lurk anywhere. The now standard ordering of the whole collection derives from H. Stephanus, *Poetae Graeci principes heroici carminis & alii nonnulli* (Basel 1566), although the Vatican sequence of 1–18 was already followed in the *editio princeps* (Milan 1480) and the Aldine of 1495.[90]

Information in this edition about MSS readings derives from Gallavotti (3rd ed.) and Gow; where possible, reports of papyri have been checked against the original publication. The apparatus which accompanies the text is extremely selective: silence should never be interpreted as a sign that the tradition is unanimous, and those requiring more detailed information should consult Gallavotti and Gow.

---

[88] Gallavotti's 3rd edition, as well as Gow's Introduction, must be consulted for the manuscript history; cf. also Gallavotti (1952) 65–75.

[89] In the following list I omit the poems of Moschus, Bion etc. which often follow after T. in our MSS.

[90] Cf. Gallavotti 361–2.

SIGLA

1. PAPYRI

Π^1 *Perg. Louvre* 6678 + *Perg. Rainer* (saec. v)[1]

Π^2 *P. Berol.* 17073 (saec. IV)

Π^3 *P. Antinoae* (saec. v–vi)[2]

Π^4 *P. Oxy.* 3545 (saec. II)

Π^5 *P. Oxy.* 2064 + 3548 (saec. II)

Π^6 *P. Oxy.* 3547 (saec. II)

Π^7 *P. Oxy.* 1618 (saec. v)

Π^8 *P. Berol.* 21182 (saec. VI)

Π^9 *P. Oxy.* 3549 (saec. II)

Π^{10} *P. Oxy.* 694 (saec. II)

Π^{11} *P. Oxy.* 4430 (saec. II)

Π^{12} *P. Oxy.* 4432 (saec. II)

2. MANUSCRIPTS AND PRINTED BOOKS

a.   K   Ambrosianus 886 (C 222 inf.) saec. XIII

b.   P   Laurentianus 32. 37 saec. XIII–XIV
     Q   Parisinus gr. 2884 AD 1301[3]
     W   Laurentianus Conv. soppr. 15 saec. XIV

c.   A   Ambrosianus 390 (G 32 sup.) saec. XIII
     G   Laurentianus 32. 52 saec. XIII
     L   Parisinus gr. 2831 saec. XIII–XIV
     N   Athous Iberorum 161 saec. XIII–XIV
     U   Vaticanus gr. 1825 saec. XIV

d.   M   Vaticanus gr. 915 saec. XIII
     S   Laurentianus 32. 16 AD 1280

---

[1] Cf. Gow 1 l–li, J. Bingen, *CdE* 113/14 (1982) 309–16.

[2] Cf. A. S. Hunt and J. Johnson, *Two Theocritus papyri* (London 1930).

[3] Cf. A. Turyn, *Studies in the manuscript tradition of the tragedies of Sophocles* (Urbana 1952) 41 n. 31.

Tr	Parisinus gr. 2832 saec. xiv
Mosch.	Codd. Moschopulei saec. xiv, xv[4]
Non.	Salmanticensis 295 saec. xvi[5]

e.
ed. princ.	editio princeps, Bonus Accursius, Milan 1480
Ald.	Aldine edition, Venice 1495
Iunt.	Editio Philippi Iuntae, Florence 1516

f.
codd.	consensus codicum omnium
Ω	consensus codicum plurimorum
l	consensus codicum PQW
v	consensus codicum familiae Vaticanae[6]
Σ	scholiasta, scholia

3. ABBREVIATIONS

K a.c.	K ante correctionem
K p.c.	K post correctionem
K[v.l.]	varia lectio in K
K[s.l.]	K supra lineam
K[1]	manus prima in K
K[2]	manus secunda in K
Σ[lem]	lemma scholiastae

[4] Cf. Gow i xliv, Gallavotti 327–34.

[5] Cf. Gow i xlvi–ii.

[6] In practice this means (following Gallavotti): Idyll 1, AGS; Idyll 3, AGNU; Idyll 4, AGU; Idyll 6, AGLU; Idylls 7, 13 ALU; Idylls 10, 11 ALNU.

THEOCRITUS
A SELECTION

I IDYLL 1

ΘΥΡΣΙΣ Η ΩΙΔΗ

ΘΥΡΣΙΣ

ἁδύ τι τὸ ψιθύρισμα καὶ ἁ πίτυς, αἰπόλε, τήνα,
ἁ ποτὶ ταῖς παγαῖσι, μελίσδεται, ἁδὺ δὲ καὶ τύ
συρίσδες· μετὰ Πᾶνα τὸ δεύτερον ἆθλον ἀποισῆι.
αἴ κα τῆνος ἕληι κεραὸν τράγον, αἶγα τὺ λαψῆι·
αἴ κα δ' αἶγα λάβηι τῆνος γέρας, ἐς τὲ καταρρεῖ   5
ἁ χίμαρος· χιμάρω δὲ καλὸν κρέας, ἔστε κ' ἀμέλξηις.

ΑΙΠΟΛΟΣ

ἅδιον, ὦ ποιμήν, τὸ τεὸν μέλος ἢ τὸ καταχές
τῆν' ἀπὸ τᾶς πέτρας καταλείβεται ὑψόθεν ὕδωρ.
αἴ κα ταὶ Μοῖσαι τὰν οῖιδα δῶρον ἄγωνται,
ἄρνα τὺ σακίταν λαψῆι γέρας· αἰ δέ κ' ἀρέσκηι   10
τήναις ἄρνα λαβεῖν, τὺ δὲ τὰν ὄιν ὕστερον ἀξῆι.

ΘΥΡΣΙΣ

λῆις ποτὶ τᾶν Νυμφᾶν, λῆις, αἰπόλε, τεῖδε καθίξας,
ὡς τὸ κάταντες τοῦτο γεώλοφον αἴ τε μυρῖκαι,
συρίσδεν; τὰς δ' αἶγας ἐγὼν ἐν τῶιδε νομευσῶ.

ΑΙΠΟΛΟΣ

οὐ θέμις, ὦ ποιμήν, τὸ μεσαμβρινὸν οὐ θέμις ἄμμιν   15
συρίσδεν. τὸν Πᾶνα δεδοίκαμες· ἦ γὰρ ἀπ' ἄγρας
τανίκα κεκμακὼς ἀμπαύεται· ἔστι δὲ πικρός,
καί οἱ ἀεὶ δριμεῖα χολὰ ποτὶ ῥινὶ κάθηται.

I   6 κρέας Heinsius: κρῆς codd.   11 ἀξῆι S²: ἀξῆς vel ἀξεῖς Ω   13 ὡς
KPQ: ἐς Wv   17 ἔστι Stobaeus 3.20.3: ἔντι codd.   γε Kl

ἀλλὰ τὺ γὰρ δή, Θύρσι, τὰ Δάφνιδος ἄλγε᾽ ἀείδες
καὶ τᾶς βουκολικᾶς ἐπὶ τὸ πλέον ἵκεο μοίσας,   20
δεῦρ᾽ ὑπὸ τὰν πτελέαν ἐσδώμεθα τῶ τε Πριάπω
καὶ τᾶν Κρανιάδων κατεναντίον, ἅιπερ ὁ θῶκος
τῆνος ὁ ποιμενικὸς καὶ ταὶ δρύες. αἰ δέ κ᾽ ἀείσῃς
ὡς ὅκα τὸν Λιβύαθε ποτὶ Χρόμιν ἆισας ἐρίσδων,
αἶγά τέ τοι δωσῶ διδυματόκον ἐς τρὶς ἀμέλξαι,   25
ἃ δύ᾽ ἔχοισ᾽ ἐρίφως ποταμέλγεται ἐς δύο πέλλας,
καὶ βαθὺ κισσύβιον κεκλυσμένον ἁδέι κηρῶι,
ἀμφῶες, νεοτευχές, ἔτι γλυφάνοιο ποτόσδον.
τῶ ποτὶ μὲν χείλη μαρύεται ὑψόθι κισσός,
κισσὸς ἑλιχρύσωι κεκονισμένος· ἁ δὲ κατ᾽ αὐτόν   30
καρπῶι ἕλιξ εἰλεῖται ἀγαλλομένα κροκόεντι.
ἔντοσθεν δὲ γυνά, τι θεῶν δαίδαλμα, τέτυκται,
ἀσκητὰ πέπλωι τε καὶ ἄμπυκι· πὰρ δέ οἱ ἄνδρες
καλὸν ἐθειράζοντες ἀμοιβαδὶς ἄλλοθεν ἄλλος
νεικείουσ᾽ ἐπέεσσι· τὰ δ᾽ οὐ φρενὸς ἅπτεται αὐτᾶς·   35
ἀλλ᾽ ὅκα μὲν τῆνον ποτιδέρκεται ἄνδρα γέλαισα,
ἄλλοκα δ᾽ αὖ ποτὶ τὸν ῥιπτεῖ νόον· οἳ δ᾽ ὑπ᾽ ἔρωτος
δηθὰ κυλοιδιόωντες ἐτώσια μοχθίζοντι.
τοῖς δὲ μετὰ γριπεύς τε γέρων πέτρα τε τέτυκται
λεπράς, ἐφ᾽ ἆι σπεύδων μέγα δίκτυον ἐς βόλον ἕλκει   40
ὁ πρέσβυς, κάμνοντι τὸ καρτερὸν ἀνδρὶ ἐοικώς.
φαίης κεν γυίων νιν ὅσον σθένος ἐλλοπιεύειν,
ὧδέ οἱ ὠιδήκαντι κατ᾽ αὐχένα πάντοθεν ἶνες
καὶ πολιῶι περ ἐόντι· τὸ δὲ σθένος ἄξιον ἅβας.
τυτθὸν δ᾽ ὅσσον ἄπωθεν ἀλιτρύτοιο γέροντος   45
†πυρναίαις† σταφυλαῖσι καλὸν βέβριθεν ἀλωά,
τὰν ὀλίγος τις κῶρος ἐφ᾽ αἱμασιαῖσι φυλάσσει
ἥμενος· ἀμφὶ δέ μιν δύ᾽ ἀλώπεκες, ἃ μὲν ἀν᾽ ὄρχως

21 Πριάπω Brunck: Πριήπω codd.   22 Κρανιάδων Tr²: κρανίδων
Ω   24 ὅκα K: ποκα *lv*   25 τέ *l*: δέ KAG: νύ S   29 ποτὶ K*v*: περὶ *l*
30 κεκονιμένος PW   32 ἔκτοσθεν Π²   36 γέλαισα Wilamowitz: -οῖσα
KAGS²: -ᾶσα PQ²: -εῦσα QW   42 κα Ahrens   48 μιν Π³ codd.: νιν
Ziegler

φοιτῆι σινομένα τὰν τρώξιμον, ἃ δ᾽ ἐπὶ πήραι
πάντα δόλον τεύχοισα τὸ παιδίον οὐ πρὶν ἀνησεῖν   50
φατὶ πρὶν ἢ ἀκράτιστον ἐπὶ ξηροῖσι καθίξηι.
αὐτὰρ ὅγ᾽ ἀνθερίκοισι καλὰν πλέκει ἀκριδοθήραν
σχοίνωι ἐφαρμόσδων· μέλεται δέ οἱ οὔτε τι πήρας
οὔτε φυτῶν τοσσῆνον ὅσον περὶ πλέγματι γαθεῖ.
παντᾶι δ᾽ ἀμφὶ δέπας περιπέπταται ὑγρὸς ἄκανθος,   55
αἰπολικὸν θάημα· τέρας κέ τυ θυμὸν ἀτύξαι.
τῶ μὲν ἐγὼ πορθμῆι Καλυδνίωι αἶγά τ᾽ ἔδωκα
ὦνον καὶ τυρόεντα μέγαν λευκοῖο γάλακτος·
οὐδέ τί πω ποτὶ χεῖλος ἐμὸν θίγεν, ἀλλ᾽ ἔτι κεῖται
ἄχραντον. τῶι κά τυ μάλα πρόφρων ἀρεσαίμαν   60
αἴ κά μοι τύ, φίλος, τὸν ἐφίμερον ὕμνον ἀείσηις.
κοὔτι τυ κερτομέω. πόταγ᾽, ὠγαθέ· τὰν γὰρ ἀοιδάν
οὔ τί παι εἰς Ἀίδαν γε τὸν ἐκλελάθοντα φυλαξεῖς.

ΘΥΡΣΙΣ

ἄρχετε βουκολικᾶς, Μοῖσαι φίλαι, ἄρχετ᾽ ἀοιδᾶς.

Θύρσις ὅδ᾽ ὡς Αἴτνας, καὶ Θύρσιδος ἁδέα φωνά.   65
πῆ ποκ᾽ ἄρ᾽ ἦσθ᾽, ὅκα Δάφνις ἐτάκετο, πῆ ποκα, Νύμφαι;
ἦ κατὰ Πηνειῶ καλὰ τέμπεα, ἢ κατὰ Πίνδω;
οὐ γὰρ δὴ ποταμοῖο μέγαν ῥόον εἴχετ᾽ Ἀνάπω,
οὐδ᾽ Αἴτνας σκοπιάν, οὐδ᾽ Ἄκιδος ἱερὸν ὕδωρ.

ἄρχετε βουκολικᾶς, Μοῖσαι φίλαι, ἄρχετ᾽ ἀοιδᾶς.   70

τῆνον μὰν θῶες, τῆνον λύκοι ὠρύσαντο,
τῆνον χὠκ δρυμοῖο λέων ἔκλαυσε θανόντα.

---

50 κεύθοισα Σ^{v.l.}   51 versus corruptus   52 -θήκαν QW   56 αἰολικὸν
Σ^{v.l.} Hesych. s.v.   θάημα Porson: τι θάημα Kυ: τι θαῦμα l   57 πορθμῆι
Ahrens: -μεῖ vel -μῆ codd.   Καλυδνίωι Σ^{v.l.}: Καλυδωνίωι codd.   60 κά
Ahrens: καί Kυ: κέν l   61 κά Ahrens: κέ(ν) codd. Π¹   62 κερτομέω Kυ:
φθονέω lυ²   65 ἅδε ἁ P᾽Q²W   67 Πίνδον Ahrens   69 οὐκ Αἴτνας Π⁴
p.c.   71 ὠδύραντο KG²

ἄρχετε βουκολικᾶς, Μοῖσαι φίλαι, ἄρχετ' ἀοιδᾶς.

πολλαί οἱ πὰρ ποσσὶ βόες, πολλοὶ δέ τε ταῦροι,
πολλαὶ δὲ δαμάλαι καὶ πόρτιες ὠδύραντο.   75

ἄρχετε βουκολικᾶς, Μοῖσαι φίλαι, ἄρχετ' ἀοιδᾶς.

ἦνθ' Ἑρμᾶς πράτιστος ἀπ' ὤρεος, εἶπε δὲ "Δάφνι,
τίς τυ κατατρύχει; τίνος, ὠγαθέ, τόσσον ἔρασαι;"

ἄρχετε βουκολικᾶς, Μοῖσαι φίλαι, ἄρχετ' ἀοιδᾶς.

ἦνθον τοὶ βοῦται, τοὶ ποιμένες, ὡπόλοι ἦνθον·   80
πάντες ἀνηρώτευν τί πάθοι κακόν. ἦνθ' ὁ Πρίαπος
κἦφα "Δάφνι τάλαν, τί νυ τάκεαι; ἁ δέ τυ κώρα
πάσας ἀνὰ κράνας, πάντ' ἄλσεα ποσσὶ φορεῖται –

ἄρχετε βουκολικᾶς, Μοῖσαι φίλαι, ἄρχετ' ἀοιδᾶς –

ζάτεισ'· ἃ δύσερώς τις ἄγαν καὶ ἀμήχανος ἐσσί.   85
βούτας μὰν ἐλέγευ, νῦν δ' αἰπόλωι ἀνδρὶ ἔοικας.
ὡπόλος, ὅκκ' ἐσορῆι τὰς μηκάδας οἷα βατεῦνται,
τάκεται ὀφθαλμὼς ὅτι οὐ τράγος αὐτὸς ἔγεντο.

ἄρχετε βουκολικᾶς, Μοῖσαι φίλαι, ἄρχετ' ἀοιδᾶς.

καὶ τὺ δ' ἐπεί κ' ἐσορῆις τὰς παρθένος οἷα γελᾶντι,   90
τάκεαι ὀφθαλμὼς ὅτι οὐ μετὰ ταῖσι χορεύεις."
τὼς δ' οὐδὲν ποτελέξαθ' ὁ βουκόλος, ἀλλὰ τὸν αὐτῶ
ἄννε πικρὸν ἔρωτα, καὶ ἐς τέλος ἄννε μοίρας.

ἄρχετε βουκολικᾶς, Μοῖσαι, πάλιν ἄρχετ' ἀοιδᾶς.

ἦνθέ γε μὰν ἀδεῖα καὶ ἁ Κύπρις γελάοισα,   95
λάθρη μὲν γελάοισα, βαρὺν δ' ἀνὰ θυμὸν ἔχοισα,
κεῖπε "τύ θην τὸν Ἔρωτα κατεύχεο, Δάφνι, λυγιξεῖν·
ἦ ῥ' οὐκ αὐτὸς Ἔρωτος ὑπ' ἀργαλέω ἐλυγίχθης;"

78 ἔρασσαι QW   81 Πρίηπος v   82 νυ l: τὺ Kv   τυ Brunck: τι l: τοι
KAG   83 πάσας ... κράνας Π⁴l: πᾶσαν ... κράναν Kv   85 ζάτεισ' ἃ
Π⁴K²: ζάτεισα K: -οῖσ' ἃ vel -οῖσα lv   86 μὰν Π⁴ Tr: μὲν Ω   90
γελᾶντι KQ: -ῶντι PWS²: -εῦντι v   96 λάθρη codd.: ἀδέα Hermann

ἄρχετε βουκολικᾶς, Μοῖσαι, πάλιν ἄρχετ᾽ ἀοιδᾶς.

τὰν δ᾽ ἄρα χὠ Δάφνις ποταμείβετο· ''Κύπρι βαρεῖα,   100
Κύπρι νεμεσσατά, Κύπρι θνατοῖσιν ἀπεχθής,
ἤδη γὰρ φράσδηι πάνθ᾽ ἄλιον ἄμμι δεδύκειν·
Δάφνις κἤν Ἀίδα κακὸν ἔσσεται ἄλγος Ἔρωτι.

ἄρχετε βουκολικᾶς, Μοῖσαι, πάλιν ἄρχετ᾽ ἀοιδᾶς.

οὐ λέγεται τὰν Κύπριν ὁ βουκόλος; ἕρπε ποτ᾽ Ἴδαν,   105
ἕρπε ποτ᾽ Ἀγχίσαν· τηνεὶ δρύες ἠδὲ κύπειρος,
αἱ δὲ καλὸν βομβεῦντι ποτὶ σμάνεσσι μέλισσαι.

ἄρχετε βουκολικᾶς, Μοῖσαι, πάλιν ἄρχετ᾽ ἀοιδᾶς.

ὡραῖος χὠδωνις, ἐπεὶ καὶ μᾶλα νομεύει
καὶ πτῶκας βάλλει καὶ θηρία πάντα διώκει.   110

ἄρχετε βουκολικᾶς, Μοῖσαι, πάλιν ἄρχετ᾽ ἀοιδᾶς.

αὖτις ὅπως στασῆι Διομήδεος ἄσσον ἰοῖσα,
καὶ λέγε 'τὸν βούταν νικῶ Δάφνιν, ἀλλὰ μάχευ μοι.'

ἄρχετε βουκολικᾶς, Μοῖσαι, πάλιν ἄρχετ᾽ ἀοιδᾶς.

ὦ λύκοι, ὦ θῶες, ὦ ἀν᾽ ὤρεα φωλάδες ἄρκτοι,   115
χαίρεθ᾽· ὁ βουκόλος ὕμμιν ἐγὼ Δάφνις οὐκέτ᾽ ἀν᾽ ὕλαν,
οὐκέτ᾽ ἀνὰ δρυμώς, οὐκ ἄλσεα. χαῖρ᾽, Ἀρέθοισα,
καὶ ποταμοὶ τοὶ χεῖτε καλὸν κατὰ Θύβριδος ὕδωρ.

ἄρχετε βουκολικᾶς, Μοῖσαι, πάλιν ἄρχετ᾽ ἀοιδᾶς.

Δάφνις ἐγὼν ὅδε τῆνος ὁ τὰς βόας ὧδε νομεύων,   120
Δάφνις ὁ τὼς ταύρως καὶ πόρτιας ὧδε ποτίσδων.

ἄρχετε βουκολικᾶς, Μοῖσαι, πάλιν ἄρχετ᾽ ἀοιδᾶς.

ὦ Πὰν Πάν, εἴτ᾽ ἐσσὶ κατ᾽ ὤρεα μακρὰ Λυκαίω,
εἴτε τύγ᾽ ἀμφιπολεῖς μέγα Μαίναλον, ἔνθ᾽ ἐπὶ νᾶσον

106 ἠδὲ Meineke: ὧδε codd.   versum delevit Valckenaer   107 αἱ δὲ
Meineke: ὧδε codd.   109 μῆλα Ahrens   114 post 115 l   118 Θύβριδος
PQΣᵛ·ˡ·: Θύμβρ- WᵤΣᵛ·ˡ·: Δύβρ- KΣᵛ·ˡ·

τὰν Σικελάν, Ἑλίκας δὲ λίπε ῥίον αἰπύ τε σᾶμα   125
τῆνο Λυκαονίδαο, τὸ καὶ μακάρεσσιν ἀγητόν.

λήγετε βουκολικᾶς, Μοῖσαι, ἴτε λήγετ᾽ ἀοιδᾶς.

ἔνθ᾽, ὦναξ, καὶ τάνδε φέρευ πακτοῖο μελίπνουν
ἐκ κηρῶ σύριγγα καλὸν περὶ χεῖλος ἑλικτάν·
ἦ γὰρ ἐγὼν ὑπ᾽ Ἔρωτος ἐς Ἅιδαν ἕλκομαι ἤδη.   130

λήγετε βουκολικᾶς, Μοῖσαι, ἴτε λήγετ᾽ ἀοιδᾶς.

νῦν ἴα μὲν φορέοιτε βάτοι, φορέοιτε δ᾽ ἄκανθαι,
ἁ δὲ καλὰ νάρκισσος ἐπ᾽ ἀρκεύθοισι κομάσαι,
πάντα δ᾽ ἄναλλα γένοιτο, καὶ ἁ πίτυς ὄχνας ἐνείκαι,
Δάφνις ἐπεὶ θνάσκει, καὶ τὰς κύνας ὤλαφος ἕλκοι,   135
κἠξ ὀρέων τοὶ σκῶπες ἀηδόσι γαρύσαιντο."

λήγετε βουκολικᾶς, Μοῖσαι, ἴτε λήγετ᾽ ἀοιδᾶς.

χὢ μὲν τόσσ᾽ εἰπὼν ἀπεπαύσατο· τὸν δ᾽ Ἀφροδίτα
ἤθελ᾽ ἀνορθῶσαι· τά γε μὰν λίνα πάντα λελοίπει
ἐκ Μοιρᾶν, χὢ Δάφνις ἔβα ῥόον. ἔκλυσε δίνα   140
τὸν Μοίσαις φίλον ἄνδρα, τὸν οὐ Νύμφαισιν ἀπεχθῆ.

λήγετε βουκολικᾶς, Μοῖσαι, ἴτε λήγετ᾽ ἀοιδᾶς.

καὶ τὺ δίδοι τὰν αἶγα τό τε σκύφος, ὥς κεν ἀμέλξας
σπείσω ταῖς Μοίσαις. ὦ χαίρετε πολλάκι, Μοῖσαι,
χαίρετ᾽· ἐγὼ δ᾽ ὔμμιν καὶ ἐς ὕστερον ἅδιον ἀισῶ.   145

ΑΙΠΟΛΟΣ

πλῆρές τοι μέλιτος τὸ καλὸν στόμα, Θύρσι, γένοιτο,
πλῆρες δὲ σχαδόνων, καὶ ἀπ᾽ Αἰγίλω ἰσχάδα τρώγοις
ἁδεῖαν, τέττιγος ἐπεὶ τύγα φέρτερον ἄιδεις.
ἠνίδε τοι τὸ δέπας· θᾶσαι, φίλος, ὡς καλὸν ὄσδει·

---

129 καλὸν Fritzsche: καλὰν codd.   134 ἄναλλα Π⁵l: ἔναλλα Κυ   135
τὰς Π⁵W: τὼς Ω   136 ἀηδόνι Π⁵   138 ἀνεπαύσατο Π⁵QW²   143
δίδοι Π⁵ˢ·ˡ·: δίδου Π⁵ codd.

Ὡρᾶν πεπλύσθαι νιν ἐπὶ κράναισι δοκησεῖς.   150
ὧδ' ἴθι, Κισσαίθα· τὺ δ' ἄμελγέ νιν. αἱ δὲ χίμαιραι,
οὐ μὴ σκιρτασεῖτε, μὴ ὁ τράγος ὕμμιν ἀναστῇ.

II IDYLL 3

ΑΙΠΟΛΟΣ Η ΚΩΜΑΣΤΗΣ

κωμάσδω ποτὶ τὰν Ἀμαρυλλίδα, ταὶ δέ μοι αἶγες
βόσκονται κατ' ὄρος, καὶ ὁ Τίτυρος αὐτὰς ἐλαύνει.
Τίτυρ', ἐμὶν τὸ καλὸν πεφιλημένε, βόσκε τὰς αἶγας,
καὶ ποτὶ τὰν κράναν ἄγε, Τίτυρε· καὶ τὸν ἐνόρχαν,
τὸν Λιβυκὸν κνάκωνα, φυλάσσεο μή τυ κορύψῃ.   5

ὦ χαρίεσσ' Ἀμαρυλλί, τί μ' οὐκέτι τοῦτο κατ' ἄντρον
παρκύπτοισα καλεῖς, τὸν ἐρωτύλον; ἦ ῥά με μισεῖς;
ἦ ῥά γέ τοι σιμὸς καταφαίνομαι ἐγγύθεν ἦμεν,
νύμφα, καὶ προγένειος; ἀπάγξασθαί με ποησεῖς.
ἠνίδε τοι δέκα μᾶλα φέρω· τηνῶθε καθεῖλον   10
ὧ μ' ἐκέλευ καθελεῖν τύ· καὶ αὔριον ἄλλα τοι οἰσῶ.
θᾶσαι μάν· θυμαλγὲς ἐμὶν ἄχος. αἴθε γενοίμαν
ἁ βομβεῦσα μέλισσα καὶ ἐς τεὸν ἄντρον ἱκοίμαν,
τὸν κισσὸν διαδὺς καὶ τὰν πτέριν ἅ τυ πυκάσδει.
νῦν ἔγνων τὸν Ἔρωτα· βαρὺς θεός· ἦ ῥα λεαίνας   15
μαζὸν ἐθήλαζεν, δρυμῶι τέ νιν ἔτραφε μάτηρ,
ὅς με κατασμύχων καὶ ἐς ὀστίον ἄχρις ἰάπτει.
ὦ τὸ καλὸν ποθορεῦσα, τὸ πᾶν λίθος, ὦ κυάνοφρυ
νύμφα, πρόσπτυξαί με τὸν αἰπόλον, ὥς τυ φιλήσω·
ἔστι καὶ ἐν κενεοῖσι φιλήμασιν ἁδέα τέρψις.   20
τὸν στέφανον τῖλαί με καταυτίκα λεπτὰ ποησεῖς,

---

152 σκιρτασεῖτε Porson: -σῆτε codd.

II 10 τηνῶ δὲ *l*   11 ἄλλα τοι αὔριον Π¹¹   12 ἐμὶν Π⁵: ἐμὸν codd.
14 πυκάσδει Q: -σδηι Ω   16 νιν Stobaeus 4.20.60: μιν codd.   ἔτραφε
Π⁵A Stobaeus: ἔτρεφε Ω   17 ὀστίον Bergk: -έον codd.   18 λίπος Σ^{v.l.}

τόν τοι ἐγών, Ἀμαρυλλὶ φίλα, κισσοῖο φυλάσσω,
ἀμπλέξας καλύκεσσι καὶ εὐόδμοισι σελίνοις.
ὤμοι ἐγών, τί πάθω, τί ὁ δύσσοος; οὐχ ὑπακούεις.

τὰν βαίταν ἀποδὺς ἐς κύματα τηνῶ ἀλεῦμαι,   25
ὧπερ τὼς θύννως σκοπιάζεται Ὄλπις ὁ γριπεύς·
καἴ κα μὴ 'ποθάνω, τό γε μὰν τεὸν ἁδὺ τέτυκται.

ἔγνων πρᾶν, ὅκα μοι, μεμναμένωι εἰ φιλέεις με,
οὐδὲ τὸ τηλέφιλον ποτεμάξατο τὸ πλατάγημα,
ἀλλ' αὔτως ἁπαλῶι ποτὶ πάχεϊ ἐξεμαράνθη.   30

εἶπε καὶ ἁ γραία τἀλαθέα κοσκινόμαντις,
ἁ πρᾶν ποιολογεῦσα Παραιβάτις, οὕνεκ' ἐγὼ μέν
τὶν ὅλος ἔγκειμαι, τὺ δέ μευ λόγον οὐδένα ποιῆι.

ἦ μάν τοι λευκὰν διδυματόκον αἶγα φυλάσσω,
τάν με καὶ ἁ Μέρμνωνος ἐριθακὶς ἁ μελανόχρως   35
αἰτεῖ· καὶ δωσῶ οἱ, ἐπεὶ τύ μοι ἐνδιαθρύπτηι.

ἄλλεται ὀφθαλμός μευ ὁ δεξιός· ἆρά γ' ἰδησῶ
αὐτάν; ἀισεῦμαι ποτὶ τὰν πίτυν ὧδ' ἀποκλινθείς,
καί κέ μ' ἴσως ποτίδοι, ἐπεὶ οὐκ ἀδαμαντίνα ἐστίν.

Ἱππομένης, ὅκα δὴ τὰν παρθένον ἤθελε γᾶμαι,   40
μᾶλ' ἐν χερσὶν ἑλὼν δρόμον ἄνυεν· ἁ δ' Ἀταλάντα
ὡς ἴδεν, ὡς ἐμάνη, ὡς ἐς βαθὺν ἅλατ' ἔρωτα.

τὰν ἀγέλαν χὠ μάντις ἀπ' Ὄθρυος ἄγε Μελάμπους
ἐς Πύλον· ἁ δὲ Βίαντος ἐν ἀγκοίναισιν ἐκλίνθη
μάτηρ ἁ χαρίεσσα περίφρονος Ἀλφεσιβοίας.   45

τὰν δὲ καλὰν Κυθέρειαν ἐν ὤρεσι μῆλα νομεύων
οὐχ οὕτως Ὤδωνις ἐπὶ πλέον ἄγαγε λύσσας,
ὥστ' οὐδὲ φθίμενόν νιν ἄτερ μαζοῖο τίθητι;

ζαλωτὸς μὲν ἐμὶν ὁ τὸν ἄτροπον ὕπνον ἰαύων

24 ὑπακούει Hermann   27 μὴ codd.: δὴ Graefe   μὰν codd.: μὲν Denniston   28 ὅκα μοι Greverus: ὅκ' ἔμοιγε KQW: ὅκα μευ AGNU   30 ἁπαλῶι ποτὶ πάχει Mosch.: -ῶ π. -εος Ω   31 ἁ γραία Heinsius: Ἀγροιῶ codd.: ἁ Γροιὼ Σᵛˡ·   39 ἐστί P: ἐντί Ω: de Π⁵ non liquet   41 ἔχων Π⁵   42 ὡς εἶδ' Π¹¹   ἅλατ' Hemsterhusius: ἄλλατ' K: ἄλ(λ)ετ' Ω   44 ἀγκοίναισιν Winterton: -ηισιν codd.   46 μῆλα P: μᾶλα Ω

Ἐνδυμίων· ζαλῶ δέ, φίλα γύναι, Ἰασίωνα,   50
ὃς τόσσων ἐκύρησεν, ὅσ' οὐ πευσεῖσθε, βέβαλοι.

ἀλγέω τὰν κεφαλάν, τὶν δ' οὐ μέλει. οὐκέτ' ἀείδω,
κεισεῦμαι δὲ πεσών, καὶ τοὶ λύκοι ὧδέ μ' ἔδονται.
ὡς μέλι τοι γλυκὺ τοῦτο κατὰ βρόχθοιο γένοιτο.

III IDYLL 4

ΝΟΜΕΙΣ

ΒΑΤΤΟΣ

εἰπέ μοι, ὦ Κορύδων, τίνος αἱ βόες; ἦ ῥα Φιλώνδα;

ΚΟΡΥΔΩΝ

    οὔκ, ἀλλ' Αἴγωνος· βόσκεν δέ μοι αὐτὰς ἔδωκεν.
ΒΑ. ἦ πάι ψε κρύβδαν τὰ ποθέσπερα πάσας ἀμέλγες;
ΚΟ. ἀλλ' ὁ γέρων ὑφίητι τὰ μοσχία κἠμὲ φυλάσσει.
ΒΑ. αὐτὸς δ' ἐς τίν' ἄφαντος ὁ βουκόλος ᾤχετο χώραν;   5
ΚΟ. οὐκ ἄκουσας; ἄγων νιν ἐπ' Ἀλφεὸν ᾤχετο Μίλων.
ΒΑ. καὶ πόκα τῆνος ἔλαιον ἐν ὀφθαλμοῖσιν ὀπώπει;
ΚΟ. φαντί νιν Ἡρακλῆι βίαν καὶ κάρτος ἐρίσδεν.
ΒΑ. κἤμ' ἔφαθ' ἁ μάτηρ Πολυδεύκεος εἶμεν ἀμείνω.
ΚΟ. κᾤχετ' ἔχων σκαπάναν τε καὶ εἴκατι τουτόθε μᾶλα.   10
ΒΑ. πείσαι κα Μίλων καὶ τὼς λύκος αὐτίκα λυσσῆν.
ΚΟ. ταὶ δαμάλαι δ' αὐτὸν μυκώμεναι αἵδε ποθεῦντι.
ΒΑ. δείλαιαί γ' αὗται, τὸν βουκόλον ὡς κακὸν εὗρον.

52 ἀεισῶ nescioquis   53 ἔδονται Π⁶ US: -οντι Ω

III 2 βόσκειν Κ   8 βίαν Π⁵: βίην codd.   ἐρίσδειν Κ   9 ἦμεν *v*
10 μῆλα Ahrens   11 κα Ahrens: κε Κ: τοι Ω   13 γ' PSTr: δ' Ω

ΚΟ. ἦ μὰν δείλαιαί γε, καὶ οὐκέτι λῶντι νέμεσθαι.
ΒΑ. τήνας μὲν δή τοι τᾶς πόρτιος αὐτὰ λέλειπται   15
  τὠστία. μὴ πρῶκας σιτίζεται ὥσπερ ὁ τέττιξ;
ΚΟ. οὐ Δᾶν, ἀλλ᾽ ὅκα μέν νιν ἐπ᾽ Αἰσάροιο νομεύω
  καὶ μαλακῶ χόρτοιο καλὰν κώμυθα δίδωμι,
  ἄλλοκα δὲ σκαίρει τὸ βαθύσκιον ἀμφὶ Λάτυμνον.
ΒΑ. λεπτὸς μὰν χὠ ταῦρος ὁ πυρρίχος. αἴθε λάχοιεν   20
  τοὶ τῶ Λαμπριάδα, τοὶ δαμόται ὅκκα θύωντι
  τᾶι Ἥραι, τοιόνδε· κακοχράσμων γὰρ ὁ δᾶμος.
ΚΟ. καὶ μὰν ἐς Στομάλιμνον ἐλαύνεται ἔς τε τὰ Φύσκω,
  καὶ ποτὶ τὸν Νήαιθον, ὅπαι καλὰ πάντα φύοντι,
  αἰγίπυρος καὶ κνύζα καὶ εὐώδης μελίτεια.   25
ΒΑ. φεῦ φεῦ βασεῦνται καὶ ταὶ βόες, ὦ τάλαν Αἴγων,
  εἰς Ἀίδαν, ὅκα καὶ τὺ κακᾶς ἠράσσαο νίκας,
  χἀ σῦριγξ εὐρῶτι παλύνεται, ἅν ποκ᾽ ἐπάξα.
ΚΟ. οὐ τήνα γ᾽, οὐ Νύμφας, ἐπεὶ ποτὶ Πῖσαν ἀφέρπων
  δῶρον ἐμοί νιν ἔλειπεν· ἐγὼ δέ τις εἰμὶ μελικτάς,   30
  κεῦ μὲν τὰ Γλαύκας ἀγκρούομαι, εὖ δὲ τὰ Πύρρω.
  αἰνέω τάν τε Κρότωνα — "Καλὰ πόλις ἅ τε
                        Ζάκυνθος ..." —
  καὶ τὸ ποταῶιον τὸ Λακίνιον, ἅιπερ ὁ πύκτας
  Αἴγων ὀγδώκοντα μόνος κατεδαίσατο μάζας.
  τηνεὶ καὶ τὸν ταῦρον ἀπ᾽ ὤρεος ἆγε πιάξας   35
  τᾶς ὁπλᾶς κῆδωκ᾽ Ἀμαρυλλίδι, ταὶ δὲ γυναῖκες
  μακρὸν ἀνάυσαν, χὠ βουκόλος ἐξεγέλασσεν.
ΒΑ. ὦ χαρίεσσ᾽ Ἀμαρυλλί, μόνας σέθεν οὐδὲ θανοίσας
  λασεύμεσθ᾽· ὅσον αἶγες ἐμὶν φίλαι, ὅσσον ἀπέσβης.
  αἰαῖ τῶ σκληρῶ μάλα δαίμονος ὅς με λελόγχει.   40
ΚΟ. θαρσεῖν χρή, φίλε Βάττε· τάχ᾽ αὔριον ἔσσετ᾽ ἄμεινον.
  ἐλπίδες ἐν ζωοῖσιν, ἀνέλπιστοι δὲ θανόντες,
  χὠ Ζεὺς ἄλλοκα μὲν πέλει αἴθριος, ἄλλοκα δ᾽ ὕει.
ΒΑ. θαρσέω. βάλλε κάτωθε τὰ μοσχία· τᾶς γὰρ ἐλαίας

17 γᾶν K   νιν PG: μιν Ω   21 θύωντι Valckenaer: -οντι codd.   22
δᾶμος codd.: ταῦρος Σ^{v.l.}   28 ἐπάξω K²QW   37 ἐξεγέλαξε Tzetzes,
Chil. 2.588   39 φίλαι ὅσσον KS: φίλαι τόσσον Ω

τὸν θαλλὸν τρώγοντι, τὰ δύσσοα. ΚΟ. σίτθ᾽, ὁ
45   Λέπαργος,
σίττ᾽ ὦ Κυμαίθα, ποτὶ τὸν λόφον. οὐκ ἐσακούεις;
ἠξῶ, ναὶ τὸν Πᾶνα, κακὸν τέλος αὐτίκα δωσῶν,
εἰ μὴ ἄπει τουτῶθεν. ἴδ᾽ αὖ πάλιν ἅδε ποθέρπει.
αἶθ᾽ ἧς μοι ῥοικόν τι λαγωβόλον, ὥς τυ πάταξα.
ΒΑ. θᾶσαί μ᾽, ὦ Κορύδων, πὸτ τῶ Διός· ἁ γὰρ ἄκανθα   50
ἁρμοῖ μ᾽ ὧδ᾽ ἐπάταξ᾽ ὑπὸ τὸ σφυρόν. ὡς δὲ βαθεῖαι
τἀτρακτυλλίδες ἐντί. κακῶς ἁ πόρτις ὄλοιτο·
εἰς ταύταν ἐτύπην χασμεύμενος. ἦ ῥά γε λεύσσεις;
ΚΟ. ναὶ ναί, τοῖς ὀνύχεσσιν ἔχω τέ νιν· ἅδε καὶ αὐτά.
ΒΑ. ὀσσίχον ἐστὶ τὸ τύμμα, καὶ ἁλίκον ἄνδρα δαμάσδει.   55
ΚΟ. εἰς ὄρος ὄκχ᾽ ἕρπῃς, μὴ νήλιπος ἔρχεο, Βάττε·
ἐν γὰρ ὄρει ῥάμνοι τε καὶ ἀσπάλαθοι κομόωντι.
ΒΑ. εἶπ᾽ ἄγε μ᾽, ὦ Κορύδων, τὸ γερόντιον ἦ ῥ᾽ ἔτι μύλλει
τήναν τὰν κυάνοφρυν ἐρωτίδα τᾶς ποκ᾽ ἐκνίσθη;
ΚΟ. ἀκμάν γ᾽, ὦ δείλαιε· πρόαν γε μὲν αὐτὸς ἐπενθών   60
καὶ ποτὶ τᾶι μάνδραι κατελάμβανον ἆμος ἐνήργει.
ΒΑ. εὖ γ᾽, ὤνθρωπε φιλοῖφα. τό τοι γένος ἢ Σατυρίσκοις
ἐγγύθεν ἢ Πάνεσσι κακοκνάμοισιν ἐρίσδει.

IV IDYLL 7

ΘΑΛΥΣΙΑ

ἧς χρόνος ἀνίκ᾽ ἐγών τε καὶ Εὔκριτος εἰς τὸν Ἅλεντα
εἴρπομες ἐκ πόλιος, σὺν καὶ τρίτος ἄμμιν Ἀμύντας.
τᾶι Δηοῖ γὰρ ἔτευχε θαλύσια καὶ Φρασίδαμος

44–5 sic Wilamowitz   possis etiam ΒΑ. θαρσέω. ΚΟ. βάλλε κτλ.   46
σίττ᾽ ὦ Ω: σίτθ᾽ ἁ GUMosch.: σίτθ᾽ ὦ Α   49 ἧς Toup: ἦν codd.   τυ P:
τὸ Ω   πάταξα Κ¹: -ξω Ω   53 ῥά γε ed. princ.: ῥά τε Κν: ἄρα *l*   56
νήλιπος Κ: ἀνήλ- vel ἀνάλ- Ω: ἀναλ- Π¹²   57 ῥάμνοι codd.: κάκτοι
Π¹²Σᵛ·ˡ·: βάττου Π¹²ᵛ·ˡ· ut vid.   61 τᾶι μάνδραι ΚΡΟ²: τὰν μάνδραν Ω: τὰν
μάκτραν Σᵛ·ˡ·   63 ἐρίσδεις Κ¹

IV 1 ἐγών Π⁵: ἐγώ codd.   2 ἁμὶν Apoll. Dysc., *GG* II 1.42, 2.177

44   IDYLL 7

κἀντιγένης, δύο τέκνα Λυκωπέος, εἴ τί περ ἐσθλόν
χαῶν τῶν ἐπάνωθεν ἀπὸ Κλυτίας τε καὶ αὐτῶ   5
Χάλκωνος, Βούριναν ὃς ἐκ ποδὸς ἄνυε κράναν
εὖ ἐνερεισάμενος πέτραι γόνυ· ταὶ δὲ παρ' αὐτάν
αἴγειροι πτελέαι τε ἐύσκιον ἄλσος ὕφαινον
χλωροῖσιν πετάλοισι κατηρεφέες κομόωσαι.
κοὔπω τὰν μεσάταν ὁδὸν ἄνυμες, οὐδὲ τὸ σᾶμα   10
ἁμῖν τὸ Βρασίλα κατεφαίνετο, καί τιν' ὁδίταν
ἐσθλὸν σὺν Μοίσαισι Κυδωνικὸν εὕρομες ἄνδρα,
οὔνομα μὲν Λυκίδαν, ἦς δ' αἰπόλος, οὐδέ κέ τίς μιν
ἠγνοίησεν ἰδών, ἐπεὶ αἰπόλωι ἔξοχ' ἐώικει.
ἐκ μὲν γὰρ λασίοιο δασύτριχος εἶχε τράγοιο   15
κνακὸν δέρμ' ὤμοισι νέας ταμίσοιο ποτόσδον,
ἀμφὶ δέ οἱ στήθεσσι γέρων ἐσφίγγετο πέπλος
ζωστῆρι πλακερῶι, ῥοικὰν δ' ἔχεν ἀγριελαίω
δεξιτερᾶι κορύναν. καί μ' ἀτρέμας εἶπε σεσαρώς
ὄμματι μειδιόωντι, γέλως δέ οἱ εἴχετο χείλευς·   20
"Σιμιχίδα, πᾶι δὴ τὺ μεσαμέριον πόδας ἕλκεις,
ἀνίκα δὴ καὶ σαῦρος ἐν αἱμασιαῖσι καθεύδει,
οὐδ' ἐπιτυμβίδιοι κορυδαλλίδες ἠλαίνοντι;
ἦ μετὰ δαῖτ' ἄκλητος ἐπείγεαι, ἤ τινος ἀστῶν
λανὸν ἔπι θρώισκεις; ὥς τοι ποσὶ νισσομένοιο   25
πᾶσα λίθος πταίοισα ποτ' ἀρβυλίδεσσιν ἀείδει."
τὸν δ' ἐγὼ ἀμείφθην· "Λυκίδα φίλε, φαντί τυ πάντες
ἦμεν συρικτὰν μέγ' ὑπείροχον ἔν τε νομεῦσιν
ἔν τ' ἀματήρεσσι. τὸ δὴ μάλα θυμὸν ἰαίνει
ἀμέτερον· καίτοι κατ' ἐμὸν νόον ἰσοφαρίζειν   30
ἔλπομαι. ἁ δ' ὁδὸς ἅδε θαλυσιάς· ἦ γὰρ ἑταῖροι
ἄνερες εὐπέπλωι Δαμάτερι δαῖτα τελεῦντι

5 ἐπάνωθεν Reiske: ἔτ' ἀν- codd.: ἐπ' ἄνωθεν Ald.   6 Βούρειαν QWΣ
7 εὖ Π⁵: εὖ γ' codd.   8 ὕφαινον Heinsius: ἔφ- codd.   11 τιν' Q²WS²
Mosch.: τὸν Ω   12 ἐσλὸν Π⁵   13 νιν Π⁷ a.c. Ziegler   14 ἀγνοιη- Π⁵
18 πλοκερῶι Σᵛ·ˡ·   23 ἠλαίνοντι Galen 12.361 Kühn, Iunt.: -ται codd.
24 δαῖτ' ἄκλητος Iunt. Σᵛ·ˡ·: δαῖτα κλητὸς codd.   28 ἦμεν Wilamowitz:
ἔμμεν uel ἔμμεναι codd.   30 ἰσοφαρίσδεν lv

ὄλβω ἀπαρχόμενοι· μάλα γάρ σφισι πίονι μέτρωι
ἁ δαίμων εὔκριθον ἀνεπλήρωσεν ἀλωάν.
ἀλλ' ἄγε δή, ξυνὰ γὰρ ὁδὸς ξυνὰ δὲ καὶ ἀώς,   35
βουκολιασδώμεσθα· τάχ' ὥτερος ἄλλον ὀνασεῖ.
καὶ γὰρ ἐγὼ Μοισᾶν καπυρὸν στόμα, κἠμὲ λέγοντι
πάντες ἀοιδὸν ἄριστον· ἐγὼ δέ τις οὐ ταχυπειθής,
οὐ Δᾶν· οὐ γάρ πω κατ' ἐμὸν νόον οὔτε τὸν ἐσθλόν
Σικελίδαν νίκημι τὸν ἐκ Σάμω οὔτε Φιλίταν   40
ἀείδων, βάτραχος δὲ ποτ' ἀκρίδας ὥς τις ἐρίσδω."
ὣς ἐφάμαν ἐπίταδες· ὁ δ' αἰπόλος ἁδὺ γελάσσας,
"τάν τοι", ἔφα, "κορύναν δωρύττομαι, οὕνεκεν ἐσσί
πᾶν ἐπ' ἀλαθείαι πεπλασμένον ἐκ Διὸς ἔρνος.
ὥς μοι καὶ τέκτων μέγ' ἀπέχθεται ὅστις ἐρευνῆι   45
ἶσον ὄρευς κορυφᾶι τελέσαι δόμον Ὡρομέδοντος,
καὶ Μοισᾶν ὄρνιχες ὅσοι ποτὶ Χῖον ἀοιδόν
ἀντία κοκκύζοντες ἐτώσια μοχθίζοντι.
ἀλλ' ἄγε βουκολικᾶς ταχέως ἀρξώμεθ' ἀοιδᾶς,
Σιμιχίδα· κἠγὼ μέν – ὅρη, φίλος, εἴ τοι ἀρέσκει   50
τοῦθ' ὅτι πρᾶν ἐν ὄρει τὸ μελύδριον ἐξεπόνασα.

ἔσσεται Ἀγεάνακτι καλὸς πλόος ἐς Μυτιλήναν,
χὤταν ἐφ' ἑσπερίοις Ἐρίφοις νότος ὑγρὰ διώκηι
κύματα, χὠρίων ὅτ' ἐπ' ὠκεανῶι πόδας ἴσχει,
αἴ κα τὸν Λυκίδαν ὀπτεύμενον ἐξ Ἀφροδίτας   55
ῥύσηται· θερμὸς γὰρ ἔρως αὐτῶ με καταίθει.
χἀλκυόνες στορεσεῦντι τὰ κύματα τάν τε θάλασσαν
τόν τε νότον τόν τ' εὖρον, ὃς ἔσχατα φυκία κινεῖ,
ἀλκυόνες, γλαυκαῖς Νηρηίσι ταί τε μάλιστα
ὀρνίχων ἐφίληθεν, ὅσοις τέ περ ἐξ ἁλὸς ἄγρα.   60
Ἀγεάνακτι πλόον διζημένωι ἐς Μυτιλήναν

39 Δᾶν Ω: γᾶν Κ   40 Φιλίταν Croenert: -ηταν codd.   42 γελάσσας S
Mosch.: -άσας ΚΡΑ¹: -άξας Ω   46 Ὡρομέδοντος vel Ὠρο- Π³Κ/LU:
Εὐρυ- ΑU² Σ^{v.l.}   52 Μιτυλήναν ΚΑU   54 ἴσχει Q¹S: -ηι Ω   55 κα
Wilamowitz: κεν codd.   60 ὅσοις Greverus: -αις codd.   61 Μιτυλήναν
ΚΑU

ὥρια πάντα γένοιτο, καὶ εὔπλοος ὅρμον ἵκοιτο.
κἠγὼ τῆνο κατ' ἆμαρ ἀνήτινον ἢ ῥοδόεντα
ἢ καὶ λευκοΐων στέφανον περὶ κρατὶ φυλάσσων
τὸν Πτελεατικὸν οἶνον ἀπὸ κρατῆρος ἀφυξῶ   65
πὰρ πυρὶ κεκλιμένος, κύαμον δέ τις ἐν πυρὶ φρυξεῖ.
χἀ στιβὰς ἐσσεῖται πεπυκασμένα ἔστ' ἐπὶ πᾶχυν
κνύζαι τ' ἀσφοδέλωι τε πολυγνάμπτωι τε σελίνωι.
καὶ πίομαι μαλακῶς μεμναμένος Ἀγεάνακτος
†αὐταῖσιν† κυλίκεσσι καὶ ἐς τρύγα χεῖλος ἐρείδων.   70
αὐλησεῦντι δέ μοι δύο ποιμένες, εἷς μὲν Ἀχαρνεύς,
εἷς δὲ Λυκωπίτας· ὁ δὲ Τίτυρος ἐγγύθεν ἀισεῖ
ὡς ποκα τᾶς Ξενέας ἠράσσατο Δάφνις ὁ βούτας,
χὠς ὄρος ἀμφεπονεῖτο καὶ ὡς δρύες αὐτὸν ἐθρήνευν
Ἱμέρα αἵτε φύοντι παρ' ὄχθαισιν ποταμοῖο,   75
εὖτε χιὼν ὥς τις κατετάκετο μακρὸν ὑφ' Αἷμον
ἢ Ἄθω ἢ Ῥοδόπαν ἢ Καύκασον ἐσχατόωντα.
ἀισεῖ δ' ὥς ποκ' ἔδεκτο τὸν αἰπόλον εὐρέα λάρναξ
ζωὸν ἐόντα κακαῖσιν ἀτασθαλίαισιν ἄνακτος,
ὥς τέ νιν αἱ σιμαὶ λειμωνόθε φέρβον ἰοῖσαι   80
κέδρον ἐς ἀδεῖαν μαλακοῖς ἄνθεσσι μέλισσαι,
οὕνεκά οἱ γλυκὺ Μοῖσα κατὰ στόματος χέε νέκταρ.
ὦ μακαριστὲ Κομᾶτα, τύ θην τάδε τερπνὰ πεπόνθεις·
καὶ τὺ κατεκλάισθης ἐς λάρνακα, καὶ τὺ μελισσᾶν
κηρία φερβόμενος ἔτος ὥριον ἐξεπόνασας.   85
αἴθ' ἐπ' ἐμεῦ ζωοῖς ἐναρίθμιος ὤφελες ἦμεν,
ὥς τοι ἐγὼν ἐνόμευον ἀν' ὥρεα τὰς καλὰς αἶγας
φωνᾶς εἰσαΐων, τὺ δ' ὑπὸ δρυσὶν ἢ ὑπὸ πεύκαις
ἁδὺ μελισδόμενος κατεκέκλισο, θεῖε Κομᾶτα.''

χὠ μὲν τόσσ' εἰπὼν ἀπεπαύσατο· τὸν δὲ μέτ' αὖθις   90
κἠγὼν τοῖ' ἐφάμαν· ''Λυκίδα φίλε, πολλὰ μὲν ἄλλα

62 ὥρια Σᵛˑˡ.   εὔπλοος Schaefer: -ον codd.   70 αὐταῖς ἐν Valckenaer
75 αιτεφνοντο Π⁵: αιτ' εφύοντο Π⁷   76 κατατάκετο Π⁵P   86 ἐμεῦ PG:
ἐμοὶ Π⁷Ω   89 κατακέκλισο Q²υ   90 ἀνεπαύσατο K

Νύμφαι κἠμὲ δίδαξαν ἀν' ὤρεα βουκολέοντα
ἐσθλά, τά που καὶ Ζηνὸς ἐπὶ θρόνον ἄγαγε φάμα·
ἀλλὰ τόγ' ἐκ πάντων μέγ' ὑπείροχον, ὧι τυ γεραίρεν
ἀρξεῦμ'· ἀλλ' ὑπάκουσον, ἐπεὶ φίλος ἔπλεο Μοίσαις. 95

Σιμιχίδαι μὲν Ἔρωτες ἐπέπταρον· ἦ γὰρ ὁ δειλός
τόσσον ἐρᾶι Μυρτοῦς ὅσον εἴαρος αἶγες ἔρανται.
Ὥρατος δ' ὁ τὰ πάντα φιλαίτατος ἀνέρι τήνωι
παιδὸς ὑπὸ σπλάγχνοισιν ἔχει πόθον. οἶδεν Ἄριστις,
ἐσθλὸς ἀνήρ, μέγ' ἄριστος, ὃν οὐδέ κεν αὐτὸς ἀείδεν 100
Φοῖβος σὺν φόρμιγγι παρὰ τριπόδεσσι μεγαίροι,
ὡς ἐκ παιδὸς Ἄρατος ὑπ' ὀστέον αἴθετ' ἔρωτι.
τόν μοι, Πάν, Ὁμόλας ἐρατὸν πέδον ὅστε λέλογχας,
ἄκλητον κείνοιο φίλας ἐς χεῖρας ἐρείσαις,
εἴτ' ἔστ' ἄρα Φιλῖνος ὁ μαλθακὸς εἴτε τις ἄλλος. 105
κεἰ μὲν ταῦτ' ἔρδοις, ὦ Πὰν φίλε, μήτι τυ παῖδες
Ἀρκαδικοὶ σκίλλαισιν ὑπὸ πλευράς τε καὶ ὤμους
τανίκα μαστίζοιεν, ὅτε κρέα τυτθὰ παρείη·
εἰ δ' ἄλλως νεύσαις, κατὰ μὲν χρόα πάντ' ὀνύχεσσι
δακνόμενος κνάσαιο καὶ ἐν κνίδαισι καθεύδοις· 110
εἴης δ' Ἠδωνῶν μὲν ἐν ὤρεσι χείματι μέσσωι
Ἕβρον πὰρ ποταμὸν τετραμμένος ἐγγύθεν Ἄρκτω,
ἐν δὲ θέρει πυμάτοισι παρ' Αἰθιόπεσσι νομεύοις
πέτραι ὕπο Βλεμύων, ὅθεν οὐκέτι Νεῖλος ὁρατός.
ὔμμες δ' Ὑετίδος καὶ Βυβλίδος ἁδὺ λιπόντες 115
νᾶμα καὶ Οἰκοῦντα, ξανθᾶς ἕδος αἰπὺ Διώνας,
ὦ μάλοισιν Ἔρωτες ἐρευθομένοισιν ὁμοῖοι,
βάλλετέ μοι τόξοισι τὸν ἱμερόεντα Φιλῖνον,
βάλλετ', ἐπεὶ τὸν ξεῖνον ὁ δύσμορος οὐκ ἐλεεῖ μευ.
καὶ δὴ μὰν ἀπίοιο πεπαίτερος, αἱ δὲ γυναῖκες, 120

92 κἠμ' ἐδίδαξαν Π⁷   93 Ζανὸς Π⁵ l L   97 ἔραντι Kl   102 ὀστίον
Fritzsche   104 κείνοιο Π⁵Π⁷ Ω: τήνοιο S   107 ὤμως Valckenaer   109
νεύσαις Π⁵Π⁷ lv: -εις K   112]ρω παρ ποταμω Π⁷ p.c.   κεκλιμένος K² l
Ἄρκτω S: -ου Ω   116 Οἰκοῦντα Hecker:]ντα Π⁷: -εῦντα ΣΣ: -εῦντες Ω
120 καὶ δὴ μὰν suspectum   μὰν v: μάλ' Kl

'αἰαῖ', φαντί, 'Φιλῖνε, τό τοι καλὸν ἄνθος ἀπορρεῖ'.
μηκέτι τοι φρουρέωμες ἐπὶ προθύροισιν, Ἄρατε,
μηδὲ πόδας τρίβωμες· ὁ δ' ὄρθριος ἄλλον ἀλέκτωρ
κοκκύσδων νάρκαισιν ἀνιαραῖσι διδοίη·
εἷς δ' ἀπὸ τᾶσδε, φέριστε, Μόλων ἄγχοιτο παλαίστρας.   125
ἄμμιν δ' ἀσυχία τε μέλοι, γραία τε παρείη
ἅτις ἐπιφθύζοισα τὰ μὴ καλὰ νόσφιν ἐρύκοι.''

τόσσ' ἐφάμαν· ὁ δέ μοι τὸ λαγωβόλον, ἁδὺ γελάσσας
ὡς πάρος, ἐκ Μοισᾶν ξεινήιον ὤπασεν ἦμεν.
χὠ μὲν ἀποκλίνας ἐπ' ἀριστερὰ τὰν ἐπὶ Πύξας   130
εἷρφ' ὁδόν· αὐτὰρ ἐγών τε καὶ Εὔκριτος ἐς Φρασιδάμω
στραφθέντες χὠ καλὸς Ἀμύντιχος ἔν τε βαθείαις
ἀδείας σχοίνοιο χαμευνίσιν ἐκλίνθημες
ἔν τε νεοτμάτοισι γεγαθότες οἰναρέοισι.
πολλαὶ δ' ἄμμιν ὕπερθε κατὰ κρατὸς δονέοντο   135
αἴγειροι πτελέαι τε· τὸ δ' ἐγγύθεν ἱερὸν ὕδωρ
Νυμφᾶν ἐξ ἄντροιο κατειβόμενον κελάρυζε.
τοὶ δὲ ποτὶ σκιαραῖς ὀροδαμνίσιν αἰθαλίωνες
τέττιγες λαλαγεῦντες ἔχον πόνον· ἁ δ' ὀλολυγών
τηλόθεν ἐν πυκιναῖσι βάτων τρύζεσκεν ἀκάνθαις·   140
ἄειδον κόρυδοι καὶ ἀκανθίδες, ἔστενε τρυγών,
πωτῶντο ξουθαὶ περὶ πίδακας ἀμφὶ μέλισσαι.
πάντ' ὦσδεν θέρεος μάλα πίονος, ὦσδε δ' ὀπώρας.
ὄχναι μὲν πὰρ ποσσί, παρὰ πλευραῖσι δὲ μᾶλα
δαψιλέως ἁμῖν ἐκυλίνδετο, τοὶ δ' ἐκέχυντο   145
ὄρπακες βραβίλοισι καταβρίθοντες ἔραζε·
τετράενον δὲ πίθων ἀπελύετο κρατὸς ἄλειφαρ.
Νύμφαι Κασταλίδες Παρνάσιον αἶπος ἔχοισαι,
ἆρά γέ παι τοιόνδε Φόλω κατὰ λάινον ἄντρον
κρατῆρ' Ἡρακλῆι γέρων ἐστάσατο Χίρων;   150
ἆρά γέ παι τῆνον τὸν ποιμένα τὸν ποτ' Ἀνάπωι,

125 ἀπὸ Π⁵KQ²Σ^lem: ὑπὸ v: ἐπὶ l Σ   128 γελάσσας U²S Mosch.: -άξας
Π⁵Π⁸Ω   129 εἶμεν Kl   130 Φύξας Σ^v.l.   135 ἁμὶν Eustath. Hom.
1112.37   147 τετράενον Von der Mühll: -ενες codd.: ἑπτάενες Σ^lem

τὸν κρατερὸν Πολύφαμον, ὃς ὤρεσι νᾶας ἔβαλλε,
τοῖον νέκταρ ἔπεισε κατ' αὔλια ποσσὶ χορεῦσαι,
οἷον δὴ τόκα πῶμα διεκρανάσατε, Νύμφαι,
βωμῶι πὰρ Δάματρος ἀλωίδος; ἅς ἐπὶ σωρῶι   155
αὖτις ἐγὼι πάξαιμι μέγα πτύον, ἃ δὲ γελάσσαι
δράγματα καὶ μάκωνας ἐν ἀμφοτέραισιν ἔχοισα.

V IDYLL 10

ΕΡΓΑΤΙΝΑΙ Η ΘΕΡΙΣΤΑΙ

ΜΙΛΩΝ

ἐργατίνα Βουκαῖε, τί νῦν, ὠιζυρέ, πεπόνθεις;
οὔτε τὸν ὄγμον ἄγειν ὀρθὸν δύναι, ὡς τὸ πρὶν ἄγες,
οὔθ' ἅμα λαιοτομεῖς τῶι πλατίον, ἀλλ' ἀπολείπηι,
ὥσπερ ὄις ποίμνας, ἅς τὸν πόδα κάκτος ἔτυψε.
ποῖός τις δείλαν τὺ καὶ ἐκ μέσω ἄματος ἐσσῆι,   5
ὃς νῦν ἀρχόμενος τᾶς αὔλακος οὐκ ἀποτρώγεις;

ΒΟΥΚΑΙΟΣ

Μίλων ὀψαμᾶτα, πέτρας ἀπόκομμ' ἀτεράμνω,
οὐδαμά τοι συνέβα ποθέσαι τινὰ τῶν ἀπεόντων;
ΜΙ.   οὐδαμά. τίς δὲ πόθος τῶν ἔκτοθεν ἐργάται ἀνδρί;
ΒΟ.   οὐδαμά νυν συνέβα τοι ἀγρυπνῆσαι δι' ἔρωτα;   10
ΜΙ.   μηδέ γε συμβαίη· χαλεπὸν χορίω κύνα γεῦσαι.
ΒΟ.   ἀλλ' ἐγώ, ὦ Μίλων, ἔραμαι σχεδὸν ἐνδεκαταῖος.
ΜΙ.   ἐκ πίθω ἀντλεῖς δῆλον· ἐγὼ δ' ἔχω οὐδ' ἅλις ὄξος.
ΒΟ.   τοιγὰρ τὰ πρὸ θυρᾶν μοι ἀπὸ σπόρω ἄσκαλα
                                        πάντα.

152 νᾶας Heinsius: λᾶας codd.   154 διακρανώσατε Π⁵Σᵛ·ˡ· Etym. Mag.
273.41 v   155 ἀλωάδος v

V 2 οὔτε τὸν MTr: οὐ τεὸν Κ: οὔθ' ἐὸν lv   5 δείλαν τὺ Κ²Μ: δ, τε
KQWv: δειλαῖε P   6 οὐδ' ἀπο- Hunter   14 τοιγὰρ τὰ PS: τοιγάρτοι Ω

ΜΙ. τίς δέ τυ τᾶν παίδων λυμαίνεται;   15
ΒΟ.   ἁ Πολυβώτα,
ἇ πρᾶν ἀμάντεσσι παρ' Ἱπποκίωνι ποταύλει.
ΜΙ. εὗρε θεὸς τὸν ἀλιτρόν· ἔχεις πάλαι ὧν ἐπεθύμεις·
μάντις τοι τὰν νύκτα χροϊξεῖται καλαμαία.
ΒΟ. μωμᾶσθαί μ' ἄρχηι τύ· τυφλὸς δ' οὐκ αὐτὸς ὁ
Πλοῦτος,
ἀλλὰ καὶ ὠφρόντιστος Ἔρως. μὴ δὴ μέγα μυθεῦ.   20
ΜΙ. οὐ μέγα μυθεῦμαι· τὺ μόνον κατάβαλλε τὸ λᾶιον,
καί τι κόρας φιλικὸν μέλος ἀμβάλευ. ἅδιον οὕτως
ἐργαξῇ. καὶ μὰν πρότερόν ποκα μουσικὸς ἦσθα.

ΒΟ.   Μοῖσαι Πιερίδες, συναείσατε τὰν ῥαδινάν μοι
παῖδ'· ὧν γάρ χ' ἄψησθε, θεαί, καλὰ πάντα ποεῖτε.   25
Βομβύκα χαρίεσσα, Σύραν καλέοντί τυ πάντες,
ἰσχνάν, ἁλιόκαυστον, ἐγὼ δὲ μόνος μελίχλωρον.
καὶ τὸ ἴον μέλαν ἐστί, καὶ ἁ γραπτὰ ὑάκινθος·
ἀλλ' ἔμπας ἐν τοῖς στεφάνοις τὰ πρᾶτα λέγονται.
ἁ αἲξ τὰν κύτισον, ὁ λύκος τὰν αἶγα διώκει,   30
ἁ γέρανος τὤροτρον· ἐγὼ δ' ἐπὶ τὶν μεμάνημαι.
αἴθε μοι ἦς ὅσσα Κροῖσόν ποκα φαντὶ πεπᾶσθαι·
χρύσεοι ἀμφότεροί κ' ἀνεκείμεθα τᾶι Ἀφροδίται,
τὼς αὐλὼς μὲν ἔχοισα καὶ ἢ ῥόδον ἢ τύγε μᾶλον,
σχῆμα δ' ἐγὼ καὶ καινὰς ἐπ' ἀμφοτέροισιν ἀμύκλας.   35
Βομβύκα χαρίεσ', οἱ μὲν πόδες ἀστράγαλοί τευ,
ἁ φωνὰ δὲ τρύχνος· τὸν μὰν τρόπον οὐκ ἔχω εἰπεῖν.

ΜΙ. ἦ καλὰς ἄμμε ποῶν ἐλελάθει Βοῦκος ἀοιδάς·
ὡς εὖ τὰν ἰδέαν τᾶς ἁρμονίας ἐμέτρησεν.

16 πρὰν S: πρὶν Ω   ἀμάντεσσι Ahrens: ἀμώντ- codd.   ποκ' αὔλει
Κl   18 μάντις τὰν Κv   χροιξεῖται Σᵛ·ˡ·: -ξεται Q: -ξῆται A: -ζεῖται vel
-ζεται Ω   καλαμαία Valckenaer: ἁ καλαμαία codd.   20 μὴ δὴ ΚΜ:
μηδὲ(ν) Ω   28 ἐντί l   32 ποκα Κ²Ρ: ἔχειν ποκα ΚQ: ἔχειν AL: om.
NU   34 τύγε μᾶλ(λ)ον v: μᾶλ(λ)ον τύ Κl   fortasse τύγα μᾶλον   38
ἐλελάθει Wilamowitz: -ήθη vel -ήθει codd.

ὤμοι τῶ πώγωνος, ὃν ἀλιθίως ἀνέφυσα.   40
θᾶσαι δὴ καὶ ταῦτα τὰ τῶ θείω Λιτυέρσα.

Δάματερ πολύκαρπε, πολύσταχυ, τοῦτο τὸ λᾶιον
εὔεργόν τ' εἴη καὶ κάρπιμον ὅττι μάλιστα.
σφίγγετ', ἀμαλλοδέται, τὰ δράγματα, μὴ παριών
τις
εἴπηι "ὑύκινοι ἄνδρες· ἀπώλετο χοῦτος ὁ μισθός."   45
ἐς βορέαν ἄνεμον τᾶς κόρθυος ἁ τομὰ ὔμμιν
ἢ ζέφυρον βλεπέτω· πιαίνεται ὁ στάχυς οὔτως.
σῖτον ἀλοιῶντας φεύγειν τὸ μεσαμβρινὸν ὕπνον·
ἐκ καλάμας ἄχυρον τελέθει τημόσδε μάλιστα·
ἄρχεσθαι δ' ἀμῶντας ἐγειρομένω κορυδαλλῶ   50
καὶ λήγειν εὔδοντος, ἐλινῦσαι δὲ τὸ καῦμα.
εὐκτὸς ὁ τῶ βατράχω, παῖδες, βίος· οὐ μελεδαίνει
τὸν τὸ πιεῖν ἐγχεῦντα· πάρεστι γὰρ ἄφθονον αὐτῶι.
κάλλιον, ὦ 'πιμελητὰ φιλάργυρε, τὸν φακὸν ἕψειν,
μὴ 'πιτάμηις τᾶν χεῖρα καταπρίων τὸ κύμινον.   55

ταῦτα χρὴ μοχθεῦντας ἐν ἁλίωι ἄνδρας ἀείδειν,
τὸν δὲ τεόν, Βουκαῖε, πρέπει λιμηρὸν ἔρωτα
μυθίσδεν τᾶι ματρὶ κατ' εὐνὰν ὀρθρευοίσαι.

VI IDYLL 11

ΚΥΚΛΩΨ

οὐδὲν πὸτ τὸν ἔρωτα πεφύκει φάρμακον ἄλλο,
Νικία, οὔτ' ἔγχριστον, ἐμὶν δοκεῖ, οὔτ' ἐπίπαστον,

---

45 εἴπηι P: -οι Ω   48 ἀλοιῶντες υ   τὸ ALN: τὸν K*l*U   51 λήγην
Π⁹   53 πιῆν Π³Π⁹LN   ἐγχεῦντα vel ἐνχεῦντα Π³Π⁹MS: ἐκχ- Ω   55
χῆρα Π⁹   56 μοχθεῦντας Π⁹ codd.: μοχθεντας Π³

VI   2 οὐδ' ἐπίπιστον υ

ἢ ταὶ Πιερίδες· κοῦφον δέ τι τοῦτο καὶ ἁδύ
γίνετ' ἐπ' ἀνθρώποις, εὑρεῖν δ' οὐ ῥάιδιόν ἐστι.
γινώσκειν δ' οἶμαί τυ καλῶς ἰατρὸν ἐόντα   5
καὶ ταῖς ἐννέα δὴ πεφιλημένον ἔξοχα Μοίσαις.
οὕτω γοῦν ῥάιστα διᾶγ' ὁ Κύκλωψ ὁ παρ' ἀμῖν,
ὡρχαῖος Πολύφαμος, ὅκ' ἤρατο τᾶς Γαλατείας,
ἄρτι γενειάσδων περὶ τὸ στόμα τὼς κροτάφως τε.
ἤρατο δ' οὐ μάλοις οὐδὲ ῥόδωι οὐδὲ κικίννοις,   10
ἀλλ' ὀρθαῖς μανίαις, ἁγεῖτο δὲ πάντα πάρεργα.
πολλάκι ταὶ ὄιες ποτὶ τωὔλιον αὐταὶ ἀπῆνθον
χλωρᾶς ἐκ βοτάνας· ὁ δὲ τὰν Γαλάτειαν ἀείδων
αὐτὸς ἐπ' ἀιόνος κατετάκετο φυκιοέσσας
ἐξ ἀοῦς, ἔχθιστον ἔχων ὑποκάρδιον ἕλκος,   15
Κύπριδος ἐκ μεγάλας τό οἱ ἥπατι πᾶξε βέλεμνον.
ἀλλὰ τὸ φάρμακον εὗρε, καθεζόμενος δ' ἐπὶ πέτρας
ὑψηλᾶς ἐς πόντον ὁρῶν ἄειδε τοιαῦτα·

ὦ λευκὰ Γαλάτεια, τί τὸν φιλέοντ' ἀποβάλληι,
λευκοτέρα πακτᾶς ποτιδεῖν, ἁπαλωτέρα ἀρνός,   20
μόσχω γαυροτέρα, φιαρωτέρα ὄμφακος ὠμᾶς;
φοιτῆις δ' αὖθ' οὕτως ὅκκα γλυκὺς ὕπνος ἔχηι με,
οἴχηι δ' εὐθὺς ἰοῖσ' ὅκκα γλυκὺς ὕπνος ἀνῆι με,
φεύγεις δ' ὥσπερ ὄις πολιὸν λύκον ἀθρήσασα;
ἠράσθην μὲν ἔγωγε τεοῦς, κόρα, ἀνίκα πρᾶτον   25
ἦνθες ἐμᾶι σὺν ματρὶ θέλοισ' ὑακίνθινα φύλλα
ἐξ ὄρεος δρέψασθαι, ἐγὼ δ' ὁδὸν ἁγεμόνευον.
παύσασθαι δ' ἐσιδών τυ καὶ ὕστερον οὐδ' ἔτι παι νῦν
ἐκ τήνω δύναμαι· τὶν δ' οὐ μέλει, οὐ μὰ Δί' οὐδέν.
γινώσκω, χαρίεσσα κόρα, τίνος οὕνεκα φεύγεις·   30
οὕνεκά μοι λασία μὲν ὀφρὺς ἐπὶ παντὶ μετώπωι

4 ἀνθρώποις KS: -ους lv   10 οὐδὲ Kl: οὐδ' αὖ v   ῥόδωι MS: ῥόδοις Ω
11 ὀρθαῖς K Iunt.: ὁλοαῖς Ω Σ^{v.l.}   14 αὐτὸς Q¹WNon.: -τῶ vel -τοῦ Ω
20 ἀρνός MS: δ' ἀρνός Ω   25 ἔγωγα Valckenaer   τεοῦς KA²: τεῶς
PQ²: τεῦ QWNU   πρᾶτον Q: πρῶτον Ω   28 παι K: πω A: τὰ Ω

ἐξ ὠτὸς τέταται ποτὶ θώτερον ὡς μία μακρά,
εἷς δ' ὀφθαλμὸς ὕπεστι, πλατεῖα δὲ ῥὶς ἐπὶ χείλει.
ἀλλ' οὗτος τοιοῦτος ἐὼν βοτὰ χίλια βόσκω,
κἠκ τούτων τὸ κράτιστον ἀμελγόμενος γάλα πίνω·   35
τυρὸς δ' οὐ λείπει μ' οὔτ' ἐν θέρει οὔτ' ἐν ὀπώραι,
οὐ χειμῶνος ἄκρω· ταρσοὶ δ' ὑπεραχθέες αἰεί.
συρίσδεν δ' ὡς οὔτις ἐπίσταμαι ὧδε Κυκλώπων,
τίν, τὸ φίλον γλυκύμαλον, ἁμᾶι κἠμαυτὸν ἀείδων
πολλάκι νυκτὸς ἀωρί. τράφω δέ τοι ἕνδεκα νεβρώς,   40
πάσας μαννοφόρως, καὶ σκύμνως τέσσαρας ἄρκτων.
ἀλλ' ἀφίκευσο ποθ' ἁμέ, καὶ ἑξῆς οὐδὲν ἔλασσον,
τὰν γλαυκὰν δὲ θάλασσαν ἔα ποτὶ χέρσον ὀρεχθεῖν·
ἅδιον ἐν τὤντρωι παρ' ἐμὶν τὰν νύκτα διαξεῖς.
ἐντὶ δάφναι τηνεί, ἐντὶ ῥαδιναὶ κυπάρισσοι,   45
ἔστι μέλας κισσός, ἔστ' ἄμπελος ἁ γλυκύκαρπος,
ἔστι ψυχρὸν ὕδωρ, τό μοι ἁ πολυδένδρεος Αἴτνα
λευκᾶς ἐκ χιόνος ποτὸν ἀμβρόσιον προΐητι.
τίς κα τῶνδε θάλασσαν ἔχειν καὶ κύμαθ' ἕλοιτο;
αἰ δέ τοι αὐτὸς ἐγὼν δοκέω λασιώτερος ἦμεν,   50
ἐντὶ δρυὸς ξύλα μοι καὶ ὑπὸ σποδῶ ἀκάματον πῦρ·
καιόμενος δ' ὑπὸ τεῦς καὶ τὰν ψυχὰν ἀνεχοίμαν
καὶ τὸν ἕν' ὀφθαλμόν, τῶ μοι γλυκερώτερον οὐδέν.
ὤμοι, ὅτ' οὐκ ἔτεκέν μ' ἁ μάτηρ βράγχι' ἔχοντα,
ὡς κατέδυν ποτὶ τὶν καὶ τὰν χέρα τεῦς ἐφίλησα,   55
αἰ μὴ τὸ στόμα λῆις, ἔφερον δέ τοι ἢ κρίνα λευκά
ἢ μάκων' ἁπαλὰν ἐρυθρὰ πλαταγώνι' ἔχοισαν·
ἀλλὰ τὰ μὲν θέρεος, τὰ δὲ γίνεται ἐν χειμῶνι,
ὥστ' οὔ κά τοι ταῦτα φέρειν ἅμα πάντ' ἐδυνάθην.
νῦν μάν, ὦ κόριον, νῦν αὐτίκα νεῖν γε μαθεῦμαι,   60

33 ὕπεστι Winsem: ἔπ- codd.   40 τράφω Paris. Suppl. Gr. 1024: τρέφω
Ω   41 μαννοφόρως Σ^{v.l.}: ἀμνοφ- codd.   42 ἀφίκευσο PGΣ Iunt.: ἀφίκευ
QW: ἀφίκευ τὺ Ω   46–7 ἔστ(ι) KP ter: ἐντὶ ... ἔντ' ... ἐντὶ Ω   49 κα
Brunck: κᾶν vel ἂν vel τὰν codd.   καὶ Ahrens: ἢ codd.   52 τεῦς K
Iunt.: τεῦ lv   55 τεῦς K Iunt.: τεῦ lv   59 οὔ κά Wilamowitz: οὐκ ἂν
codd.   60 αὐτίκα Paley: αὐτόγα KPW: τόγε Q² v

αἴ κά τις σὺν ναῗ πλέων ξένος ὧδ᾽ ἀφίκηται,
ὡς εἰδῶ τί ποχ᾽ ἁδὺ κατοικεῖν τὸν βυθὸν ὔμμιν.
ἐξένθοις, Γαλάτεια, καὶ ἐξενθοῖσα λάθοιο,
ὥσπερ ἐγὼν νῦν ὧδε καθήμενος, οἴκαδ᾽ ἀπενθεῖν·
ποιμαίνειν δ᾽ ἐθέλοις σὺν ἐμὶν ἅμα καὶ γάλ᾽ ἀμέλγειν   65
καὶ τυρὸν πᾶξαι τάμισον δριμεῖαν ἐνεῖσα.
ἁ μάτηρ ἀδικεῖ με μόνα, καὶ μέμφομαι αὐτᾶι·
οὐδὲν πήποχ᾽ ὅλως ποτὶ τὶν φίλον εἶπεν ὑπέρ μευ,
καὶ ταῦτ᾽ ἆμαρ ἐπ᾽ ἆμαρ ὁρεῦσά με λεπτύνοντα.
φασῶ τὰν κεφαλὰν καὶ τὼς πόδας ἀμφοτέρως μευ   70
σφύσδειν, ὡς ἀνιαθῇι, ἐπεὶ κἠγὼν ἀνιῶμαι.
ὦ Κύκλωψ Κύκλωψ, πᾶι τὰς φρένας ἐκπεπότασαι;
αἴ κ᾽ ἐνθὼν ταλάρως τε πλέκοις καὶ θαλλὸν ἀμάσας
ταῗς ἄρνεσσι φέροις, τάχα κα πολὺ μᾶλλον ἔχοις νῶν.
τὰν παρεοῖσαν ἄμελγε· τί τὸν φεύγοντα διώκεις;   75
εὑρησεῗς Γαλάτειαν ἴσως καὶ καλλίον᾽ ἄλλαν.
πολλαὶ συμπαίσδεν με κόραι τὰν νύκτα κέλονται,
κιχλίζοντι δὲ πᾶσαι, ἐπεί κ᾽ αὐταῗς ὑπακούσω.
δῆλον ὅτ᾽ ἐν τᾶι γᾶι κἠγών τις φαίνομαι ἦμεν.

οὕτω τοι Πολύφαμος ἐποίμαινεν τὸν ἔρωτα   80
μουσίσδων, ῥᾶιον δὲ διᾶγ᾽ ἢ εἰ χρυσὸν ἔδωκεν.

VII IDYLL 6

ΒΟΥΚΟΛΙΑΣΤΑΙ ΔΑΜΟΙΤΑΣ ΚΑΙ ΔΑΦΝΙΣ

Δαμοίτας χὠ Δάφνις ὁ βουκόλος εἰς ἕνα χῶρον
τὰν ἀγέλαν ποκ᾽, Ἄρατε, συνάγαγον· ἧς δ᾽ ὃ μὲν αὐτῶν
πυρρός, ὃ δ᾽ ἡμιγένειος· ἐπὶ κράναν δέ τιν᾽ ἄμφω

69 λεπτύνοντα Meineke: λεπτὸν ἐόντα codd.   74 κα Ahrens: κεν S: καὶ
Ω   79 ἦμεν MS: εἶναι Ω

VII 1 καὶ PQAU

ἐσδόμενοι θέρεος μέσωι ἄματι τοιάδ' ἄειδον.
πρᾶτος δ' ἄρξατο Δάφνις, ἐπεὶ καὶ πρᾶτος ἔρισδεν.   5

ΔΑΦΝΙΣ

βάλλει τοι, Πολύφαμε, τὸ ποίμνιον ἁ Γαλάτεια
μάλοισιν, δυσέρωτα καὶ αἰπόλον ἄνδρα καλεῦσα·
καὶ τύ νιν οὐ ποθόρησθα, τάλαν τάλαν, ἀλλὰ κάθησαι
ἁδέα συρίσδων. πάλιν ἅδ', ἴδε, τὰν κύνα βάλλει,
ἅ τοι τᾶν ὀΐων ἕπεται σκοπός· ἁ δὲ βαΰσδει   10
εἰς ἅλα δερκομένα, τὰ δέ νιν καλὰ κύματα φαίνει
ἅσυχα καχλάζοντος ἐπ' αἰγιαλοῖο θέοισαν.
φράζεο μὴ τᾶς παιδὸς ἐπὶ κνάμαισιν ὀρούσηι
ἐξ ἁλὸς ἐρχομένας, κατὰ δὲ χρόα καλὸν ἀμύξηι.
ἁ δὲ καὶ αὐτόθε τοι διαθρύπτεται· ὡς ἀπ' ἀκάνθας   15
ταὶ καπυραὶ χαῖται, τὸ καλὸν θέρος ἁνίκα φρύγει,
καὶ φεύγει φιλέοντα καὶ οὐ φιλέοντα διώκει,
καὶ τὸν ἀπὸ γραμμᾶς κινεῖ λίθον· ἦ γὰρ ἔρωτι
πολλάκις, ὦ Πολύφαμε, τὰ μὴ καλὰ καλὰ πέφανται.

τῶι δ' ἐπὶ Δαμοίτας ἀνεβάλλετο καὶ τάδ' ἄειδεν.   20

ΔΑΜΟΙΤΑΣ

εἶδον, ναὶ τὸν Πᾶνα, τὸ ποίμνιον ἁνίκ' ἔβαλλε,
κοὔ μ' ἔλαθ', οὐ τὸν ἐμὸν τὸν ἕνα γλυκύν, ὧι ποθορῶιμι
ἐς τέλος (αὐτὰρ ὁ μάντις ὁ Τήλεμος ἔχθρ' ἀγορεύων
ἐχθρὰ φέροι ποτὶ οἶκον, ὅπως τεκέεσσι φυλάσσοι)·
ἀλλὰ καὶ αὐτὸς ἐγὼ κνίζων πάλιν οὐ ποθόρημι,   25

---

7 καὶ Meineke: τὸν codd.   9 ἅδ' ἴδε Ω: ἀδὶ PΣ^v.l.   12 καχλάζοντος SΣ:
-οντα Ω   15 αὐτόθε P: -θι Ω   16 φρύγει S: -γῆ KWALU: -ξῆι PG: φλέ-
γει Q   20 καὶ τάδ' ἄειδεν Kυ: καλὸν ἀείδε(ι)ν l Σ^v.l.   22 τὸν ἕνα Ω: ἕνα
KL   ποθορῶιμι Heinsius: -ωμαι US: -ημαι Ω   24 φέροι ποτὶ A²L² U
Mosch.: φέρει vel φέρηι ποτὶ KAL: φέροιτο ποτ' lG   25 ποθόρημι A
Mosch.: -ημαι Ω

ἀλλ' ἄλλαν τινὰ φαμὶ γυναῖκ' ἔχεν· ἃ δ' ἀίοισα
ζαλοῖ μ', ὦ Παιάν, καὶ τάκεται, ἐκ δὲ θαλάσσας
οἰστρεῖ παπταίνοισα ποτ' ἄντρα τε καὶ ποτὶ ποίμνας.
σίξα δ' ὑλακτεῖν νιν καὶ τᾶι κυνί· καὶ γὰρ ὅκ' ἤρων
αὐτᾶς, ἐκνυζεῖτο ποτ' ἰσχία ῥύγχος ἔχοισα.   30
ταῦτα δ' ἴσως ἐσορεῦσα ποεῦντά με πολλάκι πεμψεῖ
ἄγγελον. αὐτὰρ ἐγὼ κλαιξῶ θύρας, ἔστε κ' ὀμόσσηι
αὐτά μοι στορεσεῖν καλὰ δέμνια τᾶσδ' ἐπὶ νάσω·
καὶ γάρ θην οὐδ' εἶδος ἔχω κακὸν ὥς με λέγοντι.
ἦ γὰρ πρᾶν ἐς πόντον ἐσέβλεπον, ἦς δὲ γαλάνα,   35
καὶ καλὰ μὲν τὰ γένεια, καλὰ δέ μοι ἁ μία κώρα,
ὡς παρ' ἐμὶν κέκριται, κατεφαίνετο, τῶν δέ τ' ὀδόντων
λευκοτέραν αὐγὰν Παρίας ὑπέφαινε λίθοιο.
ὡς μὴ βασκανθῶ δέ, τρὶς εἰς ἐμὸν ἔπτυσα κόλπον·
ταῦτα γὰρ ἁ γραία με Κοτυτταρὶς ἐξεδίδαξε   40
[ἃ πρᾶν ἀμάντεσσι παρ' Ἱπποκίωνι ποταύλει].

τόσσ' εἰπὼν τὸν Δάφνιν ὁ Δαμοίτας ἐφίλησε·
χὠ μὲν τῶι σύριγγ', ὃ δὲ τῶι καλὸν αὐλὸν ἔδωκεν.
αὔλει Δαμοίτας, σύρισδε δὲ Δάφνις ὁ βούτας·
ὡρχεῦντ' ἐν μαλακᾶι ταὶ πόρτιες αὐτίκα ποίαι.   45
νίκη μὲν οὐδάλλος, ἀνήσσατοι δ' ἐγένοντο.

VIII IDYLL 13

ΥΛΑΣ

οὐχ ἁμῖν τὸν Ἔρωτα μόνοις ἔτεχ', ὡς ἐδοκεῦμες,
Νικία, ὧιτινι τοῦτο θεῶν ποκα τέκνον ἔγεντο·
οὐχ ἁμῖν τὰ καλὰ πράτοις καλὰ φαίνεται ἦμεν,

29 σίξα Ruhnken: σῖγα vel σίγα vel σιγᾶι codd.   ὑλακτεῖν νιν v: ὑλακτεῖ
Κ¹Σ^{v.l.}: ὑλακτεῖν l   30 ἐκνυζεῖτο Κ²Ρ: -ᾶτο Ω: -οῖτο Σ^{lem}: -ῆτο S Greg.
Cor. 79   36 δέ μοι Κl: δ' ἐμὶν v: δέ μευ Ahrens   41 (= 10.16) om. Κ
46 μὲν Κl: μὰν v

VIII 3 ἦμεν S: εἶμεν Κ: εἶμες PQ: ἦμες Wv

οἳ θνατοὶ πελόμεσθα, τὸ δ' αὔριον οὐκ ἐσορῶμες·
ἀλλὰ καὶ Ἀμφιτρύωνος ὁ χαλκεοκάρδιος υἱός,   5
ὃς τὸν λῖν ὑπέμεινε τὸν ἄγριον, ἤρατο παιδός,
τοῦ χαρίεντος Ὕλα, τοῦ τὰν πλοκαμῖδα φορεῦντος,
καί νιν πάντ' ἐδίδασκε, πατὴρ ὡσεὶ φίλον υἱόν,
ὅσσα μαθὼν ἀγαθὸς καὶ ἀοίδιμος αὐτὸς ἔγεντο·
χωρὶς δ' οὐδέποκ' ἦς, οὔτ' εἰ μέσον ἆμαρ ὅροιτο,   10
οὔθ' ὅκχ' ἁ λεύκιππος ἀνατρέχηι ἐς Διὸς ἀώς,
οὔθ' ὁπόκ' ὀρτάλιχοι μινυροὶ ποτὶ κοῖτον ὁρῶιεν,
σεισαμένας πτερὰ ματρὸς ἐπ' αἰθαλόεντι πετεύρωι,
ὡς αὐτῶι κατὰ θυμὸν ὁ παῖς πεπονᾱμένος εἴη,
†αὐτῶι δ' εὖ ἕλκων† ἐς ἀλαθινὸν ἄνδρ' ἀποβαίη.   15
ἀλλ' ὅτε τὸ χρύσειον ἔπλει μετὰ κῶας Ἰάσων
Αἰσονίδας, οἱ δ' αὐτῶι ἀριστῆες συνέποντο
πασᾶν ἐκ πολίων προλελεγμένοι ὧν ὄφελός τι,
ἵκετο χὠ ταλαεργὸς ἀνὴρ ἐς ἀφνειὸν Ἰωλκόν,
Ἀλκμήνας υἱὸς Μιδεάτιδος ἡρωίνας,   20
σὺν δ' αὐτῶι κατέβαινεν Ὕλας εὔεδρον ἐς Ἀργώ,
ἅτις κυανεᾶν οὐχ ἅψατο Συνδρομάδων ναῦς,
ἀλλὰ διεξάιξε βαθὺν δ' εἰσέδραμε Φᾶσιν,
αἰετὸς ὥς, μέγα λαῖτμα, ἀφ' οὗ τότε χοιράδες ἔσταν.
ἆμος δ' ἀντέλλοντι Πελειάδες, ἐσχατιαὶ δέ   25
ἄρνα νέον βόσκοντι, τετραμμένου εἴαρος ἤδη,
τᾶμος ναυτιλίας μιμνάσκετο θεῖος ἄωτος
ἡρώων, κοίλαν δὲ καθιδρυθέντες ἐς Ἀργώ
Ἑλλάσποντον ἵκοντο νότωι τρίτον ἆμαρ ἀέντι,
εἴσω δ' ὅρμον ἔθεντο Προποντίδος, ἔνθα Κιανῶν   30
αὔλακας εὐρύνοντι βόες τρίβοντες ἄροτρα.
ἐκβάντες δ' ἐπὶ θῖνα κατὰ ζυγὰ δαῖτα πένοντο
δειελινοί, πολλοὶ δὲ μίαν στορέσαντο χαμεύναν.

8 ἐδίδασκε Π³: -αξε codd.   υἱόν Π³: υἱέα K: υἷα Ω   10 οὔτ' Sauppe:
οὐδ' codd.   11 οὔθ' *lv*: οὐδ' K   ὅκχ' ed. princ.: ὅκα codd.: ὁπόχ'
Graefe   ἀνατρέχηι Wilamowitz: -χει codd.: -χοι Schaefer   12 οὔθ' *lv*:
οὐδ' K   ὁπόκ' S: ὁπότ' Ω   19 ἀφνειὸν Ἰωλκόν K: ἀφνειὰν Ἰαολκόν
lv   22 ἅψατο Brunck: ἠψ- codd.   23 Φᾶσιν codd.: Πόντον Griffiths
24 delevit Meineke   30 ἔθεντο codd.: ἵκοντο Π¹⁰   33 δειελινήν KM²

λειμὼν γάρ σφιν ἔκειτο, μέγα στιβάδεσσιν ὄνειαρ,
ἔνθεν βούτομον ὀξὺ βαθύν τ' ἐτάμοντο κύπειρον.   35
κὦιχεθ' Ὕλας ὁ ξανθὸς ὕδωρ ἐπιδόρπιον οἴσων
αὐτῶι θ' Ἡρακλῆι καὶ ἀστεμφεῖ Τελαμῶνι,
οἳ μίαν ἄμφω ἑταῖροι ἀεὶ δαίνυντο τράπεζαν,
χάλκεον ἄγγος ἔχων. τάχα δὲ κράναν ἐνόησεν
ἡμένωι ἐν χώρωι· περὶ δὲ θρύα πολλὰ πεφύκει,   40
κυάνεόν τε χελιδόνιον χλωρόν τ' ἀδίαντον
καὶ θάλλοντα σέλινα καὶ εἰλιτενὴς ἄγρωστις.
ὕδατι δ' ἐν μέσσωι Νύμφαι χορὸν ἀρτίζοντο,
Νύμφαι ἀκοίμητοι, δειναὶ θεαὶ ἀγροιώταις,
Εὐνίκα καὶ Μαλὶς ἔαρ θ' ὁρόωσα Νύχεια.   45
ἤτοι ὁ κοῦρος ἐπεῖχε ποτῶι πολυχανδέα κρωσσόν
βάψαι ἐπειγόμενος· ταὶ δ' ἐν χερὶ πᾶσαι ἔφυσαν·
πασάων γὰρ ἔρως ἁπαλὰς φρένας ἐξεφόβησεν
Ἀργείωι ἐπὶ παιδί. κατήριπε δ' ἐς μέλαν ὕδωρ
ἀθρόος, ὡς ὅτε πυρσὸς ἀπ' οὐρανοῦ ἤριπεν ἀστήρ   50
ἀθρόος ἐν πόντωι, ναύτας δέ τις εἶπεν ἑταίροις
"κουφότερ', ὦ παῖδες, ποιεῖσθ' ὅπλα· πλευστικὸς οὖρος."
Νύμφαι μὲν σφετέροις ἐπὶ γούνασι κοῦρον ἔχοισαι
δακρυόεντ' ἀγανοῖσι παρεψύχοντ' ἐπέεσσιν·
Ἀμφιτρυωνιάδας δὲ ταρασσόμενος περὶ παιδί   55
ὤιχετο, Μαιωτιστὶ λαβὼν εὐκαμπέα τόξα
καὶ ῥόπαλον, τό οἱ αἰὲν ἐχάνδανε δεξιτερὰ χείρ.
τρὶς μὲν Ὕλαν ἄυσεν, ὅσον βαθὺς ἤρυγε λαιμός·
τρὶς δ' ἄρ' ὁ παῖς ὑπάκουσεν, ἀραιὰ δ' ἵκετο φωνά
ἐξ ὕδατος, παρεὼν δὲ μάλα σχεδὸν εἴδετο πόρρω.   60
[ὡς δ' ὁπότ' ἠυγένειος ἀπόπροθι λὶς ἐσακούσας]
νεβροῦ φθεγξαμένας τις ἐν οὔρεσιν ὠμοφάγος λίς
ἐξ εὐνᾶς ἔσπευσεν ἑτοιμοτάταν ἐπὶ δαῖτα·

---

34 γάρ σφιν ἔκ. codd.: σφιν πα[Π¹⁰: πάρ σφιν ἔκ. Griffiths   48 ἐξεφόβησεν M²: ἐξεφηβόβησεν K: ἀμφεκάλυψεν Ω   49 ἀργείωι
Bonanno   51 ναύτας Brunck: -ταις codd.   ἑταίροις K: -ρος lv   52
πνευστικὸς K   55 ἐπὶ παιδί K   58 βαρὺς K   60 versum delevit
Griffiths   61 om. Π¹ΚΣ

Ἡρακλέης τοιοῦτος ἐν ἀτρίπτοισιν ἀκάνθαις
παῖδα ποθῶν δεδόνητο, πολὺν δ' ἐπελάμβανε χῶρον.   65
σχέτλιοι οἱ φιλέοντες, ἀλώμενος ὅσσ' ἐμόγησεν
οὔρεα καὶ δρυμώς, τὰ δ' Ἰάσονος ὕστερα πάντ' ἦς.
†ναῦς μὲν ἄρμεν' ἔχοισα μετάρσια τῶν παρεόντων,
ἱστία δ' ἡμίθεοι μεσονύκτιον ἐξεκάθαιρον†
Ἡρακλῆα μένοντες. ὃ δ' ᾇ πόδες ἆγον ἐχώρει   70
μαινόμενος· χαλεπὸς γὰρ ἔσω θεὸς ἧπαρ ἄμυσσεν.
οὕτω μὲν κάλλιστος Ὕλας μακάρων ἀριθμεῖται·
Ἡρακλέην δ' ἥρωες ἐκερτόμεον λιποναύταν,
οὕνεκεν ἡρώησε τριακοντάζυγον Ἀργώ,
πεζᾶι δ' ἐς Κόλχους τε καὶ ἄξενον ἵκετο Φᾶσιν.   75

66 ὡς ἐμόγ. K   68–9 μὲν codd: γέμεν Hermann   ἤιθεοι *lv*   73 Ἡρα-
κλέη K

COMMENTARY

I Idyll 1

A shepherd, whose name, Thyrsis, we learn in 19, compliments a goatherd on his syrinx-playing and is in turn complimented as a singer. The goatherd persuades Thyrsis to sing 'the sufferings of Daphnis' in return for a goat and a wooden bowl with marvellous decoration; the bowl is described in detail (27–60). Thyrsis then sings the story of Daphnis' resistance to Aphrodite and ultimate death (64–145). The poem ends with the handing over of the bowl. There is no explicit setting, but Thyrsis comes from Etna (65) and sings a Sicilian song; it is not improbable that the setting is a stylised Sicilian countryside, cf. 24, 57nn.

Idyll 1 seems always to have been placed first in ancient collections of T.'s poetry, and it is not hard to see why. At its heart lies the story of Daphnis, variously the first 'bucolic' singer and the original subject of 'bucolic' song; Thyrsis' song begins with an invocation to the Muses to 'begin the bucolic song' (64), and so the placing of this poem at the head of a collection entitled Βουκολικά would be unsurprising. The author of the *Hypothesis* ascribes its position in the collection known to him to the fact that it 'possesses more charm (χάρις) and art' than the other poems. Be that as it may, its 'programmatic' character is clear. It begins with the crucial idea of poetic 'pleasure' (1n.), and the description of the marvellous cup (27–61n.) evokes a style of poetry as well as a work of art, cf. Halperin (1983a) 169–76, Cairns (1984). The programmatic significance of the subject is matched metrically and stylistically: there is a relatively high number of guaranteed epic forms, and a very high incidence of bucolic diaeresis accompanied by period or colon end, cf. Di Benedetto (1956) 54–5, Van Sickle (1975) 55·

There is, however, no compelling reason to think that Idyll 1 was originally designed or subsequently redesigned to fit within a collection (contrast, e.g., Eclogue 1), nor that it was written against a background of a pre-existing body of 'bucolic' poems to which it could form a programmatic introduction, cf. above, Intro. Section 5. What is more important than the possible relation between Idyll 1 and any hypothesised early (or even authorial) collection is the sense of tradition which is written into the poem. Thyrsis is already a 'master poet' (20) and the 'sufferings of Daphnis' have been sung many times before (19); Thyrsis has taken part in song contests which still live in the memory (24); even the carved scenes on the cup suggest a pre-existing tradition of poetry (27–61n.). The extreme courtesy and mutual praise of the opening verses both play off *against* an expectation of antagonism (Idyll 5), and are distinctly agonistic in form (1–11, 12–23nn.). T. may, moreover, be exploiting the poetry of Stesichorus for the song of Thyrsis (cf. below); if so, he is laying claim to a model from the ranks of high literature, rather as Callimachus uses Hipponax in the *Iambi*. In short, whatever the original circumstances of writing and performance, Idyll 1 conjures up a pre-existing 'bucolic' tradition, while itself founding such a tradition, cf. Van Sickle (1975) 54–8, (1976) 22. Moreover, the three refrains which punctuate the song of Thyrsis chart the move from 'beginning' to 'repetition' – that move by which all acts of cultural foundation are marked – and ultimately to 'cessation'. Thyrsis' song inaugurates and completes a whole genre.

Idyll 1 raises a popular song tradition to the level of high art: as the cup is an elaborate version of a common, rustic object, so the song of Thyrsis suggests the popular in both style (the refrains) and subject (Daphnis), but we may well believe that nothing like it had ever been heard or read before. Like the cup, the poem itself is 'a marvel of the goatherd's world, a τέρας to amaze your heart' (56n.). Its power derives from the fact that it does not fit readily into familiar categories (this is what a τέρας is), and it stands under the sign of Pan (3, 123–30), himself both 'a marvel of the goatherd's world' and a τέρας (above, p. 15). Moreover, Idyll 1 is specifically music performed for prizes of a goat or a sheep (1–11, 25). βουκολιασμός was believed to be a pre-literate song (Intro. Section 2), and 1–11 evoke the related τραγωιδία, 'goat song', which was variously etymologised in antiquity: 'song sung by goat-men' and 'song for [the prize of] a goat' would both have been known to T.'s audience, cf. Dioscorides, *Anth. Pal.* 7.410 (= *HE* 1585–90), Eratosthenes fr. 22 Powell, Pickard-Cambridge (1962) 112–24. The opening verses thus suggest a historical narrative for 'bucolic' which is analogous to the familiar account of tragedy's origins. Later Peripatetic theory seems in fact to have invented an origin for bucolic on the pattern of the story told about the origins of comedy (Intro. Section 2); T. himself, however, has already inscribed a related history in the fabric of Idyll 1. 'Bucolic' here is literally a kind of 'tragedy', with Pan taking the place of Dionysos, that Olympian to whom Pan stands nearest (*h. Pan* 46); Pan, Dionysos and the nymphs are indeed also found together in a 'pastoral' epigram of Leonidas (*Anth. Pal.* 6.154 = *HE* 2555–62). It is Dionysos who is evoked by Thyrsis' name (19n.), and the decoration on the 'ivy-cup' specifically recalls a famous Dionysiac miracle (29–31n.). The boy weaving his cricket-cage, who is at one level a figure of the poet, is set within the Dionysiac *locus* of a ripening vineyard (cf. the story of the young Aeschylus' poetic 'initiation' by Dionysos (Paus. 1.21.2 = Aesch. *Test.* III Radt)). At another level, the 'sufferings of Daphnis' clearly resemble a tragic *pathos* (cf. A. Parry, *YCS* 15 (1957) 11–13), and the θρῆνος or lament offers another vision of pre-tragedy, the kind of song which, taken in another direction, led to 'drama'. Idyll 1 thus shares the very strong literary-historical orientation of much third-century poetry (cf. Hunter (1998)). Dionysos plays an important rôle also in the 'bucolic foundation' of Idyll 7 (7.154n.).

The marvellous cup is another Dionysiac artefact, but the 'mimetic realism' of the scenes, their contemporary or at least timeless setting, and their subjects – erotic rivalry, rustic labour – suggest perhaps the traditions of comedy, and comedy's forebear, the *Odyssey*, rather than those of tragedy and the *Iliad*. Where the story of Daphnis, like so many tragedies, blocks generational passage, the cup, like both the *Odyssey*, from which the κισσύβιον ultimately derives, and New Comedy, lays great stress upon 'the ages of man' and the activities appropriate to each. The 'goat-song' of Pan will thus be as double as the god himself, and the Aristotelian distinction between the *pathos* of the *Iliad* and the *ethos* of the *Odyssey* (*Poetics* 1459b14–15), a distinction which later theory applied to tragedy and comedy (cf. Quintilian 6.2.20, Halperin (1983a) 239–43, C. Gill, *CQ* 34 (1984) 149–66), is played out in the counterpoint of the song and the cup. In Daphnis and the Cyclops of Idylls 6 and 11 (the original owner of a κισσύβιον) T. constructed two proto-bucolic poets, both Sicilian herdsmen, both in other versions blinded, but one tragic and one comic, one a hero of *pathos*, the other of *ethos*: 'bucolic' was to encompass them both. For a different view of *pathos* and *ethos* in Idyll 1 cf. Walsh (1985).

The song of Thyrsis, the ἄλγεα Δάφνιδος, is mysterious and allusive. In the east of Sicily (68–9) Daphnis 'wastes away', a verb often used of the sufferings of unsatisfied love. He is visited by Hermes and his fellow-herdsmen who enquire as to his trouble; next comes Priapos who tells him that ἁ κώρα is searching madly for him, and the god calls him δύσερώς τις ἄγαν καὶ ἀμήχανος. To these visitors Daphnis makes no reply but 'saw his bitter love through to the end appointed by fate' (92–3). Next comes Aphrodite who claims that Daphnis had vowed to defeat Eros, but he himself has now been defeated; Daphnis responds abusively to her, and then delivers a lyrical farewell to nature and Pan, as he acknowledges that Death is at hand (130). Fate has now run its course and, though Aphrodite would have wished it otherwise, 'Daphnis went to the stream (ἔβα ῥόον), and the whirlpool washed over the man who was dear to the Muses and no enemy of the Nymphs' (140–1). Minimally, we may infer that Daphnis is 'in love', perhaps with the girl who is searching for him, but refuses to satisfy that love, even though he knows that that refusal means death (103). The manner of his death remains mysterious, but he *may* merely have 'wasted away' (cf. 7.73–7).

The very allusiveness of Thyrsis' narrative demands a different, but related, mode of reading to that necessary in the reading of an *ekphrasis*, such as the goatherd's description of the cup. As *ekphrasis* offers more 'than is actually there' (the thoughts and emotions of the figures, for example), so the song offers less 'than is actually there', no matter whether we are to bring to our reading of the song knowledge of a pre-existing Daphnis story (cf. below) or whether our very strong feeling of ellipse is purely a product of the poet's 'invention of tradition', his ability to evoke a historical and generic sense within a creation which is wholly new. This is not merely a transposition to hexameters of the allusive techniques of lyric. The nameless figures on the cup, with their timeless and generic quality, provoke us to enquire after particulars – 'What *is* the story of the woman and her suitors?', whereas Thyrsis' song of Daphnis, by its very particularity and apparent intertextual evocation of a familiar narrative, invites us to look to the general and universal.

Some of our later sources for the story of Daphnis may have been written to explain Idyll 1, and as such must be treated with caution, but the ancient tradition is fairly consistent; for useful surveys cf. Prescott (1899), *LIMC* III 1.348–52, Zimmerman (1994) 25–37. Our principal sources are as follows (omitting minor variants which have no obvious connection with T.).

(i) 7.72–7 'Tityros shall sing how Daphnis the oxherd once loved Xenea, and how the mountain grieved and the oak trees, which grow on the banks of the River Himeras, mourned him as he wasted (κατετάκετο) like snow on tall Haimos or Athos or Rhodope or furthest Kaukasos.'

(ii) Parthenius, *Narr. amat.* 29 'Concerning Daphnis. The story occurs in the *Sikelika* of Timaeus [*FGrHist* 566 F83]. Daphnis was born in Sicily; he was the son of Hermes, and a fine syrinx player and very handsome. He did not consort with most men, but stayed in the countryside both winter and summer herding cattle (βουκολῶν) on Etna. The story is that the nymph Echenais fell in love with him, and told him not to sleep with (?another) woman, for if he disobeyed he would lose his eyesight. For some time he held out, though many women were crazy about him, but finally a Sicilian princess got him drunk and roused his desire to sleep with her. Thus it was that, like the Thracian Thamyras, an act of thoughtlessness caused him to be blinded.' The attribution to Timaeus, a Sicilian historian of the late fourth or early third century, is due not to Parthenius but to a later annotator (cf. Knox (1993) 63–4), but it is not implausible, particularly in view of the next source.

(iii) Diod. Sic. 4.84 'In the Heraean mountains [SE Sicily, inland from Syracuse], so the story goes, was born Daphnis, a son of Hermes and a nymph, and he, because of the bay (δάφνη) which grew there in profusion, was called Daphnis. He was brought up by the nymphs, and possessed very many herds of cattle which he tended very carefully. For this reason he earned the name 'Boukolos'. He was a naturally gifted musician and invented bucolic poetry and song (τὸ βουκολικὸν ποίημα καὶ μέλος), which persists throughout Sicily to the present day. The story is that Daphnis hunted with Artemis and found favour with the goddess, and that he delighted her exceedingly with his syrinx playing and bucolic singing (βουκολική μελωιδία). They say that one of the nymphs fell in love with him and warned him that, if he slept with another woman, he would lose his sight. A king's daughter made him drunk and he slept with her, whereupon he was blinded in accordance with the nymph's warning.'

(iv) Aelian, *VH* 10.18 'Some say that Daphnis the *boukolos* was Hermes' *eromenos*, others that he was his son ... His mother was a nymph and she exposed him in a bay bush (ἐν δάφνηι). They say that his cattle were from the same stock as the cattle of the sun, of which Homer tells in the *Odyssey* (12.127ff.). When he was herding his cattle in Sicily, a nymph fell in love with him; he was beautiful and young, with his first beard, and she slept with him. She got him to agree not to sleep with anyone else, and she threatened that if he transgressed the agreement he would be blinded ... Some time later the daughter of a king fell in love with him, and under the influence of wine he broke his agreement by sleeping with the princess. As a result of this, bucolic song was sung for the first time (τὰ βουκολικὰ μέλη πρῶτον ἤισθη) and its subject was what happened (τὸ πάθος) to his eyes. Stesichorus of Himera [*PMGF* 279] began this kind of lyric (τῆς τοιαύτης μελοποιίας ὑπάρξασθαι).'

The meaning of the last phrase is unclear: are the 'first singing' and Stesichorus' poem intended to be the same, or is Stesichorus being credited with raising 'bucolic song' from a sub-literary to a literary form? Halperin (1983a) 79 understands the verb to mean 'inherited [from Daphnis]', but Aelian is not explicit that Daphnis himself sang the story of his suffering, and such an interpretation, though in itself credible, finds no support in Diodorus. Doubts have been expressed about whether the famous Stesichorus of Himera, rather than a fourth-century namesake, really sang (or even mentioned in passing) the story of Daphnis, but there is no compelling reason to reject the traditional interpretation (cf. L. Lehnus, *SCO* 24 (1975) 191–6, O. Vox, *Belfagor* 41 (1986) 311–17), and the reference to the River Himeras at 7.75 – Himera stands at its mouth on the north coast of Sicily – makes it not implausible that T. associated the story with his great Sicilian forebear.

(v) Σ 8.93 'The story is that Daphnis was loved by a nymph whom Sositheos [*TrGF* 1 99 F1] calls Thaleia. She told him not to sleep with another woman and when he disobeyed she came to hate him. So Theocritus says that the nymph rejected him, but that he persisted in his love for her and died of grief; but he also says that Daphnis rejected her and loved another, "how Daphnis once loved Xenea" [7.73]. Others say that he was blinded and fell over a cliff as he wandered around.'

(vi) [Servius] on Virg. *Ecl.* 5.20 adds that after he was blinded 'Daphnis called for aid to his father Mercury [Hermes], and the god snatched Daphnis up to heaven and caused a fountain to appear where Daphnis had been; there the Sicilians hold annual sacrifices.' Such an aetiological reference would not be out of place in T., and 7.76, 'Daphnis was wasting like snow', is at least suggestive in this context.

Sources (iii) and (iv) connect the story of Daphnis with the origin of 'bucolic song', as also apparently does Idyll 1. As an aetiological figure, Daphnis finds a close parallel in Menalkas, whose story was told by Clearchus (late fourth to early third century) in his *Erotika* (fr. 32 Wehrli = Ath. 14 619c–d): 'Eriphanis, the lyric poetess (ἡ μελοποιός), fell in love with Menalkas while he was hunting, and in her desire she too went hunting. She wandered and roamed over all the woods of the mountains ... so that not only the most heartless men, but also the most savage beasts, wept at her suffering (συνδακρῦσαι τῶι πάθει), for they perceived the lover's delusion. Hence, they say, she composed poetry and wandered through the wilderness calling out and singing the so-called "pastoral song" (νόμιον), in which occur the words "Tall are the oaks, Menalkas".' Here are many familiar elements – unrequited love, a madly searching girl, the 'pathetic fallacy', the origin of a rustic poetry; those elements are differently distributed from their occurrence in any version of the Daphnis story, but the similarities are clear. Daphnis and Menalkas (originally a Euboean figure) are connected in various sources – Hermesianax apparently made them lovers (Σ 8.55 = fr. 2 Powell) – and they may have been rival 'first inventors' whom poets liked to bring together as competitors, *à la* Homer and Hesiod, cf. Idylls 8 and 9, Sositheos *TrGF* 99 F1. Clearchus' account suggests, though does not state explicitly, that Menalkas rejected the love of Eriphanis. The hunting motif (cf. (iii) above) *might* in fact suggest that Menalkas rejected all *eros*, like Hippolytus, Atalanta (3.40–2n.) and perhaps Daphnis.

The nature of Daphnis' death (140–1) remains a tantalising puzzle. For some critics, Daphnis is in love with a water-nymph – perhaps has been punished by Aphrodite with this love – and finally can hold out no longer; he thus throws himself into her pool and 'dies' in the manner of Hylas (cf., e.g., H. W. Prescott, *CQ* 7 (1913) 176–87, H. White, *AC* 46 (1977) 578–9). Comparable perhaps is Call. *Epigr.* 22 (= *HE* 1211–14) in which Astakidas, who has been 'snatched from the mountain by a nymph', usurps Daphnis' position as a subject for shepherds' song (above, p. 3 n. 8). Line 103, however, seems to be a cry of ultimate defiance. For others, Daphnis refuses to satisfy his love for a mortal girl (ἁ κώρα), because of a boast or a general vow of chastity (cf. Hutchinson (1988) 149), or because of his oath to the nymph to which 97 may allude (cf. F. J. Williams, *JHS* 89 (1969) 121–3). In the latter case, he may drown in the nymph's pool as revenge for the breaking of his oath. Nevertheless, 140–1 are intended to be mysterious: the 'hero' dies in a manner unlike that of ordinary 'oxherds', cf. Segal (1981) 50–3. The emphasis on the watery nature of his end – whether it is understood literally or meta-phorically (71–5n.) – seems to point to a specific narrative and not *simply* to be an elaborate way of saying 'went to the Underworld', though the words must also evoke such an idea (140n., A. M. Van Erp Taalman Kip, *Hermes* 115 (1987) 249–51). Daphnis may, for example, have wasted away to nothing and the place of his death been marked by a spring.

Thyrsis' song shapes the story of Daphnis as a myth, that is 'as a narrative about the deeds of gods and heroes ... handed on as a tradition ... and of collective significance to a particular social group or groups' (Buxton (1994) 15), and it also brilliantly displays what has been called the 'improvisatory character of myth' (J. Bremmer in J. Bremmer (ed.), *Interpretations of Greek mythology* (London 1987) 4). In the Hellenistic age traditional tales, like the story of Daphnis, were very commonly fashioned into aetiologies for ritual practice; 'bucolic song' is the recurrent commemoration of the *pathos* of Daphnis, and in the threnodic form of Idyll 1 is very close to ritual. As a myth, the story of Daphnis has clear analogues. Daphnis' resistance to *eros* brings him close to the Phaedra of Euri-pides' *Hippolytos*, although as a male who insults Aphrodite he stands closer to Hippolytos; with Hippolytos he shares an almost obsessive self-concern, a sense of his own worth and position (120–1n.). For both figures this 'radical refusal of the "other"' inevitably means 'that when desire comes, it will turn not outward but rather within' (Zeitlin (1996) 223, 279). Zimmerman (1994) has in fact argued that we are to read Daphnis' story as largely parallel to that of Narcissos (cf. 133): Daphnis' 'wasting' is due to the effect of 'the evil eye' to which his scorn for love left him vulnerable, and his death is a lique-faction into the stream beside which he has been lying and in which he had seen his own reflection.

The story of Daphnis (as indeed that of Hippolytos) has clear sim-ilarities to eastern stories of the *paredroi* of great female divinities (Dumuzi and Inanna etc.). Such young men, regularly shepherds or herdsmen, are part son, part lover, and are characterised by great beauty and essential passivity; their death causes great grief to the goddess (even though she may be in part responsible for it) and upheaval in nature, and is usually commemorated in song (cf. again Hippolytos, Eur. *Hipp.* 1428–30). The most familiar of these figures is Adonis (cf. 3.46–8, Idyll 15); 109–10 in which Daphnis taunts Aphrodite with her lost favourite might also be an acknowledgement of the affinity of Daphnis and Adonis. Bion certainly drew heavily upon the song of Thyrsis for his *Lament for Adonis* (cf. A. Porro, *Aevum Antiquum* 1 (1988) 211–21), and the Daphnis of Eclogue 5 owes much to Adonis (cf. esp. lines 22–3). Reconstruction of a 'chain of trans-mission' from the east to T. is fraught with difficulty, but as 'the pathetic fallacy' also seems to look eastwards (71–5n.), the similarities cannot be dismissed. Cf. further W. Berg, *Early Virgil* (London 1974) 15–22, Halperin (1983b), Griffin (1992).

Title. Θύρσις ἢ Ὠιδή (Σ and some MSS), Ποιμὴν καὶ Αἰπόλος *vel sim.* *cett.*

Modern discussions. Cairns (1984); Calame (1992) 59–85; Edquist (1975) 101–8; Griffin (1992); Gutzwiller (1991) 83–104; Halperin (1983a) 161–89; Lawall (1967) 14–33; Miles (1977) 145–56; Ott (1969) 85–137; Schmidt (1987) 57–70; Segal (1981) 25–46, 50–3; Stanzel (1995) 248–68; Walsh (1985) 2–11; Zimmerman (1994). For further bibliography on the *ekphrasis* of the cup cf. 27–61n.

1–11 In sound, dialect and rhythm the opening exchange announces a 'new' poetry to which our ears must become accustomed, cf. D. Donnet, *AC* 57 (1988) 158–75. Bucolic diaeresis is observed throughout, and until 9 no verse has more than one spondee; the opening verses thus strongly align T.'s poetic 'whisper' with 'modern' poetic taste, though his overall practice is somewhat different (Intro. Section 4). Bucolic poetry is to be a 'clear' and 'sharp' sound, like that of the syrinx itself which is evoked by the repeated *i* and *ü* sounds of the opening verses (cf. *Ecl.* 1.1 *Tityre tu ...*, *Arg.* 1.577–8 σύριγγι λιγείηι | καλὰ μελιζόμενος). [Arist.], *De audib.* 804a22–5 lists cicadas, grasshoppers and nightingales as examples of creatures whose song is λιγυρόν 'sharp' and λεπτόν 'thin', and all are associated by T. with 'bucolic song' (cf. 52, 136, 7.139).

The 'competition' of compliments with which the poem opens does not necessarily mean that the goatherd is to be imagined as playing the syrinx and Thyrsis 'singing' before the poem begins (7–8n.); these are the usual skills of the two characters. Rather, this 'competition' corresponds to the opening exchange of abuse in Idyll 5: in both poems a poetic exchange, though of very different kinds, follows; so too in Idyll 7 the preliminary sparring of Lykidas and Simichidas is a form of 'bucolic *agon*'. In Idyll 1, however, *eris* (24) is a thing of the past, now recollected only in art, whether on the cup or in the song of Thyrsis; the present is marked by reciprocal φιλία, the past by the bitterness of *eris* and *eros*. T. thus not merely explores the shifting relationship between frame and included song, but also suggests the timelessness of bucolic conventions in a poem which is actually going to 'invent' those conventions. The second structure which informs 1–11 is that of the 'priamel', in this case of the simple 'A is fine, B is fine, but C is finest' type, cf. Asclepiades, *Anth. Pal.* 5.169 (= *HE* 812–15), 'Sweet it is to drink ice-water when thirsty in summer, and sweet for sailors is the sight of the spring Garland after winter storms, but sweeter it is when one blanket covers lovers ...' Thyrsis uses one version of this to compliment the goatherd (1–3), but then the goatherd caps the compliment by incorporating Thyrsis' priamel into a larger priamel structure: the opening 'sweeter ...' suggests that Thyrsis' song surpasses not just the sound of splashing water, but also the music of 1–3. In both herdsmen's priamels, however, the final, and hence privileged, sound is that of human music – syrinx-playing and song: T.'s poetry both derives from and surpasses the music of nature.

1–3 > *Ecl.* 1.1. 'Something sweet, goatherd, the whispering [which] that pine-tree by the springs sings, and sweet also is your syrinx-playing.' The construction combines ἁδύ ... ἁδὺ δέ with καὶ ... καί. The goatherd's playing (and hence T.'s poetry) has the same qualities as nature itself, but this poetic vision of 'nature' will be a highly 'artful' one, as signalled here by the mannered word-order and phrasing (ψιθύρισμα ... μελίσδεται), which juxtaposes two key features of the bucolic *locus*, the music of nature and nature itself; both ψιθύρισμα and μελίσδεται are transferred from the human sphere to that of nature to emphasise the relationship. The link between nature and the 'rustic music' is further reinforced by the assonance of ψιθύρισμα ... συρίσδες, and prepares for the 'pathetic fallacies' of Thyrsis' song (71–5n.).

1 ἁδύ: 'sweetness' is to be the key quality of T.'s bucolic verse, cf. 65, 145, 148, Call. fr. 1.11 (Mimnermus as γλυκύς). ἁδύ suggests the quality of the sound of the syrinx itself (cf. Eur. *El.* 703 μοῦσα ἡδύθροος of Pan's playing) and the 'pleasure' it gives both men and animals (cf. Aristid. Quint. 2.5); the beauty of that sound mirrors and repays the beauty of the *locus* in which it is performed and the calm ease of the singer or piper (cf. 5.31–4 ἅδιον ἀισῆι | τεῖδ' ὑπὸ τὰν κότινον κτλ., 6.9, Edquist (1975) 102–3). Behind ἁδύ lies also a long-standing debate about the purposes and value of 'literature'. The 'pleasure' (τὸ τερπνόν, *dulce, iucundum*) that poetry brings had been a battleground for Plato and Aristotle, and one branch of Hellenistic theory, particularly associated with Eratosthenes (cf. Pfeiffer (1968) 166–7), privileged poetry's emotional appeal, its ψυχαγωγία, over any moral or educational claims it might have. On this view, 'bucolic poetry' will have no effect in the world in which it is performed – goats go on being goats, and Daphnis' *pathos* will become, like the marvellous cup, purely a subject for our aesthetic appreciation. Like, however, the 'sweet (γλυκερή) voice' of the Hesiodic poet (*Theog.* 96–103), bucolic poetry, the 'sufferings of Daphnis', can make us forget our own sufferings and induce a sense of ἀσυχία. In later rhetorical theory, ἡδονή, like γλυκύτης, was a quality of thought and writing particularly associated with 'bucolic' and images of nature, cf. Hunter (1983b) 92–8. In particular, the description of nature in terms properly applicable to men, such as 'the pine whispering', was considered 'sweet', and the 'pathetic fallacy' of 71–5 would be an excellent example of 'sweet' ideas; T. may have already been influenced by such critical categories. **ψιθύρισμα:** the soft (and sensual, cf. 2.141, 27.67–8) rustle of the leaves, cf. 27.58 ἀλλήλαις λαλέουσι τεὸν γάμον αἱ κυπάρισσοι, Ar. *Clouds* 1008 ἦρος ἐν ὥραι, χαίρων ὁπόταν πλάτανος πτελέαι ψιθυρίζηι, Anyte, *Anth. Pl.* 228.2 (= *HE* 735) ἁδύ τοι ἐν χλωροῖς πνεῦμα θροεῖ πετάλοις, *Ecl.* 8.22 *argutumque nemus pinusque loquentis.* **πίτυς:** this name for the pine may have been particularly associated with Pan and Arcadia, cf. Pind. fr. 95 Maehler, Thphr. *HP* 3.9.4, Leonidas, *Anth. Pal.* 6.334 (= *HE* 1966–71); T. uses πεύκη only at 7.88 (where see n.) and 22.40. The story of Pan's love for the nymph Pitys is largely attested in imperial sources, but cf. *Syrinx* 4, Prop. 1.18.19–20. **αἰπόλε:** the goatherd remains nameless throughout the poem. In all the other 'bucolics', as also in Idylls 2, 11, 13, 14 and 15 and in later imitations, there is at least one proper name in the first or second verses, cf. J. Hubaux, *RBPh* 6 (1927) 603–16, Clausen on *Ecl.* 1.1. Here the repeated generic addresses, αἰπόλε ... ποιμήν ... αἰπόλε ... ποιμήν (1, 7, 12, 15), establish the antithetical bucolic, cf. Hunter (1993b) 40.

2 παγαῖσι: the presence of cool water is inevitable for any Mediterranean *locus amoenus.* T. uses παγά only here, perhaps for the alliterative effect. **μελίσδεται:** μελι- (connected with μέλος, 'song' cf. 7) suggests τὸ μέλι 'honey', thus emphasising the 'sweetness' of bucolic, cf. 128 μελίπνουν, 146–8n.

3 συρίσδες: Doric -ες for -εις in the 2nd pers. sing. is never metrically guaranteed in T., cf. Molinos Tejada 279–81; a Cyrenean inscription of the second century BC (*SEG* xx 719) gives ποτοισές for ποτοισεῖς, cf. Ruijgh (1984) 60 n.10. The syrinx is Pan's instrument and that of the bucolic world. The herdsmen depicted on the Shield of Achilles 'delight themselves with the syrinx' (*Il.* 18.526) in a scene which is constructed as antithetical to the world of martial epic; here too the syrinx functions as an image of a new poetic world. It was constructed out of reeds cut (usually) to the same length and held together with wax, and differential pitch was created by stopping each reed with wax at a different point, cf. [Arist.] *Probl.* 19.919b8, Gow on 1.129, West (1992) 109–12; in the Roman period a syrinx constructed of reeds of descending length became standard.

ἆθλον: the idea of competition for a prize appeals not merely to the agonistic Greek spirit (cf. 22.70–2) but also introduces a familiar feature of 'bucolic poetry' cf. 5.21–9. *EB* 55–6 revises the conceit, 'Pan might be afraid to play Bion's syrinx, lest he take second prize.'

4–6 Of three possible prizes the goatherd will always receive the one immediately below Pan's prize in value. Pan 'takes' a goat when it is sacrificed to him, and this prepares for the idea in καταρρεῖ.

5 ἐς τὲ καταρρεῖ lit. 'flows down to you', not merely 'falls to your lot', though the verb may have been used colloquially in this way; as part of a pattern of water imagery, the word evokes the 'flowing' collapse of the kid, as it is sacrificed and then (6) eaten, cf. *MD* 32 (1994) 165–8. The Doric accusative τέ is all but certainly restored also at 5.14.

6 ἁ χίμαρος 'young she-goat', one stage older than an ἔριφος 'kid'. The point of Thyrsis' assurance – to a goatherd who may be expected to understand such things – is that it is not only the ἔριφος which is good to eat: so too is a young goat before she has had her own kids, cf. Hes. *WD* 591–2 on the pleasures of summer, βοὸς ὑλοφάγοιο κρέας μή πω τετοκυίης | πρωτογόνων τ' ἐρίφων. With rustic cunning, Thyrsis proposes a diminution only of the goatherd's flocks; the goatherd will respond in kind (9–11). κρέας: the transmitted κρῆς is a good Doric form (Sophron fr. 25 Kaibel, Ar. *Ach.* 795, Buck (1955) 39) and might be right; such an intrusive breach of 'Naeke's Law' (130n.), however, would disturb the otherwise uniform rhythm of the opening verses. A long monosyllable in the second half of the fourth foot is very rare at all periods, and partial parallels at 5.132, 15.62 and 22.114 do not lessen the oddity, cf. O'Neill (1942) 123, 139. At 5.140 καλὸν κρέας is universally transmitted in the same *sedes*.

7–8 > *Ecl.* 5.45–8, 84. Either 'Your song, shepherd, flows down more sweetly than that water [flows down]' or 'Sweeter, shepherd, [is] your song than that plashing water [which] flows down from the rock on high ...'; the syntactical ambiguity matches that of 1–2 (cf. Ott (1969) 88), just as the κ and λ alliteration, indicative of flowing water (cf. 7.137, 22.37–9, 49–50, *Arg.* 3.71), matches the sound effects of the opening verses. Whereas the opening verses move from nature to human music, 7–8 move from the shepherd's song to natural phenomena. The principal models are Hes. *Theog.* 786–7 (the fearsome

Styx is rewritten as a nameless and pleasant waterfall) and *Od.* 17.209–10 (the spring at which Melantheus, Eumaeus and Odysseus meet, cf. Idyll 7, Intro.); both models mark bucolic as a re-writing and re-evaluation of epic. Although 'your song' refers primarily to special performances of the kind cited in 24 and exemplified by the Daphnis-song which is to follow, 1–6 are also part of 'Thyrsis' song' here praised by the goatherd. It is amusing that the goatherd is so full of praise for a 'song' which was full of praise for him, but this technique also calls attention to the relation between 'frame' and 'song', or rather explores the distinction between them, cf. 143–5n.

9–11 Here the prizes are of equal value, which caps Thyrsis' offer of a hierarchy of prizes; the Muses, however, who are to song what Pan is to syrinx-playing, get *first* choice. The association of the Muses with sheep may go back to Hesiod's 'initiation' while herding his lambs (*Theog.* 23).

9 Μοῖσαι: T. seems to have used this Aeolic and Pindaric form rather than the common Doric Μῶσαι; he may also have used Μοῦσαι, but (if so) the rationale of the choice is unclear, cf. 117 Ἀρέθοισα, Nöthiger (1971) 93, Molinos Tejada 55–8.   **οἴιδα:** this accusative does not occur elsewhere (cf. Pfeiffer on Call. fr. 513); disyllabic ὄιν in 11 offers a mannered contrast.

10 σακίταν 'fed in the stall (σηκός)', rather than being allowed to graze with its mother.   **δέ** may appear in the apodosis of a conditional, usually as here with a pronoun, cf. 29.17, Denniston 180–1.

12–23 The characters now 'contest' both the nature of the performances to follow and their location, cf. 5.31–61. Attempts to provide a spatial map of the geography of the setting are doomed to failure; typical features of the *locus amoenus* (7.135–47n.) are divided between the speakers and hence multiplied and stylised, cf. Elliger (1975) 326–7, Pearce (1988) 295–6.

12 λῆις: λῆν 'to be willing' is completely absent from epic and high lyric, but is one of the most persistent features of literary Doric at 'lower' levels.   **Νυμφᾶν:** it may be that we are to imagine statues of the Nymphs in the vicinity, cf. 22n.   **τεῖδε** 'here'; the form occurs on a first-century BC papyrus of Epicharmus (fr. 99 Kaibel = *CGFPR* 83). The standard variants are τεῖνδε and τῆδε, cf. Molinos Tejada 338–9, West on Hes. *WD* 635.

13 ὡς 'where', a marked dialect feature. This verse recurs at 5.101.   **μυρῖκαι** 'tamarisks', cf. Lindsell (1937) 80, Lembach (1970) 105–6. It was perhaps this verse that prompted Virgil to make *humiles myricae* a symbol of Theocritean pastoral (*Ecl.* 4.2).

14 συρίσδεν: cf. 16. Both -εν and -ειν or -ην infinitives are metrically guaranteed in T. (Molinos Tejada 312–17); the short form occurs also in the traditional language of high lyric (Nöthiger (1971) 96–9).   **τὰς δ᾽ αἶγας κτλ.:** singing or playing the syrinx may be conceived as an alternative to ordinary pastoral activities (Idylls 1, 3) or as taking place during those activities (Idylls 4, 5).

15–18 The heat of midday is the traditional time for meeting gods and when gods are most dangerous, cf. 7.21, Call. *h.* 5.72–4 (with Bulloch's note), T. D. Papanghelis, *Mnem.* 42 (1989) 54–61, Roscher s.v. *Meridianus daemon.* Piping would annoy the god when he is trying to rest, but singing, so the goatherd alleges, carries no similar danger. Like Priapos and the Nymphs, Pan will thus be 'present' to hear a song in which he is closely involved.

16 δεδοίκαμες: perhaps 'we goatherds'.

17 ἔστι: cf. 3.37–9n.

18 χολὰ ποτὶ ῥινί: cf. Herodas 6.37–8 μὴ δή, Κοριττοῖ, τὴν χολὴν ἐπὶ ῥινός | ἔχ᾽ εὐθύς. The phrase combines semi-Homeric diction (cf. *Il.* 18.322 δριμὺς χόλος) with a colloquial expression. At *Od.* 24.318–19 δριμὺ μένος moves along Odysseus' nostrils as he watches his father weeping.

19 γάρ: 'anticipatory' γάρ (Denniston 69–70) explains the proposition of 21–3.   **Θύρσι:** not otherwise attested, except in imitations of Idyll 1 (*Epigr.* 6, Myrinus, *Anth. Pal.* 7.703 (= *GP* 2568–73)). Θύρσος is not uncommon (*LGPN* I s.v.), and Θύρσις may suggest Dionysos, cf. above, p. 62.   **τὰ Δάφνιδος ἄλγε᾽:** at 5.20 the phrase is used as proverbial for the worst fate which can befall a herdsman. **ἀείδες:** probably present (3n.), rather than an unaugmented imperfect (ἄειδες). To (be able to) 'sing the sufferings of Daphnis' is virtually the same as 'reaching mastery in bucolic song' (20).

20 βουκολικᾶς: cf. Intro. Section 2.   **πλέον:** cf. 3.46–8n.

21 > *Ecl.* 5.3. As the opening suggested a parallelism between the sounds of nature and bucolic song, so the central narrative is to be a projection from the environment of the characters: Thyrsis and the goatherd sit near statues of Priapos and the nymphs for Thyrsis' song

in which Priapos and the nymphs have important rôles.   **Πριάπω:**
Πρίαπος is Attic / *koine* and passed to the Romans, whereas Πρίηπος
is the Ionic form used in the god's Lampsacene homeland. For T.
certainty is hardly possible, but a Doric poet might well prefer the
form with long -α. The cult of Priapos, the ithyphallic son of (variously) Dionysos and Aphrodite, Dionysos and a nymph or Hermes
and a nymph, spread from Lampsakos on the Hellespont all over the
Greek world; in Hellenistic times he was particularly associated with
Dionysos, and their images were carried together in the great procession of Ptolemy Philadelphos (Ath. 5 201c–d). His prominent rôle
in Idyll 1 is thus a typically Hellenistic retrojection of 'the present'
into the mythic past. In essence a fertility deity, the protector of
crops and fruit, his functions clearly overlapped those of Pan;
Pausanias says that he is honoured 'wherever goats or sheep are
pastured or there are swarms of bees' (9.31.2). Springs, as sources
of irrigation and fertility, were an obvious site for statues of the god
(cf. *Epigr.* 4), as they were for Pan and the nymphs (Nikarkhos, *Anth.
Pal.* 9.330 (= *HE* 2727–36) etc.). Cf. in general H. Herter, *De Priapo*
(Giessen 1932).

22 Κρανιάδων '[statues of] Nymphs of the spring', the νύμφαι
κρηναῖαι of *Od.* 17.240, cf. 13.43–5, Leonidas, *Anth. Pal.* 9.326 (= *HE*
1978–83), *Arg.* 1.1228–9 etc.; for the form cf. *SH* 978.14–15 ἐπὶ
πηγὴν | τήνδε μετ᾽ εὐνομίης βαίνετε Κρηνιάδες (probably not much
later than T.). The transmitted κρανίδων would most naturally
mean 'springs' (cf. Eur. *Hipp.* 208, Call. fr. 751), rather than 'spring
nymphs', because in the latter sense the -ι- might be expected to be
short (cf. *EB* 29). Like Priapos, nymphs are to play a major rôle in
Thyrsis' song, and it is important that bucolic narrative and bucolic
emotion are seen to grow out of the context in which they are set.

24 This line presupposes (and thereby inaugurates) the existence
of song 'contests', the rustic equivalent of the aristocratic games at
which a Homer or a Hesiod competed and the dramatic contests of
Athens. Thyrsis is most naturally understood to have sung 'the griefs
of Daphnis' in this contest; this is his 'masterpiece', as Daphnis is the
prime subject of 'bucolic song'. In an amusing fantasy, Chromis may
be imagined to have travelled from Libya to take part in one of
these rustic 'matches', as Hesiod crossed the sea to Euboea (*WD*
650–7) and as Theocritus and his contemporaries regularly travelled

to poetic festivals; the most familiar institutions of classical poetry are thus to have their bucolic equivalents. 'Chromis of Libya' (or his family) may, however, have settled in the area long before, and he may have been no more a recent arrival than the Libyan goat of 3.5. Χρόμις is a Homeric name (*Il.* 2.858) and a fish of uncertain identification (Thompson, *Fishes* s.v.), but it may be relevant that among the people called Χρόμιος known to literature is a Syracusan patron of Pindar (Nemeans 1, 9).

25 ἐς τρὶς ἀμέλξαι 'for milking three times', i.e. I will let you milk her three times; for the 'infinitive of purpose' cf. Goodwin §770.

26 ποταμέλγεται ἐς δύο πέλλας 'produces two pails of milk in addition [to the milk for her kids]'. The repeated numerals in these verses mark the goatherd's 'naïve' eagerness to convince Thyrsis.

27–61 As Hesiod won a tripod, Thyrsis is to be rewarded with a marvellous cup; Cairns (1984) 106 sees here a reminder to T.'s patrons that they should be equally generous. The *ekphrasis* of the bowl is the goatherd's 'masterpiece' to match the song which Thyrsis will sing. In the bucolic world of reciprocal exchange rather than financial transaction, cup is to be exchanged for song: both are of an equal value (56n.), which is that of a goat and a large cheese (57–8). The description of the wooden cup evokes contemporary ceramics, metalwork, and statuary in a fantastic τέρας (56), which is at once both 'realistic' and quite 'unrealistic'; like Thyrsis' song, the cup is a highly wrought and artistic version of an essentially humble and popular form. For Hellenistic *ekphrasis* in general cf. D. P. Fowler, *JRS* 81 (1991) 25–35, Hunter (1993a) 52–9, Goldhill (1994), M. Fantuzzi, *Der neue Pauly* s.v. 'Ekphrasis'. On the cup cf. also Dale (1952), Gallavotti (1966), Nicosia (1968) 15–47, Manakidou (1993) 51–83.

The three scenes all have analogues on the Shield of Achilles, and it is clear that the cup is to be seen as a 'bucolicisation' of the Shield, where the first 'bucolic poets' of literature appear (the herdsmen playing the syrinx, *Il.* 18.525–6). Just as Homer's shield was interpreted as a comprehensive picture of the world (cf. P. R. Hardie, *JHS* 105 (1985) 11–31), so the cup offers a view of the wider world against which the limited concerns of 'bucolic' poetry are played out. In turning the Shield of war into a rustic bowl of peace, T. exploited a familiar opposition, perhaps under the influence of the roughly similar shape of the objects, cf. Ar. *Ach.* 583–6 (Lamachos' shield used as a vomit-bowl), *Lys.* 185–237 (a large *kylix* is substituted for an Aeschylean shield), Aristophon fr. 13.2 Κ–Α τῶν θηρικλείων εὐκύκλωτον ἀσπίδα, Arist. *Poet.* 1457b19–22, *Rhet.* 3 1407a15–18 (a shield and a drinking-bowl (φιάλη) are 'analogous', as the latter is to Dionysos as the former to Ares); as on a shield, the decoration is on the outside (cf. below). The cup is not a simple representation of the bucolic world – there are, e.g., no flocks – because the ecphrastic relation here constructed between a described object and the poem in which it occurs is not that of 'original' and 'copy'. The three scenes cover the three principal 'ages of man' (maturity, old age and childhood), as the Shield divided existence into 'war' and 'peace'; so too, emotional (the lovers) and physical (the fisherman) πόνος give way to a labour (the boy's weaving) which suggests poetic πόνος (7.51n.). That the art of poetry is expressed through an image ('a boy weaving a cage') is itself a manifestation of how poetry works; so too is the fact that the goatherd's account of the scene does not follow the 'natural' order of child – adult – old man, cf. Ettin (1984) 116.

The fisherman and the boy in the vineyard suggest contemporary 'realistic' trends in art, cf. Himmelmann (1980), id., *Alexandria und der Realismus in der griechischen Kunst* (Tübingen 1983), Laubscher (1982), Pollitt (1986) 141–7. An old fisherman is represented in famous statues in the Vatican and the Louvre and was clearly a widespread sculptural type (cf. 43n., Pollitt fig. 155, Ridgway (1990) 334–6); these may have had predecessors close in time to T., but relief work on pottery and metal will have been the principal influence, cf. U. Hausmann, *Hellenistische Reliefbecher aus attischen und böotischen Werkstätten* (Stuttgart 1959), E. A. Zervondaki, *MDAI(A)* 83 (1968) 1–88; for a relief vase depicting fishermen cf. Zervondaki p. 35 with *Tafel* 26.4–5. By suggesting that the subjects of his poetry have already been copied into art, only then to be re-inscribed in literature through the device of *ekphrasis*, T. reinforces the sense of tradition in his poetry; in describing works of art, literature erects a hierarchy in which art is both derivative from literature and also needs the written word if its narratives are to be explained, and indeed from a later period survive relief bowls decorated with scenes from epic and tragedy (cf. Hausmann op. cit.). For an early nineteenth-century silver version (by Paul Storr) of T.'s cup cf. Gallavotti (1966) 431, W. G. Arnott, *QUCC* 29 (1978) 129–34.

27–31 > *Ecl.* 3.36–9.

27 κισσύβιον: a rustic wooden bowl or pail (*Od.* 9.346, 16.52) which could doubtless double, as here (cf. 55, 149), as a drinking vessel, cf. Dale (1952), Halperin (1983a) 167–76. After Homer the word may have been restricted to literature. The most common etymology was 'a bowl made of ivy-wood (κισσός)' (cf. Eur. *Cycl.* 390–1, Ath. 11 476f–7e), but such bowls are technologically improbable, and the word is perhaps non-Greek in origin, cf. C. A. Mastrelli, *SIFC* 23 (1948) 97–112. T. may wish to etymologise as 'decorated with an ivy pattern' (cf. 30, Pollux 6.97). **κεκλυσμένον:** wooden vessels might be sealed with wax for protection and to prevent seepage into the wood, cf. Ovid, *Met.* 8.668–70; Cato, *De agr.* 111 says that ivy-wood is porous to wine. κλύζειν is the technical term for such sealing (Ammonius, *De diff.* 274 Nickau). **ἀδέι κηρῶι:** the wax shares the principal quality of bucolic poetry (1n.).

28 ἀμφῶες 'two-handled', a *hapax* corresponding to the Homeric *hapax* ἄμφωτος (*Od.* 22.10), used of the beautiful golden cup from which Antinous is about to drink when Odysseus kills him; the change from precious object to wooden bowl is a pointed marker of the move from epic to bucolic. ἀμφῶες may also suggest 'double': the cup is both 'a cup' and an image of poetry, it is 'ambiguous'. **νεοτευχές** carries a 'programmatic' charge: this poetry is something quite new. The bowl still 'smells of the knife'; the reference is not merely to the shaping of the bowl, but specifically to the carving of the decoration. Thus the inside of the bowl will be fragrant with the sealing wax, whereas the outside still carries the smell of wood-carving, cf. Könnecke (1917) 290–1.

29–31 'Up towards the cup's lip weaves ivy, ivy intertwined with helichryse; along the flower winds the ivy-tendril rejoicing in its [own] yellow fruit.' The intricate word-order is mimetic of the interwoven plants; the anaphora of κισσός across a verse-division displays the curling ivy. The principal model is the description at *h. Dion.* 40–1 of ivy curling over the mast of the ship carrying the god, ἀμφ' ἱστὸν δὲ μέλας εἰλίσσετο κισσὸς | ἄνθεσι τηλεθάων, χαρίεις δ' ἐπὶ καρπὸς ὀρώρει, cf. K. J. Gutzwiller, *AJP* 107 (1986) 253–5; one Dionysiac miracle prompting amazement (*h. Dion.* 37) is used to describe another. The language of weaving (μαρύεται, κεκονισμένος) associates the cup with the 'cricket-trap' depicted on it (52–4): both artefacts suggest poetry.

Except for one particular, the above translation broadly follows Gallavotti (1966). Both sides of the bowl (as defined by the two handles) carry a pattern of interwoven ivy and helichryse rising from the base and running around the top to form a frame closed at the base by an acanthus pattern (55). On the cup, as in the text, the two flower patterns frame the asymmetrical carved scenes (29–31, 55). Both painted pottery and Hellenistic silver-ware offer examples of such work. (Among those who have placed the decoration on the outside of the cup, the most popular alternative has been to see a line of ivy round the rim of the bowl with the ἕλιξ 'opposite it' (κατ' αὐτόν) and the scenes between the two; this, however, leaves the position and purpose of the acanthus unexplained. It is doubtful whether the imitations at *Ecl.* 3.36–40 and Nonnus 19.130–1 should be used to try to explain T.'s text.)

29 ποτί: *lectio difficilior.* Particularly in later Greek, ποτί can denote 'near' in a fairly vague sense, but Gallavotti's interpretation gives it point.   **μαρύεται** (i.e. μηρύεται) 'winds', intransitive middle.

30 ἑλιχρύσωι: probably *Helichrysum siculum*, cf. Polunin–Huxley 183–4. A notice in the *Suda* (ε 874), glossing a quotation from Call. *Hecale* (fr. 274 = 45 Hollis), alleges that ἑλίχρυσον can be the ivy-flower; there is, however, no other evidence for this meaning. ἑλιχρ- ... ἕλιξ ... εἰλεῖται reinforces the mimetic word-order; *Et. Mag.* 330.29 Gaisford derives ἕλιξ from ἑλίσσω.   **κεκονισμένος** 'interwoven', from the rare κονίζειν, continuing the image in μαρύεται, cf. Hesychius δ 1070, Latte (1968) 668–9; Σ glosses as συμπεπλεγμένος. κεκονι(σ)μένος has more usually been derived from κονίω, and interpreted as 'dusted' or 'sprinkled'.   **κατ' αὐτόν** 'along the helichryse'.

31 καρπῶι: the tendril 'rejoices in / prides itself upon' its saffron-coloured fruit (cf. *Epigr.* 3.3–4 τὸν κροκόεντα ... κισσόν), a good example of γλυκύτης (above, p. 70) which illustrates the genesis of one kind of 'pathetic fallacy', for here the viewer shares the plant's 'joy'. Gallavotti, however, understood the 'fruit' to be the yellow flowers of the helichryse.

32 ἔντοσθεν 'within [the frame of the plants]'. The oldest witness reads ἔκτοσθεν, which would remove the potential ambiguity of 'inside', i.e. 'inside the frame' or 'inside the cup', but seems an unnecessary specification; it may have arisen precisely to remove the ambiguity.   γυνά, τι θεῶν δαίδαλμα: cf. 15.79 (the tapestries) θεῶν περονάματα φασεῖς, 57n. δαίδαλμα belongs to the standard language of *ekphrasis*, cf. *Il.* 18.482, *Arg.* 1.729, Moschus, *Europa* 43, but here evokes Pandora, the most famous 'fashioned' woman of Greek story, an emblem of women's power to cause 'grievous desire and body-devouring cares' (Hes. *WD* 66) for men, cf. Miles (1977) 147.

34–5 καλόν: adverbial neuter.   **ἐθειράζοντες:** this *hapax* could refer to either beard or hair, but the latter, the normal sense of ἔθειρα, seems more likely.   **ἀμοιβαδὶς ... | νεικείουσ' ἐπέεσσι:** the scene rewrites the 'legal' νεῖκος of the Homeric Shield (*Il.* 18.497–508), cf. 506 ἀμοιβηδὶς δὲ δίκαζον; a case of murder has become a fruitless erotic quest. νεικείουσ' is a non-Doric form of an epic word, and ἔπος also is otherwise absent from the bucolic Idylls, cf. Hunter (1996a) 43–4; the diction thus marks the 'epic' origin of the scene. The men stand on either side of the woman and argue their case alternately (cf. the imitation at Longus, *D&C* 1.15.4–17.1). The principle of alternation suggests the bucolic *agon*, and ἔπη hints at the performance of hexameters; it is noteworthy that at 7.48 ἐτώσια μοχθίζοντι is used of unsuccessful poets. Other Theocritean lovers do not, however, 'contest' before their rivals, cf. Idylls 3, 10, 11: such a stylised and controlled display is possible only in the freezing grip of pictorial art.

36–7 ὅκα μὲν ... | ἄλλοκα δ': a Doric version of the epic ὁτὲ μὲν ... ἄλλοτε δέ, cf. 4.17–19, *Il.* 18.599–602, Call. *h.* 3.192–3, Chantraine, *GH* 2.360–1.   **γέλαισα:** if correctly restored, this will be the athematic participle of a thematic verb (< *γέλα-νσα), cf. 85 ζάτεισα, 6.8 ποθόρησθα, 7.40 νίκημι. The phenomenon is standard in Lesbian Aeolic, but examples occur also in Cyrene and Cos; γελάοισα is, however, metrically guaranteed at 95–6. The woman laughs while the men suffer from the *eros* for which she is responsible; here is the mortal equivalent of 'laughing' Aphrodite (95–6) and Daphnis.   **ποτὶ τόν** 'to the other'.

38 The first *spondeiazon* of the poem completes the scene; the heavy rhythm is mimetic of the men's wasted labour. **κυλοιδιόωντες** 'with bags under their eyes', presumably caused by the sleeplessness typical of those in love; κύλα are the tender parts under the eyes and κυλοιδιᾶν ... τοὺς ὀφθαλμούς is a symptom of love at Heliod. 4.7.7.   ἐτώσια μοχθίζοντι: cf. 7.48. They 'labour in vain' because, as Σ observes, 'who could persuade a statue?' As in 35, the 'naïve' interplay between the narrative and the carving explores the principles of ecphrastic description.

39 τοῖς δὲ μετά 'near them' or perhaps 'in addition to these' (17.84, 25.129).   **γριπεύς:** a fisherman with his net is depicted on the Hesiodic *Shield* (*Aspis* 213–15), and cf. *Il.* 16.406–8 (simile of a fisherman on a rock); the Homeric Shield depicts various workmen – ploughmen, reapers, harvesters – but not fishermen. Some contemporary epigrammatists, notably Leonidas of Tarentum, specialised in the depiction of working people, and a fisherman appears in Idyll 3; Idyll 21 depicts the hard and frustrating life of the fisherman, but is certainly later than T.

40 ἐς βόλον: perhaps 'for [i.e. to make] a cast' rather than 'for a catch'. Such an interpretation suits the uncertainty and chanciness of the fisherman's life.

41 τὸ καρτερόν: adverbial, cf. 3.3–5n.   **ἐοικώς:** the standard language of *ekphrasis*, cf. Hes. *Aspis* 215 (the fisherman) ἀπορρίψοντι ἐοικώς, Arat. *Phaen.* 63–7 μογέοντι ... ἀνδρὶ ἐοικὸς κτλ., *Arg.* 1.739 (Zethos) μογέοντι ἐοικώς. All such figures are merely 'like' because they are not 'real', but the phrasing also foregrounds the rôle of the interpreter in literary *ekphrasis*.

42 'You would say that he was fishing with [lit. as to] all the strength of his limbs.'   **φαίης κεν:** a Homerism, which might protect the epic-lyric κεν against Ahrens' κα, cf. 34–5n. In Homer φαίης κεν is used by both the poet and his characters (cf. De Jong (1987) 57–60, Richardson (1990) 174–8); T. uses it only here (150 Ὡρᾶν ... δοκησεῖς and 15.79 θεῶν περονάματα φασεῖς are related forms), and the phrase will have particular significance in an *ekphrasis* concerned with the viewer's production of meaning, cf. Arat. *Phaen.* 196 (the constellation Cassiepeia) φαίης κεν ἀνιάζειν ἐπὶ παιδί, Herodas 4.28 (an *ekphrasis* in the mouth of a humble character) οὐκ ἐρεῖς ...; Here the form plays against the precious poeticisms γυίων and ἐλλοπιεύειν: would *anyone* 'say' such a thing?   **ἐλλοπιεύειν:** ἔλλοψ (probably 'scaly') occurs as an epithet of fish in T.'s Hesiodic model (*Aspis* 212), and is used as a noun for fish in Hellenistic poetry. As fish were proverbially dumb, the standard etymology is ἐλλείπειν τὴν ὀπά, cf. *Syrinx* 18 ἔλλοπι κούραι of Echo, who has no voice of her own, Hesych. ε 2168, *Et. Mag.* 331.51–2 Gaisford. This verb, which is found only here, may therefore have special point for a work of art which cannot speak.

43 'Realistic' depiction of veins, muscles and sinews is a familiar feature of Hellenistic statuary and *ekphrasis*, cf. 22.44–50, 25.148–9, and is particularly prominent on the 'Louvre fisherman' (27–61n.). In *Epist.* 3.6 Pliny describes a bronze figure which he believes to be *uetus et antiquum: effingit senem stantem; ossa musculi nerui, uenae rugae etiam ut spirantis adparent; rari et cadentes capilli . . .*

44 πολιῶι: perhaps little more than 'old', but the ecphrastic mode allows the goatherd to 'see' colours on the *kissubion*, no less than the poet describes the colours on Achilles' shield.   ἄβας: ἄβα is Aeolic and ἤβα the original Doric, but ἄβα in third-century literary Doric would not be surprising, cf. Ruijgh (1984) 85, Cassio (1993); a second-century inscription from Tenos has both ἐφηβεύσαντες and ἔφαβοι (*IG* XII 5.911).

45–54 A vineyard at harvest-time is depicted on the Shield of Achilles (*Il.* 18.561–72, cf. Hes. *Aspis* 292–300): young men and girls collect grapes in 'woven baskets' (cf. 52, *Ecl.* 10.71 which combines 52 with its Homeric model), while a παῖς plays the lyre and sings λεπταλέηι φωνῆι. So too the boy on the cup is an image of the bucolic poet, constructing something beautiful from 'natural materials' (52–3), cf. Call. *fr.* 1.6 παῖς ἅτε, Cairns (1984) 102–5, S. Goldhill, *ICS* 12 (1987) 1–6.

45 τυτθὸν δ' ὅσσον ἄπωθεν (lit.) '[It is] a little how distant from . . .', i.e. 'very close to . . .'   ἀλιτρύτοιο: Leonidas calls fishermen ἀλιπλάγκτοι . . . δικτυβόλοι (*Anth. Pal.* 6.4.4 = *HE* 2286).

46 Cf. *Il.* 18.561–2 ἐν δὲ τίθει σταφυλῆισι μέγα βρίθουσαν ἀλωήν | καλὴν χρυσείην; the unusually close reworking acknowledges the significance of the Homeric passage as a founding 'bucolic' text. †πυρναίαις†: quite obscure and presumably corrupt. Briggs's περκναῖσι (περκναίαις *iam* Ribbeck) has won much favour (cf. ὑποπερκάζουσιν of the grapes in Alcinous' orchard, *Od.* 7.126). τὸ πύρνον is 'bread', 'food', and 'ready for eating' would make good sense (cf. 49), but the adjective is unattested; πυρνοτόκος 'producing food' occurs as an epithet of ἄρουρα (*IG* XII 5.739, line 45). Wilamowitz understood 'of Pyrnos' in Caria; Ahrens proposed πυρραίαις, and

Campbell (*CQ* 25 (1931) 90) γενναίαις. (There is no evidence for any other reading, cf. J. Bingen, *CdE* 113/114 (1982) 313.)

48 The two foxes echo and invert the two men who strove for the attention of the beautiful woman. Vineyards are a standard place to find foxes, cf. 5.112–13, Ar. *Knights* 1076–7, Song of Songs 2.15 etc.　　μιν: the Doric is νιν, but the transmission is very unstable in such details (Molinos Tejada 248–53); epic colouring is appropriate in this *ekphrasis*, and ἀμφὶ δέ μιν is a Homeric verse-beginning (*Od.* 3.467, 4.404 etc.).

49 τὰν τρώξιμον: a collective σταφυλά may be understood, 'grapes ripe for eating (τρώγειν)', but the expression may also be a colloquialism in which the absence of a noun is no longer felt. The *Digest* states that τρώξιμοι were grapes grown for eating rather than pressing (50.16.205).

50–1 The textual and interpretative problems in these verses have as yet found no satisfactory solution. The second fox presumably has designs on the boy's own food (bread – τὰ ξηρά – carried in the pouch referred to in 53?), but the final four words of 51 defy explanation. ἀκρατίζεσθαι is 'to breakfast', but if ἀκράτιστον means 'having breakfasted' and καθίξηι is intransitive, the minimum necessary change will be ἀκράτιστος to agree with the fox, 'will not let the boy go until she has sat down having feasted upon dry food'; the word is, however, probably corrupt. ἢ ἀκρ- must be scanned as a single syllable by synizesis, but ἤ could be excised as an interpolation. To the commentaries add J. Edmonds, *CR* 26 (1912) 241–2, A. Y. Campbell, *CQ* 25 (1931) 90–102, A. D. Knox, *CQ* 25 (1931) 205–11.　　τεύχοισα: cf. above, p. 26.　　φατί 'thinks to herself', cf. LSJ s.v. 1b.

52 > *Ecl.* 10.71.　　ἀνθερίκοισι 'asphodel stalks'.　　πλέκει: weaving as an image for poetry occurs already in the archaic period (Bacchylides 5.9–10 ὑφάνας | ὕμνον, 19.8), and becomes a commonplace of Latin poetry.　　ἀκριδοθήραν 'a trap for crickets'; the variant ἀκριδοθήκαν 'a cricket-cage' is not impossible – the two variants also occur in the Longan imitation of this passage (*D&C* 1.10.2) – but 'traps' may also function as 'cages', as does the modern glass jar, and -θήκη words seem to be confined to containers for the dead or inanimate (P. Kretschmer and E. Locker, *Rückläufiges Wörterbuch der griechischen Sprache* (Göttingen 1963) 86). 'Pet' crickets are the subject of a number of contemporary epigrams (e.g. Leonidas, *Anth. Pal.* 7.198 = *HE* 2084–91). Other ἀκρίδες posed a threat to grapes (cf. 5.108–9), but it is unlikely that 'locusts' were the boy's prey; for the terminological problems cf. Davies–Kathirithamby 135–44. The boy has become entirely absorbed in the task, and μέλεται δέ οἱ κτλ. captures both the 'frozenness' of art and the innocent unconcern which is built into the pastoral vision from the earliest texts, cf. *Il.* 18.526, 21.39, Griffin (1992) 198–9; we are here close to an ancient expression of 'art for art's sake'.

53 σχοίνωι ἐφαρμόσδων 'joining [the asphodel] to rush'; σχοίνωι is collective singular. The asphodel will give strength, while the more pliant rushes bind the trap together.

55 > *Ecl.* 3.45. The acanthus design runs round the base of the cup.   **δέπας:** in 27 the cup was a κισσύβιον and in 143 will be a σκύφος; such use of synonyms is a common feature of Hellenistic poetry, which always sought variety rather than sameness. **περιπέπταται** 'is spread around', perfect passive of περιπετάννυμι. **ὑγρός** 'pliant', 'able to bend in supple ways'.

56 The expression of admiration refers to the acanthus, but colours the description of the whole cup, to which it forms the conclusion; after the section-by-section account, we learn that the *whole* cup is a τέρας, as acanthus surrounds the *whole* cup.   **αἰπολικὸν θάημα** 'a marvel of the goatherd's world', an expression appropriate to the speaker. Despite Hes. *Aspis* 318, θαῦμα ἰδεῖν καί Ζηνὶ βαρυκτύπωι, 'a thing at which a goatherd would marvel' seems less natural, although the difference is slight. For the variant αἰολικόν cf. Wilamowitz (1906) 36–8. θάημα is the Doric form of θέαμα '(marvellous) sight', which was rightly connected in antiquity with θαῦμα words, cf. *Etym. Mag.* 443.37–48 Gaisford; the language of 'wonder' is standard in ancient *ekphrasis*, cf. *Il.* 18.377, *Arg.* 1.767, Moschus, *Europa* 49, *LfgrE* s.v. θαῦμα, and see next n.   **τέρας κέ τυ θυμὸν ἀτύξαι** 'it would amaze your heart as a wonder'. τυ θυμόν is a double accusative of 'whole and part', cf. K–G 1 289–90. Contemplation of the cup, like listening to the song of Thyrsis, produces not just 'wonder' but 'amazement'; ἀτύζειν is a strong word of high poetry. The cup is a τέρας, i.e. a manifestation of the supernatural, and this associates viewing the cup with the reception of poetry. 'Pleasure' as an aim of poetry (1n.) was closely linked by Hellenistic theorists with ἔκπληξις, the 'amazing' of the mind and senses, a ὑπερβολὴ θαυμασιότητος (Arist. *Top.* 4 126b14); this was most important for tragedy and epic, but not limited to them, cf. Polyb. 2.56.11, Strabo 1.2.17, R. Heinze, *Virgil's epic technique* (Eng. trans., Bristol 1993) 370, 384–5. 'Longinus' 15.1–2 makes ἔκπληξις the purpose of poetic φαντασία, which is 'when inspiration and emotion make you appear actually to see what you describe and bring it before your hearers' eyes'; the goatherd thus inscribes both his technique and our reaction into the text. As cup and song are reciprocal artefacts, so the effect of the cup upon Thyrsis will be the same as that of Thyrsis' song upon the goatherd.

57 τῶ μὲν κτλ. 'For it [i.e. in exchange for it] I gave ... as price ...'; the genitive resembles a genitive of price, cf. *Od.* 11.326–7 Ἐριφύλην | ἣ χρυσὸν φίλου ἀνδρὸς ἐδέξατο τιμήεντα, K–G 1 378. **πορθμῆι Καλυδνίωι** 'a ferryman from Kalydna', an island (modern Kalimno) or set of small islands off the NW coast of Cos, cf. *Il.* 2.677, *RE* x 1768–71. The geographical specificity increases the mystery of the cup's origin: a ferryman might well have received the cup from a passenger, perhaps indeed from a god (which would give added point to 32); we might think of the story of Aphrodite and the ferryman Phaon. It would be hazardous to seek to draw conclusions from this phrase about the setting or place of composition of Idyll 1, cf. above, p. 2. (The text is not certain: the MSS have πορθμεῖ Καλυδωνίωι 'ferryman of Calydon', which lies on the edge of the mountains towards the NW end of the Corinthian Gulf; this may have arisen from familiarity with the πορθμὸς Καλυδώνιος, Heliodorus 5.17.1 etc.)

58 τυρόεντα: meaning and text are uncertain. Hesychius glosses the word as πλακοῦντα 'cake', but it may simply = τυρόν; ἄρτος τυρόεις is 'cheese bread' (cf. Sophron fr. 14 Kaibel). Elsewhere, however, the first syllable of τυρός is long; unless this is an unparalleled exception, -οε- is scanned (by synizesis) as a long syllable or we should read τυρῶντα or the text is corrupt.

59 > *Ecl.* 3.43, 47. ποτὶ ... θίγεν: tmesis, although the verb normally governs the genitive rather than the accusative.

60 ἄχραντον: like νεοτευχές (28), 'unstained' suggests the novelty of T.'s undertaking, cf. Call. *h.* 2.111 (the programmatic epilogue) καθαρή τε καὶ ἀχράαντος. There is humour in the implication that, had a goatherd drunk from the cup, it would no longer be 'pure'. κά: cf. 42n.

61 φίλος: cf. 149. φίλος as a nominative address occurs already in Homer, cf. *Il.* 9.601, 21.106, M. L. West, *Glotta* 44 (1967) 139–44; in many cases the form seems to convey great urgency.   τὸν ... ὕμνον 'that ... hymn [we have mentioned before]'. ὕμνος is here not simply 'song': the 'song of Daphnis' is an encomiastic commemoration of a 'bucolic hero'.

62 κερτομέω: an allusion to the expected agonistic rivalry between musical herdsmen, cf. 5.77 τύγα μὰν φιλοκέρτομος ἐσσί. πόταγ' 'Come on!'

63 ἐκλελάθοντα 'which causes forgetfulness', a strong aorist participle from ἐκληθάνω, cf. *Il.* 2.599–600 (of the Muses taking away Thamyris' musical skill). Hades wipes out memory (cf. Ar. *Frogs* 186, Pl. *Rep.* 10 621a), and this is particularly cruel for a singer, as the Muses are the daughters of Mnemosyne; cf. the variation at *EB* 22 παρὰ Πλουτῆι μέλος Ληθαῖον ἀείδει. The goatherd's rhetoric is reinforced by the assonance of ἀοιδάν ... Ἀίδαν, and looks forward to Daphnis' abandonment of music as he dies (128–30). The idea of an underworld river of *Lethe*, 'forgetfulness', is largely post-classical (cf. Roscher s.v., *RE* XII 2141–3).

64–145 On the manner and subject of Thyrsis' song cf. above, pp. 63–8. Later antiquity developed a complex and confused scheme of classification for lamentatory poems: Thyrsis' song may be described as an ἐπικήδειον, in which praise of the dead played a major rôle, but very little generic importance should be attached to the label. Whether or not it is relevant that the *Suda* Life ascribes Ἐπικήδεια to T. is unclear. There are major reworkings of the song in Bion's *EA*, the *EB*, in Eclogue 5 (cf. I. M. DuQuesnay, *PVS* 16 (1976/7) 18–41) and Eclogue 10.

64 > *Ecl.* 8.21, 25 etc. The song is punctuated by three different refrains; to judge from Σ, the changeover verses are 94 and 127 (where see n.), but the transmission is far from unanimous. The refrains, which divide the song into short but irregular units, suggest both popular βουκολιασμός – Wilamowitz compared them to a 'real-life' blast on the syrinx – and the antiphonal refrains of the threnodic tradition, cf. Wilamowitz (1906) 148–51, Alexiou (1974) 131–7.   ἄρχετε: the invocation to the Muses is of a traditional kind (cf. *PMG* 14a, 27, 278 etc.), but here it carries a particular charge: not only are the 'sufferings of Daphnis' the original subject of 'bucolic' song, but Idyll 1 is also a foundational poem (above, p. 61). **βουκολικᾶς:** cf. Intro. Section 2.   **Μοῖσαι φίλαι:** cf. 9–11n. Singers are 'dear to the Muses', cf. 141, 7.95 etc. Mortals call gods 'dear' when they have a special relationship with them and/or are asking a favour, cf. 2.142 (Simaitha and Selene), 7.106, 22.23.

65 A *sphragis* 'seal' which marks the song as the property of the singer; although this normally concludes rather than begins the song (cf., e.g., Theognis 19–24, Eratosthenes fr. 35.18 Powell τοῦ Κυρηναίου τοῦτ' Ἐρατοσθένεος), there are exceptions (Sousarion fr. 1 K–A), and the historiographical tradition may be influential here, cf. Hecataeus, *FGrHist* 1 F1 Ἑκαταῖος Μιλήσιος ὧδε μυθεῖται κτλ., Hdt. 1.1 Ἡροδότου Ἁλικαρνησσέος ἀπόδεξις ἥδε κτλ. For the *sphragis* in general cf. W. Kranz, *Studien zur antiken Literatur und ihrem Fortwirken* (Heidelberg 1967) 27–78.   **Αἴτνας:** whether this is the mountain (cf. 69) or the homonymous town at its foot, Thyrsis comes from the same area as the story of Daphnis which he is to sing; the *sphragis* therefore also gives authority to his song. The Cyclops is another proto-bucolic poet 'from Etna', cf. 11.47.   **Θύρσιδος ἁδέα φωνά:** probably, 'sweet is the voice of Thyrsis' rather than '[this is] the sweet voice of Thyrsis'. 'Sweetness' echoes the beginning of the poem (1–3n.), a repetition which questions the relation between the frame and the song: which constitutes 'bucolic song'?   **ἁδέα:** such feminine forms occur first in Homer, and then sporadically in both Doric and Ionic, cf. 3.20, 7.78, both in the same *sedes*.

66–9 > *Ecl.* 10.9–12 (where see Clausen's note). The fact that the Nymphs did not save Daphnis can only be understood on the assumption that they were elsewhere at the time; a feature of major gods – that they may be either present (ἐπίδημος) or absent (ἀπόδη-μος) – is here transferred to nymphs, who are usually closely connected with a single locality. There are three further points. The Nymphs knew that Daphnis was to die, and gods keep away from death, even (or especially) the death of those close to them (cf. Eur. *Hipp.* 1437–9). Secondly, the absence of the nymphs from the lamentation for Daphnis, himself the son of a nymph, reverses the pattern of Achilles, at whose funeral his mother, her fellow Nereids and the Muses all lamented (*Od.* 24.47–59, *Aethiopis* p. 47 Davies). Finally, T.

tends to associate the Muses with 'mythological' poetry and the Nymphs with the lives of his fictional herdsmen, cf. 7.148n., Fantuzzi (1998b).

66 πῆ: the form used by T. is quite uncertain. Doric dialects knew πεῖ (cf. 15.33, ?2.1), πᾶι and πῆ, cf. Buck (1955) 103, Gow on 15.33, Hunter (1996b) 156.   ἆρ' marks an urgent question, cf. Denniston 39–40, LSJ s.v. β2.

67 The Peneios rises in the Pindos range, which divides Thessaly from Epiros, and flows NE to emerge at the sea between Olympos and Ossa; the last part of its journey is through the 'lovely valley of Tempe' (cf. Hdt. 7.173.1, Aelian, *VH* 3.1, *RE* VA 473–9). In later poetry τέμπεα could be used more generally of any 'beautiful glade', but Πηνειῶ here could hardly fail to evoke the famous 'Tempe'. If Πίνδω is correct – Ahrens proposed Πίνδον, but cf. Virgil's *nam neque Parnasi uobis iuga, nam neque Pindi* (*Ecl.* 10.11) – we have here an intermediate stage in which 'Tempe' is clearly dominant, but τέμπεα is sliding towards a wider application. The present verse may in fact have been influential in the fondness of Roman poets for the wider use (Virg. *Georg.* 2.469, Hor. *C.* 3.1.24 etc.). The 'beauty spots' of northern Greece are an obvious place for nymphs, but Thyrsis' choice may carry a sarcastic rebuke: while Daphnis was wasting (a verb which suggests *heat* and melting), the nymphs were carefree in the *cool* mountains. So also, both wild and domesticated animals, other gods and mortals came, but not the nymphs . . .

68 εἶχετ': the standard verb for gods 'haunting' / 'protecting' / 'dwelling in' a place, cf. LSJ s.v. A3.   Ἀνάπω: the Anapos flows from the hills into the sea at Syracuse.

69 'The holy stream of Akis' flows from the foothills of Etna to the sea north of Catania (cf. modern Acireale, Aci Castello). Ovid tells the story of how it got its name from Galatea's lover, who was killed by the Cyclops (*Met.* 13.870–97).

71–5 In a startling narrative anticipation, the song begins after Daphnis' death, thus confirming the power of Daphnis' farewell and the efficacy of his call to nature: 115–21 (where see n.) closely rework 71–5 to make this point. No convincing alternative has been suggested, though some sense of awkwardness remains. If 140 (where see n.) means that Daphnis' death involved his disappearance, it is odd that the cattle mourn his corpse; at 7.73–7 the lamentation of nature for Daphnis takes place *while* he wastes away, and cf. *Ecl.* 10.14–16. Either, therefore, 140 is purely 'metaphorical' or 74–5 refer to a time when Daphnis was wasting but not yet dead, while clearly evoking the imagery of death (cf. 74n.); so too could 71–2, if θανόντα is emended or explained.

The strong 'pathetic fallacy', in which nature responds to human events, rather than just mirroring them, is found also in connection with Daphnis at 7.73–7, and cf. 4.12–14, 6.45. It may be connected with Eastern lament traditions (cf. Griffin (1992) 204–9), just as Daphnis himself resembles figures such as Adonis (above, p. 68): cf. *Epic of Gilgamesh* p. 94 Sandars (Gilgamesh weeps for Enkidu) 'And the beasts we hunted, the bear and the hyena, tiger and panther, leopard and lion, the stag and the ibex, the bull and the doe [weep for you]', *EA* 32–6. The weeping of Achilles' immortal horses for the fate of Patroclus (*Il.* 17.426–40) shows Homer moulding the device to his own stylised view of the epic world. For the 'pathetic fallacy' in Greek poetry cf. F. O. Copley, *AJP* 58 (1937) 194–209, B. F. Dick, *Comp. Lit.* 20 (1968) 27–44, J. L. Buller, *Ramus* 10 (1981) 35–52, Reed (1997) 215. T.'s discretion in the use of the figure is marked by a distinction between the wild animals of 71–2 and Daphnis' own herds of 74–5. Whereas the latter gather around the dying or dead hero, the 'crying' of the former is more naturally located in their usual habitats, thus showing that in their case the 'fallacy' depends upon an interpretation by the singer of the sounds of nature, rather than upon a manifest and extraordinary event; cf. Leonidas, *Anth. Pal.* 7.657.5 (= *HE* 2088), the request of a dead shepherd, βληχήσαιντ' ὄιές μοι. T.'s usually neat separation of wild and domesticated was another distinction which subsequent bucolic abandoned, cf. A. Perutelli, *ASNP* III 6.3 (1976) 763–98. The 'pathetic fallacy' was to become one of the most familiar tropes of the Western pastoral tradition; it is already ironised by Meliboeus as a generic marker at *Ecl.* 1.38–9.

71–2 > *Ecl.* 5.20–1, 27–8, 10.13–15. The pattern of 71, *sssds*, is very rare (cf. 22.39), and 72 is also heavily spondaic: the verses imitate the mournful howling of the animals. For a related effect in the same context cf. *Ecl.* 5.24 *non ulli pastos illis egere diebus*. **ὠρύσαντο:** the standard verb for the howling of wolves etc. (Livrea on Colluthus 116); it is nowhere else constructed with an accusative, 'howl for', but the extension is not difficult. Nevertheless, the variant ὠδύραντο cannot be dismissed out of hand, particularly given T.'s fondness for mannered repetition; either corruption would be very easy to explain. (ὠρύσαντο seems to be imitated at Quint. Smyrn. 12.518; ὠδύραντο at *EA* 18 may derive from 75, but is in any case itself problematic). **δρυμοῖο:** cf. 3.15–17n. **λέων:** Sicily may never have known lions, as was already objected in antiquity (cf. Σ, Virg. *Ecl.* 5.27 perhaps 'correcting' T.), but this is 'myth' (cf. Eur. *Cycl.* 248), and the proximity of Sicily to North Africa means that no great leap of imagination is required.

74 Another heavily spondaic verse continues the lamentation. **πὰρ ποσσί:** the animals gather 'round [Daphnis'] feet', like mourners at the feet of a corpse, a scene represented on very many archaic vases. Aelian, *HA* 10.13 reports that Daphnis' dogs wept for him and then chose to die with him.

75 Another *spondeiazon*. δέ is treated as long 'in ictus'.

77 Although some later sources make Hermes Daphnis' father (cf. above, p. 64–5), it is his pastoral rôle as Hermes νόμιος which is crucial here (cf. *h. Herm.* 567–71, Ar. *Thesm.* 977–8 etc.). He comes from 'the mountain', the place of summer pasturage, and an area naturally associated with this god of margins, cf. Buxton (1994) 81–96. Hermes is Pan's father and, like his son, was credited with the invention of the syrinx (*h. Herm.* 511–12); like Priapos, who is also sometimes Hermes' son (21n.), Hermes is often depicted as ithyphallic, and may in general be credited with a fairly straightforward view of sexual passion (cf. *Od.* 8.338–42). It is he and Priapos, rather than Aphrodite herself, who here take over the rôle of Aphrodite from Sappho fr. 1.

78 ἔρασαι: the middle syllable is long, as at 2.149, but this anomaly remains unexplained.

80 > *Ecl.* 10.19–21. The repeated verb imitates a Homeric mannerism, cf. *Od.* 3.430–5, 8.322–3 (the gods coming to laugh at Ares and Aphrodite). In T.'s stylised countryside, unlike that of the poet of 9.17, there are no mixed herds of sheep and goats, cf. 6.6–7n. Later scholarly theory constructed a 'bucolic hierarchy' with oxherds at the top and goatherds at the bottom (cf. *Proleg.* c Wendel, Donatus, *Vit. Verg.* 49, Longus, *D&C* 1.16.1), and this verse may be thought to foreshadow that structure; 'goatherd (in matters of love)' is a jibe aimed at the *amour propre* of a βουκόλος in 86 (where see n.) and a shepherd in 6.7. In Idyll 1 a shepherd and a goatherd exchange songs about the originary figure of an oxherd, so that the latter is necessarily privileged in this 'bucolic' song. Elsewhere in the genuine 'bucolics', the only real oxherds are Daphnis himself (cf. Idyll 6, Intro.), the errant Aigon of Idyll 4, Lykopas (5.62), and Damoitas (6.1–2n.); neither Aigon nor Lykopas actually appears, and Aigon's social status seems rather higher than that of the other characters, cf. further 7.91–2n. As for shepherds and goatherds, there is no sign that the shepherds of Idylls 1 and 5 are a *social* cut above the goatherds, though a sheep would normally be reckoned more valuable than a goat (5.25–30, 16.90–3), cf. Schmidt (1987) 37–5.

81 ἀνηρώτευν: cf. 3.18–20n.   **τί πάθοι κακόν:** a standard question to those in love (cf. 10.1, Sappho fr. 1.15, *Arg.* 3.675 etc.) or, as perhaps here, resisting love.   **Πρίαπος:** cf. 21n. On the situation presupposed by Priapos' speech cf. the Introduction to this poem. He tries to be kind and helpful (Σ rightly identify elements of consolation in his speech); for him, the situation has a straightforward physical solution. There is no reason to think, with Σ82–5(e), that Priapos is teasing Daphnis because Daphnis himself is searching for the girl, rather than vice versa.

82–3 > *Ecl.* 10.22–3.   **τάλαν** here expresses sympathy, but elsewhere this vocative may suggest surprise or anger, cf. 6.8 (to another δύσερως, the Cyclops), 4.26 (to the thoughtless Aigon). The form is very common in Menander, where it is used almost exclusively by women (cf. D. Bain, *Antichthon* 18 (1984) 33–5); Hellenistic poetry, however, does not observe this distinction.   **νυ** is common in questions of this kind (LSJ s.v. νῦν II 4), and seems more likely than τύ, particularly if accusative τυ is correct later in the verse. At 5.41, ἀνίκ' ἐπύγιζόν τυ, τὺ δ' ἄλγεες, there is a pointed contrast between the characters to justify the repeated pronoun (cf. 5.39 ἐγὼν παρὰ τεῦς). The -τ- alliteration of Priapos' rhetoric, matched by -π- alliteration in 83, is not spoiled by νυ.   **τάκεαι:** cf. above, p. 63. Daphnis is an extreme case of the traditional thinness and wasting of lovers (McKeown on Ovid, *Am.* 1.6.5–6).   **πάσας:** in the accusative plural of the first and second declensions T. uses forms with a short final syllable, as well as the familiar forms (cf. 90 τὰς παρθένος, 134 ὄχνας, 3.2 αὐτάς, 6.32 θύρας); such short-vowel forms, which arise from the loss of -ν- from *-ονς and *-ανς without compensatory lengthening, occur in some Doric dialects (including Cos and Cyrene) cf. Buck (1955) 68, Molinos Tejada 163–8. **ποσσὶ φορ-εῖται** suggests the randomness of a wild search, cf. 13.70 (Heracles in a similar situation), 13.64–71n.

Bion draws upon both Idylls 1 and 13 for his description of Aphrodite's frenzied search for the wounded Adonis; *EA* 23 δι' ἄγκεα φορεῖται reworks the present verse (with πόσιν, line 24, as a mannered variation on ποσσί?).

85 ζάτεισ': cf. 36n. The enjambment of the participle across the refrain emphasises the length and desperation of the girl's search, cf. 2.104–6 (a moment of suspense). **δύσερως:** at 6.6–7 Galateia is alleged to flirt with Polyphemos and call him δύσερωτα καὶ αἰπό-λον; that song assumes a situation in which Polyphemos could have Galateia but holds back. So here, Priapos probably considers Daphnis δύσερως, 'perverse with regard to love', because he is not taking an easy opportunity. The precise nuance will, however, depend on the situation envisaged: elsewhere the word may connote an obses-sive desire for the unattainable (F. Williams, *JHS* 89 (1969) 122–3), and either this or 'hopelessly in love (with another girl)' have been proposed as interpretations, cf. above, p. 67.   **ἀμήχανος:** for Priapos, any man who does not know what to do when a girl is 'after' him is both 'helpless' and beyond help. Here it is the lover, rather than love itself (Sappho's γλυκύπικρον ἀμάχανον ὄρπετον, fr. 130 Voigt), who is ἀμήχανος; at 14.52–3 τὸ φάρμακον ... ἀμηχα-νέοντος ἔρωτος | οὐκ οἶδα, Aischinas' love is ἀμήχανος because the object of his desire has fallen in love with another.

86–91 The listening goatherd apparently approves of this description of his kind as much as of the rest of the song (146–8); the framing context never completely disappears. As for the verses themselves, Σ86a explains that oxherds were self-controlled in mat-ters of sex, whereas goatherds were notoriously licentious; this, how-ever, seems entirely contrary to Priapos' point, which rather implies Daphnis' *rejection* of the girl who is seeking him. Schmitt (1997) argues from Σ that 'goatherd love' is so overwhelming that any attempt to satisfy it would be pointless, as Daphnis knows; others explain that the goatherd gets upset because he-goats can indulge themselves whereas he has no easily available woman, but neither explanation accounts for the analogy Priapos draws between the goatherd's behaviour and Daphnis' desire to 'dance with the maidens' (90–1). Even if Priapos is not a model logician, some relationship between the situations is inevitable; the analogy is reinforced by the virtual rhythmical identity of 87–8 and 90–1. Priapos' point may be that the goatherd is δύσερως because, although having in his (female) goats a ready supply of outlets for desire, he longs for the impossible (transformation into a he-goat) rather than merely doing what a Priapos would do to the nearest available she-goat. Unlike the he-goat (151–2), the goatherd places emotional barriers and impossible wishes in the way of sexual satisfaction; the contrast is repeated in that between Tityros and 'the goatherd' in Idyll 3 (below, p. 112), and is important for the whole construction of bucolic *eros*. The inimitable model is Pan, the goatherds' god and 'he who mounts the she-goats' (αἰγιβάτης), for he has achieved 'metamorphosis' in being half-man, half-goat, cf. above, p. 15. Daphnis, according to Priapos, longs to join 'the maidens' in their dance; Priapos perhaps sees this as a strategy of seduction (cf. Achilles on Scyros). Priapos presumably simplifies to assimilate a situation which is beyond his understanding to the categories in which he sees the world, but in one sense at least he is right: to 'dance with the maidens', actually to become a παρθένος, would be to escape the anguish of sexual desire, and this is indeed what Daphnis wishes (cf. Miles (1977) 150, Zimmerman (1994) 52–3). Both he-goats and παρθένοι are represented as free of the erotic suffering felt by both 'goatherds' and Daphnis, but neither suggested transformation is possible.

86 μάν: an emphatic Doric particle, 'you were indeed called', cf. Denniston 330–1, Gallavotti (1984) 20–1, Wakker (1996); Daphnis was indeed ὁ βούτας *par excellence*. μάν is *lectio facilior*, as μέν would be treated as long 'in ictus' (cf. 75, 6.46), but the latter probably arose under the influence of the following δέ.

87 βατεῦνται 'are mounted [by the he-goats]'.

88 τάκεται ὀφθαλμώς: 'wastes/melts in his eyes' is chosen as a way of saying 'cries' (cf. *Od.* 19.204–9, Onians (1954) 201–3), to echo both Daphnis' wasting condition (66) and the 'bags under the eyes' of the lovers on the cup (38). Whether this phrase and the corresponding one in 91 evoke the blinding of Daphnis may be debated. Zimmerman (1994) 52 connects this phrase with the 'evil eye', one of whose typical effects is 'wasting'.

90 παρθένος: cf. 82–3n.

92 Daphnis' silence, broken only after Aphrodite's final provocation, marks him as a tragic figure.   **τώς:** i.e. τούς 'them', Priapos and the herdsmen.   **ποτελέξαθ'** 'addressed', cf. 25.192, Livrea on *Arg.* 4.833.   **αὐτῶ:** cf. 15.131 τὸν αὐτᾶς ... ἄνδρα. Zimmerman (1994) 54–5 sees here an ambiguity explained by the similarity of Daphnis and Narcissos, i.e. both 'his love' and 'love of himself'.

93 ἄνυε 'bore to its end', 'saw it through', though no exact parallel is at hand, cf. 2.164 οἰσῶ τὸν ἐμὸν πόθον.   **ἐς τέλος ... μοίρας** 'to the end [determined by] fate'. Wilamowitz's μοῖραν, 'bore his fate to the end', makes explicit what is darkly suggested by the transmitted reading, which should therefore be retained.

94 The change of refrain marks the arrival of Aphrodite, Daphnis' 'enemy'.

95–6 Desperately difficult, and perhaps corrupt, verses. The laughter of Aphrodite may convey indulgence (cf. Sappho fr. 1) or triumphant glee (*h. Aphr.* 49 etc.), but both what she says to Daphnis and his reply suggest that here it is the latter, cf. Cameron (1995) 412–13. θυμός covers a range of emotions, from grief to anger. Here it is normally interpreted as the former: if she is griefstricken now (i.e. βαρύθυμος, cf. Hopkinson on Call. *h.* 6.80), as she may well be later (138–9), she must be hiding the grief and feigning a sense of mocking triumph, cf. G. Crane, *HSCP* 91 (1987) 161–84. Such a reading can, however, make no adequate sense of λάθρη, unless it is taken (unconvincingly) to mean 'openly but treacherously', and it is not clear that the second half of 96 can mean 'holding (?back) deep grief'. The first knot would be cut by adopting Hermann's attractive ἀδέα for λάθρη, which could be explained as an intrusive gloss. Others understand Aphrodite to be 'laughing inside' but feigning grief (like Clytemnestra at Aesch. *Ch.* 738–9), a pose through which Daphnis sees; ἀνέχειν will thus mean 'hold out', 'display', which seems possible, if very unusual, with an emotion as object, cf. G. Zuntz, *CQ* 10 (1960) 37–40. If, however, we give weight to the apparently mocking tone of Aphrodite's speech in which nothing suggests 'grief' (cf. below on ἀργαλέω), we may be rather inclined to see 'anger' on display here: Aphrodite is 'secretly' indulgent towards her Adonis-like favourite, but (with Zuntz's interpretation of ἀνέχειν) puts on a display of angry mockery. This interpretation suits Aphrodite's subsequent wish to 'save' Daphnis (138–9). Daphnis, facing death and not party to the real motives and schemes of the immortals, takes his tormentor at her word and hurls abuse at her. This is as far as interpretation of the transmitted text can go. As an alternative, it should be noted that ἀνὰ θυμόν may mean 'in the heart' (*Il.* 2.36 etc.), and βαρύν may have replaced (e.g.) χόλον or even πόθον, perhaps under the influence of Κύπρι βαρεῖα in 100. Nonnus 34.303, εἶχε νόον γελόωντα, χόλον δ' ἀνέφηνε προσώπωι, is at least suggestive. For the pattern of 96 cf. 7.61–2n.   γε μάν marks the climactic point of an enumeration, cf. Denniston 349, Wakker (1996) 258.   ἀδεῖα: probably neuter plural with γελάοισα, though many construe as feminine singular, cf. G. Tarditi in *Filologia e forme letterarie. Studi offerti a Francesco Della Corte* (Urbino 1987) 1 347–52. Ott (1969) 124–5 suggests that, as a feminine, the meaning is ἡσθεῖσα 'pleased' (cf. LSJ s.v. ἡδύς II 2); this would sit well with the interpretation of 96 offered above.

97 κατεύχεο 'bound yourself with an oath'. In the standard version of the myth, Daphnis had not vowed 'to worst Eros' but rather 'to remain faithful' to one girl; Aphrodite (and much of Greek tradition) sees the two things as equivalent – faithfulness is a triumph over ordinary sexual feelings. Others understand the verb as 'boasted', an easy extension from the simple εὔχεσθαι.   **λυγιξεῖν** 'to bind', apparently a wrestling term denoting having an unbreakable hold on one's opponent; the metaphor arises from the intertwining of arms and legs which such a hold entails, cf. λύγοι 'withes'. Kypris is a wrestler at Soph. fr. 941.13 Radt, and Eros is represented as a boxer (Anacreon, *PMG* 396.2, Soph. *Tr.* 442).

98 ἀργαλέω 'hard to bear (let alone defeat)', as Daphnis has found to his cost; Aphrodite is under no illusions about what *eros* entails. ἀργαλέος is connected with ἄλγος (*Et. Mag.* 135.19 Gaisford), which gives point to Daphnis' response at 103.

100 βαρεῖα: cf. 3.15–17n.

101 *dsssd* is a rare shape at all periods (Brioso Sanchez (1976) 39 counts 11 examples in the genuine corpus); the heavy rhythm displays Daphnis' bitterness, as does the rising tricolon with anaphora. **νεμεσσατά** 'spiteful', 'nursing resentment', cf. *Il.* 11.649 (Patroclus about Achilles).

102 'Do you think that every sun has set for me?', an apparently proverbial way of saying 'I am not beaten by you yet', cf. Diod. Sic. 29.16, Livy 39.26.9. The suggestion that the sun will shine on Daphnis even in the Underworld underlines his extraordinary defiance of 'the natural order' (cf. *Od.* 12.382–3). The implication of γάρ is 'Do you say this (i.e. 97–8) because . . . ?'   **δεδύκειν:** cf. 11.11n.

103 Δάφνις: the use of his own name evokes his *kleos*; this is the Daphnis 'who everyone will know' did not yield to *eros*.   **ἄλγος:** cf. 98n. Daphnis will continue after death to be a source of 'bitter pain' to Eros, because Eros (and Aphrodite) will always know that one man at least rejected their power, and this man will be the subject of a song, the ἄλγεα Δάφνιδος, which will be constantly re-sung. Daphnis' 'triumph' over the obliteration of death contrasts with the projected fate of the singer (63).

105 Daphnis now turns from persistent defiance to Aphrodite's own love-making with a βουκόλος, an episode which remained a μέγ' ὄνειδος for the goddess (cf. *h. Aphr.* 247); she herself proved too weak to resist the *eros* with which she taunts Daphnis. Somewhat similar is the abuse which Gilgamesh hurls at Ishtar: 'Your lovers have found you like a brazier which smoulders in the cold, a backdoor which keeps out neither squall of wind nor storm . . . Which of your lovers did you ever love for ever? What shepherd of yours has pleased you for all time? Listen to me while I tell the tale of your lovers . . .' (*Gilgamesh* p. 86 Sandars), cf. P. Walcot, *Ugarit-Forschungen* 1 (1969) 118, Halperin (1983b) 190–1. As close in tone, however, is Helen's abuse of Aphrodite at *Il.* 3.406–9 ἧσο παρ' αὐτὸν [i.e. Paris] ἰοῦσα κτλ.; there Helen, like Daphnis, rejects love-making, although in her case the goddess is to prove too strong.   **οὐ λέγεται κτλ.:** for the 'polite' omission of, and hence suggestion of, a verb of sexual intercourse cf. Meleager, *Anth. Pal.* 5.184.5 (= *HE* 4374) οὐχ ὁ περίβλεπτός σε Κλέων;, Ter. *Eun.* 479 *ego illum eunuchum, si opus siet, uel sobrius, Ecl.* 3.8–9, J. N. Adams, *Phoenix* 35 (1981) 120–8.   **Ἴδαν:** Ovid's Alcithoe sets the story of Daphnis on Ida (*Met.* 4.276–8), perhaps under the influence of this passage.

106–7 > *Ecl.* 7.12–13. The transmitted text implies a contrast between the oaks of Mt Ida at Troy (cf. *Il.* 23.117–18, Thphr. *HP* 3.8.2) and the galingale and bees of Daphnis' location; there must be a pointed reference to the rôle of oaks in the story of Anchises (*h. Aphr.* 264), of which Aphrodite does not wish to be reminded. No point has, however, been discovered in a contrast between oaks and galingale (for attempts cf. Giangrande (1977) 177–86, Di Gregorio (1984) 280–2). Bees, on the other hand, are notoriously pure and asexual, so that at 107 Daphnis could be saying 'Ida is where you belong; this place is chaste', or perhaps he is alluding to a belief (see below) that bees sting adulterers, and thus giving Aphrodite some 'good advice'. Some critics (cf. Wilamowitz (1906) 229–35) have seen an allusion to an otherwise unattested story that it was bees, rather than lightning, which were the instrument of Anchises' punishment by blinding when he finally revealed the story of how he slept with Aphrodite (*h. Aphr.* 286–8, Soph. fr. 373.2 Radt, Austin on Virg. *Aen.* 2.649); Daphnis need not, however, make the point that Anchises, like Adonis, came to an unhappy end – Aphrodite's disgrace is sufficient.

Valckenaer deleted 106, as an intrusion from 5.45 (together perhaps with Ἀγχίσαν arising from a gloss on βουκόλος). Nevertheless, a sixteenth-century Latin version of a lost discussion by Plutarch of why bees tend to sting adulterers suggests an alternative approach (*QN* fr. 36 Bernadakis = *Mor.* v 3, p. 28 Hubert–Pohlenz): *apud Theocritum iocose Venus ad Anchisen a pastore ablegatur uti apum aculeis propter adulterium commissum pungatur:*

> te confer ad Idam,
> confer ad Anchisen, ubi quercus atque cypirus
> crescit, apum strepit atque domus melliflua bombis.

Meineke noted that this translation seemed to imply a text of 106–7 with ἠδὲ κύπειρος | αἱ δὲ καλὸν κτλ. In this case Daphnis would be sending Aphrodite off to a *locus amoenus* with a real sting in its tail; far from suggesting chastity, the similarity of Κύπρις and κύπειρος, and the latter's use in garlands (cf. Alcman, *PMG* 58, P. E. Easterling, *PCPS* 20 (1974) 38–40), suggests that 'galingale' is an appropriate plant for a 'love-nest'. ἠδὲ κύπειρον ends a hexameter at *Il.* 21.351, and although this would be the only use of ἠδέ in the bucolics (cf. Hunter (1996a) 41), there are more than enough epic touches in the rest of the poem to allow the reading. The corruption may be explained as assimilation to 5.45–6. On balance, this seems to be the best option, but the weak MS attestation of 108 and the problems attending 109–13 suggest that there can be little confidence in this passage of text.

109–10 > *Ecl.* 10.18. 'Adonis too [i.e. as well as Anchises] is in his prime [i.e. ripe for sex] since . . .', cf. 3.46–8n. Adonis' activities, as listed by Daphnis, move from the harmless to the ultimately fatal, as Adonis was killed by a wild boar, a death which moved Aphrodite to paroxysms of grief, cf. Bion, *EA*. Adonis is the kind of seductive shepherd favoured by Aphrodite (cf. Paris) and thus ὡραῖος for her. On the rhythm of 109 cf. 130n. **μᾶλα:** this 'hyperdorism' for μῆλα 'sheep' is found on a third-century papyrus of Stesichorus (*PMGF* 222b.241); it is customarily dismissed from the text of T.'s genuine poems, but too little is known about the construction of his literary Doric to allow any confidence in such matters, cf. 3.46–8n., 4.10, Gallavotti (1984) 7–8, Cassio (1993) 907–10.

112–13 Diomedes wounded and mocked Aphrodite in a famous sequence of *Il.* 5 (lines 335–430): Diomedes, Dione and Zeus all advise Aphrodite to stay away from war, so Daphnis' choice of martial language is particularly pointed. **αὖτις** 'again', 'for a second time'. Cf. *Il.* 3.432–3 (Helen to Paris) ἀλλ' ἴθι νῦν προκάλεσσαι ἀρηίφιλον Μενέλαον | ἐξαῦτις μαχέσασθαι ἐναντίον. **ὅπως στασῆι:** this imperative form with the future indicative is a colloquial Attic usage (Goodwin 94–5), not otherwise attested in T. Alternative proposals include making ὅπως στασῆι a final clause dependent upon 105 with 109–10 being treated as a parenthesis ('off to Ida – or if you prefer there is Adonis – so that . . .', cf. Könnecke (1917) 294–8), and wholesale deletion. Text and interpretation must be considered uncertain.

115–21 Daphnis' farewell reworks 71–5: 115–17 re-orders 71–2 and substitutes bears for lions, and 120–1 picks up 74–5 but omits 'heifers'. The appeal to the surroundings recalls the final speeches of tragic heroes, cf. Soph. *Phil.* 936–8 ὦ λιμένες, ὦ προβλῆτες, ὦ ξυνουσίαι | θηρῶν ὀρείων, ὦ καταρρῶγες πέτραι, | ὑμῖν τάδ' κτλ., *Ajax* 859–65, Eur. *Hipp.* 1092–7.

115 A tricolon begins the farewell in impressively rhetorical style. Daphnis' relation with wild animals is that he pastured his cattle in country which really belonged to those animals and devoted his life to protecting his cattle from them. To this extent he is no different from 'ordinary' herdsmen. The animals' grief, however, marks his death as the event which ultimately separated man from nature, as Prometheus' deception separated men from the gods. **ὦ θῶες, ὦ**

ἀν' κτλ.: -ες is treated as long in arsis (cf. Legrand (1898) 316–18) and the following ὦ shortened ('correpted') before ἀν', cf. 15.123 ὦ ἔβενος, ὦ χρυσός, ὦ ἐκ λευκῶ κτλ. In both cases the prosody is expressive of the speaker's emotion.   φωλάδες ἄρκτοι 'bears who dwell in caves', rather than 'bears in hibernation' (φωλεία), which would explain their absence from the lamentation of 71–2 but might tip *pathos* into bathos; the phrase also occurs at *IG* XII 5.739, line 46 (a first-century Isis hymn from Andros). The Cyclops, another Sicilian singer from mythical time, keeps bear-cubs (11.41).

116–17 ὁ βουκόλος ... Δάφνις '*the* [famous] oxherd Daphnis'. Cf. the Sophoclean Ajax's last words, τοῦθ' ὑμὶν Αἴας τοῦπος ὕστατον θροεῖ κτλ.   ὕμμιν: the so-called 'ethic' dative (K–G I 423) expresses Daphnis' conception of the animals' interest in him. οὐκέτ' ... οὐκέτ' evokes the language of epitaphs, cf. *CEG* 2.680.6, Anyte, *Anth. Pal.* 7.202.1 (= *HE* 704), 7.215.1 (= *HE* 708).   ὕλαν: marginal wooded land where animals could be grazed; this aspect of the Theocritean landscape comes to dominate Virgil's *Musa siluestris*, cf. *Ecl.* 1.2, 5, 4.3 etc.

117–18 Cf. Ajax's farewell to the waters, κρῆναί τε ποταμοί θ' οἵδε (Soph. *Ajax* 862).   Ἀρέθοισα: the famous spring of Syracuse; for the form cf. 9n.   Θύβριδος: an unidentified geographical feature 'down from which' waters rush (cf. *Il.* 9.15 = 16.4 ἥ τε κατ' αἰγίλιπος πέτρης δνοφερὸν χέει ὕδωρ). Servius on *Aen.* 3.500 alleges that Athenian prisoners were compelled by the Syracusans to dig a ditch for a moat around Syracuse, and that this was called Thybris ἀπὸ τῆς ὕβρεως; such a ditch would fit Daphnis' words, but we might rather think of a natural feature. 'Thybris' (or 'Thymbris') has therefore often been identified with Monte Crimiti above Syracuse; the waters from this set of rocky gorges would, in T.'s day, have been channelled down to Syracuse, and such a fusion of mythic and present time would be very much in the manner of Hellenistic poetry, cf. K. Ziegler, *RE* VIA 659–61.

120–1 > *Ecl.* 5.43–4. Line 120 recalls 65 to associate Daphnis with Thyrsis, like all bucolic singers a 'descendant' of Daphnis. As Virgil saw (and made explicit), Daphnis here writes his own epitaph. Hector designed the epitaph of a Greek, whom he intended to kill, for a tomb which would be a source of eternal *kleos* for himself (*Il.* 7.89–90), but Daphnis' self-contemplation brings him rather closer to Hippolytos, cf. above, p. 67, Eur. *Hipp.* 1078–9, 1363–6 Ζεῦ, Ζεῦ, τάδ' ὁρᾶις; | ὅδ' ὁ σεμνὸς ἐγὼ καὶ θεοσέπτωρ | ὅδ' ὁ σωφροσύνηι πάντας ὑπερσχών, | προῦπτον ἐς Ἅιδην στείχω κτλ.

123–6 > *Ecl.* 10.15, *Georg.* 1.16–18. It is standard in prayers and invocations to list possible places where the god may be found (cf. *Il.* 16.514–16, Aesch. *Eum.* 292–8, Ar. *Clouds* 269–74), just as one tries to list all the titles by which a god may wish to be known, cf. Norden (1913) 143–63.

123 Πὰν Πάν: such doubling is common in address to a divinity, cf. Aesch. *Ch.* 246 Ζεῦ Ζεῦ, θεωρὸς τῶνδε πραγμάτων γενοῦ, J. Wills, *Repetition in Latin poetry* (Oxford 1996) 50. **Λυκαίω:** Lykaion was a mountain in SW Arcadia with a famous sanctuary of Pan (cf. Pausanias 8.38); here the name seems to be used for the whole range west of Megalopolis. Pan is, of course, quintessentially a god of the ὄρος, cf. *h. Pan* (19) 6–21.

124 Μαίναλον: a mountain lying between Megalopolis and Mantinea, and also associated with Pan, cf. Call. *h.* 3.88–9, Pausanias 8.36.8, *RE* xiv 576–7. **ἔνθ' = ἔλθ(ε).**

125 Ἑλίκας: T. here plays with the mythic history of Arcadia. The founding family was as follows:

Pelasgos

|

Lykaon

|

Kallisto (Helike) = Zeus

|

Arkas

As early as Hesiod (fr. 163 M–W) 'the Great Bear' constellation seems to have been identified as the (only) daughter of Lykaon, usually called Kallisto. When the Great Bear was subsequently identified with Helike, one of the Cretan nurses of Zeus (cf. 'Epimenides' 3 F23 D–K, Aratus, *Phaen.* 37, *Arg.* 2.360, 3.745, *RE* vii 2858–61), an assimilation of Kallisto to Helike was inevitable; for the various versions cf. Kannicht on Eur. *Hel.* 375–85, Borgeaud (1988) 29–34. 'The peak of Kallisto/Helike' might be any Arcadian mountain, though 123 makes it not improbable that it is here Mt Lykaion, just as 'the high tomb of the descendant of Lykaon, i.e. Arkas' is probably to be identified with Mainalos (cf. Pausanias 8.9.3–4). Pausanias 8.35.8 identifies 'the tomb of Kallisto' as an Arcadian site, and Bosius conjectured λίπ' ἠρίον; λίπεν ῥίον occurs, however, in the same *sedes* at *Il.* 14.225, 19.114.

Σ interpret very differently: Helike is the Achaean town of that name on the Corinthian Gulf, Rhion the promontory near Patrai at the western end of the Gulf, and 'the descendant of Lykaon' is Aipytos, a grandson of Arkas (Pausanias 8.4.7, 16.1–3) whose tomb near Mt Kyllene, the highest Arcadian mountain, is mentioned in the *Iliad* (2.605) and was still a tourist attraction in Pausanias' day. 'Rhion of Helike' makes little sense, however, (the two places are not adjacent), and there is no obvious connection with Pan. Nevertheless, the *Iliad* passage is the start of the 'catalogue of Arcadians' and its striking word-play might have attracted any Hellenistic poet: οἳ δ' ἔχον Ἀρκαδίην ὑπὸ Κυλλήνης ὄρος αἰπύ, | Αἰπύτιον παρὰ τύμβον. The whole manner of 125–6 suggests the 'mythological games' of which Hellenistic poets were fond, and αἰπύ τε σᾶμα presumably signals by its allusion to the *Iliad* that more than one 'decoding' of this phrase (Arkas or Aipytos?) is possible. τῆνο 'that well known . . .' adds to the learned tease.

126 μακάρεσσιν ἀγητόν: the allusion remains mysterious, for the association of gods with mountains and tombs seems too weak an explanation.

127 > *Ecl.* 8.61. The Muses are called upon to end the song just as Daphnis abandons his syrinx (cf. 63n.).

128–30 > *Ecl.* 2.36–8, Longus, *D&C* 1.29.2–3 (cf. Hunter (1983b) 81–2).

128 φέρευ πακτοῖο: this articulation seems more likely than the active φέρ' εὐπακτοῖο (both were known in antiquity): contrast the reworking at *EB* 55 Πανὶ φέρω τὸ μέλισμα;   **μελίπνουν** 'breathing sweetly [from the wax]'; the syrinx shares the sweetness of cup (ἑλικτάν recalls 30–1) and poem cf. 1n., 27–8, 149–50. The sweet aroma of the binding wax forms an associative unity with the sweet breath of the syrinx-player and the sweet sound of the musical 'airs'.

129 καλὸν περὶ χεῖλος ἑλικτάν lit. 'well bound-around [as to] the lip'; καλόν is adverbial, περὶ ... ἑλικτάν in tmesis, and χεῖλος accusative of respect. The reference will be to binding near the lip which aids the wax between the reeds in holding the syrinx together; for περὶ ... ἑλικτάν of the object around which the bindings are wrapped rather than the bindings themselves cf. 2.121–2 λεύκαν ... πορφυρέαισι περὶ ζώστραισιν ἑλικτάν. The interwoven word-order is clearly imitative of the sense. Both text and interpretation are, however, doubtful. The transmitted καλάν may be defended by 8.18 σύριγγ' ... καλάν and *Epigr.* 2.1 καλᾶι σύριγγι (both in same *sedes*), but is flat and rhythmically inferior to καλόν, cf. also 5.134–5 ὅκ' αὐτῶι | τὰν σύριγγ' ὤρεξα, καλόν τί με κάρτ' ἐφίλησεν. If καλόν is adopted, it could also be taken as an adjective with χεῖλος. White (1979) 39–44 follows Σ in understanding the final words as 'turned around ⟨the player's⟩ lip', in reference to the mode of playing the syrinx; it is, however, (as White recognises) the lips rather than the syrinx which move, and this can hardly be derived from the Greek. There is, moreover, no reason why Daphnis would say such a thing to Pan.

130 Ἀίδαν: word-break after a fourth-foot spondee (a breach of one of the Callimachean rules, 'Naeke's Law') is very rare in the genuine 'bucolics' (cf. 6n., 109, mitigated by prepositive καί, 5.132, Intro. Section 4); how sensitive T. was to such matters can be seen from the fact that there are two examples in Idyll 10, six in Idyll 11 (including line 1), and thirteen in Idyll 15 (of which eleven fall in the conversational lines 1–99), cf. 11.1n., Legrand (1898) 336, Fantuzzi (1995a) 231, 239. All third-century poets except Callimachus show sporadic infringements of this 'Law'; Call. has only *h.* 4.226 (where Maas's emendation is often accepted). Ἀίδος, a familiar dactylic form in Homer, would remove the anomaly, but it is hard to believe that the heavy (? ugly) rhythm does not evoke the Death of which Daphnis speaks.   **ἕλκομαι:** the verb would suit (*inter alia*) disappearance into a pool, cf. *Arg.* 1.1239 (Hylas and the nymph) ἔσπασε.

132–6 > *Ecl.* 3.89, 5.34–9, 8.26–8, 52–6 (cf. L. Braun, *Phil.* 113 (1969) 292–7). Daphnis sees his life as so fundamental to nature that his death, unlike that of Adonis who was able to return, should be marked by an overturning of the natural order, cf. Walsh (1985) 3. *Ecl.* 5.34–9 combines this with the Hesiodic–Aratean abandonment of the earth by the gods: *postquam te* [sc. *Daphnin*] *fata tulerunt,* | *ipsa Pales agros atque ipse reliquit Apollo.* | *grandia saepe quibus mandauimus hordea sulcis,* | *infelix lolium et steriles nascuntur auenae* etc. For some similar passages in other cultures cf. D. E. Gershenson, *SCI* 1 (1974) 24–8. Daphnis' mode of expression is the *adynaton* (cf. 5.124–7), a statement of phenomena contrary to the natural order; such statements may be made either as a promise that nothing extraordinary *will* happen ('lead will rise from the sea-floor before …', cf. *Ecl.* 1.59–63) or in response to an extraordinary event ('Now I could believe …', cf. Archilochus fr. 122 West); the form becomes very common in Latin poetry, cf. E. Dutoit, *Le thème de l'adynaton dans la poésie antique* (Paris 1936), Nisbet–Hubbard on Hor. *C.* 1.29.10, 1.33.7. Daphnis' death is not in fact *contra naturam*, but his obsessive concern with his own position places him, in his own eyes, at the very centre of the natural order. The rhyming verse-ends of 132–4 have the effect of a magical incantation, working the changes of which Daphnis speaks.

133 κομάσαι: cf. Virg. *Georg.* 4.122–3 *sera comantem* | *narcissum.* A more regular expression would be 'let the juniper flower with the narcissus' (cf. 7.9, Call. *h.* 3.41, *Arg.* 3.928); there is no need to see a play on κομᾶν ἐπί in the sense of 'pride oneself upon' (Lembach (1970) 87). The thorny juniper makes an appropriate opposition to 'the beautiful narcissus'.

134 ἄναλλα 'changed', a very rare word, as also is the alternative ἔναλλα; the former might be thought *lectio difficilior*, because of the easy association of ἔναλλα with ἐναλλάσσειν, and the possibility of taking ἀν- as privative. That Virgil knew a text with ἔναλλα has been attractively deduced from *Ecl.* 8.58 *omnia uel medium fiat mare*; he would be playfully connecting ἔναλλα with ἐνάλια 'things in the sea'. **πίτυς:** the very symbol of the 'natural' world, cf. 1, is to revolt.

135 > *Ecl.* 8.28. We might have expected 'Daphnis' death' to come after all the *adynata*, but 'the natural tendency toward terminal weight is blocked … Inventory is put at the service of disorder' (Rosenmeyer (1969) 264–5). **τὰς κύνας:** hunting-hounds are usually (at least in literature) female, cf. Xen. *Cyn. passim*, LSJ s.v. κύων. **ἔλκοι** 'worry', 'tear apart', rather than 'drag back' (Call. *h.* 3.93).

136 Daphnis closes with a final *spondeiazon.* **γαρύσαιντο:** here constructed with a dative, 'cry in competition with …', i.e. 'rival' (cf.

8.6 λῆις μοι ἀεῖσαι), rather than just 'cry to . . .' However unpleasant the cry of the scops owl (cf. Σ), whose name was etymologised from σκώπτειν, and however firmly this bird is linked with the woods, that it should 'compete with nightingales from the mountains' is not obviously a real revolution in nature. One zoological tradition distinguished ἀείσκωπες, the common, noisy type, from σκῶπες cf. [Arist.] HA 9 617b32–618a8, Call. fr. 418); the latter were rare and voiceless, (so rare in fact that they are unknown to modern ornithology). To give the σκῶψ a voice would then be a piece of 'learning' on a par with the mythological games of 125–6. At another level, it is clear that Daphnis identifies himself with the nightingale, the singer (Hes. WD 203–12) whose sweet song is surpassed only by Pan himself (cf. h. Pan (19) 16–18), cf. 1–11n., 8.38; it was for this reason that Daphnis handed his syrinx to Pan. After his death this beautiful song will be replaced by the harsh sounds of lesser singers trying, in an unequal song-contest, to rival his sweetness as they sing of his death (cf. 7.41). ἀηδόνι is thus perhaps to be preferred to the better attested plural (cf. ὤλαφος), but confidence would be unwarranted, cf. 5.136 ποτ' ἀηδόνα κίσσας ἐρίσδειν (immediately followed by a plural), Anth. Pal. 9.380.2 τολμῶιεν δ' ἐρίσαι σκῶπες ἀηδονίσιν. The nightingale is par excellence the bird of lamentation, and Daphnis is both the first singer and first subject of a song of ἄλγεα, a θρῆνος in fact. As this suggests 'tragedy', the bird of σκώπτειν evokes its opposite, 'comedy', and it is in the fusion of the two that the foundation of 'bucolic' song is to be located.

138 ἀπεπαύσατο evokes the final 'cessation' in death, without making it as explicit as would the variant ἀνεπαύσατο (LSJ s.v. ΙΙ 2c), cf. 7.90, Segal (1981) 32.   **Ἀφροδίτα:** T. uses this name for the goddess only at verse-end; Apollonius and Callimachus in hexameters avoid the name entirely as it involves treating the initial α- as short before -φρ- ('Attic correption'), cf. Fantuzzi (1988) 155–63.

139–40 ἀνορθῶσαι 'set him on his feet', cf. Barrett on Eur. Hipp. 198; the verb also suggests 'raise him [from death]'. That gods can do nothing about the certainty of human death is familiar from the Iliad on; that Aphrodite wanted to save Daphnis marks the heroic and tragic nature of his death. It seems more likely that her wish arises from a (?new-found) concern for Daphnis than that she wants him alive so that she can continue to make him suffer (Vaughn (1981)

58). See further 95–6n., 152n.   λίνα ... | ἐκ Μοιρᾶν 'the threads [assigned] by the Moirai', cf. Bulloch on Call. *h.* 5.104–5.   λελοίπει 'had run out', cf. *Od.* 14.213 νῦν δ' ἤδη πάντα λέλοιπεν (where interpretation is disputed). λείπειν is here used like ἐπιλείπειν. ἔβα ῥόον: cf. above, p. 67.   δίνα: in poetry this need mean little more than 'water', but Apollonius uses δίνη of the pool which closes over Hylas (*Arg.* 1.1239), and the word is likely to have a strong meaning here. *Arg.* 1.644–5 refers to the Ἀχέροντος | δίνας ἀπροφάτους and both Catullus (65.5) and Virgil (*Aen.* 6.296) associate the Underworld with a *gurges*; cf. already Simonides, *PMG* 522 πάντα γὰρ μίαν ἱκνεῖται δασπλῆτα Χάρυβδιν.

141 The song of Thyrsis closes with the death of Daphnis and, as it had begun (64 6), with the Muses and the Nymphs. Daphnis belongs both to the mythical world of the Muses and the bucolic world of the Nymphs, cf. 66–9n., Fantuzzi (1998b).   οὐ Νύμφαισιν ἀπεχθῆ: 'litotes', or pointed understatement, cf. Eur. *Helen* 16–17 οὐκ ἀνώνυμος | Σπάρτη, K–G II 180. Σ explains the phrase with reference to the love of a nymph for Daphnis, and there is certainly a clear allusion to the details of the story.

143–5 These lines stand outside the song proper, but the promise and hymnic farewell to the Muses which link 144 to 141, the echo of 65 in 145 (ἐγώ – Θύρσις ὅδ', ἄδιον – ἀδέα), and the fact that the expectation has been created that the refrain of 142 will introduce a new stanza all blur the boundary between the two; cf. Goldhill (1991) 245. The promise to 'sing a sweeter song in the future' takes the place of the standard αὐτὰρ ἐγὼ καὶ σεῖο καὶ ἄλλης μνήσομ' ἀοιδῆς with which the *Homeric Hymns* close: the 'sufferings of Daphnis' have a stature equal to the doings of the gods.

143 δίδοι: an imperative form found in Pindar and archaic Boeotian inscriptions (*CEG* 326, 334, 358), but also almost certainly in a Corinthian text (*IG* IV 213), cf. K. Strunk, *Glotta* 39 (1961) 114–23, Gallavotti (1984) 4–5.   σκύφος occurs only here in T., reflecting its one appearance, in the rustic context of Eumaios' entertainment of Odysseus, in Homer (*Od.* 14.112); Virgil too uses it only once (*Aen.* 8.278), cf. J. Farrell in C. Martindale (ed.), *The Cambridge companion to Virgil* (Cambridge 1997) 226–8.

146–8 Poets are traditionally nourished by bees and have mouths 'full of sweet honey' (cf. 7.80–5, Ar. fr. 598 K–A, Waszink (1974));

these motifs have been present throughout the poem, cf. 1n., 2 μελίσδεται, 128 μελίπνουν. A wish that Thyrsis *be rewarded* with a mouth full of honey, honeycombs and figs may simply be a naïvely humorous way of saying that he deserves to be on a par with the most famous legendary singers, but there is also a humorous distortion of the conventional motifs, showing that the goatherd's critical response is at a very different level from the poem to which we and he have been listening, cf. 15.145–9, Miles (1977) 155–6. The imitation at 8.82–3 reverts to the conventional expression.

147 Αἰγίλω: Aigilos was the eponymous hero of the Attic deme Aigilia, apparently famous for its figs (Ath. 14 652e). This 'realistic' touch emphasises how mundane are the goatherd's concerns beside the song we have just heard.

148 τέττιγος: the singer *par excellence*, cf. Pl. *Phdr.* 258e–9d, Call. fr. 1 etc. Cicadas notoriously lived only on dew (4.15–16n.), so there may be humour in the juxtaposition of this image to the eating of figs.

149–50 The stress on the sweet smell of the cup marks the completion of the promise of 27–8, as πεπλύσθαι varies κεκλυσμένον (27).   **φίλος:** cf. 61n.   **Ὡρᾶν:** the Hours, daughters of Zeus and Themis, are associated with beauty and fruitfulness – their Attic cult names were Θαλλώ and Καρπώ. They are closely linked with Aphrodite and the Graces: the attraction of the bowl, as of 'bucolic', is an erotic one, cf. Hes. *Theog.* 901–3 (with West's note), *LIMC* s.v. Horai. The 'spring of the Hours' is not explicitly attested elsewhere, but continues the water imagery which has dominated the poem; a washing in that spring confers upon the bowl (and upon T.'s poetry) the same power to amaze and arouse desire as the Hours confer upon Aphrodite herself before her presentation to the immortals (*h. Aphr.* (6) 5–18). It is a related idea when Callimachus asks for 'the oil of the Graces' to flow over his poetry (fr. 7 = 9 Massimilla). Giangrande (1981) 352 sees here rather a reference to 'seasonal' rain-water.   **ἐπί:** cf. *Arg.* 3.876–7 λιαροῖσιν ἐφ᾽ ὕδασι Παρθενίοιο . . . λοεσσαμένη (with Hunter's n.).   **δοκησεῖς:** cf. 42n.

151–2 For the earthy ending cf. 4.58–63, 5.147–50. We move from the mysterious eroticism of the bowl and Daphnis' death to the straightforward animality of rutting goats, cf. 86–91n. **Κισσαίθα:** Σ derive the first part of the name from κισσός 'ivy', of which goats are said to be fond, or κισσᾶν 'to crave', 'to conceive'; the second part they derive from αἴθω or αἰθός ('white'). Κυμαίθα is a cow at 4.46 and Κιναίθα a goat at 5.102.   αἱ δὲ χίμαιραι: this form of address is perhaps a colloquial survival of the demonstrative force of the article; it is used only to inferiors or animals, cf. 4.45–6, 8.50, Ar. *Frogs* 521 ὁ παῖς ἀκολούθει.   σκιρτασεῖτε: the future is normal in this form of prohibition, but the transmitted subjunctive may be possible also, cf. Goodwin §§ 297, 301, 364.   ἀναστῆι: i.e. 'get up' from where he is now lying in order to rut. Unlike Daphnis (139), the he-goat can 'rise up', cf. Segal (1981) 34. A *double entendre*, 'have an erection', would suit the tone of these verses; such puns may occur at Antiphanes fr. 19.6 K–A, Men. *Dysk.* 895, and cf. Ovid, *Am.* 1.9.29 *resurgunt*.

II Idyll 3

A nameless goatherd leaves his goats in the charge of Tityros (cf. 1–2n.) while he serenades his beloved Amaryllis outside her cave; lack of success leads to despair and thoughts of suicide. There is very little indication of a geographical setting (cf. 25–7n.). Very little too can be conjectured about the poem's literary sources. A probably fourth-century lyric poem by Lykophronides (*PMG* 844) included a goatherd who was in love with a girl 'beautiful and dear to the Graces', cf. Stanzel (1995) 193–4; T.'s interest in post-classical lyric is clear from his use of Philoxenus in Idyll 11 (cf. Idyll 11, Intro.), another komastic poem with much in common with Idyll 3 (cf. Cairns (1972) 145–7). There are some indications of Philitan influence (40–51n.).

Idyll 3 offers a rustic version of the *komos*, that familiar literary event, which no doubt had 'real life' analogues, in which one or more young men, often rather the worse for drink, proceeded through the town to the house of a boy or lady to sing songs outside the house; a late source (Plut. *Mor.* 753b) preserves the name παρα- κλαυσίθυρον for these songs of the *lacrimans exclusus amator* (Lucr. 4.1177). Elements of the *komos* are found in many cultures (cf. Song of Songs 2.8–14, 5.2–6) and in virtually every classical literary genre (first in Alcaeus fr. 374 Voigt), and in the third century komastic epigrams become very numerous; Asclepiades seems to have been a formative influence in this, as in so many, fields. 'Rustic' *komoi* also occur in Bion fr.11 and Euripides' *Cyclops*, in which the chorus tease Polyphemos, as he wants to set out on a *komos*, that a τέρεινα νύμφα awaits him 'within his dewy cave' (515–16). On the *komos* in T. cf. Sicherl (1972) 57–62 and, more generally, Headlam on Herodas 2.34–7, F. O. Copley, *Exclusus amator* (Baltimore 1956), Cairns (1972) Index s.v. *komos*, P. Pinotti, *GIF* 8 (1977) 60–71, S. L. Tarán, *The art of variation in the Hellenistic epigram* (Leiden 1979) 52–114, McKeown's Introduction to Ovid, *Am.* 1.6. Despite the clear parallels with Idyll 11, most of the komastic *topoi* which are here 'bucolicised' must be illustrated from later poetry; this obviously carries the danger of undervaluing the innovative *poiesis* of Idyll 3, but the procedure is justified by the state of our evidence.

Of particular importance for Idyll 3 are *komoi* within dramatic and quasi-dramatic modes. In addition to Eur. *Cycl.*, *komoi* occur in Aristophanes (*Eccl.* 938–75) and Plautus (*Curc.* 1–157), and Menander constantly varies and inverts the idea (the end of *Dysk.*, the openings of *Mis.* and Ter. *Eun.*). A solo 'performance' such as Idyll 3 brings us rather closer, however, to mimic performances of the kind described by Athenaeus: 'The player called a *magode* (μαγῳδός) carries tambourines and cymbals, and all his clothes are women's garments. He makes rude gestures (σχινίζεται), and all his actions lack decency, as he plays the part of adulterous women or bawds (μαστροπούς), *or a man drunk and going on a revel to his mistress*. Aristoxenus [fr. 110 W²] says that *hilarodia* is serious and derives from tragedy (παρὰ τὴν τραγῳδίαν εἶναι), whereas *magodia* derives from comedy (παρὰ τὴν κωμῳδίαν). For often *magodes* took comic scenarios (ὑποθέσεις) and acted them in their own style and manner' (Ath. 14 621c–d). As early as the fifth century we hear of Gnesippos ὁ παιγνιαγράφος who wrote 'night-time songs with which adulterers could call out women', presumably like the songs of Ar. *Eccl.* 938–75, cf. Ath. 14 638d, Eupolis fr. 148 K–A, Plut. *Mor.* 712e. A second-century papyrus preserves the so-called *Fragmentum Grenfellianum* (*CA* pp. 177–9, cf. Hunter (1996a) 7–10), a *paraklausithyron* of a locked-out woman; for mimic *komoi* cf. also *Mim. Adesp.* 2–3 Cunningham. Idyll 3 offers a sophisticated hexameter version of this semi-dramatic form, which was always 'parasitic' upon high poetry. 'Parody' is thus an inadequate description of the style and function of Idyll 3. It is true that the transference to the countryside of an essentially urban form (the *komos*) lays bare the conventional absurdities and absurd conventions of that form, but the poem reproduces a mode already based on a displacement from 'serious' styles.

Idyll 3 is highly 'dramatic', not only in its pathos, but also in the structure which allows the speaker to pause (?and gesture), or utter asides, after each small song-section. Refocusing of scene after 5 would also have clear links with a quasi-dramatic tradition, cf. the change of scene after 27.48. Moreover, the change of tone after 5, from the practical and ordinary concerns of a goatherd to a senti- mental and self-pitying serenade, emphasises the goatherd's quasi- dramatic 'rôle-playing'. We are, at one level, offered an infatuated and deluded goatherd, who is entirely free of self-knowledge, but does, after his own fashion, what he thinks 'lovers' do: so deluded is he that, whereas the *exclusus amator* is normally forced to his despair- ing position by the rejection of the one he loves, here the rejection (6–7n.) and perhaps even the beloved herself (8–9n.), are part of his fantasy. He *could* just walk into the cave and find . . . ? On the other hand, as the knowing 'generic' announcement of κωμάσδω makes clear, we are also offered, and always remain conscious of, a 'per- formance' (by a master mime-actor?) of 'the goatherd as komast' (cf. Herodas 2, 'the pimp as forensic orator'); we laugh collusively, not so much at the foolishness of the goatherd, but at the brilliance of the script. The audience, whether we ourselves or 'Amaryllis', are to be won over not by the individual arguments, but by the virtuosity of the whole.

Structurally, there is a clear 'stanzaic' pattern (cf. Wilamowitz (1906) 144): 1–5; 6–11 (3 couplets); 12–23 (4 triplets); 24; 25–36 (5 triplets); 37–9; 40–51 (4 triplets); 52–4. The 'narrative' of the song follows this division, but does not do so exactly, and this too is in keeping with Theocritean practice elsewhere. After 5 the goatherd turns to address Amaryllis, and there may be a refocusing of the set- ting (1–5n.); between 6 and 23 we may imagine a pause after each unit while the goatherd waits in vain for Amaryllis to respond. Line 24 marks his recognition that he is not getting anywhere; as a result of this, he decides (25–7n.) to cure himself or die, though he hopes that this too will draw Amaryllis out. In 28–33 he lists the earlier indications that should have warned him that his suit was helpless, but these verses too are gambits to lure Amaryllis out. In 34–6 he tries again ('a last throw of the dice'), with another bribe and the weapon of jealousy. He is rewarded with a favourable omen (37–9) which leads to the mythological song of 40–51, a 'performance' within a performance. When this too achieves nothing he returns to the 'moral blackmail' of death (52–5). Clear parallelism between 27 and 54 divides the poem also into two halves, thus accentuating the marked structuring characteristic of 'folksong'. For other proposed structures cf. Ott (1969) 183–4.

Title. MSS and Σ label the poem with some part or combination of Ἀμαρυλλὶς ἢ Αἰπόλος [or Αἰπολικὸν] ἢ κωμαστής, cf. 1; the simple Κῶμος is much less well attested.

Modern discussions. Damon (1995) 104–12; Gutzwiller (1991) 115–23; Isenberg–Konstan (1984); Lawall (1967) 34–41; Ott (1969) 174–89; Segal (1981) 193–8; Stanzel (1995) 131–7, 191–206.

1–5 κωμάσδω most naturally suggests that the *komos* is already under way, as in the standard scenario of komastic epigrams, and cf. an early fifth-century red-figure cup on which a man holding a lyre is singing εἶμι κωμάζων ὑπ' αὐ[λοῦ (F. Lissarrague, *Un flot d'images. Une esthétique du banquet Grec* (Paris 1987) 127–8). Lines 1–5 are thus an 'entrance monologue' in which 1–2 are addressed, as in comedy, to 'the audience', and 3–5 to Tityros who is 'offstage', cf. Hunter (1993b) 41. Hermogenes (second century AD) cites 1–2a as an example of 'naïve simplicity' (ἀφέλεια) because the goatherd explains what he is doing when no one has asked him (p. 322 Rabe), but the phenomenon is regular in comedy. It makes little difference whether we imagine these verses spoken on the way to the cave or after it has already been reached. Such scenic vagueness must have been normal in mime-performances.

　　1–2 > *Ecl.* 5.12. The frame, '*komos* ... goats', and the clear indication that it is day-time (4), although the *komos* is usually a nocturnal activity, establish the paradoxical narrative. The use of the definite article with proper names is a feature of less formal speech, and is accordingly much more common in the 'Doric' than in the 'epic' Idylls, cf. Leutner (1907) 38–45; here the speaker's narrow horizons are established ('my Amaryllis', 'my Tityros', cf. K–G 1 598). In 1 the central caesura falls between the article and its noun, cf. 2.8, 97 (Simaitha), 10.29 (rustic song), 21.47; although the effect is somewhat weakened by the fact that 'the article is preceded by a preposition to which it can become enclitic' (Bulloch on Call. *h.* 5.103), this metrical 'roughness' may be an opening marker of the character of the speaker.   Ἀμαρυλλίδα: the name is found once in imperial Athens (*LGPN* II s.v.), but is otherwise restricted to pastoral literature; it is the name of Philetas' beloved in *Daphnis & Chloe* (2.5.3). ἀμαρύσσειν 'to glitter', 'to sparkle', 'to flash' is frequently connected with female beauty (Sappho fr. 16.18 Voigt, Campbell on *Arg.* 3.288), and the Hesiodic formula Χαρίτων ἀμαρύγματ' ἔχουσα (frr. 70.38, 196.6 M–W) gives special point to χαρίεσσ' Ἀμαρυλλί in 6 (cf. 4.38). There is probably a particular reference to the brightness of the eyes from which desire radiates, cf. Asclepiades, *Anth. Pal.* 5.153.4 (= *HE* 823) γλυκεροῦ βλέμματος ἀστεροπαί, *Arg.* 3.288, 1018; the association of the name with fire gives point to ἀπέσβης, lit. 'you were extinguished', in 4.39. Virgil perhaps chose 'Tityrus' and 'Amaryllis' for his programmatic First Eclogue under the influence of biographical scholarship on T. Tityrus was early identified with Virgil (cf. *Ecl.* 6.4), just as the komast of Idyll 3 was later identified as T. because σιμός in 8 points to the Σιμιχίδας of Idyll 7 (so Munatius of Tralles (second century AD), cited in the *Hypothesis*, cf. Wendel (1920) 74–7). Cf. further Bowie (1985) 80–1.   Τίτυρος ... ἐλαύνει: for 'Tityros' and Sicily cf. above, p. 10. Among later explanations are that τίτυρος means κάλαμος 'reed', 'pipe', and that it is a dialect term either for a satyr (or *silenos*), cf. Aelian, *VH* 3.40, or for a he-goat. The first would suit 7.72 (a singing Tityros, cf. n. ad loc.) and Eclogue 1 (*Tityre ... auena* frame the opening couplet), but the goatherd of Idyll 3 certainly has satyr-like features (8–9n.), and so may his friend. Tityros may, however, be the leading he-goat who has been left in charge of the flock; to address a goat as 'my wonderfully dear friend' would be naïvely 'sweet' in the manner approved by later rhetoricians (cf. Hermogenes p. 335.8–23 Rabe; Aulus Gellius, *NA* 9.9.7–11, discussing Virgil's translation of 3–5 at *Ecl.* 9.23–5), and has an obvious model in the Homeric Cyclops' address to his favourite ram (*Od.* 9.447–60 κριὲ πέπον κτλ.). ἐλαύνειν normally means 'drive [from one site of pasture to another]', whereas here it seems to mean simply 'graze'; this may lend colour to the suggestion

(Hunter (1983b) 127 n. 12, H. White, *MPhL* 7 (1986) 147–9) that there is here a *double entendre*, as ἐλαύνειν is a not uncommon vulgarism with sexual sense (cf. Eng. 'bang', 'screw'). The he-goat will seize whatever opportunities are offered by the absence of the goatherd, one of whose jobs was to prevent unwanted mating (cf. 5.147–50); κορύπτειν (5) is the *uox propria* for fighting between rival he-goats or rams (cf. Σ 5, 5.147, Lyc. *Alex.* 558), though it could doubtless also have a wider application. Such an earthy opening would stand in obvious counterpoint to the pathetic emotion and frustrated desire of the rest of the poem (cf. 1.86–91n.); animals do not suffer in this way. If, on the other hand, Tityros is a human figure, the *double entendre* persists and the picture is an even earthier one (for bestial relations cf. 4.58–63n.); Tityros, unlike his friend, knows the cure for sexual longing.   αὐτάς: cf. 1.83n.

3–5 > *Ecl.* 3.96, 9.23–5, cf. Aulus Gellius, *NA* 9.9.7–11.

3 τὸ καλὸν πεφιλημένε 'my wonderfully dear friend', cf. 18, 1.41, 7.98, Call. *Epigr.* 52.1 (= *HE* 1067) τὸν τὸ καλὸν μελανεῦντα Θεόκριτον, Asclepiades, *Anth. Pal.* 12.105.3 (= *HE* 910) ἀζήλωτα φιληθείς, Headlam on Herodas 1.54. Gellius describes this phrase as *dulcissimum ... uerba hercle non translaticia, sed cuiusdam natiuae dulcedinis.* Virgil reproduces the *captatio beneuolentiae* of the address by having his goatherd note that he will not be gone for long, *Tityre, dum redeo, breuis est uia* (*Ecl.* 9.23).

4 ἐνόρχαν: both 'sexually mature' and 'uncastrated'. There is nothing vulgar in this rare word (cf. *Il.* 23.147, Ar. *Birds* 569), but the context gives it particular point: the goatherd will never get a chance to show that he too is ἐνόρχης.

5 τὸν Λιβυκὸν κνάκωνα 'the tawny Libyan' (cf. 7.16). Already in the *Odyssey* Libya is the true home of nomadic pastoralism (4.85, with West's note), cf. Virg. *Georg.* 3.339–47.

6–7 These lines imply that the goatherd has previously enjoyed some success with his courting, but doubts persist, as they do about Amaryllis herself (8–9n.).   **χαρίεσσ':** cf. 13.7n. To the komast of Ar. *Eccl.* his girl is Χαρίτων θρέμμα (line 973).   **τοῦτο κατ' ἄντρον** 'out from [the mouth of] this cave'. This use of κατά, where ἐκ (cf. 8.72) or διά is expected, lacks exact parallels, but the preposition can mean 'through [gates etc.]', cf. *Il.* 12.469, Thucyd. 4.67.3. At 7.149 the phrase means 'in the cave'.   **καλεῖς, τὸν ἐρωτύλον**

'invite me, your beloved, in', rather than 'call me your beloved'; for the verb cf. 7.104n. ἐρωτύλος occurs first here, and is presumably a hypocoristic term of affection which the goatherd fondly hopes that Amaryllis may apply to him; cf. τὰν κυάνοφρυν ἐρωτίδα at 4.59 (where see n.).

8–9 > Ecl. 2.7 mori me denique cogis? (v.l. coges).   σιμός 'snub-nosed', a characteristic regarded as ugly (so, most famously, Socrates), and ascribed to goats (8.50), satyrs and non-Greeks; cf. the 'broad nose' of the lovesick Cyclops, 11.33. Physiognomic writers make snub noses a sign of randy lustfulness ([Arist.] Physiog. 811b2, SPG I 228.19–29, 376.5, A. S. F. Gow, JHS 71 (1951) 82.   ἐγγύθεν 'on close inspection', with the (hopeful) implication, 'I am not obviously ugly ...'   νύμφα: to the goatherd Amaryllis is his (future) 'bride' (cf. 19). νύμφα is used in high poetry both of marriageable girls (Il. 9.560, Hes. Theog. 298) and of married women (Stesichorus, PMGF 209.1), cf. V. Andò, QUCC 52 (1996) 47–79; there is a similarly pointed ambiguity at [Bion] 2.28. On the other hand, the νύμφαι which one normally finds in a cave are (despite 8.72–3) indeed 'nymphs', and we may guess that the goatherd has fallen in love with a 'nymph' whom he has presumably never seen and whose existence is, at best, shadowy, cf. DuQuesnay (1979) 44 ('his goddess, his diuina puella'), Gutzwiller (1991) 118–19, and nn. on 18–20 and 37–9 below. Our uncertainty about Amaryllis' existence mirrors a central uncertainty in the audience's perception of any dramatic character who is not 'on-stage'. 'Nymphs' are also the object of the persistent sexual advances of satyrs, and this fits well with other indications about the goatherd.   προγένειος 'with a full [untrimmed] beard', a prominent characteristic of satyrs, cf. Lissarrague (1990). So too, the Cyclops of 6.36 is naïvely proud of his beard, though this is not a view which Galateia might share; cf. Virg. Ecl. 8.34 hirsutumque supercilium promissaque barba.   ἀπάγξασθαι: the speaker's frustration is perhaps marked by the absence, for the first time in the poem, of 'bucolic diaeresis'. This childishly petulant threat is actually carried out by the komast of Idyll 23, and cf. Ovid, Met. 14.716–38 (Iphis).

10–11 > Ecl. 3.70–1, cf. 2.51–2. Apples are a very common love-token in ancient poetry, cf. 6.7, 11.10, A. R. Littlewood, HSCP 72 (1967) 147–81, and 40–2n. below; for apples as komastic gifts cf. 2.120, Propertius 1.3.24. The naïve goatherd does not, however, understand symbolism, and so he brings Amaryllis many apples (and promises more tomorrow), as though their value was purely functional; cf. the Cyclops' 'practical' objections to the effusions of love-poetry at 11.58–9. Moreover, he casts himself as Herakles, bringing back from North Africa the golden apples of the Hesperides at the behest of Eurystheus (Bond on Eur. *HF* 394–9), cf. 29.37–8, 'for you I would fetch the golden apples and Kerberos, watchdog of the dead', Prop. 2.23.7–8, 2.24.34; that the golden apples had been a wedding gift to Hera from Earth (Pherecydes, *FGrHist* 3 F16) is appropriate in this address to his 'bride'. Amaryllis *may* have given him this instruction, but surely only as a tease ('Of course I'll kiss you if …'); for such tasks imposed by the beloved cf. the story of Leukokomas and Euxynthetos at Strabo 10.4.12 (= Thphr. fr. 560 Fortenbaugh). For Amaryllis to accept the apples would have signalled submission, cf. *Anth. Pal.* 5.79 (= 'Plato', Epigr. IV Page) τῶι μήλωι βάλλω σε· σὺ δ' εἰ μὲν ἑκοῦσα φιλεῖς με, | δεξαμένη, τῆς σῆς παρθενίης μετάδος κτλ. **τηνῶθε** 'from that place' = ἐκεῖθεν (cf. Ar. *Ach.* 754); the variant τηνῶ δέ is not impossible (cf. 25), but the asyndeton (like the repetition καθεῖλον … καθελεῖν) suits the simple speaker.

12–14 What should Amaryllis look at? Perhaps we are to recall that satyrs were in an 'almost permanent state of erection' (Lissarrague (1990) 55), and there would thus indeed be a visible sign of the goatherd's distress; this would prepare for the imagery of the sexual penetration of the female in lines 13–14. Others take θᾶσαι with ἄχος, which is improbable, or with the apples of 10–11, but this seems unlikely in this system of self-contained 'stanzas' (though cf. 40–2n.). θυμαλγὲς ἐμὶν ἄχος can hardly be a vocative addressed to Amaryllis.

The goatherd's wish for metamorphosis is of a familiar kind in the erotic poetry of many cultures (cf. *PMG* 900–1, *Anth. Pal.* 5.83–4, Nonnus 15.258–66, Ovid, *Am.* 2.15, M. L. West, *HSCP* 73 (1969) 132, Petropoulos (1994) 35–6), and may have been a komastic *topos*, cf. 11.54–5. He could just walk through 'ivy and fern', but he has got to play out the rôle he has designed for himself. The bee – the definite article shows that he sees a bee enter the cave – is a familiar element of a *locus amoenus*, cf. 7.142, *Od.* 13.106, but here there is a special point. Bees were free of sexual longing and therefore had no need to play at being *exclusae*; whether or not bees copulated was a famous problem of ancient zoology (cf. Arist. *GA* 3 759a8–60b33, Virg. *Georg.* 4.197–9). Σ raises the possibility that he wishes to be a bee in order to sting Amaryllis; however unlikely this seems, the bee image does take its starting-point from his θυμαλγὲς ἄχος, for the comparison of the pain of love to a bee-sting is (at least in later poetry) common, cf. Idyll 19, Meleager, *Anth. Pal.* 5.163 (= *HE* 4248–53). Σ also recalls a story in which a bee acted as a go-between for Rhoikos of Knidos in his relations with a nymph, but there seems to be no necessary reference to that story here.

12 ἐμίν: ἐμόν with metrical lengthening is not impossible, particularly in this emotional outburst.

14 ἅ τυ πυκάσδει 'which conceals you'. Alternatives include ἅι τὺ πυκάσδηι, 'by which you are concealed' and ἅι τυ πυκάσδεις, 'by which you conceal yourself' (cf. *Il.* 17.551, Wilamowitz (1906) 81 n. 1).

15–17 > *Ecl.* 8.43–5. This is the only 'stanza' between 6 and 39 without an explicit reference to Amaryllis; we are perhaps to conceive of it as an 'aside' spoken to himself or 'the audience'. Lucretius 3.294–8 associates the rage of angry lions with their 'hot bodies', but the curious sequence of thought in these verses is plain evidence of the goatherd's suffering.

15 ἔγνων: the aorist can mean simply 'know' (cf. 2.5, Meleager, *Anth. Pal.* 5.184.1–2 (= *HE* 4370–1) etc.), but the goatherd's realisation has been a slow one, hence νῦν. Cf. Ovid, *Met.* 13.762 (the Cyclops) *quid sit amor sensit.* **βαρύς** 'hard', 'grievous', cf. 1.100 Κύπρι βαρεῖα, 2.3 (of the beloved), Eubulus fr. 40.5–7 K–A, Lat. *durus.* **ἦ ῥα λεαίνας κτλ.:** one of many extant reworkings of *Il.* 16.33–5 (Patroclus to Achilles), 'Pitiless one, horseman Peleus was not your father nor Thetis your mother; the grey sea and the high cliffs bore you, so unbending is your mind'; cf. Theognis 1231, Pease on Virg. *Aen.* 4.365–7. Eros' parentage was a notorious problem (13.1–2n.), but the lioness is chosen as a creature lacking all human sympathy, whose savagery passed to its cubs through its milk, cf. 23.19 (a cruel *eromenos*), Catullus 60, 64.154, Ovid, *Met.* 9.615 (Byblis about Caunus) *nec lac bibit ille leaenae.*

16 δρυμῶι: δρυμοί are dense 'thickets' or 'undergrowth', often with thorns (cf. 13.64–7); for the association with lions cf. 1.72, 25.134–5. The point is that the *erastes* must endure a painful existence in a harsh environment. **ἔτραφε:** probably imperfect, cf. ἐθήλαζε, 11.40–1n.

17 κατασμύχων: cf. 8.90, *Arg.* 3.446 (Medea) κῆρ ἄχει σμύχουσα, 762–3 (the pain of love attacks Medea) σμύχουσα διὰ χροὸς ἀμφί τ' ἀραιὰς | ἶνας καὶ κεφαλῆς ὑπὸ νείατον ἰνίον ἄχρις, Pease on Virg. *Aen.* 4.2. For the bones as the site of this attack cf. 7.102, 30.21 etc.   **ἰάπτει:** although the verb means 'hurt', 'torture' (cf. LSJ s.v. A), the phrasing also evokes ἰάπτειν = 'shoot [arrows etc.]' (LSJ s.v. B). The pains of love are figured as the arrows of the Erotes in the very similar *Arg.* 3.761–5 (previous note), and cf. Propertius 2.34.60 *quem tetigit iactu certus ad ossa deus.*

18 τὸ καλὸν ποθορεῦσα '[maiden] whose glance is beauty', cf. 3n., 13.45n.; the phrase suggests the etymology of Amaryllis' name (1–2n.). The participle is formed as though from -ὀρέω rather than -ὀράω; for this Doric feature cf. 4.53, 5.85, 6.31, 7.55, 11.69, K–B 1 124, Buck (1955) 125.   **λίθος:** appropriate both to Amaryllis' existence in a cave and to her 'stony' heart, cf. 37–9n., 23.20 λάϊνε παῖ, *Il.* 16.33–5 (quoted above). Gutzwiller (1991) 120 notes that as ὀφρῦς can mean both 'eyebrow' and 'mountain-ridge', κυάνοφρυ continues the conceit: has the goatherd fallen in love with a stone statue of a nymph? The phrase sits somewhat oddly between two complimentary addresses, and Σ record the variant λίπος; λιπαρός 'sleek', 'shining' is used as a compliment for women (Bacchyl. 5.169, 7.1), as well as men, whose use of oil in the gymnasium gave the adjective particular point (cf. 2.78–80, 102). 'All unguent' would be a 'naïve' way of conveying the compliment.   **κυάνοφρυ:** cf. 4.59; in the *Iliad* both Zeus and Hera have 'dark brows' (1.528, 15.102, 17.209), and Ibycus gives Eros himself κυάνεοι βλέφαροι (*PMG* 287.1–2). Here too Amaryllis is distanced into poetry and myth.

19 πρόσπτυξαι: a poetic word, in keeping with the goatherd's stylistic ambitions; πρόσ-, rather than πότ-, is perhaps determined by euphony, cf. Hunter (1996a) 42. 'Embrace me, your goatherd, so that I may kiss you' is deliberately naïve; the definite article conveys more than a touch of pride (cf. 5.90 κῆμὲ ... τὸν ποιμένα, 1n., Leutner (1907) 59–60), though kissing goatherds had its down side (cf. Longus, *D&C* 1.16.2 on the smell).

20 ἔστι καὶ κτλ.: 20 is identical to line 4 of the spurious Idyll 27, where it is perhaps to be understood as a 'quotation' of T. 'Empty' kisses are usually understood as 'not progressing to sexual inter-course' (Dover), but at 27.3–4 'insignificant', 'carrying no serious implications' seems the more likely sense; thus the goatherd is offer-ing Amaryllis the 'sweet delight' of kisses which need not signify any emotional attachment on her part (cf. 12.32–7). She is unlikely to fall for that one. ἀδέα: cf. 1.65n.

21–3 Garlands were standard wear for both komasts and bride-grooms (cf. Blech (1982) 63–81), but here perhaps we have a special garland which the goatherd has made and 'is keeping' for Amaryllis as a 'wedding gift' (cf. Chariton 3.2.16, Lucian, *Hdt.* 5). If so, the flowers will be very faded by the time Amaryllis sees them. For φυλάσσω 'save' cf. 34; at 7.64 στέφανον περὶ κρατὶ φυλάσσων, 'around my head' makes all the difference. The komast often aban-doned his garlands at the door of the beloved (cf. 2.153, Asclepiades, *Anth. Pal.* 5.145 (= *HE* 860–5) etc.), but this goatherd threatens not even to do that.

21 τὸν στέφανον κτλ. 'You will make me shred [lit. 'pluck'] the garland into little pieces [cf. *Od.* 12.174 τυτθὰ διατμήξας] this very moment.' καταυτίκα is not otherwise attested, but cf. καταυτόθι; it may be a very prosaic touch in the goatherd's threat. Σ, however, explains the syntax as κατατῖλαι τὸν στέφανον αὐτίκα εἰς λεπτά, i.e. with 'anastrophic tmesis' of κατά, cf. 8.74, Bühler (1960) 221–8.

22 κισσοῖο: in view of her surroundings (14) one might suppose that ivy was not something for which Amaryllis had great need or which she would value very highly. The Dionysiac associations of ivy (cf. 26.4, Lembach (1970) 120), however, make it an appropriate offering for the satyr-like goatherd.

23 ἀμπλέξας: ἀναπλέκειν more usually governs the part of the body which is garlanded rather than the wreath to which subsidiary decorations are added, for which the regular verb is συμπλέ-κειν. καλύκεσσι: probably '[rose] buds', as the marginal Σ in Π[5] explains, cf. 11.10 (roses as a love-gift), Strato, *Anth. Pal.* 12.8.5, 12.204.3. εὐόδμοισι σελίνοις: Theophrastus ascribes the pleas-ant smell of 'wild celery' to the sap (*HP* 1.12.2). Being πολύγναμπ-τον (7.68), it was very suitable for garlands, cf. *PMG* 410, Hor. *C.* 1.36.16 (with Nisbet–Hubbard ad loc.), 2.7.23–4, 4.11.3, A. C. Andrews, *CP* 44 (1949) 91–9.

24 A despairing 'aside', cf. above, p. 109; Hermann's ὑπακούει may be right (cf. 37–9), but is not necessary (cf. 52–4). In the first half of the verse the goatherd strikes a Homeric pose of despair (*Od.* 5.465, *Il.* 11.404).   **ἐγών:** literary Doric seems to use both ἐγώ and ἐγών before consonants; MSS will count for little in such a matter, but here it is tempting to see a 'Doricisation' of a Homeric sequence. **δύσσοος** 'wretched', possibly a Doric colloquialism with a similar semantic range to κακοδαίμων, cf. 4.45, *RIGI* 8 (1924) 266 (a Sicilian curse tablet); εὔσοος occurs at 24.8, and the noun at Soph. *OC* 390, fr. 122 Radt and probably Alcaeus fr. 286a 6 Voigt.

25–7 > *Ecl.* 8.59–60. To throw oneself over a cliff was a typical lover's death; Hermesianax had told how Menalkas (above, p. 66) threw himself to his death in despair over one Euhippe (fr. 3 Powell); the goatherd's threat may, therefore, evoke the experience of one of his models, cf. 5.15–16. Nevertheless, the most famous such leap was Sappho's supposed leap off a cliff on the island of Leukas in her 'crazed desire' (Menander fr. 258 K–T) for Phaon, cf. the Ovidian *Epistula Sapphus*, *RE* xix 1790–5, G. Nagy, *HSCP* 77 (1973) 137–77; subsequently, it was believed that those who repeated Sappho's leap and survived would be cured of their passion, cf. Strabo 10.2.9, Photius, *Bibl.* 153a–b (= 3.70–2 Henry). Amaryllis' lack of response thus leads the goatherd to the final alternative – death or a cure. μή may therefore be retained in 27, despite the obvious attractions of Graefe's δή, because Amaryllis will be happy if he is cured of his love and pesters her no more. Damon (1995) 108 suggests a break after 25 to allow a response, before he defines the rock from which he will leap; the text does not require such an articulation, but 'scripts' always allow more than one performance.

25 τὰν βαίταν ἀποδύς: the act itself is not naïve, because (if μή is retained) this is not a simple attempt at suicide; what is ἀφελές, like the opening verses, is saying what does not need saying.

26 θύννως: cf. Ar. *Knights* 313, Oppian, *Hal.* 3.631–40 'Abundant and wondrous is the spoil for fishermen when the host of tunnies set forth in the spring ... first a skilful tunny-watcher (θυννοσκόπος) ascends a steep high hill, who remarks the various shoals, their kind and size, and informs his comrades' (trans. Mair). The place, sometimes specially constructed, from which the look-out was kept was a θυννοσκοπεῖον or σκοπιά/σκοπή. Tunnies are particularly associated with the seas around Sicily (Mair on line 627), and this may suggest a setting for Idyll 3. Ὄλπις 'Oil-flask', λήκυθος, cf. 2.156, 18.45, Pfeiffer on Call. fr. 534; the word is also used of a ladle or jug for pouring wine (Sappho fr. 141.3 Voigt, Ion *TrGF* 19 F10). The name perhaps suggests the fisherman's physical shape, but Σ make other suggestions based on 'fish' words (λεπίς, ἔλλοψ); ὄλπις is an anagram of λοπίς 'fish-scale'. Sophron wrote a mime (about which nothing is known) called Θυννοθήρας, and the name might derive from that. Amaryllis is presumably expected to know that Olpis' cliff is the highest in the locality: the verses again show the narrowness of the goatherd's horizons.

27 καῖ κα μὴ 'ποθάνω κτλ. 'Even if I do not kill myself, your pleasure will certainly be done.' τὸ τεὸν ἁδύ is 'your pleasure', cf. Eur. *Hec.* 120 τὸ σὸν ἀγαθόν, although Σ interpret 'it will be pleasant as far as you are concerned' (cf. Pl. *Prt.* 338c5, Pind. *Pyth.* 11.41). **γε μάν** 'certainly', cf. Denniston 348. γε μέν (Denniston) would mean 'nevertheless'.

28–30 'I realised recently when I was giving thought [and wondering] whether you loved me, and not even did the smack make the love-in-absence cling, but it withered on my smooth forearm.' Text and interpretation are again uncertain. 'Clearly this was a kind of "she loves me, she loves me not" divination in which a man smacked a petal or leaf on to the hairless underside of his arm and got his answer from whether it remained stuck to him when the arm was held normally ... or curled and fell off. It was later believed (by Σ, among others) that the sound made by the smack was crucial' (Dover, cf. G. Kaibel, *Hermes* 36 (1901) 606–7). Pollux 9.127 offers a different explanation involving the fingers of the left hand and the hollow palm of the right. For modern parallels cf. Petropoulou (1959) 67–70.

28 ἔγνων πρᾶν stands in naïve counterpoint to νῦν ἔγνων (15).

29 τηλέφιλον: the 'love-in-absence' is, according to Σ, a poppy leaf; poppy petals could be called πλαταγώνια, cf. 11.57, Lembach (1970) 163–4.

30 αὔτως 'to no purpose', 'without accomplishing the desired result'. **ἁπαλῶι ... πάχεϊ:** the transmitted genitive could perhaps imply 'it withered [and fell off from]', with ποτί chosen for variation before ἐξεμαράνθη; the dative is, however, much easier.

31 ἁ γραία: cf. 6.40 (where the interpolation of line 41 (= 10.16) supports Heinsius' emendation here). The transmitted Ἀγροιώ, 'Lady of the fields', makes 32 very difficult, but the text must be regarded as uncertain; ἁ Γροιώ would suggest γραῦς, and for the resulting word order cf. *Il.* 1.11 τὸν Χρύσην ... ἀρητῆρα. **κοσκινόμαντις:** 'sieve-diviners' perhaps worked by sieving beans (*vel sim.*) and 'reading' the subsequent pattern, though other methods are also recorded in more recent times, cf. *RE* xi 1481–3, Petropoulou (1959) 72–5, W. G. Arnott, *Mnem.* 31 (1978) 27–32. They were probably a familiar feature of the ancient countryside. Magic plays a very prominent role in Roman love poetry (A. Tupet, *La Magie dans la poésie latine* (Paris 1976)), and 28–32 are a lowlife anticipation of that. There is an obvious irony here: no special 'gifts' would be required to ascertain the goatherd's condition and Amaryllis' lack of interest.

32 ποιολογεῦσα 'cutting grass' or, more likely, 'gathering magical herbs', which perhaps played some rôle in the sieve-divining (cf. Nicander, *Ther.* 497, LSJ s.v. πόα 1 2); Σ understands 'making sheaves' (cf. Idyll 10), but there is no evidence that the verb could mean that.   **Παραιβάτις** does not occur elsewhere, but the masculine form is very common (*LGPN* i s.v.). As an adjective the meaning would be 'as she walked beside me'.

33 τὶν ὅλος ἔγκειμαι 'I am completely devoted to you', cf. Parthenius, *Erot.* 23.1 πᾶσα δὲ ἐνέκειτο Ἀκροτάτωι, Herodas 5.3; πρόσκειμαι is more common in this sense (LSJ s.v. II 2), but one can ἐγκεῖσθαι πόθωι (Archil. fr. 193.1 West), just as desire can ἐγκεῖσθαι mortals (Ar. *Eccl.* 956). Much the same meaning is differently expressed at 2.96 πᾶσαν ἔχει με τάλαιναν ὁ Μύνδιος.

34–6 > *Ecl.* 2.40–4.

34 λευκὰν διδυματόκον αἶγα: cf. 1.25. This is a rustic version of the small animals (hares, cocks etc.) which are the standard love-gifts of erotic literature and art, cf. Dover (1978) 92. White was presumably a prized colour in a goat, and there is particular point in that it is going to be given to a 'dark' girl; that it has borne twins suggests that it will yield a rich supply of milk.

35 ἐριθακίς 'serving-girl', 'hired labourer'; Σ also notes the possibility of Ἐριθακίς, i.e. 'Erithakis, servant [rather than 'daughter'] of Mermnon', cf. 10.15 ἁ Πολυβώτα.   **μελανόχρως:** the goatherd tries to provoke Amaryllis by the mention of an inferior rival; whatever her exact status (8–9n.), the cave-dwelling Amaryllis is likely, in the goatherd's imagination, to have desirable white skin. μέλας can simply mean 'with a dark complexion' (as judged by a Greek), 'swarthy', cf. Pl. *Rep.* 5 474e1; on the other hand, Greeks judged all members of some races (Egyptians, Ethiopians) to be 'dark'. Within Egypt μελάγχρως was one of a graded series of skin-colour terms used in official documents, cf. Preisigke s.v., Cameron (1995) 233–5. There is not enough evidence to decide the ethnic identity of this 'serving girl', nor whether she affords any clue to the setting of the poem. Cf. further 10.26–8.

36 ἐνδιαθρύπτηι 'play the tease with me', cf. 6.15 (Galateia and Polyphemos). The goatherd accuses Amaryllis of 'playing hard to get'.

37–9 An aside, prompted by an omen, breaks off the series of pleas to Amaryllis and introduces the mythological catalogue of 40–51. The twitching of the right eye (always a good omen) is an example of the involuntary physical movements around which a whole para-science (παλμῶν μαντική) developed in later antiquity, cf. *PRyl.* 1 28, Plaut. *Pseud.* 107, *Suda* π 113, 2110, S. G. Oliphant, *AJP* 31 (1910) 203–8. ἄλλεσθαι 'to quiver' is the standard term in discussions of such movements. The goatherd's superstition will belong, however, to a simpler age before systematisation.

37 ἰδησῶ: this future is not otherwise attested. If the form was noticeably prosaic or colloquial, it may be significant that it occurs in a 'spoken' aside.

38 ἀισεῦμαι: 6–23 and 25–36 have been 'songs', but now that he has fond hopes of success, he will raise the stylistic register and produce a more elaborate performance.   **ἀποκλινθείς:** poetic for -κλιθείς. The goatherd now adopts the sitting posture of the bucolic-erotic poet, cf. 1.12, 21, 6.4, 7.89, Virg. *Ecl.* 1.1, 3.55, 8.16 *incumbens tereti Damon sic coepit oliuae* (with Clausen's note); this gives particular point to πεσών in 53. In Aristainetos' account, based upon Callimachus, Akontios laments his love for Kydippe 'sitting beneath oaks or elms' (1.10.57 Mazal). Cf. further 40–51n. This self-conscious pose may suggest that the pine-tree (*inter al.*) was already associated with the production of poetry (cf. 1.1); the Theocritean goatherd strikes a pose constructed from T.'s own poems. These considerations make the interpretation 'stepping to one side' less likely.

39 ποτίδοι 'give me a look', not just 'catch sight of me'. For hia-

tus at the central caesura cf. 11.45–8n. ἀδαμαντίνα: 'adamant'
was (in the poetic imagination) a wondrously hard metal typically
associated with gods, cf. West on Hes. *Theog.* 161, H. Troxler, *Sprache
und Wortschatz Hesiods* (Zurich 1964) 19–21. For the present conceit
cf. 13.5–6n., Pind. fr. 123.4 (imperviousness to desire), Ovid, *EP*
4.12.31–2 *quae nisi te moueant, duro tibi pectora ferro | esse uel inuicto clausa
adamante putem*, Prop. 1.16.29–32 (in a *paraklausithyron*), McKeown on
Ovid, *Am.* 1.11.9–10. ἐστίν: most MSS offer ἐντί (cf. 1.17, 5.21),
which is first attested as a singular in third-century inscriptions and
Hellenistic Doric literary texts; it has some claims to be retained in
the text of T., cf. Gallavotti 42, Molinos Tejada 320–1, W. Blümel
and R. Merkelbach, *ZPE* 112 (1996) 151–2. The reading of the papyrus here is uncertain: Parsons notes 'the trace suggests εσσα[ι; the
suprascript correction might be -τ[ι or -τ[αι'.

40–51 The goatherd's new song is formally distinguished from
what has gone before both by its stylistic pretension (epicisms,
Homeric phrases etc.) and mythological subject matter, and also –
until the end – the absence of *explicit* reference to Amaryllis and the
singer's own position; except for the suggestion in χώ (43n.), the
parallels between the mythological exempla and the framing narrative are, however clear, merely implicit, and the question of 47–8 is
not explicitly addressed to Amaryllis. The goatherd thus offers a formal poetic composition, rather than the 'extemporised' *ad feminam*
verses which have preceded. The world of the countryside, peopled
by such as Olpis and Mermnon, gives way to the world and exotic
names of myth. Four of the five myths (at least) appear to have links
with the poetry of Hesiod, and the song apes in form the 'catalogue'
poems, inspired by Hesiod's *Catalogue of women*, which were popular
in the Hellenistic period. Of particular importance is a long tradition of elegiac poems, in which poets consoled themselves for the
loss of, or lack of requital from, beloved women: Mimnermus' *Nanno*,
Antimachus' *Lyde*, Hermesianax's *Leontion* and the *Bittis* of Philitas
perhaps all fell into this category, cf. Knox (1993) 66–7, Cameron
(1995) 380–6, V. J. Matthews, *Antimachus of Colophon* (Leiden 1996)
26–39. The long fragment of Hermesianax's poem (fr. 7 Powell)
shares both the Hesiodic inspiration and the short units of the goatherd's song, even if the structure of the latter is exaggeratedly regular, in keeping with the character of the singer (cf. above, p. 109).

Philitas may have been an important model: Longus' Philetas loved
an Amaryllis (2.5.3), and the poet somewhere referred to Atalanta
and Hippomenes (40–2n.). For other bucolic catalogues cf. 20.34–41
(another attempt to persuade a haughty girl), Longus, *D&C* 4.17.6.

All five myths had, in various versions, endings other than bliss-
fully requited love, and the ironic gap between the singer's inten-
tions and limited 'learning' and our fuller knowledge is clearly important, cf. Fantuzzi (1995b) 22–7. Others see the apparent optimism
of 40–5, created by the good omen of 37–9, giving way to increasing
despair in 46–51, cf. Lawall (1967) 39–40, R. Whitaker, *Myth and personal experience in Roman love-elegy* (Göttingen 1983) 49–52. What is
crucial, however, is that, just as the transference to a (highly artificial) countryside of the apparently 'natural' manners of erotic poetry
lays bare those manners for the cultural conventions they are, so the
goatherd's mythology reveals how the very process of adducing
'mythological parallels' depends entirely upon an audience's willing-
ness to 'forget' much of what it knows.

40–2 Atalanta, daughter of Schoineus of Boeotia, lived (like
Amaryllis) in the wild and, again like Amaryllis, spurned men; she
was ἡ φεύγουσα γάμον (Theognis 1293), cf. 40 τὰν παρθένον. Her
suitors were compelled to compete with her in a running race, and
those who lost were killed. She was finally 'caught' by Hippomenes
of Onchestos (or in other versions Melanion), who dropped golden
apples at strategic points of the race. Hesiod told the story at some
length, and enough survives for us to gain an impression of his telling (frr. 72–6 M–W). Hippomenes' apples were a gift of Aphrodite
from her own garden or from the garland of Dionysos (Call. fr. 412,
cf. 2.120) or of the Hesperides (cf. *Ecl.* 6.61), a story already evoked
by the goatherd's apples (10–11n.). At least in later versions, Atalanta
and Hippomenes were metamorphosed into lions as punishment for
making love in a temple. For the myth cf. Frazer on [Apollodorus]
3.9.2, M. Detienne, *Dionysus slain* (Baltimore 1979) 26–34, P. M. C.
Forbes Irving, *Metamorphosis in Greek myths* (Oxford 1990) 59–95, A.
Ley, *Nikephoros* 3 (1990) 31–72; in Ovid's *Met.* the story is told as a
warning by Venus to her beloved Adonis (*Met.* 10.560–707, cf. 46–8).
Σ 2.120 reports that Philitas told how Aphrodite gave Hippomenes
'apples of Dionysos' and that these 'stirred Atalanta to love' (fr. 18
Powell); an allusion to Philitas here would certainly not surprise.

42 ὡς ἴδεν ὡς κτλ.: cf. 2.82, *Ecl.* 8.41. The model is *Il.* 14.293–4 (Hera's 'deception of Zeus') ἴδε δὲ νεφεληγερέτα Ζεύς. | ὡς δ' ἴδεν, ὥς μιν ἔρως πυκινὰς φρένας ἀμφεκάλυψεν; for other reworkings cf. Call. fr. 260.2, Moschus, *Europa* 74. The second and third ὡς are probably demonstrative with the emphasis on simultaneity, 'as she saw, so ...', i.e. 'no sooner did she see than ...', cf. Gow on 2.82, S. Timpanaro, *Contributi di filologia e di storia della lingua latina* (Rome 1978) 233–70. In the *Iliad* Hera too comes, like Hippomenes, with a powerful gift from Aphrodite (the *kestos*, *Il.* 14.214–17), and we are to understand that the apples exercise powerful aphrodisiac magic. A papyrus of Augustan date (*P. Berol.* inv. 21243) preserves a hexameter spell to be said over an apple: whichever girl picks up the apple or eats it, 'may she set everything else aside and go mad (μαίνοιτο, cf. ἐμάνη) for my love', cf. R. W. Daniel and F. Maltomini, *Supplementum Magicum* II (Opladen 1992), no. 72, C. A. Faraone, *Phoenix* 44 (1990) 230–8. So too in Hesiod, Atalanta is *instantly* attracted to the apples (fr. 76.17–19).   **ἐς βαθὺν ἅλατ' ἔρωτα:** cf. 25–7, where it is the goatherd (not Amaryllis) who does the 'leaping'. 'Deep' here is influenced by this earlier passage, but is otherwise very rare as an adjective of ἔρως, cf. Nonnus 15.209 (in an episode where T. is an important model); it may, however, have had a wider currency: Cat. 68.107–8, 117 *sed tuus altus amor barathro fuit altior illo* are particularly suggestive. The association between Kypris and the (stormy) sea helps, cf. 7.52–89n., Nisbet–Hubbard on Hor. *C.* 1.5.16.

43–5 The seer Melampous helped his brother Bias by recovering from Phylake in Thessaly, at the cost of a year's imprisonment, cattle belonging to the family of Neleus of Pylos which had been taken there by Phylakos (or his son Iphiklos); this recovery was the price demanded by Neleus for the hand of his daughter Pero with whom Bias was in love. Cf. *Od.* 11.281–97, 15.230–8, Pherecydes, *FGrHist* 3 F33, Σ *Arg.* 1.118–21. The story was told in the Hesiodic *Catalogue* (fr. 37 M–W), and also in the *Melampodia* (frr. 270–9 M–W). The 'rustic' elements of the story allow the goatherd to exploit it. Lines 43–4 are a 'virtuoso' variation of *Od.* 11.288–92, οὐδέ τι Νηλεὺς | τῶι ἐδίδου ὃς μὴ ἕλικας βόας εὐρυμετώπους | ἐκ Φυλάκης ἐλάσειε βίης Ἰφικλ- ηείης | ἀργαλέας· τὰς δ' οἶος ὑπέσχετο μάντις ἀμύμων | ἐξελάαν, enhanced by the *figura etymologica* in ἀγέλαν ... ἄγε (cf. *Et. Mag.* 7.42 Gaisford); no wonder the goatherd had a headache after this effort.

Fantuzzi (1995b) 24 argues that T. here constructs, or extrapolates from the Homeric passages, a version in which Melampous wanted Pero for himself, but Bias enjoyed the fruits of his brother's labours, cf. *Arg* 1.118–21, Prop. 2.3.51–4. If this is correct, we (but not the goatherd) will understand δέ in 44 as 'but'; in any event, it is clear that any similarities the goatherd has are with Melampous rather than Bias.

43 τὰν ἀγέλαν: the article suggests 'his herd' (cf. 6.2), thus bringing Melampous closer to the goatherd.   **χὦ:** i.e. 'in addition [to me, for I too have driven a herd]'. A herd of cattle thus becomes a wedding-gift for Pero (cf. 27.34), as the goatherd has offered Amaryllis a single kid. The disjunction between the mythic and the 'real' is not dissimilar to that between Hippomenes' golden apples and the goatherd's ordinary fruit. Alternatively, καί is either postponed and simply joins the two myths, cf. δέ in 46, or means 'in addition (to Hippomenes)' who also used a rustic gift to win a lady.   **Ὄθρυος:** a mountain range in southern Thessaly, lying in fact to the south of Phylake, but the goatherd uses a little poetic licence. This does not merely stress the difficulty of Melampous' task, but also again brings him closer to the goatherd, who knows all about herding in the mountains (cf. 2), as well as to Adonis.

44 ἀγκοίναισιν: a high poeticism, used by Homer only of women sleeping in the arms of Zeus (*Il.* 14.213, *Od.* 11.261).

45 χαρίεσσα: like Amaryllis (6).   **μάτηρ ... περίφρονος Ἀλφεσιβοίας:** the periphrasis perhaps holds out to Amaryllis the prospect of the joys of motherhood, if she yields to the goatherd's suit. This child of Bias and Pero appears only here and in the parallel narrative in Pherecydes; her name, 'she who brings cattle', is obviously derived from the story in which she appears, cf. W. J. Verdenius, *Hermeneus* 29 (1957) 4–7, Edwards on *Il.* 18.593. περίφρων, which is very common in *Od.*, particularly of Penelope, wittily points to her obscurity: there is nothing to say about her, so a 'standard' epithet must be used by our struggling poet. It can hardly be an accident that, according to Hesiod (fr. 139 M–W), Alphesiboia was the name of Adonis' mother; she thus forms a link between this myth and the next, and the 'confusion' between two homonyms is of a kind very familiar in Hellenistic and Roman poetry.

46–8 Adonis, a Hellenisation of the Mesopotamian Tammuz or the Sumerian Dumuzi, had a vital link with agriculture, and bucolic poetry thus naturally represents him as a shepherd, cf. 1.109–10n., 20.35–6, *Ecl.* 10.18. The youthful beloved of Aphrodite was killed by a boar sent by a jealous rival, but was allowed an annual return to the embrace of Aphrodite, rather than that of Persephone, when his festival was celebrated (cf. Idyll 15). Adonis' death is thus suitably evoked by a goatherd preoccupied with thoughts of suicide. On the Adonis myth, which was probably at least mentioned in the Hesiodic *Catalogue*, cf. M. Detienne, *The gardens of Adonis* (Hassocks, Sussex 1977), W. Burkert, *Structure and history in Greek mythology and ritual* (Berkeley 1979) 105–11, J. D. Reed, *CA* 14 (1995) 317–47, Reed (1997).

46 καλάν: like Amaryllis (18). **Κυθέρειαν:** interpreted in antiquity (cf. Hes. *Theog.* 198) as 'lady of Kythera', although the island is Κύθηρα (cf. G. Morgan, *TAPA* 108 (1978) 115–20, Burkert (1992) 190). Pausanias 3.23.1 describes the temple of Aphrodite Ourania on the island as 'the most holy and ancient of all Greek shrines of Aphrodite'. The title occurs in a Sapphic lament for Adonis (fr. 140 Voigt), and T. may have associated it particularly with the Adonis story. **ἐν ὤρεσι:** like the goatherd (2). **μῆλα:** cf. 1.109n. μᾶλα 'apples' in 41 argues for μῆλα here.

47 ἐπὶ πλέον ... λύσσας 'to the highest point of crazed desire'; for this comparative cf. 1.20, Arat. *Phaen.* 1048.

48 οὐδὲ φθίμενον: gods normally avoided the pollution of human death, cf. Eur. *Hipp.* 1437–8, Parker (1983) 33–7. **ἄτερ μαζοῖο τίθητι:** the present tense evokes the repeated representation of the scene in ritual and art (cf. 15.84–6). ἄτερ seems to be unparalleled in this sense, and Gallavotti deleted the whole triplet.

Aphrodite's embrace of the dying Adonis (cf. Bion, *EA* 40–62) is the embrace both of the grieving lover and of the mother who has lost her son (the *pietà* figure). The suggestion in this verse that the dead Adonis drinks from Aphrodite's breast catches a central paradox: Adonis is both new-born and dead (φθίμενος 'wasted away' points to the fertile growth which the new-born, or resurrected, Adonis brings). In some versions, Aphrodite first saw Adonis when he was a baby and then entrusted him to Persephone (cf. Apollod. 3.14.4 = Panyassis fr. 22A Davies), and the notion that she suckled him after he had burst forth from the tree into which his mother had metamorphosed was an obvious narrative step. In *Met.* 10 Ovid does not explicitly exploit the quasi-incestuous dimension of the Adonis story, but he does place it after the stories of Pygmalion and Myrrha, a sequence which is at least suggestive. '[The goatherd] brings within the limited enclosure of his conventional and trivial amorous problems the gigantic archetypes and the tragic universality of primal fertility myths' (Segal (1981) 71–2).

49–51 The final triplet brings a change from narrative to *makarismos*, and also contains two myths rather than one; these features may be a mark of the goatherd's growing despair.

49–50a Endymion, like Adonis, was a hunter and/or shepherd, and was loved by Selene who visited him in the 'Latmian cave' in Caria; the goddess's love led him to fall into an eternal sleep, either because she was scared of a rival or through the agency of Zeus. The principal sources for the story are collected by Σ on this passage and on *Arg.* 4.57; it was treated, *inter alios*, by Sappho. The sleep of Endymion in his cave looks forward to the goatherd's melodramatic collapse outside Amaryllis' cave.   ἄτροπον ὕπνον: the phrase catches the sleep/death ambiguity so familiar from epitaphs, cf. 22.204, Call. *Epigr.* 9, 16, *EA* 71, M. B. Ogle, *MAAR* 11 (1933) 81–117, E. Vermeule, *Aspects of death in early Greek art and poetry* (Berkeley 1979) 145–56; analogous expressions from earlier poetry include χάλκεος ὕπνος (*Il.* 11.241) and ἀτέλευτος ὕπνος (Aesch. *Ag.* 1451). Ἄτροπος was the name of one of the Moirai (Hes. *Theog.* 905), and this confirms the powerful ambiguity of the phrase. Endymion's sleep is ἄτροπος – and hence he is ζαλωτός – in two senses. He does not 'toss and turn', because (so the goatherd imagines) his love is requited; tormented insomnia etc. is a standard mark of the unhappy lover, cf. Ovid, *Am.* 1.2.1–4 with McKeown's notes, and the motif may go back to Achilles' grief for the dead Patroclus (*Il.* 24.3–12). Secondly, his sleep 'allows no release', i.e. he is dead and not suffering as the goatherd suffers; this gives point to ἐμίν, with which the goatherd sets his judgement against that of the world at large.

50b–1 Ἰασίωνα: lover of Demeter 'in a thrice-turned field' and father of Ploutos, he was killed by Zeus's lightning (Hom. *Od.* 5.125–8, Hes. *Theog.* 969–74, Diod. Sic. 5.49.4). The Hesiodic *Catalogue* told this story of Eetion (fr. 177 M–W), but Eetion and Iasion are identified as early as Hellanicus (*FGrHist* 4 F23). The union of Iasion and Demeter was plainly 'the mythical correlate of the ancient agrarian ritual' (West on *Theog.* 971), and Iasion was figured as a *protos heuretes* of agriculture (cf. Hellanicus, *FGrHist* 4 F135). The similarities to Eleusinian myth are obvious; Iasion was celebrated as the founder of the Samothracian mysteries ('about which it is lawful only for the initiated to hear' Diod. Sic. 5.48.4, cf. 51) and was also connected with the mysteries of the Great Mother. The Samothracian mysteries were actively supported by Ptolemy Philadelphos and Arsinoe, and so by implying that the mysteries have touched the world even of this goatherd, T. may be complimenting real or potential patrons, cf. Fantuzzi (1995b) 26–7. Something similar may be true of the allusion to Aphrodite and Adonis, cf. Idyll 15. In the goatherd's eyes, Iasion (even the Homeric figure) is lucky, because Demeter 'yielded to passion for him' (*Od.* 5.126), and his violent death then spared him prolonged erotic suffering. The address to Amaryllis, φίλα γύναι, like ἐμίν in 49, points the paradox: the goatherd's suffering has brought him a perspective different to that of most people. More-over, his claim to privileged knowledge – as though *he* was an initiate – is held out as a final teasing bribe to Amaryllis; 'you (pl.) *profani* will never know' means 'people like you, Amaryllis'. It may well be true that Amaryllis will never (wish to) know the pleasures of making love with this goatherd in an open field; the verses thus play with a familiar representation of sex as a 'mystery'. βέβαλοι 'unin-itiated', 'profane' cf. 26.14, Hopkinson on Call. *h.* 6.3.

52–4 The goatherd's headache (cf. 11.70–1) may be part of the komastic pose (a hangover following too much drinking), and/or a symptom of love (cf. perhaps Eustath. Macr. 6.3).

52 οὐκέτ' ἀείδω: the 'formal' song is over, and the performance as a whole is drawing to a close; the present tense indicates 'no more singing for me', but ἀεισῶ deserves at least a place in the apparatus.

53 κεισεῦμαι δὲ πεσών 'I shall lie where I have fallen', i.e. 'I will not try to get up', cf. Ar. *Eccl.* 962 καταπεσών κείσομαι; the image is of a defeated competitor in the *palaistra*, rather than one who has merely been thrown, cf. Aesch. *Eum.* 590, Ar. *Clouds* 126, Meleager, *Anth. Pal.* 12.48.1 (= *HE* 4078) κεῖμαι· λὰξ ἐπίβαινε κατ' αὐχένος, ἄγριε δαῖμον κτλ., Di Marco (1995b). Plato lists 'sleeping in front of doors' among the ignominies of the lover (*Symp.* 183a6), and this – the so-called θυραυλία – is a standard ending to the literary *komos*, cf. F. O. Copley, *TAPA* 73 (1942) 101–7. **ὧδε** 'here'. The wolves which normally attack lame or abandoned kids will now attack the goatherd as he lies in despair, cut off from the society of such as Tityros.

54 μέλι: the jingle with μέλει may be bitterly reproachful.   βρόχθοιο 'throat'. The word is precious rather than vulgar, but the wish suggests an equation between Amaryllis and the wolves of 53; 'wolves' are standardly associated with prostitutes (cf. Lat. *lupa, lupanar*), so there may be a sting for Amaryllis here.

III Idyll 4

A conversation between Battos and Korydon, who is looking after Aigon's cows while the latter is away at the Olympic Games, about the state of the cattle, Aigon's athletic prowess and a deceased local beauty; Battos gets a thorn in his foot which Korydon extracts, and the end of the poem reverts to local gossip. Korydon seems to be a free hired labourer (1–2n.). As for Battos, 38–40 *may* imply that he is, or has been, a goatherd (cf. n. ad loc.); he is, however, not up with the latest local gossip (1–2) and 56–7 perhaps suggest that he is not as much of a countryman as Korydon; in 26–8 and 38–40 he produces mildly parodic versions of 'bucolic' song, and in 21–2 shows some interest in wider issues. The contrast between the two characters has something in common with that between the urban Simichidas and the rustic Lykidas in Idyll 7 (the jesting, the conversational strategies etc.), but in keeping with the mimetic, rather than narrative, structure, neither character is 'explained' in any depth.

As in Idyll 5, the scene is set in southern Italy, near Kroton at the western entrance to the Gulf of Tarentum. Why T. set these two poems in southern Italy is unclear; it is not impossible that he associated such rustic meetings with a particularly localised tradition of poetic *agon* (cf. Intro. Section 2). Although Idyll 5 is far more agonistic than Idyll 4, and contains an explicit song contest, Idyll 4 also explores the dynamics of conversation and in 26–43 (at least) offers a kind of exchange of song. Battos constantly jests at the expense of Korydon and others, whereas Korydon is a conversational literalist who ignores (or is unaware of) irony, dealing rather in 'facts'. Put broadly, the poem moves from a series of exploratory agonistic gambits by Battos, which are parried by Korydon's literalism, to a

sense of equilibrium and harmony in the shared enjoyment of the
thought of a lustful old man; to this extent the movement of the
poem is closer to Idyll 6 than to Idyll 5, despite the formal similarities between the endings of the two 'Italian poems'. The matching triplets of the central section reinforce the sense of an *agon*, even
without the formal structure and 'rules' of Idyll 5. As with the written record of any (real or imagined) conversation, there is often
room for doubt about tone and implication, and this is in part responsible for the very different interpretations which this poem has
prompted; a recognition of the open-endedness of conversation and
the importance of voice and gesture is written into the mimetic tex-
ture of the poem.

Formally, Idyll 4 is loosely structured into four roughly equal sections followed by a briefer coda: 1–14, Aigon and his cows (14 lines),
15–28 the state of the cattle (14 lines), 29–43 song and Amaryllis
(15 lines), 44–57 cows and a thorn (14 lines), 58–63 sex on the farm
(6 lines), cf. Van Sickle (1970) 74. The sections are also distinguished
by form: the regularity of 1–14 (stichomythia) and 15–28 (a couplet
followed by four triplets) gives way to a greater diversity, but is
restored by a final series of couplets marking the harmonious close
of the poem. This structure is neither rigid nor strongly marked –
thus, for example, 26–8 belong both with the theme of the cattle
and with the following section of song – but is one of a number of
formal features which emphasise the poem as a *mimesis*. We are
offered a 'realistic' conversation in hexameters, whose artifice is
emphasised by patterns of stichomythia and matching couplets and
triplets, and a language replete with echoes of Homer and the high
style of traditional poetry, and perhaps also of contemporary élite
poetry (35–7n.). The scene in which Battos is pricked by a thorn
directs our attention to contemporary art (50–7 n.) as a means of
displaying the stylisation of this *mimesis*. The very detail of the references to local people and places, the 'effects of the real', thus both
creates and works against the 'mimetic realism' of the bucolic world.

Thematically, that world is constructed by opposition. The world
of Battos and Korydon is *not* the world of Homer, nor the world of
the great pan-Hellenic festivals and the poetry associated with them.
On the other hand, the bucolic world only exists by comparison with
this 'other' world; Milon and probably Aigon (1–2n.) have names

which evoke figures of Kroton's legendary past, because the bucolic present replays and is measured against that past. 'As we progress from Herakles to Aigon to Korydon ... we are continually confronted with diminished versions of what we have left behind' (Haber (1994) 24). In particular, the poem rewrites the central bucolic myth of Daphnis. Aigon's disappearance, a 'death' (5n.) caused by an evil *eros* (27), threatens the existence of the bucolic world: his cows do not eat, and music, symbolised by the syrinx, is abandoned (28, cf. 1.1–3n., 1.128–30). Talking and singing (26–8n.) about the disappearance of Aigon ὁ βουκόλος (37) repeats in a different mimetic register the central bucolic act of commemoration. Aigon's feats have indeed already passed into song (33–7); if *he* has not literally died, 'Amaryllis', the absent beloved at the heart of bucolic, has. The promise never to forget her (38–9) is a promise for the continuation of 'bucolic' song, just as the rhapsode promises to 'remember and not forget' the subject of his song (*h. Ap.* 1, cf. 1.143–5n.).

During the late fourth and early third centuries Kroton was involved in almost constant warfare, and was sacked by the people of Rhegion during Rome's wars with Pyrrhus in the 270s; the city was depopulated (cf. Livy 24.3.1–2) and never recovered. It is tempting to associate this poem's concern with the heroic past of the city, and more generally with the present as an echo of the past sounding in a different register, with these catastrophic events (cf. Barigazzi (1974) 309–11), but this is not strictly necessary. The theme of athletics is naturally connected with Kroton (6n.), and we cannot assume that political and demographic changes looked as stark then as they do to us with our very fragmentary hindsight.

Title. Very variously given in MSS and Σ: Νομεῖς or Νομεῖς Βάττος καὶ Κορύδων are perhaps the best attested. R. W. Daniel, *ZPE* 27 (1977) 82–3, suggests that one transmitted title, Φιλαλήθης (i.e., presumably, Battos, though Meillier (1989) understands Korydon), is an error for Φιλαθλητής (i.e. Aigon).

Modern discussions. Barigazzi (1974); Giangrande (1980) 97–105; Gutzwiller (1991) 147–57; Haber (1994) 20–5; Lawall (1967) 42–51; Meillier (1989); Ott (1969) 43–56; Sanchez-Wildberger (1955) 41–8; Segal (1981) 85–109; Van Sickle (1969); Vox (1985); Walker (1980) 48–53.

1–2 > *Ecl.* 3.1–2. The abrupt opening question, like the *in medias res* opening of a Platonic dialogue, is in the tradition of the mime, cf. Herodas 5.1 λέγε μοι σύ, Γαστρων, ἤδ' ὑπερκορὴς οὕτω κτλ. Such an opening shuts off the temptation to construct our own narrative beyond the 'facts' of the poem (Where does Battos come from? Why is he ignorant of local events? etc.); at the centre of the poem will lie the narrative of Aigon, and Battos' ignorance is necessary to prompt the telling of that tale. Battos knows, however, that the cattle cannot belong to Korydon himself; the latter is, therefore, probably a poor but free man.   **Κορύδων** 'Mr Lark'; both Κόρυδος and Κορυδαλλός are attested as names and nicknames (cf. Arnott (1996) 166–7). That we do not learn Battos' name until 41 may be due to a wish to avoid too stylised or agonistic an opening (contrast 5.1–4). **Φιλώνδα:** genitive, cf. 7.75n. The name occurs also at 5.114 (also S. Italy) and is attested on Euboea and Rhodes (*LGPN* I s.v.). **Αἴγωνος:** in this context Αἴγων, attested both in Athens and the Aegean (*LGPN* I–II s.v.), suggests 'Mr Goat'. An Aigon from Kroton is named as a follower of Pythagoras at Iambl. *Vit. Pyth.* 267 (p. 143 Deubner); as with Milon (6n.), therefore, T. may have a chosen a name with local associations as part of the sense of the present re-creating the past, cf. above, p. 131.   **βόσκεν:** cf. 1.14n.

3 > *Ecl.* 3.5–6. 'I imagine you find some way to milk them all secretly in the evening'; the remark seems more like a jest than an attempt 'to provoke a quarrel by accusing Korydon of theft' (Gutzwiller (1991) 148).   **ψε** for σφε occurs also at 15.80 (so *P. Hamb.* 201) in the mouth of a Syracusan resident in Alexandria, and Sophron fr. 94 Kaibel, whence the grammatical tradition regarded it as 'Syracusan'; it is, however, also attested on Crete (Buck (1955) 74, 98), cf. Hunter (1996b) 153–4.   **τὰ ποθέσπερα:** the singular is more usual with such neuter accusatives, cf. 1.15, 7.21, 10.48. **ἀμέλγες:** cf. 1.3n. In 46, however, ἐσακούεις is unanimously transmitted.

4 ἀλλ' 'No, for ...'   **ὁ γέρων:** Σ suggests that this is the absent Aigon's father, cf. 58–63n., *Ecl.* 3.33–4 *est mihi namque domi pater, est iniusta nouerca,* | *bisque die numerant ambo pecus, alter et haedos*; the lack of specificity is mimetic of colloquial conversation.

5 αὐτὸς ... ὁ βουκόλος 'their master ... the cowherd', cf. 12, LSJ s.v. αὐτός I 1.   **ἄφαντος ... ὤιχετο:** the tone is mockingly grand, cf., e.g., Aesch. *Ag.* 657 ὤιχοντ' ἄφαντοι. The suggestion of death, however, introduces the theme of Aigon as a 'Daphnis' who has left the countryside, cf. Intro. above, 12–14n. ἄφαντος is common in high lyric and tragedy, but not found in prose until very late.

6 The last two words echo the close of 5; the effect is perhaps to mark the significance of the news he has to impart, rather than to tease Battos for his ignorance.   **Ἀλφεόν:** the river of Olympia, frequently used in poetry to denote Olympia itself.   **Μίλων:** the name of a (rather macho) character in Idyll 10 and well attested at all periods, but here it must recall Milon, the famous sixth-century wrestler who won 31 victories at pan-Hellenic games, including six Olympic victories, and was closely associated with Kroton and the Pythagorean circle, cf. Strabo 6.1.12, Paus. 6.14.5, *RE* xv 1672–6, H. A. Harris, *Greek athletes and athletics* (London 1964) 110–13. The precise relationship between his latter-day namesake and Aigon is left unspecified: it is often assumed that Milon was Aigon's trainer, but nothing in the poem justifies this.

7 'And when did he [Aigon] ever behold oil?', implying not only that, to Battos' knowledge, Aigon has never had any interest in athletics, but also that Aigon would be quite out of his depth in the sophisticated world of athletics and the gymnasia (cf. 2.77–80). High-flown language (ἐν ὀφθαλμοῖσιν ὁρᾶν is a common Homeric locution) mocks Aigon's pretentiousness in departing for the primary athletic festival of the Greek world.   **ὀπώπει:** cf. 11.1n.

8 Herakles was not only the greatest Greek athletic hero, but also the legendary founder of Kroton (*RE* xi 2020).   **βίαν καὶ κάρτος:** Korydon defends Aigon with a Homeric phrase of his own (*Od.* 4.415, 13.143, 18.139), used perhaps more in naïve respect than mockery. The Ionic and Homeric βίην might tip the tone towards the latter, but decision is very difficult.   **ἐρίσδεν:** cf. 1.14n.

9 For Polydeukes, the divine boxer without peer (cf. 22.2–3), and Herakles together in a 'serious' epinician, cf. Simonides, *PMG* 509.   **ἁ μάτηρ** 'my mother'.

10 σκαπάναν 'pick-axe' or 'shovel'. Σ explains that athletes used digging as a form of training to increase upper-body strength, as modern athletes lift weights.   **τουτόθε** 'from here'.   **μᾶλα:** cf. 1.109–10n. The sheep are Aigon's 'rations' for his absence from the farm. Athletes, like Herakles, were traditionally associated with a

meat diet and were a standard object of satire for their gluttony, cf.
34n., Ath. 10 412d–414d, Hunter (1983a) 92. Korydon may not
intend his image of Aigon setting off with pick-axe and twenty sheep
to be amusing, but to Battos it is pure madness (cf. 11).

11 'Milon might also persuade the wolves to go crazy at once.'
Taking 20 sheep away from the flock produces the same result as
would be achieved by crazed wolves, or perhaps the sense is that
leaving the animals in Korydon's care is an open invitation to the
wolves (cf. 13). λυσσῆν is normally used of rabid *dogs*, and Σ suggests
that the point is that if Milon can persuade Aigon to take up athletics, he could also produce a revolution in nature; one might, however, have expected a more improbable *adynaton* (1.132–6n.) than
crazed wolves, and the verse itself suggests, perhaps rightly, an etymological link between λύκος and λυσσᾶν. According to a story not
certainly attested before Strabo 6.1.12, the famous Milon (6n.) was in
fact killed by wolves (or dogs) in a wood, and the present line could
be a malicious wish that a like fate befall his namesake 'straightaway', cf. Fantuzzi (1998a).

12–14 Korydon interprets the lowing of the cattle as πόθος for
their absent master, in a gesture towards the 'pathetic fallacy' (1.71–
5n.). Aigon is a ridiculous Daphnis, whose absence (5n.) is mourned
by a bovine threnody, cf. *EB* 23–4 (after Bion's death) αἱ βόες αἱ
ποτὶ ταύροις | πλαζόμεναι γοάοντι καὶ οὐκ ἐθέλοντι νέμεσθαι, *Ecl.*
5.24–6. Korydon assimilates the situation to human *eros*: the heifers
waste away in longing for the absent male, as human lovers stop eating, grow thin (15–16n.), and express their longing in song (cf. Idylls
3 and 11). Subsequent verses and the pointed ambiguity of 13 – is the
βουκόλος Aigon or Korydon? – invite us rather to interpret the cattle's lowing as a sign of hunger.

12 αὐτόν 'their master', cf. 5n.

13 δείλαιαί γ' αὗται: the better attested δ' would be a case of δέ
in 'passionate or lively exclamation, where no connexion appears to
be required' (Denniston 172).

15–16 > *Ecl.* 3.100–2. The change from single-line stichomythia is
marked by the delay of τὠστία to the start of 16 ('enjambment').
τὠστία: the heifer's condition resembles that of the lovesick
Simaitha, 2.89–90 αὐτὰ δὲ λοιπά | ὀστί' ἔτ' ἦς καὶ δέρμα.
πρῶκας 'dew-drops'; that this was the sole element in a cicada's diet
is a belief attested as early as Hes. *Aspis* 393–5 and repeated con-

stantly by both poets (cf. *Ecl.* 5.77) and technical writers, cf. Arist. *HA* 4 532b13, 5 556b16, Davies–Kathirithamby 123–4. Cicadas notoriously lacked physical strength (cf. *Il.* 3.151) and their 'skeletons', like those of the cattle in Battos' jest, seem visible to the naked eye. Perhaps Battos jokes that the 'grieving' cattle risk a fate similar to Plato's cicada-men (*Phaedrus* 259c1–2, above, p. 14).

17–19 Korydon takes Battos' jest seriously: he in fact takes good care to provide excellent fodder. The adjectives in 18, 'a lovely bundle of soft grass', reflect Korydon's view (or hope) of the calf's pleasure, much as some people today talk to babies, cats and dogs; there is a similar effect in 24–5.   **οὐ Δᾶν:** cf. 6.21–2, 7.39 nn. **ἀλλ' ὅκα μὲν ... ἄλλοκα δέ:** cf. 1.36–7n.   **Αἰσάροιο:** the Aisaros (modern Esaro) flowed into the sea at Kroton, cf. Strabo 6.1.12, Ovid, *Met.* 15.53–9.   **Λάτυμνον:** said by Σ to be a mountain near Kroton, but there is no other evidence.

20 > *Ecl.* 3.100.   **πυρρίχος:** cf. 7.132n.

20–2 'May Lampriadas' people be allotted such [a beast] when the demesmen sacrifice to Hera! That deme's a bad lot.' A skinny bull would (presumably) fail to please Hera and provide a less than satisfactory feast after the sacrifice; the practice of distributing sacrificial animals among the sacrificers by lot is attested from all over the Greek world. τοὶ δαμόται may be in apposition to τοὶ τῶ Λαμπριάδα, 'Lampriadas' people, the [?my] demesmen, when ...', but the reference to the lot and the rhythm of the sentence favour taking τοὶ δαμόται inside the temporal clause. Lampriadas is probably the eponymous hero of a local deme, though nothing else is known about him and the name is otherwise unattested (Lamprias is very common). Others understand 'the sons of Lampriadas', who would then be chief figures in their deme. It is significant that, though ignorant of local affairs, Battos is concerned with the 'politics' of sacrifice at a communal level.

22 Ἥραι: Hera Lakinia (32–3n.), the greatest goddess of Magna Graecia.   **κακοχράσμων** does not occur elsewhere and the exact nuance is unclear; there is, however, no obvious reason to assume corruption. (For κακοφράσμων cf. P. Radici Colace, *GIF* 4 (1973) 65–6.)

23–4 Korydon ignores Battos' outburst and again (17–19n.) answers the 'serious' charge of not feeding the cattle correctly. **Στομάλιμνον** 'the salt-lagoon', probably to be conceived as a particular place (hence the capital letter). Elsewhere the standard form is στομαλίμνη.   **τὰ Φύσκω:** Σ identify Physkos as a mountain. The name is suitable (φύσκων is 'pot-bellied'), but the phrase would be hard to understand. It seems more likely that Physkos is a personal name (cf. *LGPN* II s.v.), 'to Physkos' territory'. The obscurity of the reference is a device of 'mimetic realism'.   **Νήαιθον:** a river north of Kroton (Strabo 6.1.12), probably the Neto which flows into the sea some 15 km north of the site.   **καλὰ πάντα:** cf. 17–19n.

25 Cf. 13.45n. αἰγίπυρος is not securely identified, cf. Lembach (1970) 55–6; Σ claims that it is spiny. For κνύζα 'fleabane' cf. 7.67–8n. μελίτεια (Lembach (1970) 52–4) is also unidentified, though the 'honeyed' name sits well with the epithet 'sweet-smelling'; at 5.130 it is good food for sheep.

26–8 Battos breaks into a kind of lament for the cattle and for the 'bucolic world' in general. The tone is at least mock-tragic ('the cows will pass to Hades'), as it is in the corresponding 38–40; the opening spondees of 26 signal the mourning. Though the cows 'long for' him (12–14n.), Aigon has 'fallen in love' with the fashion for (καὶ τύ) athletics.

26 τάλαν: cf. 1.82–3n.

27 ὅκα is here causal, cf. LSJ s.v. ὅτε β.

28 ἐπάξα: 2nd person singular aorist middle. This ending (< -αο) is well attested in the grammatical tradition (cf. Σ, *Et. Mag.* 579.20–2 Gaisford), though it may be hyper-Doric, cf. Dover xxxiv, Hopkinson (1984) 49. ἔπαξας occurs, presumably as a correction, in some late MSS.

29 οὐ Νύμφας; cf. 6.22n. An oath by the Nymphs is appropriate as they are the patrons of rural song, cf. 7.91–2, 148nn.   **Πῖσαν:** Pisa was an old name for the site of Olympia, and is frequently used to denote it.

30 ἐμοί, only here in the bucolics, is presumably preferred to ἐμίν for euphony.   **τις ... μελικτάς** 'something of a singer'. For the link between syrinx-playing and song cf. 7.27–31n.

31 Glauke was a Chian citharode, associated in anecdote with Ptolemy Philadelphos, and renowned for the lasciviousness of her tunes, cf. Hedylus, *HE* 1883 Γλαύκης μεμεθυσμένα παίγνια Μουσέων, Plut. *Mor.* 397a, *RE* VII 1396–7. Even if her tunes were indeed very popular all over the Mediterranean, we are presumably to understand that she is at most just a name to Korydon, used to bolster his claim to musicianship. Glauke's link to Ptolemy suggests a possible patronage context for these verses – even illiterate Italians have heard of one of Philadelphos' favourites. This amusing improbability was perhaps reinforced in the 'performance' of Idyll 4 by gestures and 'play-acting' at this point. Pyrrhos is said by Σ to have been a lyric poet from Erythrae in Ionia or Lesbos, but is otherwise unknown; Meineke suggested an identification with a Milesian κιναιδολόγος called Pyres or Pyrrhos (Ath. 14 620e, *Suda* σ 871), and a reference to such lascivious verse would fit the humour here.   ἀγκρούομαι 'I strike up', cf. 10.22 ἀμβάλευ.

32–7 Korydon now gives more details of his repertory, including a summary of a comic 'epinician' for the athletic Aigon; T. here evokes a tradition of popular song which surfaces only occasionally in high literature, cf. M. Vetta, *RFIC* 112 (1984) 344–5. It may be that we are to imagine this as Korydon's own composition, but this is not necessary; echoes of Callimachus, cf. 35–7n., would make the effect particularly amusing. Less probable is to regard all of 32–7 (with 32 suitably emended) as a verbatim quotation.

32–3 'I sing the praises of Kroton – "A beautiful city is Zakynthos and ..." – the Lakinian shrine that faces the dawn ...' Korydon interrupts his summary to offer proof of what he is saying in the form of the opening words of the song (38–9n.), which was in the form of a priamel, i.e. 'Zakynthos is lovely and Y is lovely and Z is lovely, but Kroton, the home of Aigon, is loveliest', cf. Hor. *C.* 1.7, Virg. *Georg.* 2.136–9. Text and interpretation are, however, uncertain; Edmonds proposed καλὰν πόλιν ἆτε Ζάκυνθον, '[Kroton] a lovely city like Zakynthos'.   ἅ τε Ζάκυνθος: τε is not lengthened before Ζάκυνθος, in imitation of Homeric practice (cf. *Od.* 1.246, *Il.* 2.634, W. F. Wyatt, *Metrical lengthening in Homer* (Rome 1969) 183 n. 1); this licence is appropriate in a snatch of song. The beauty of the town of Zakynthos is praised by Pliny, *NH* 4.54.   τὸ ποταῶιον τὸ Λακίνιον: the great temple of Hera which stood on the headland of Lakinion, south-east of Kroton, commanding the entrance to the Gulf of Tarentum; the headland is now Capo Colonna, from the one surviving column, cf. R. Stillwell (ed.), *The Princeton encyclopedia of classical sites* (Princeton 1976) s.v. Kroton. Livy 24.3.3–7 tells of sacred cattle and 'miracles' associated with this rich shrine. Korydon's song gives an account of a comic *miraculum* which took place there.

34 This act of gluttony, and the feat of strength in 35–7, should be imagined within the context of the celebrated athletic festivals at Kroton (cf. Ath. 12 522c); such festivals were a standard site for displays of physical and intellectual prowess. The famous Milon was reported to have carried a bull on his shoulders around the stadium at Olympia and then eaten the whole animal in a single day (Ath. 10 412e–f); T.'s contemporary Alexander Aetolus mentioned an ox-eating contest between Milon and Titormos of Aetolia (fr. 11 Powell). **μόνος:** in the standard language of praise, μόνος signals the uniqueness of the achievement (cf. 38, Barrett on Eur. *Hipp.* 1281, Hunter (1983a) 96); here there is an amusing perversion of the motif – Aigon ate 'all alone'.

35–7 Similar feats of strength are recorded for other athletes: Astyanax of Miletos (Σ here), Milon (34n.), and Titormos, who won even Milon's admiration (Aelian, *VH* 12.22). Of particular interest is the story of how Theseus, son of Aigeus (cf. Aigon), captured the bull of Marathon and dragged it back alive to Athens. Callimachus' account in the *Hekale* has suggestive points of contact with these verses, cf. fr. 260 (= 69 Hollis). 4 μακρὸν ἄυσε, 9 ζωὸν ἄγων τὸν ταῦρον, 14–15 αἱ δὲ γυναῖκες | . . . στόρνῃσιν ἀνέστεφον. The celebration for Theseus takes place in the countryside, and may be seen as the heroic model for Aigon's act. There are no serious chronological objections to echoes of the *Hekale*, but the matter must remain open.

35 τὸν ταῦρον 'the bull [in the well-known story]'.

35–6 πιάξας | τᾶς ὁπλᾶς 'squeezing [i.e. grasping tightly] by the hoof'. πιάζειν is Doric for πιέζειν, cf. Molinos Tejada 109–11. **Ἀμαρυλλίδι:** cf. 3.1n. Aigon offers the bull as a 'love-token', as the goatherd offered a rich supply of apples to another Amaryllis in Idyll 3.

37 μακρὸν ἀνάυσαν: μακρὸν ἀύσας is a standard Homeric verse-ending, but form and position are here altered.   **ἐξεγέλασσεν:** cf. 7.42n.

38–40 Battos matches Korydon's song with a lament for the dead Amaryllis, an αἰπολικόν to match Korydon's βουκολικόν. It is not necessary to see here serious sentiment and pathos; Battos has no more necessary emotional attachment to its subject than he has in 26–8, cf. further 44n. There is obvious humour in this lament, but it may be debated whether we are to see a deliberate parody by

Battos of 'rustic song' or a sign that Battos is no countryman (so S. Lattimore, *GRBS* 14 (1973) 323–4). Those who see 'genuine sentiment' here may feel that Battos' hostility to Aigon is now revealed as that of a rival suitor (so Hutchinson (1988) 168).

38–9 Cf. 3.6. It is tempting to see a self-quotation by T.: Battos is 'playing the goatherd', and rustic song is amusingly figured as the opening words of one of T.'s own αἰπολικά.   **σέθεν:** only here in the genuine bucolics, presumably as a mark of (mock) high-style in a song. τεῦς would produce a breach of 'Naeke's Law' (1.130n.), but T. could doubtless have found other ways to avoid that.   **οὐδὲ ... | λασευμεσθ':** the language of epitaphs, cf. *CEG* 2.631.3–4 οὔποτ' ἐπαίνου | [λησό]μεθ'· ἦ μάλα γὰρ [σὴν φ]ύσιν ἠγασάμην κτλ. Death is not common in bucolic poetry, unless it is of figures from the mythical past. The plural λασεύμεσθ' can be interpreted strictly, 'we who remember you'; there is no contradiction with the following ἐμίν.

39 'As dear to me as are my goats, so [dear] [3.40–2n.] were you [when your light was] extinguished.' The metaphor of 'light and life' is a common one (cf. Xen. *Cyr.* 5.4.30, Leonidas, *Anth. Pal.* 7.295.7–8 (= *HE* 2080–1) etc.), but it has a particular appropriateness for 'Miss Sparkle', cf. 3.1–2n.

40 Battos strikes a 'tragic' pose, cf. Alciphron 3.13.1 (a parasite) ὦ δαῖμον, ὅς με κεκλήρωσαι καὶ εἴληχας, ὡς πονηρὸς εἶ κτλ. (= *Adesp. Trag.* 17 K–S).   **τῶ σκληρῶ ... δαίμονος:** exclamatory genitive, cf. 10.40, K–G I 389.   **λελόγχει:** cf. 11.1n.

41–3 Korydon takes Battos' song at face value, i.e. he does not understand poetic 'impersonation'; *his* poem, after all, was about 'real' events. These verses might themselves be understood as a poem of consolation, but it seems more likely that we have now reverted to the 'spoken' mode. The consolation is predictably banal, cf. Soph. *El.* 173–8, 916–19, Hor. *C.* 2.10.13–20, Tib. 2.6.19–20 *credula uitam | spes fouet et fore cras semper ait melius*; for the importance of ἐλπίς cf. also Theognis 1135–50, Lyc. *Leocr.* 60. Line 42 is singularly clumsy in the context of Amaryllis' death.

41 θαρσεῖν χρή: the idea is of course ubiquitous in consolation, but the injunction to mourners to 'cheer up' became very common on tombstones (cf. Lattimore (1962) 253), and such a resonance suits the context here.   **Βάττε:** the name ('Stammerer') is particularly associated with Cyrene (cf. Callimachus, 'son of Battos'), but is found elsewhere also (*LGPN* I s.v.), cf. further 50–4n.

42 ἀνέλπιστοι: for the epitaphic theme of the utter desolation of death cf. Lattimore (1962) 74–82.

44 θαρσέω: Battos' laconic response may signal a genuine reaction to Korydon's consolation, but it may also be an ironic acknowledgement of what has always been obvious, except to Korydon, cf. 38–40n. Ott (1969) 46 takes the first view, and suggests that the quick change of subject is a strategy by Battos to regain the conversational initiative, cf. 45n.   **βάλλε** 'drive', perhaps with the implication that this will be accomplished by throwing things at the calves, cf. Eur. *Cycl.* 51 ὠή, ῥίψω πέτρον τάχα σου, *Ecl.* 3.96 *reice.*   **τᾶς ... ἐλαίας:** collective singular, 'the olive-trees'.

45 Wilamowitz divided this verse between speakers after δύσσοα, i.e. at the bucolic diaeresis, but there are other possibilities, of which the most attractive is division after θαρσέω in 44, with βάλλε addressed by Korydon to a nameless helper or to no one in particular. The threat to the cows and knowledge of their names identify Korydon as the speaker of 45b–9, but 44–5a are more uncertain. Earlier editors give all of 44–5 to Battos, but σιτθ' ὁ Λέπαργος certainly sounds like Korydon. With any of these arrangements, this will be the only example of verse-splitting (*antilabe*) in the poem; so too, Idylls 5 and 10 have only one example each (5.66, 10.15). The poetic effect is quite different from that of Idylls 14 and 15 where *antilabe* is common: the solitary example is a stylised marker of *mimesis* and of 'the tension between the rustic illusion and the literary self-consciousness' (Segal (1981) 99).   **δύσσοα:** cf. 3.24n.   **σίτθ':** σίττα presumably represents a whistling sound, cf. 5.3, but with the same meaning as our 'hey!'   **ὁ Λέπαργος:** for the article with an injunction cf. 1.151–2n. λέπαργος, 'with white coat', is in origin an adjective, but here seems to be the name of a calf. It occurs as the name of a bull in Call. fr. 24 (= 26 Massimilla), the story from *Aitia* 1 of Herakles and Theiodamas; that fragment also has the motif of a thorn-prick in the foot and the verb ἐξεγέλασσεν (line 13, cf. 37 above), and some connection between these passages is not improbable, cf. A. Barigazzi, *Prometheus* 2 (1976) 237–8.

46 σίττ' ὦ Κυμαίθα: cf. Eur. *Cycl.* 52 ὕπαγ' ὦ ὕπαγ' ὦ κεράστα κτλ. (with Seaford's note), Sophron fr. 10 Kaibel φέρ' ὦ τὸν δρίφον;

in such cases a distinction between vocative ὦ and exclamatory ὤ is largely academic. If ὦ of the Sophron papyrus is correct, σίτθ' ὦ may be required (cf. Latte (1968) 529); σίτθ' ἁ looks like a correction designed to bring this verse into line with the preceding. For Kymaitha cf. 1.151–2n.; of the various guesses in Σ, a link with κυεῖν seems the most probable.   ἐσακούεις: cf. 3n.

47 κακὸν τέλος most obviously suggests death, cf. θανάτοιο κακὸν τέλος at *Od.* 24.124, but this would be the emptiest of threats, as Korydon's powerlessness in the matter of the cattle has already been stressed (1–4). The phrase may, however, merely indicate a beating, cf. 49, Ar. *Frogs* 552 κακὸν ἥκει τινι, Men. *Perik.* 398–9 μέγα τί σοι κακὸν | δώσω, Plaut. *Persa* 816–17 *caue sis me attigas, ne tibi hoc scipione | malum magnum dem.*

49 λαγωβόλον: cf. 7.19n.   **πάταξα:** cf. 11.55n. The subjunctive πατάξω (in most MSS) is preferred by some editors.

50–7 Battos gets a thorn in his foot and Korydon removes it. The motif is natural in poetry set in the countryside, cf. 10.3–4, but some connection with a famous motif of Greek sculpture seems certain. Single figures extracting thorns from their feet are known in various versions, the most famous being a Roman bronze of (probably) the first century, now in the Palazzo dei Conservatori, cf. R. R. R. Smith, *Hellenistic sculpture* (London 1991) 136–7 with figs. 171–2, W. Fuchs, *Der Dornauszieher* (Bremen 1958). A group of Pan attending to the foot of an injured satyr is also known in more than one copy, cf. M. Bieber, *The sculpture of the Hellenistic age* (2nd ed., New York 1961) 148, Pollitt (1986) fig. 43, and it is likely enough that the motif always had a 'pastoral' connection (cf. Himmelmann (1980) 97–8, Nicosia (1968) 90–2). This motif cannot with certainty be traced in Greek art as early as T., though it occurs in an Egyptian tomb painting of the second millenium BC (cf. E. Strouhal, *Life in ancient Egypt* (Cambridge 1992) fig. 28), but the likelihood that T. here directs his readers' attention to contemporary art is strong, cf. 24.26–33 (Herakles and the snakes); θᾶσαι (50) will act as a cue to this 'visual allusion' (cf. *Epigr.* 18 θᾶσαι τὸν ἀνδριάντα τοῦτον κτλ.). This is part of the poem's concern with the nature of bucolic *mimesis* (above, p. 130), and with the relation between 'reality' and the stylisations of literature; art is used as a suggestive analogue for the process involved. So too, Battos' foolish 'gaping' at the heifer (53) inscribes in the text a familiar reaction to the wonders of art (cf. 15.78–86, Herodas 4.20–78, Hunter (1996a) 117–19).

50 πὸτ τῶ Διός: cf. 11.1n.

51 ἐπάταξ' picks up πάταξα from 49. **ὥς:** exclamatory. **βαθεῖαι** 'thick-set', 'dense'.

52 τάτρακτυλλίδες: i.e. ταὶ ἀτρακ., a kind of thistle described by Thphr. *HP* 6.4.6: it was also called φόνος and had a bad smell. An identification with *Carthamus lanatus*, 'an orange-flowered annual thistle ... erect up to 60 cm high ... unpleasant-smelling, with reddish juice' (Polunin–Huxley 192) seems probable. **κακῶς ... ὄλοιτο:** the curse is high-flown, creating a pointed contrast with the ordinariness of its object.

53 Battos holds out his foot to Korydon. **χασμεύμενος** 'gaping'. For the form in -έομαι rather than -άομαι cf. 3.18n. There is no suggestion in the verb that Battos has actually been helping Korydon to round up the cows; rather he has been watching events without looking where he was putting his feet. Lawall (1967) 48–9 sees an erotic sense in the participle (cf. χάσκει at Anacreon, *PMG* 358.8): the thorn symbolises the *eros* he feels, but this *eros* is merely 'gross physicality'; cf. further 50–7, 58–63nn. **ἦ ῥά γε:** the text is uncertain.

54 ἔχω τέ νιν: the very rare postponement of τε (cf. Denniston 517) is indicative of Korydon's excitement.

55 Battos shows that the removal of the thorn has allowed him to recover his mood and strike another 'tragic' pose, this time involving humour at his own expense. The balanced verse, arranged around the rhyming ὀσσίχον ... ἁλίκον, has something of the flavour of a quotation or wise saw. For the 'paradox' cf. 19.5–8 (bees and Eros are tiny, but both cause big wounds). **ὀσσίχον** 'how small', cf. 7.132n.

56–7 Korydon now has a chance to tease Battos. We need not assume that Battos was so ignorant of the countryside that he did not know about thorns, or that herdsmen *never* went barefoot. Korydon repeats 'traditional wisdom', whose truth has just been demonstrated. He speaks to Battos like a mother warning a child, and it is indeed children who would be most likely to run around without any protection on their feet at all; the repetition 'to the mountain ... on the mountain ...' is structured like 'Don't walk alone through the

park. The park is full of bad men.'   νήλιπος 'barefoot', cf. 7.25–
6n.   Βάττε: it is hard to resist hearing a play with βάτος 'thorn',
cf. M. Paschalis, *RhM* 134 (1991) 205.   ῥάμνοι 'buckthorn', cf.
Thphr. *HP* 3.18.2, Lembach (1970) 77–8.   ἀσπάλαθοι are not
securely identified (?brambles), cf. Lembach (1970) 72–3.
κομόωντι: cf. 1.133n. The form combines an epic 'diektasis' with a
Doric personal ending, cf. Molinos Tejada 285–6.

58–63 Battos seeks to catch up on more local gossip. Σ59e identify
τὸ γερόντιον as Aigon's father, i.e. the γέρων of 4, and the reprise
of the opening verse in 58 supports the identification. More problematic is the identity of the 'dark-browed sweetie' of 59. It is normally assumed that she is human, but a farm animal is as likely, in
view of his choice of location for sex, the cattle-pen, and the final
comparison with satyrs and Pans, both famous for bestial practices.
If this is correct, the story of Pasiphae in *Ecl.* 6 will have a kind of
Theocritean precedent.

58 εἴπ' ἄγε μ', ὦ Κορύδων: cf. 1; the echo introduces the poem's
closure. The injunction is Homeric (*Il.* 9.673, 10.544), a style in
pointed contrast to the following γερόντιον and to the subject
matter.   μ' = μοι, cf. 7.19.   μύλλει 'milling', cf. Lat. *molere*,
permolere (Hor. *Sat.* 1.2.35); μυλ(λ)άς is given as a word for a prosti-
tute (Photios s.v., *Suda* μ 1403).

59 'that dark-browed [3.18n.] sweetie [3.7n.] for whom he once
had the itch'.   ἐκνίσθη is followed by a genitive, as with verbs of
desire and longing (cf. Legrand (1898) 292, K–G 1 351–2). The
'thorns' of desire (13.64–71n.) link this theme to the thorn-pulling
scene which has immediately preceded.

60 ἀκμάν γ' 'Yes, he's still at it.'   ὦ δείλαιε teases Battos for
his ignorance.

61 καί goes closely with what follows, 'at the very cattle-pen'; the
implication is that such activity would normally take place out in
the fields.   ἐνήργει 'was on the job', cf. Longus, *D&C* 3.18.4,
Alciphron 3.19.9 (transitive).

62 φιλοῖφα 'randy'; οἴφειν or οἰφεῖν is a synonym of βινεῖν.

62–3 'That kind is a close (ἐγγύθεν) rival of Satyrs or Pans with
their ugly shins.' This seems preferable to ἐρίσδεις continuing the
apostrophe, with τὸ γένος as an accusative of respect.   γένος: the
meaning is uncertain – the old man's 'family', or 'people like' the old

man, i.e. (?) old countrymen. The former is perhaps suggested by
ἐρίσδει picking up ἐρίσδεν in 8, cf. Stanzel (1995) 85.   **Πάνεσσι:**
plural Pans figure already in classical literature (Aesch. fr. 25b Radt,
Soph. fr. 136 Radt, Ar. *Eccl.* 1069); they are rustic *daimones*, spirits
'like Pan'. The ugliness of their shins presumably reflects the fact
that they have the straight, fleshless shins of a goat, but there is a
moral point as well: [Arist.] *Physiog.* 810a31–3 associates 'thin,
sinewy' shins with lustfulness (λαγνότης), and 812b13–14 associates
'hairy' shins with the same failing, 'on the model of he-goats', cf.
SPG I 358.5, 428.7.

IV Idyll 7

The narrator, Simichidas (21), recalls an occasion when he went
with two friends from Cos town into the countryside to join in the
harvest-festival of an old Coan family. On the way they meet a
goatherd called Lykidas who, Simichidas claims, enjoys the reputation of the best 'syrinx-player' in the countryside; Simichidas invites
him to an exchange of 'bucolic song'. Lykidas sings a song about his
passion for Ageanax, from which – during the course of the song –
he finds relief in listening to the stories of the mythical founders of
bucolic song, Daphnis and Komatas. In reply, Simichidas sings of
the passion of his friend Aratos for a boy called Philinos and he
urges him to abandon the pursuit. Lykidas then presents Simichidas
with his staff, 'as a guest-gift in the Muses', and parts company. The
narrator and his friends reach Phrasidamos' farm, where the celebration takes place in a marvellous *locus amoenus*.

First-person narratives of past events which, unlike Odysseus'
account of his travels, are not embedded in a wider context are rare
in Greek poetry. Archilochus' 'Cologne Epode' (*SLG* 478, cf. 120-1n.)
tells of a past seduction in the first person, but unfortunately the
opening is lost; centuries later, Ovid, *Amores* 1.5 uses a similar form
for a similar experience (cf. 156n.). The form seems more at home in
the 'lower' genres: some of Hipponax's poetry and the short narra-
tive of Catullus 10, *Varus me meus ad suos amores | uisum duxerat* etc.,
suggest this. If the narrating first person is not explained or embedded, then such poetry looks (auto-)biographical. Suggestive in
this regard are Horace's *Satires*, especially 1.5 and 1.9, two 'journey'

poems full of 'effects of the real' (names of contemporaries, place-names etc., casually mentioned as if familiar to the reader, cf. 7.1–11, E. Gowers, *PCPS* 39 (1993) 48–61); in neither poem is the narrator named, although 'embedding' within the book of the *Satires* must be taken into account.

Perhaps the closest Greek analogues for Idyll 7 are in Plato's dialogues. The *Lysis* begins: 'I was going from the Academy in the direction of the Lyceum by the road just beyond outside the city wall; when I was opposite the gate where the spring of Panops is located, I met Hippothales ... When Hippothales saw me approaching, he said, "Socrates, where have you come from and where are you going?".' Particularly striking is the similarity of the opening of Idyll 7 to the opening of the *Republic*: 'Yesterday I went down to Peiraeus with Glaukon the son of Ariston to pay my respects to the goddess ...'; that the narrator is called Socrates emerges a paragraph and a half later when Polemarchos addresses him by name (cf. the technique of the *Lysis*). In both of these openings there is the same concern with 'realistic' detail as in Horace's *Satires* and Idyll 7. The similarity between Plato and T. may be due in part to a shared debt to the mimes of Sophron (so Weingarth (1967) 77), and T. may even wish to appropriate Plato, who visited Syracuse, as a 'Sicilian' writer.

It is, however, the *Phaedrus* which seems closest to Idyll 7: a walk in the countryside in the heat of the day and an exchange of performances designed to win over a beautiful boy make that dialogue more specifically important for Idyll 7 than its place in the generic 'pastoral' tradition would indicate (cf. Intro. Section 3). The *Phaedrus* is a purely mimetic–dramatic dialogue without narrative frame; its mode is that of Idylls 1, 4, 5 and 10. For the rewriting of the *Phaedrus* in Idyll 7, however, T. has chosen a different, but equally Platonic, mode, namely that of the *Lysis* and the *Republic*; such virtuosity is typical of Hellenistic exploitation of the literary heritage. Whereas in the *Phaedrus* it is the city-dwelling Socrates who has 'ironic' mastery of the conversation, in Idyll 7 it is the rustic Lykidas who plays the 'Socratic' rôle; it is as though the *Phaedrus* has been transposed into a narrative related by Phaedrus. Secondly, the *Phaedrus* shows that responding epideictic performances are no substitute for the serious business of dialectic philosophy; 'bucolic', however, whether

expressed through 'capping' couplets (Idyll 5), prompt and response
(Idyll 6), or juxtaposed *epideixeis* (Idyll 7), is concerned not with intellectual progress (as the Platonic Socrates represents it), but with the
pursuit of aesthetic and emotional pleasure and ἀσυχία (cf. 1.1n.).

The relationship between T., 'the author', and Simichidas the
narrator has since antiquity been thought to be more complex than
that between Plato and Socrates. This is not a version of the (pointless) question 'Does Idyll 7 describe a real experience?', but relates
to how we are to understand the poem. It is not impossible that, just
as Asclepiades was 'Sikelidas' (40n.), so T. was known as 'Simichidas'
(for reasons we do not know), and it is just unhappy chance that we
have no other evidence for it. On the other hand, when reading, or
listening to a recitation (by T. himself?), 'Simichidas ...' in 21 could
have caused real surprise, and in this the Theocritean pattern would
differ from the Platonic. About Simichidas at the time of the festival
we learn that he is relatively young (44), a poet (37–41) and indeed
by his own account already a 'bucolic' poet (30–1, 91–5); he is
clearly very familiar with Cos and perhaps resident in Cos town (2).
τὸν ξεῖνον ... μευ in 119 might suggest that he comes from somewhere other than Aratos' home (cf. 28.6 about Nikias of Miletos);
unfortunately, Simichidas' song gives no clue to Aratos' origin,
although both he and Philinos bear names very common on Cos
(105n.). All suggested ancient connections between T. and Cos probably derive from interpretations of Idyll 7, but at least there is nothing which forbids *some kind of* identification between Simichidas and
T., and some things positively encourage us to put the two together.
Idyll 6 is addressed to an Aratos (below, p. 243), and the temptation
to identify the two characters of this name is obviously strong, thus
giving a link between the poetry of 'Simichidas' and the poetry of T.
If therefore 'Simichidas' was a name specially created for Idyll 7,
then 'Simichidas both is and is not T.' (Bowie (1985) 68); similarly,
the setting of the poem both is and is not Cos, i.e. there is *both* a
reconstructable and 'real' geography *and* a geography of the mind
and the mythic and literary tradition, just as there are real people
(T.'s patrons in whose honour the poem is written) and the fictitious
creations of song. 'Bucolic' poetry too claims to reproduce the 'real'
singing of herdsmen, but is only too conscious of its difference.

Lykidas is introduced with detail which suggests that, unlike the
characters and geography of the opening passage, he is new to us.

Simichidas, however, apparently knows his name, origin, and reputation as a poet, as Lykidas for his part knows Simichidas. Perhaps
we are to understand that Simichidas knows who this is from his
appearance, but has never met him before (Simichidas may never
have ventured into the countryside before and Lykidas never goes to
town, cf. 92n.). Lykidas 'was a goatherd', but he has no goats, materialises mysteriously, and apparently speaks only to Simichidas; he is
clearly not simply what he seems, cf. 11–14n. The meeting is in fact
modelled on Homeric 'encounter' scenes, one variety of which is the
appearance of disguised gods to mortals, often when they are on a
journey, cf. Puelma (1960), Archibald Cameron (1963) 291–307, G.
Luck, *MH* 23 (1966) 186–9. The principal such scenes are Priam
and Hermes (*Il.* 24.322–472), Odysseus and Athene (*Od.* 7.14–132),
Odysseus and Hermes (*Od.* 10.274–310), Odysseus and Athene (*Od.*
13.219–440), and Odysseus/Eumaios and Melantheus (*Od.* 17.182–
261). Two such scenes are suggestively 'bucolic'. In *Od.* 13 the disguised Athene confronts Odysseus on the Ithacan shore: 'But then
Athene drew near to him; she wore the guise of a young shepherd,
with the gentle air of a king's son; a lovely mantle fell in two folds
about her shoulders; there were sandals on her glistening feet, and
she held a javelin in her hand' (13.221–5, trans. Shewring; cf. 7.14–19
with appropriately 'un-epic' variations, F. Williams, *MPhL* 3 (1978)
219–25). The most important model, however, is the purely human
encounter of *Od.* 17 (cf. Ott (1972) 144–9, Halperin (1983a) 224–7).
Odysseus, disguised as a beggar, and Eumaios are journeying from
the countryside to the town; Odysseus has borrowed a staff from
Eumaios to support himself: 'The two walked on over the rugged
path till they neared the city and came to the fountain of fashioned
stone from whose lovely streamlet those of the town drew their
water. Ithakos had built it, with Neritos and Polyktor; encircling it
was a group of black poplars (αἴγειροι) that throve on the moist
ground; overhead, cool water ran down from the rock; above the
fountain the nymphs had an altar built to them, and passers-by
always made offerings there. At this spot the two crossed the path of
Melantheus son of Dolios; he was driving goats ... When he saw the
others he turned upon them with jeering words ...' (*Od.* 17.204–16,
trans. Shewring, adapted). Here there is a fateful meeting with a
'goatherd', at a *locus amoenus* dedicated to the nymphs and characterised by a fountain created by the eponymous heroes of the land

(cf. Bourina); Odysseus' rags are replaced by Simichidas' smart town clothes, and Melantheus' abuse by Lykidas' gentle mockery, but the motif of disguise remains, as does Melantheus' suggestion that the travellers are interested largely in their stomachs (24n.). T. thus acknowledges the 'bucolic' inspiration of the archaic epic.

A central irony of Idyll 7 is that a 'bucolic' poet, who inevitably works within the social networks of the city and for whom 'being in the countryside' is usually part of a code (91–2n.), is made to confront a 'real' creature of the land. The poem is an exploration of what is at stake in and what are the limits of this metaphorical code. Lykidas' smile is the poet's recognition of these limits. As, however, Lykidas himself embodies the essence of the bucolic (27–9), we should not be surprised that no clear answer emerges from a search to define him; as Idyll 1 has shown, 'bucolic' poetry does not fit into familiar categories. Nevertheless, the Homeric encounter scenes, particularly the scenes involving gods, are suggestive. At one level, Lykidas is fashioned as a divine being, presiding over bucolic, and therefore known by hearsay to Simichidas. For Brown (1981) Lykidas is Pan, the divine carrier of the λαγωβόλον, though the poem does not hint that he has the feet of a goat. Lawall (1967) 80–4 argued that he was modelled on the figure of a satyr, and satyric features certainly characterise other Theocritean creations (the goatherd of Idyll 3, Polyphemos in Idyll 11), as well, of course, as Socrates himself (cf. above). Much the most suggestive interpretation is that of Williams (1971): Lykidas is 'Apollo himself, in pastoral guise'. The name will suggest the Apolline title Λύκιος, changed to conform to the -idas names of poets (Simichidas, Sikelidas, cf. 40n.); Apollo Lykios has not yet been found on Cos, though the title is attested on nearby Kalymna (cf. H. Collitz and F. Bechtel, *Sammlung der gr. Dialekt-Inschriften* III 1 (Göttingen 1899), no. 3591.5). Moreover, important place-names of the poem – Kydonia (12), Horomedon (46), Pyxa (130) – have Apolline connections (see notes ad loc.). For ironies created by such an identification cf. 11–14, 95, 100–1nn. Apollo was a major Coan god (cf. Sherwin-White (1978) 299–303), and would have an obvious significance in a poem concerned with the meaning of a kind of poetry. Nevertheless, however Apolline Lykidas may be, there are also undeniable evocations of other gods (Pan and Hermes), and the end of the poem seems to emphasise the 'Dionysiac'; no Olympian existed ready-made to preside over the 'new' genre, and so T. had to fashion his own eclectic deity (cf. Lawall (1967) 84); whether we say that Lykidas *is* Apollo or merely has marked Apolline 'characteristics' may in the end be of little importance.

Bowie (1985), however, argued that Lykidas is a character from 'bucolic' poetry of Philitas (40n.) set on Lesbos, who here meets Simichidas, a creation (44 πεπλασμένον) of T. The poem, which on any interpretation is likely to be full of echoes of Philitas, is thus 'an elaborate compliment to Philitas' by a younger poet. That there is much in Idyll 7 which would become clearer if more had survived of the great Coan poet can hardly be doubted, and Bowie's case is ingenious and suggestive; a confrontation with the 'divine essence' of bucolic will, in any case, always involve a confrontation with the literary heritage in which that essence was constructed and embodied.

The Apolline elements in Lykidas were very important for Virgil. In *Ecl.* 1 Tityrus recounts how he went from the countryside to Rome where a 'divine' *iuuenis* gave him a *responsum* allowing him to continue the pastoral life. This *iuuenis* (Octavian) is figured as the prophetic Apollo (cf. Wright (1983) 118–20), and the figure in T. whose function most closely corresponds to that of the *iuuenis* is Lykidas in Idyll 7. Cf. further 72–89n.

Lykidas' rôle is also determined by echoes of the proem of Hesiod's *Theogony*, in which the Muses appeared to Hesiod as he was 'shepherding his lambs under holy Helikon' (cf. 92); the goddesses expound the possibility of both 'true' and 'false' poetry (cf. 44–8), hand Hesiod a marvellous staff, the symbol of both the rhapsode and those in authority (cf. 43, 128–9), inspire him with a divine voice and instruct him to sing 'theogonic' material. The implication is that Hesiod was not a poet before the encounter with the Muses, which therefore represents his poetic investiture (as Apollo appeared to Callimachus, fr. 1.21–8). Simichidas, however, is already a poet when he meets Lykidas, and the echoes of Hesiod do not so much explain why Simichidas (or T.) is a bucolic poet, as serve to explore the nature of bucolic itself; so too, the songs which Lykidas and Simichidas sing both deal with the torments of love, which is constructed as the essential 'bucolic' theme (cf. Intro. Section 3). It is the Muses who appear to Hesiod because it is they who are the repository of memory and true knowledge, the two prerequisites of 'true' theogonic poetry. 'Bucolic' poetry might seem on the surface to

require a 'true' knowledge of the countryside, as well as of the past
masters of bucolic form (Daphnis and Komatas); Lykidas fits this bill
perfectly, but his ever present smile marks the irony at the heart of
the 'bucolic' tradition – 'true' knowledge of the countryside is not in
fact important for the production of 'bucolic song'. T. explores the
same paradox in Idyll 10, in which the 'bucolic' song of the lovesick
Boukaios is set against the 'Hesiodic' worksong of the 'real' countryman (Id. 10, Intro.). The poem as a whole, therefore, offers us two
versions of 'bucolic', one a misprision of the other.

Hesiod's encounter with the Muses fits a widespread literary pattern of 'poetic initiation' (cf. A. Kambylis, *Die Dichterweihe und ihre
Symbolik* (Heidelberg 1965)). Of particular interest is the story of the
young Archilochus' encounter with the Muses, which was inscribed
about the middle of the third century in the 'Archilocheion' at Paros
(*SEG* xv 517; A. Kambylis, *Hermes* 91 (1963) 129–50). In the evening
the young boy was leading a cow into the town to be sold the following day; he met some ladies who joked with him and said they
would give him a fair price for the cow, which then disappeared;
in its place the boy found a lyre. Subsequent enquiries at Delphi
ascertained that the boy would become a famous poet. Here is an
encounter with the Muses which is truly βουκολικόν, takes place on
the road between the city and a specific country location ('the
Meadows') and indeed at a specific place ('Lissides'), and which
defines the kind of poet Archilochus is to become (the jesting ladies
indicate iambic poetry). In Idyll 7 Archilochus is important in the
song which Simichidas sings (120–1n.), and T. wrote an epigram in
his honour (*Epigr.* 21). In the Parian story, however, Archilochus
really is a βουκόλος, whereas for Simichidas this language has
become a code; the difference again marks T.'s recognition of the
ironic status of his generic enterprise.

The journey of Idyll 7 ends with an evocation of the promised end
of Odysseus' wanderings (156n.). That epic of exploration has been
telescoped into a brief journey into the countryside, but one which
encompasses all of mythic time in its exploration of 'bucolic' song.
So too, the style of Idyll 7 is more 'Homeric' than almost any other
'bucolic' poem (cf. Di Benedetto (1956) 55, 58), characterised by a
very sparing use of the definite article (Leutner (1907) 19).

Idyll 7 forms the primary model for *Eclogue* 9, and echoes of this poem are very common throughout the *Eclogues*; for Idyll 7 and *Eclogue* 6 cf. 72–89n.

Title. Θαλύσια (Σ, K, probably Π⁵; cf. 3–4n.), or Λυκίδας ἢ Θαλύσια (*Et. Mag.* 273.42 Gaisford, from the commentary of Amarantos (second century AD)). Other variants, e.g. Θαλύσια ἢ ἐαρινοὶ ὁδοιπόροι, also occur, cf. Gow 1 lxx.

Modern discussions. Arnott (1984) 333–46; Berger (1984); Bowie (1985); Brown (1981); Furusawa (1980); Giangrande (1980) 119–61; Goldhill (1991) 225–40; Gutzwiller (1991) 158–71; Hatzikosta (1982); Heubeck (1973); Hunter (1996a) 20–8; Hutchinson (1988) 201–12; Kelly (1983); Krevans (1983); Kühn (1958); Lawall (1967) 74–117; Monteil (1968) 99–124; Ott (1969) 138–73; Puelma (1960); Schwinge (1974); Seeck (1975b); Segal (1981) 110–75; Serrao (1971) 11–68; Stanzel (1995) 269–93; Van Groningen (1959); Van Sickle (1975); Walsh (1985) 11–19; Weingarth (1967); Williams 1971; Winter (1974).

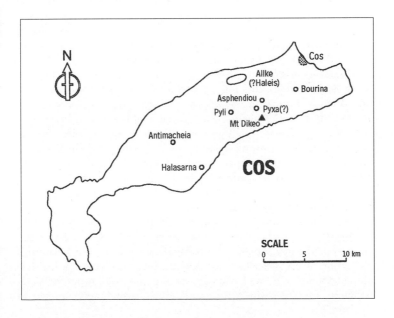

1 ἧς χρόνος ἀνίκ': in contrast to the simple ποτέ, this form suggests that the event to be described was of some duration and importance, and belongs to an era which is now closed, cf. Furusawa (1980) 98–103, T. Choitz and J. Latacz, *WJA* 7 (1981) 86–7, 92–4. The form may be used for recent events of purely personal significance, but T. here suggests a distant past appropriate to a poem which is to record a 'foundation' of bucolic poetry, cf. Critias, *TrGF* 1 43 F19 ἦν χρόνος ὅτ' ἦν ἄτακτος ἀνθρώπων βίος κτλ., Pl. *Prt.* 320c8 ἦν γάρ ποτε χρόνος ὅτε θεοὶ μὲν ἦσαν κτλ. **Εὔκριτος:** a common name throughout the Aegean (*LGPN* 1 s.v.). Hippotas, son of Eukritos, was sent from Cos on a public mission in 242 (cf. *SEG* XII 381.4, R. Herzog and G. Klaffenbach, *Asylienurkunden aus Kos* (Berlin 1952) 29), and his father might be an obvious candidate for Idyll 7. The closeness of the name to Θεόκριτος (Θεύκριτος) has seemed to some critics important.   **τὸν Ἅλεντα:** the group head west from Cos town towards the deme Haleis, about ten kilometres distant, which seems to have extended south from a coastal salt lake (modern Alike); its principal settlement may have been near Pyli, see map and 64n. The definite article would be very unusual with a deme-name, so 'the Haleis' may be a village or a river (cf. 5.123) in the deme; this form, like the unadorned names Eukritos and Amyntas, creates the illusion that both the personnel and the location are well known.

2 ἄμμιν: an ancient grammarian explicitly attests ἀμίν for this verse, as Eustathius does for 135; certainty is, however, not possible, cf. Molinos Tejada 142–7, 254–5.   **Ἀμύντας:** a very common name, attested on Kalymnos and Rhodes, though not yet on Cos (*LGPN* 1 s.v.); Bowie (1996) 99 notes that it is common in Thessaly and suggests a borrowing from Simonides. Line 132 (where see n.) suggests that Amyntas was an *eromenos* of Simichidas and/or Eukritos, and therefore may be assumed to be rather younger than his travelling companions; Horace's 'Coan Amyntas' is distinguished by his sexual prowess (*Epod.* 12.18).

3–4 'Phrasidamos' is known from both Keos and Attica, and 'Antigenes' is common all over the Greek world; Lykopeus is found only in mythology (Apollod. 1.8.6, Diod. Sic. 4.65.2), but Lykopas is the name of a cowherd at 5.62. Family cults involving the heroisation of the founder and his family were an important aspect of Coan religious life (Sherwin-White (1978) 363–7), and such a context

would certainly suit the ancestry which these Coans claimed.   τᾶι
Δηοῖ: this name for Demeter, perhaps originally a hypocoristic of
Δημήτηρ (cf. Hopkinson on Call. *h.* 6.17), occurs only here in the
bucolic corpus; it is frequently associated with Demeter's rites (esp.
those at Eleusis) and here adds an appropriate sacral tone. The cult
of Demeter was very important on Cos, and there was a sanctuary
of the goddess in the Haleis deme (Sherwin-White (1978) 305–12).
Philitas (40n.) wrote an elegiac *Demeter* which seems to have alluded
to many Coan traditions, and lines 4–11 very likely echo this poem,
cf. 4–7n.   **θαλύσια:** an offering of 'firstfruits' after the harvest; as
the term is a Homeric *hapax* (*Il.* 9.534), the elevated tone of τᾶι Δηοῖ
is continued. As a title for the poem, it is reminiscent of the pseudo-
Homeric *Eiresione* ('festal garland'), or may be seen as shorthand for,
e.g., οἱ τὰ θαλύσια ἀνατιθέμενοι.

4–7 '... the two sons of Lykopeus, the noblest [lit. [noble], if
anything is noble, ...] of those glorious by descent (ἐπάνωθεν) from
Klytia and Chalkon himself, who created the spring Bourina with his
foot, having set his knee firmly against the rock'. For the syntax cf.
Epigr. 17.4 τῶν πρόσθ' εἴ τι περισσὸν ᾠδοποιῶν, '[Anacreon]
[outstanding], if anything is outstanding, among poets of old'.
Simichidas identifies his hosts as the very cream of old Coan families
who traced their descent back to a pre-Dorian era (cf. Sherwin-
White (1978) 49). Klytia ('Famous Lady') was the daughter of Merops, the founding pre-Dorian hero of the Coans, according to Σ5–
9(c), which perhaps derives from Nikanor of Cos's commentary on
Philitas (cf. Σ5–9(o)); she is perhaps to be identified with Kos, the
daughter of Merops who gave her name to the island (*Et. Mag.*
507.55 Gaisford, Steph. Byz. s.v. Κῶς). Klytia's husband, Eurypylos,
son of Poseidon, was an early, if not the first, legendary king of Cos
(cf. *Il.* 2.677, Apollod. 2.7.1), and Chalkon was their son (cf. Hes. fr.
43a.58–60). For these legends cf. H. Dibbelt, *Quaestiones Coae myth-
ologae* (diss. Greifswald 1891), Paton–Hicks (1891) xii-xv, 361–2.

4 ἐσθλόν: this word is almost a mannerism with Simichidas, who
uses it four times elsewhere of poets or poems (12, 39, 93, 100), and is
not otherwise found in the 'bucolic' poems; it suits his opinionated
and agonistic spirit.

5 χαῶν 'noble', 'well-born'. Σ claim the word is Spartan, and the
only other certain occurrences are Ar. *Lys.* 90–1, 1157 in the mouths

of Spartans, with the meaning 'in fine condition'. Did Simichidas' hosts have Spartan connections? Cf. further Σ Aesch. *Suppl.* 858. **αὐτῶ:** the prominence given to Chalkon accords with the importance of Bourina for the poem.

6 Βούριναν: mentioned also by Philitas (fr. 24 Powell) and very likely to be identified with the modern Vourina (though that name may be a revival rather than a survival), an important water-source which supplies the modern town of Cos and lies some 5 km southwest, above the site of the Asklepieion, cf. G. Zanker, *CQ* 30 (1980) 373–7. Puelma (1960) 162–3 argued that the spring and its associated *locus amoenus* was none other than the site of the *thalysia* described at the end of the poem, but this is most unlikely, cf. 135–47n. The name, if etymologised as 'Ox-flow', clearly recalls Hippokrene, the 'horse spring' on Mt Helikon, said to have been caused by a blow from the hoof of Pegasos (Arat. *Phaen.* 216–23) and beside which Callimachus placed the encounter of Hesiod and the Muses (fr. 2 = 4 Massimilla, with Massimilla's notes, fr. 112.6); Hippokrene is here replaced by a suitably βουκολικόν alternative, in a poem which will rewrite Hesiod's encounter. In the later Hellenistic period, Hesiod was thought to have drunk from Hippokrene before composing, cf. [Asclepiades], *Anth. Pal.* 9.64 (= *HE* 1018–25), but the notion cannot certainly be traced as early as T.

Both the real etymology of Bourina and what precisely Chalkon did are unclear; Σ offer many competing versions. Nikanor (4–7n.) explained that the water flowed out from a bull's muzzle (ῥίς), either an artificial fountain-spout or a rock thought to resemble a muzzle, and this explanation is not improbable. Chalkon will have created the spring by kicking the ground or rock-face, a common aetiology of marvellous springs, cf. *Arg.* 4.1446, Matthews on Antimachus fr. 136; in this case the aetiology may have been associated with an impression in the rock said to have been made by his knee, as Achilles left both a spring and a footprint behind as he leapt ashore at Troy (Lyc. *Alex.* 245–8 ἅλμα ... ποδὸς ... ἐρείσας). Although Corinth had a statue of Pegasos with water flowing from his hoof (Paus. 2.3.5), the alternative version in Σ, that Chalkon set up a statue with water flowing from its foot, looks like a rationalising account which would not do proper justice to the marvellous family legends of Simichidas' hosts.

7–9 > *Ecl.* 9.41–2. The verses suggest that the grove miraculously came into being at the same time as Bourina; that the creation of water should lead to the growth of trees is a natural idea. For the reworking of *Od.* 17.208–10 cf. above, p. 147.

8 αἴγειροι πτελέαι τε: cf. 136n.

9 χλωροῖσιν κτλ. 'forming a roof with their rich foliage of green leaves', cf. *Arg.* 3.220 ἡμερίδες χλοεροῖσι καταστεφέες πετάλοισιν (with Campbell's n.), 3.928. This verse of four words, standing syntactically independent and with 'end-punctuation, serving to close a section of narrative with weight and solemnity' (Hopkinson on Call. *h.* 6.87), is of a common type; cf. S. E. Bassett, *CP* 14 (1919) 216–33.

10–11 > *Ecl.* 9.59–60; cf. Simaitha's fateful sighting of Delphis μέσαν κατ' ἀμαξιτόν (2.76). The absence of the 'mound of Brasilas' marks out the landscape as the presence of the tomb of the eponymous Ilos, beside which Priam encountered Hermes, marks the plain of Troy (cf. 16.75, *Il.* 24.349); this makes it likely that Brasilas was another legendary Coan figure (from the poetry of Philitas?), and his 'mound' is another way in which T. signals that his 'bucolic' poetry consciously measures its distance from the heroic model. Outside this passage the name does not recur (cf. A. Heubeck, *Živa Antika* 23 (1973) 17–18. W. G. Arnott, *QUCC* 32 (1979) 99–105, attractively identifies this mound with 'a small hill [modern 'Meso Vouno'] shaped exactly like a tumulus [which] becomes visible' about 4 km from the town.   **ἄνυμες:** a non-thematic imperfect, as if from ἄνυμι, cf. *Od.* 5.243. The imperfect suggests the steady progression of the travellers.

11–14 Lykidas is introduced as though not known to the reader (contrast the names of 1–4); whether the narrator's information about him is to be understood as something Simichidas had at the time, or something he subsequently acquired, is left mysterious.

11 τιν': the much better attested τόν is presumably a mistake arising from the position of τιν', which is not, however, unusual (K–G I 665).   **ὁδίταν:** at the end of the poem Lykidas turns off on the road to Pyxa (130n.), but here it is left deliberately unclear whether Simichidas and friends overtake him or he just 'materialises' (note the ambiguous εὕρομες); 21–3 suggest that Lykidas is too knowledgeable to travel far in the middle of the day, but at 35 Simichidas assumes (with naïve self-centredness?) that Lykidas is travelling in the same direction as himself. Of known divinities, Hermes is notoriously ὅδιος and Pan is elsewhere εὔοδος and ἐνόδιος (Brown (1981) 86).

12 ἐσθλόν: Π⁵ has ἐσλόν, which is familiar from high lyric and the Lesbian poets; it may be a 'learned' intervention in the text, but certainty is not possible. The adjective is paradoxically applied to a goatherd, as part of the suggestion that Lykidas is not quite what he seems.   **σὺν Μοίσαισι** '[found] thanks to the Muses', because the meeting will lead to an exchange of song; we may be tempted, however, also to hear '[a good man] with the Muses', which would fit Apollo as well as anyone.   **Κυδωνικόν:** the best known Kydonia was a city on the north-west coast of Crete, with no obvious connection with Cos; Steph. Byz. claims that it used to be called Apollonia, which has obvious consequences for the Apolline identification of Lykidas. Other places of this name were an island off the coast of Lesbos (Pliny, *NH* 2.232, 5.140, Bowie (1985) 73, 90–1), and cities in Sicily and Libya. No ancient Coan Kydonia is known, though Κυδωνιά ('place of the quinces') is a place-name on modern Cos, in roughly the right area near Antimacheia, cf. G. L. Huxley, *LCM* 7 (1982) 13. Brown (1981) 84–5 suggests that the phrase evokes a quince-wood statue of a god, and the passage certainly reads like an ecphrasis (cf. Call. fr. 114.7–9, the statue of Delian Apollo).

13 Λυκίδαν: not otherwise attested on Cos (though related names are), but it occurs in both Euboea and Attica (*LGPN* I–II s.v.).   **οὐδέ κέ τίς μιν κτλ.** 'nor when you saw him could you fail to recognise [that he was a goatherd]', not (as Puelma (1960) 147) 'nor when you saw him could you fail to recognise [that he was Lykidas the goatherd]'. There is a close reworking of a Homeric formulation found at *Il.* 1.536–7 (Hera realising that Zeus has been with Thetis) οὐδέ μιν Ἥρη | ἠγνοίησεν ἰδοῦσ' ὅτι κτλ. and *Od.* 5.77–8 (Kalypso recognising Hermes) οὐδέ μιν ἄντην | ἠγνοίησεν ἰδοῦσα Καλυψώ κτλ., combined with a variation of the Homeric πάντα ἐῴκει, which is standard in scenes of divine disguise. This may be a way of stressing the rightness of Simichidas' identification, but in view of the fact that in *Od.* 5 (lines 79–80) Homer goes on to explain that *gods* do not fail to recognise each other, we may rather see an allusive way of saying that Lykidas was not what he seemed, because

Simichidas is not a god and is therefore fallible. There may be a memory of this passage in *Ecl.* 1.40–1 *neque seruitio me exire licebat | nec tam praesentis alibi cognoscere diuos.*   **μιν:** the Ionic form should perhaps be retained in this rather 'epicising' poem, especially in a 'formula' which is borrowed from Homer, cf. Molinos Tejada 248–53.

14 ἠγνοίησεν: the unaugmented form in Π⁵ may be correct, cf. ὕφαινον (8).   **ἔξοχ'** 'to a T'; Lykidas looks so much like the 'ideal' of the goatherd that we may well be suspicious.

15 On the pattern of this verse cf. 61–2n.   **λασίοιο δασύτριχος:** the juxtaposition of these synonyms is odd, and its purpose unclear; the second does not look like an intrusive gloss on the first. Graefe proposed λαίοιο 'on the left side', and Kaibel λαίοιο ... ὤμοιο.

16 κναχόν 'tawny', cf. 3.5.   **ταμίσοιο:** cf. 11.65–6n.; it would have to be 'fresh' to be effective in cheese-making. The town-dwelling Simichidas has a keen nose for the smells of the country-side. Lykidas' rustic odour is a humorous variation on the sweet smell which normally attends divine epiphany, cf. *h. Dem.* 277–8 (with Richardson's n.), Moschus, *Europa* 91–2.

18 ζωστῆρι πλακερῶι 'with a broad belt', cf. *Od.* 14.72 of Eumaios; neither πλακερῶι, which Σ gloss as πλατεῖ, nor the variant πλοκερῶι occur elsewhere.   **ἀγριελαίω:** the 'wild olive' is smaller, bushier and much less valuable than the cultivated version, cf. Lembach (1970) 101.

19 κορύναν: called in 128 a λαγωβόλον, i.e. a relatively short crook, hooked or curved at one end for catching animals by the legs or throwing after them; Pan is regularly depicted carrying the 'hare-killer', cf. Gow on 4.49, Cameron (1995) 415.

19–20 'with imperturbable mockery and a smiling eye he spoke to me [μ' = μοι], and laughter hung around [lit. clung to] his lips', cf. Longus, *D&C* 1.4.2 (statues of the Nymphs) μειδίαμα περὶ τὴν ὀφρύν. In addition to his laughter, here stressed by three different words in little more than one verse, Lykidas is also characterised by an air of calm superiority; both are characteristic of the divine: for laughter cf. *Od.* 13.287, Call. *h.* 3.28 etc., for stillness Eur. *Ba.* 436–40 (Dionysos), and for the combination Plut. *Aemilius* 25.4

ἀτρέμα μειδιῶντες (the Dioskouroi).   σεσαρώς: Aelian, *VH* 3.40
derives σάτυρος from σαίρω, but the etymology does not seem to be
attested earlier.

21 > *Ecl.* 9.1 (in the mouth of 'Lycidas'). On the form of Lykidas'
opening question cf. above, p. 147. Particularly close is *Il.* 24.362–3
(Hermes to Priam), 'Where, father, are you guiding your horses and
mules through the immortal night, when other men are asleep?';
here it is midday and even the lizards are asleep. This is not the only
'Hermaic' quality of Lykidas, cf. 10–11n.   **Σιμιχίδα:** the vocative
without ὦ (cf. 27, 50, 91) is the politer form, cf. F. Williams, *Eranos* 71
(1973) 60. Lykidas seems to ignore completely Eukritos and Amyntas,
who play no further part in the poem until after Lykidas has
departed. This reverses the Hesiodic pattern in which the Muses
address a plurality of 'shepherds of the field' but give a staff to
Hesiod, who makes no mention of any companions (*Theog.* 22–34).
τύ 'you [of all people, a townsman]', rather than 'you [like myself]'.
So too, δή expresses (feigned?) surprise, cf. *Il.* 24.201, *Od.* 21.362,
Denniston 210–11.   **μεσαμέριον:** cf. 1.15–18n. Hesiod's encounter
with the Muses was later placed at midday (e.g. [Asclepiades], *Anth.
Pal.* 9.64.1 (= *HE* 1018)), though Hesiod himself gives no time indication.   **πόδας ἕλκεις:** this phrase normally denotes slow and
laboured movement, whereas the travellers are moving fast (24–6);
Lykidas' irony suggests that Simichidas' feet, if they could choose,
would not be out in the hot sun.

22 > *Ecl.* 2.9. Cold-blooded lizards may in fact become more
active in the middle of the day, but Lykidas' remark has a semi-
proverbial flavour, 'it's so hot, the lizards are asleep'.   **καὶ σαῦρος:** for the absence of the article cf. 141, but χὠ σαῦρος is worth
considering.

23 A jokingly pompous *spondeiazon* rounds off Lykidas' opening
salvo.   **ἐπιτυμβίδιοι:** the crest of the crested lark was likened to
the familiar floral ornamentation on grave-stelae; an aetiology for
the likeness was found in a story that the bird buried its father in its
head, cf. Thompson, *Birds* 96–7, Dunbar on Ar. *Birds* 472–5. Others
understand 'which frequent tombs', cf. G. Roux, *RPh* 37 (1963) 76–8.

24 μετὰ δαῖτ' ἄκλητος is to be preferred to μετὰ δαῖτα κλητός as
it suits Lykidas' teasing; the potential doubleness is, however, itself

part of that teasing. It is parasites who hurry 'uninvited' (cf. Arnott (1996) 611), and this, Lykidas suggests, is what Simichidas might be: why else would anyone travel in the heat of the day? Cf. the epithet of parasites τρεχέδειπνος (Plut. *Mor.* 726a etc.). In the Homeric model Melantheus calls Odysseus 'a troublesome beggar who spoils feasts' (*Od.* 17.220), a prototype of the later 'parasite', and in the Hesiodic proem the Muses abuse the shepherds as 'mere stomachs' (*Theog.* 26). Σ explain κλητός as a reference to the suspicions which the late arrival of an invited guest proverbially arouse.   ἀστῶν: a pointed jest: even in the countryside, Simichidas does not leave his city connections behind.

25 λανόν: probably just 'wine jar', 'container' (or perhaps the building containing them), rather than specifically 'wine press', cf. 25.28 (a similar context) ἐς ληνοὺς δ' ἱκνεῦνται ἐπὴν θέρος ὥριον ἔλθηι, *h. Herm.* 104, Preisigke s.v. Giangrande (1980) 130–5 suggests that Lykidas is teasing Simichidas with hurrying to find employment as a casual labourer who could be paid in wine.   **θρώισκεις** may suggest an attack or raid upon the wine jars, not merely the speed of movement.

25–6 'for [lit. how ... (exclamatory ὥς)] as your feet travel along, every stone sings as it stumbles from your shoes'.   **τοι:** for the dative pronoun followed by a genitive participle cf. 2.82–3, K–G ii iii, Serrao (1971) 104.   **νισσομένοιο:** the verb only here in T.; its high style, reinforced by the epic -οιο, is part of Lykidas' mockery.   **πᾶσα λίθος:** the feminine may be an epicism, as in classical and later Greek this is usually reserved for precious stones or statues, cf. 6.38, Headlam on Herodas 4.21.   **πταίοισα:** normally people stumble against stones; here the stones 'totter' away as Simichidas' hurrying boots kick against them. Lykidas' reversal both marks Simichidas' intrusion into an alien world where stones, but not Simichidas, belong and reveals his own peculiarly 'bucolic' vision. **ἀρβυλίδεσσιν** 'travelling boots' (Fraenkel on Aesch. *Ag.* 944); Lykidas may not be barefooted (cf. 4.56), but Simichidas is certainly dressed as no countryman ever would be. The epic dative form may be a further mocking touch (cf. Molinos Tejada 220–1, Hunter (1996a) 33–4).

27–31 The absence of anything such as 'So he spoke, and I ...'

and the rapid half-verse display Simichidas' eagerness to reply. He first tries to match Lykidas' jesting with an opening gambit of his own – encomium and modesty – before actually answering the questions, cf. Serrao (1971) 24–5; his words, however, reveal his commitment to an urban world of competition, self-regard and reputation. This opening exchange is itself a version of the preliminary exchanges which precede the *ekphrasis* and song in Idyll 1 (cf. 1.12–23n.) and the song contest itself in Idyll 5; whereas in those poems the herdsmen manœuvre for spatial position, here the game is rather about status.

28 συρικτὰν μέγ' ὑπείροχον: the epic adjective applied to a humble status is an attempt to match Lykidas at his own game, but Simichidas is, in any case, presented as someone who deals in simplistic value-judgements, cf. 94. 'Syrinx-player' here denotes a *bucolic* singer, who punctuates his song with piping, and there is a pointed contrast with ἀοιδόν in 38, cf. Hunter (1996a) 21–2. 'By far the outstanding syrinx-player' would in fact suit Pan very well (cf. above, p. 148). 'Herding' and 'reaping' are occupations accompanied by song, but the words have also a generic resonance in the wider context of T.'s poetry: many of his characters are 'herdsmen' – Idyll 4 is entitled Νομεῖς – and Idyll 10 is an exchange between two reapers.

29 θυμὸν ἰαίνει: another high-style epicism. Simichidas disclaims the envy and jealousy (φθόνος) which was traditionally thought to mark relations between poets (Hes. *WD* 26), but the following challenge at least complicates his generosity of spirit.

30 κατ' ἐμὸν νόον: repeated in 39, the phrase suggests how keen Simichidas is for Lykidas' approval, and it acts as a bait to lure him into an exchange of songs. Cf. 35–6n.

32 Demeter is normally portrayed in art 'in a glorious robe' (cf. Roscher 2.1339–79), but the sacral tone of the epithet suggests an answer to Lykidas' teasing: 'I'm no parasite, this is serious business . . .'

33 ὄλβῳ ἀπαρχόμενοι 'making a firstfruits offering from their wealth'. **πίονι μέτρωι** 'with overflowing measure'; Demeter is pictured as 'measuring out' the harvested grain, and the adjective which applies to the produce itself (cf. 143) is transferred to the measure she offers. Cf. Call. *h.* 6.132–3 Δηὼ | δωσεῖ πάντ' ἐπίμεστα, 'Deo will give them everything in full measure.'

34 εὔκριθον: predicative, '[has filled their threshing-floor] so that it is rich in grain'. Barley and wheat were the two most important grains throughout the Greek world, but τὸ κρῖ may be used of 'grain' in general, not specifically barley. The adjective occurs elsewhere only at Adaios, *Anth. Pal.* 6.258.6 (= *GP* 10), a farmer's prayer to Demeter accompanying a sacrifice on the threshing-floor, σὺ δὲ Κρήθωνος ἄρουραν | πᾶν ἔτος εὔκριθον καὶ πολύπυρον ἄγοις, where the sense 'rich in barley' is plain.

35–6 > Ecl. 9.64–5.   ξυνὰ ... ξυνά: for this anaphora cf. Hes. fr. 1.6 M–W, *Arg.* 1.336–7, 3.173.   **ὁδός:** cf. 11–14n.   **ἀώς:** the sense 'dawn' is sometimes felt only weakly, if at all (cf. 12.1, 16.5, 17.59, Reed (1997) 145), but here the nuance, in an utterance of semi-proverbial flavour, is perhaps 'no one owns the sunlight', cf. 'the common sun' of Men. frr. 416, 737 K–T.   **βουκολιασδώμεσθα:** cf. Intro. Section 2.   **ὀνασεῖ:** the claim that each might learn something about the technique of singing from the other is particularly amusing if Simichidas is talking to a divinity (Apollo!). Nevertheless, whereas Lykidas is a universally acknowledged master of 'syrinx-playing', Simichidas' prowess in that direction is just a matter of his own private opinion (30, cf. 92–3), although he does claim a matching reputation in the wider field of poetry; each therefore may have something to offer the other. Such altruism sharply distinguishes this 'bucolic exchange' from the contest of Idyll 5 (cf. 5.69 ὀνάσῃς). *Ecl.* 9.64 *cantantes licet usque (minus uia laedet) eamus* perhaps suggests that Virgil understood the meaning to be that song takes some of the wearisomeness out of travel.

37–41 > Ecl. 9.32–6.

37 καὶ γὰρ ἐγώ 'for indeed I ...', explaining why Lykidas might derive some benefit from the exchange of song, cf. 5.134, 6.29, Denniston 108–9, Hunter (1996a) 22. Despite *Ecl.* 9.32–3, the alternative explanation, 'for I too ...', does less justice to the inherent contrast between 'syrinx-playing' and 'poetry' in a wider sense (35–6n.).   **Μοισᾶν:** the Muses belong to the wider world of all poetry, whereas, as Simichidas knows (91–2n.), it is the Nymphs who particularly preside over 'bucolic song'.   **καπυρόν:** perhaps 'clear', 'pure', cf. *Ecl.* 9.36 *argutos ... olores*, P. E. Legrand, *REG* 20 (1907) 10–17.

38 ἐγὼ δέ τις κτλ. 'but I'm not a credulous sort of person'.

39 οὐ Δᾶν: cf. 6.22n. Δᾶν may have been felt as a dialect form of Δία, although the ancient grammatical tradition explained it as a Doric form of Γῆν, cf. H. L. Ahrens, *Phil.* 23 (1866) 206–7. At 4.17 it is placed in the mouth of an Italian herdsman.   **οὐ ... πω** 'not yet' (!).   **κατ' ἐμὸν νόον:** cf. 27–31n.   **ἐσθλόν:** cf. 4–7n.

40 Simichidas names two great poets, both rather older than T., but both probably still alive at the time of composition. 'Sikelidas' is Asclepiades of Samos (*HE* II 114–18, Fraser (1972) I 557–61, Hunter (1996a) 19–20); the origin of the name Sikelidas is unknown (Σ claim that it is a patronymic), but it does not seem to have been a 'disguise' or code-name, and Asclepiades might have used it himself, cf. Hedylos *apud* Ath. II 473a (= *HE* 1860), Meleager, *Anth. Pal.* 4.1.46 (= *HE* 3971). Almost all that survives of his poetry is epigrams, in which field he exercised great influence – his fondness for *komos*-motifs may be important for 122–4 – but we know that he also wrote lyrics (Idylls 28 and 30 are in 'asclepiads'), choliambs and hexameters; such variety foreshadows the poetic range of T. himself. There is no sign in the extant remains of 'bucolic' poetry. He is listed among the 'Telchines' who criticised Callimachus (*Schol. Flor.* to Call. fr. 1 (p. 62 Massimilla)); behind this may lie their difference of opinion as to the merits of Antimachus' *Lyde* (cf. Krevans (1993), Cameron (1995) 303–7), but there is no obvious sign that Asclepiades' relations with Callimachus are relevant here (*pace* B. Effe, *WJA* 14 (1988) 87–91). Philitas (the spelling in -ίτας accords with Coan inscriptions, cf. W. Crönert, *Hermes* 37 (1902) 212–37, C.-W. Müller in Steinmetz (1990) 27–37) was the greatest scholar and poet of the generation before Callimachus (cf. Call. fr. 1.9–12). He came from Cos, as the absence of any indication in this verse suggests, and is said to have taught both Zenodotos and the future Ptolemy Philadelphos; his poetry included epigrams and hexameter and elegiac narratives (cf. 3–4, 4–7nn.), and it was as an elegist that posterity particularly celebrated him. There are no clear signs of 'bucolic' fragments (cf. 3.40–51n.), but the remains are exiguous. For Philitas cf. *CA* pp. 90–6, Kuchenmüller (1928), Pfeiffer (1968) 88–93, Knox (1993), L. Sbardella, *QUCC* 52 (1996) 93–119, Hunter (1996a) 17–19.   **νίκημι:** Simichidas thinks in terms of (formal or informal) *agones*, cf. 6.46, 8.84; for the form of the verb cf. 1.36–7n.

41 Simichidas produces what he regards as a suitably 'bucolic' comparison (cf. 1.136, 5.29, and the following ἐπίταδες). ἀκρίδες, a word for more than one type of grasshopper or cricket (cf. Davies–Kathirithamby 135–44), were kept in cages and admired for their song (*Anth. Pal.* 7.189, 190, 192 etc.); the sound of frogs, on the other hand, is often represented as unlovely (*EB* 106) or tiresome, except of course by frogs themselves (Ar. *Frogs* 205–7, 213, 229–32). Serrao (1995) 147 suggests that the fact that frogs puff themselves up even to the point of bursting (cf. Phaedrus 1.24) is relevant here: for Simichidas to compete with Asclepiades or Philitas would be like the ludicrous frog who tries to break the bounds of nature. This explanation sits well with 47–8, but suits a competition with crickets less well than the competition with an ox of the fable tradition.

42 ἐπίταδες 'with a purpose'; everything Simichidas has said has been designed to draw Lykidas out.   **ἁδὺ γελάσσας:** cf. 19–20n., Cameron (1995) 412–15, W. Beck, *LfgrE* s.v. γελάω 1 2a 'with ἡδύ … perhaps *chuckle, chortle derisively and/or maliciously* at another's pain or humiliation'; we may therefore interpret ἁδύ rather differently than does the narrating Simichidas. The better attested γελάξας may be right; at 128 it is read by both papyri and MSS, and -άζω for -άω may have been regarded as a Sicilian feature (Herakleides *apud* Eustath. *Hom.* 1654.18, K–B 1 158–9). Such forms can, however, arise as learned 'corrections' (cf. 2.115), and Idyll 7 is an epicising poem.

43 Cf. *Ecl.* 5.88. The offer of a gift *before* the exchange of songs is a version of the wrangling about prizes at 5.21–30. That Simichidas does not give Lykidas a gift is a further sign of the latter's superiority.   **δωρύττομαι:** the required sense is 'I have it in mind to give/offer', but though verbs in -ύττω are common enough in Attic (Schwyzer 1 733), it is unclear why Lykidas should be given such a form. It may characterise Lykidas with a dialect colouring obscure to us (cf. Gallavotti (1952) 100).

44 '[because you are] a young plant all fashioned by Zeus with a view to truth [cf. LSJ s.v. ἐπί B III 2]'. Simichidas' propensity for 'truth' was evidenced in his (ironic) refusal to claim parity with Asclepiades and Philitas; Lykidas now (ironically) takes him at his word – he is indeed no match for them. That not all is as it seems is made clear by the play of paradox. πεπλασμένον, 'fashioned', 'educated' (cf. 13.14 πεπονναμένος), also suggests 'made up', 'invented', 'not true' (cf. Pl. *Tim.* 26e4–5 μὴ πλασθέντα μῦθον ἀλλ' ἀληθινὸν λόγον, LSJ s.v. πλάσσω v); Segal (1981) 170–1 well translates 'fictioned for truth'. Simichidas *is*, of course, at one level a 'poetic fiction', but his (fictional) devotion to truth recalls what had been the key issue of Greek poetics ever since Hesiod's Muses had proclaimed their ability to speak both 'lies, like real things, and the truth' (*Theog.* 27–8, cf. above, p. 149). Moreover, the apparent appropriateness of 'I will give you a staff [from an olive-tree] because you are a plant ...' is undercut by the crookedness of the staff in question (19n.); crookedness is always, particularly in Hesiod (σκολιός etc.), connected with untruthfulness and dishonesty, whereas straightness (ἰθύς etc.) is the sign of the truth. Simichidas is thus as shifting and illusory as poetry itself. Cf. further Serrao (1971) 43–52, id. (1995), who sees here the notion that a poet should confine himself to kinds of poetry to which he is naturally, 'truly' suited.

45–6 In Lykidas' view, it is as absurd and objectionable to try to compete with great poets as it is for a builder to try to build a house as tall as a mountain, presumably in the belief that there is intrinsic value in size *per se*; such activity is hybristic and is certain to end in disaster. There may be some event of recent or past history alluded to here. That Mt Dikeo is not, in fact, very high (as mountains go) suits the creation of a local, 'bucolic' world.   **τέκτων:** the craftsman or carpenter is a familiar analogue (or contrast) for the poet, cf. *Diegesis* IX 37–8 (Pfeiffer I 205) describing Callimachus, *Iambus* 13 οὐδὲ τὸν τέκτονα τις μέμφεται πολυειδῆ σκεύη τεκταινόμενον, Asper (1997) 190–3.   **Ὠρομέδοντος:** almost certainly to be identified with Mt Dikeo, the highest ridge (over 800 m) in the chain visible on the left to Lykidas and Simichidas as they walk along. In Asphendiou (130n.) at the foot of Dikeo was found an inscription attesting to a cult of Apollo Ὠρομέδων, 'ruler of the seasons', an epithet of Apollo found also in imperial texts, cf. R. Herzog, *Heilige Gesetze von Kos* (Berlin 1928) 17, 20, *IG* XII 5.893, *Epigr.* 1036.2 Kaibel; if Lykidas is in some senses Apollo, this will have a particular appropriateness, although Σ associate the mountain with Pan, as indeed all mountains are the haunts of that god. The name also occurs as that of an initiate at Samothrace in the second century, and he may come from Cos (cf. F. Salviat, *BCH* 86 (1962) 275–8). Σ know only Ὠρο-, not Ὡρο-, but they are much influenced by the etymology 'mountain-ruling'. The variant Εὐρυμέδοντος is defended by H. White, *Corolla Londiniensis* 1 (1981) 159–65.

47–8 > *Ecl.* 9.36. Lykidas' second example of pretentious self-assertion is poets who try to compete with Homer. The natural inference is that a more sensible course is to pursue a type of poetry different from the Homeric, like Lykidas' coming 'little song' (τὸ μελύδριον). Such a poetics, if it deserves the name, has obvious points of contact with Callimachean aesthetics (51n.). **Μοισᾶν ὄρνιχες:** poets are traditionally compared to birds (Nisbet–Hubbard, Introduction to Hor. *C.* 2.20), but κοκκύζοντες (cf. 124) suggests that these poets are cockerels, a notoriously aggressive and self-important bird, as well as one prone to crowing at the most inappropriate times, cf. *CPG* 2.712 'more quarrelsome than cocks', M. Cantilena, *Eikasmos* 3 (1992) 179–97, 5 (1994) 213–15. If so, the pretension of the poets is marked by the colloquial ὄρνις 'cock' (LSJ s.v. III) alongside the grand Μοισᾶν; the cockerel struts around its own narrow farmyard, but the fame of the 'singer of Chios' knows no bounds. As a contest of types of bird is envisaged, we are perhaps to understand that 'the singer of Chios' is here imaged as a swan, a bird particularly associated with Apollo (cf. Call. *h.* 4.249–54, where swans are Μουσάων ὄρνιθες, and Virgil's *olores*, *Ecl.* 9.36) or perhaps a nightingale, cf. 5.136–7 οὐ θεμιτόν, Λάκων, ποτ' ἀηδόνα κίσσας ἐρίσδειν, | οὐδ' ἔποπας κύκνοισι· τὺ δ', ὦ τάλαν, ἐσσὶ φιλεχθής. **Χῖον ἀοιδόν:** cf. 22.218, Simonides fr. eleg. 19.1 West; *h. Ap.* 172 already exploits a supposed Chian origin for Homer. The 'singer of Chios' is an instance of a common way of referring to a poet (cf. Krevans (1983) 205–7, J. Farrell, *Vergil's Georgics and the traditions of ancient epic* (New York / Oxford 1991) 27–60), but here there is a particular point. Idyll 7 evokes a vibrant world of poetry in the eastern Aegean: in order from south to north, we have Cos, Samos and Chios, and soon our thoughts will move further north to Lesbos. The 'singer of Chios' is a part of that world: indeed the suggestion may be that there can only ever be one Chian poet. **ἐτώσια μοχθίζοντι:** as in the parallel passage at 1.38 the *spondeiazon* marks the pointlessness (and unmusicality?) of the crowing. There may well be a reworking of Pind. *Ol.* 2.87–8 μαθόντες ... κόρακες ὣς ἄκραντα γαρυέτων | Διὸς πρὸς ὄρνιχα θεῖον, which was interpreted (Σ, pp. 98–9 Drachmann) as a reference to the attempts of Simonides and

Bacchylides to rival the Pindaric eagle, cf. A.-T. Cozzoli, *QUCC* 54 (1996) 14–19.

49 Cf. Intro. Section 2.

50 At this stage should come the decision as to who is going to sing first; instead of simply claiming that right, Lykidas modestly offers a 'little song', not in the hope of 'winning', but to see if it meets with Simichidas' approval. The aposiopesis suggests his diffidence, cf. Ott (1972) 140 n. 15.

51 > *Ecl.* 5.13–14.   ἐν ὄρει: cf. 92. The model here is Hesiod (*Theog.* 23), though Lykidas, unlike Simichidas, would be perfectly at home in the mountains.   ἐξεπόνασα: cf. 3.18–20n. ἐκπονεῖν suggests an ideal of highly polished work in which every word counts, cf. Thucyd. 3.38.2 τὸ εὐπρεπὲς τοῦ λόγου ἐκπονήσας, Philitas fr. 10 Powell πολλὰ μογήσας, Herodas 8.71 τοὺς ἐμοὺς μόχθους, *Ecl.* 10.1 *extremum hunc, Arethusa, mihi concede laborem,* Hor. *C.* 4.2.31–2 *operosa … carmina.* Callimachus notoriously regarded such poems as λεπτόν (fr. 1.24, *Epigr.* 27.3–4, about Arat. *Phaen.*). Such an ideal has very close links with written, as opposed to oral, composition; a solitary 'goatherd on the mountain' would have a lot of time to devote to his poem, but not normally the equipment or skills for written composition. ἐξεπόνασα thus calls attention to the ambiguous status, not just of the included songs, but of T.'s poetry as a whole: 'bucolic' poetry might be thought to demand impromptu improvisation, but Lykidas knows better than that.

52–89 Lykidas begins with the prophecy of a safe voyage for Ageanax to Mytilene, 'if he saves Lykidas from the fires of Aphrodite'. He then imagines his celebration for Ageanax's safe arrival; he will have a party and listen to songs about mythic 'bucolic' poets. Lykidas' song is obviously rich with echoes of earlier poetry, even if many of these cannot now be recovered; for Simonides fr. eleg. 22 West cf. *ZPE* 99 (1993) 11–14.

The first part of the song is a version of what came to be known as a *propemptikon*, i.e. a poem or speech (cf. Men. Rhet. pp. 126–35 R–W) wishing a safe sailing for someone departing. In view of Ageanax's destination, examples in Lesbian poetry may be particularly relevant: Sappho fr. 5 Voigt is a prayer to Kypris (?) and the Nereids (cf. 7.59) for the safe return of her brother, and fr. 15 Voigt is a scrap of what may have been a similar poem:]ευπλο.[(line 2) suggests 7.62. Alcaeus fr. 286 Voigt seems to have wished someone a safe sailing now that the winter storms are over (cf. Hor. *C.* 1.4). The form is familiar in the Hellenistic period (Call. fr. 400, probably paederastic, *SH* 404, Dioscorides, *Anth. Pal.* 12.171 (= *HE* 1515–18)) and was very popular with Roman poets (cf. Hor. *C.* 1.3 (with Nisbet–Hubbard's Introduction), Prop. 1.8 (with Fedeli's Introduction), Cairns (1972) Index s.v. propemptikon). Lykidas combines propemptic material with a sophisticated exploitation of the idea of 'the stormy sea' of love. The calming of the sea will reflect the soothing of Lykidas' torment: if Ageanax reaches Mytilene safely, then both he and Lykidas will be saved from 'shipwreck'; for these ideas cf. Men. fr. 656 K–T, Cercidas fr. 2 Livrea–Lomiento, Meleager, *Anth. Pal.* 5.190 (= *HE* 4316–19), 12.157 (= *HE* 4642–5), A. Lesky, *Thalatta. Der Weg der Griechen zum Meer* (Vienna 1947) 247–83, M. R. Falivene, *QUCC* 42 (1983) 129–42, K. Gutzwiller, *CA* 11 (1992) 199–202.

52 ἔσσεται: the assertion rather than the wish may simply denote the strength of Lykidas' desire, but it may also be a function of his 'divinity': Apollo was the god of prophecy, and Apollo Ἐμβάσιος was an obvious god to receive propemptic prayers (cf. *Arg.* 1.409–24) – here the situation is reversed and 'Apollo' himself is saying goodbye, with a paradoxically conditional prophecy. Among Apollo's *eromenoi* celebrated in poetry are Hyakinthos, Admetos (cf. Call. *h.* 2.47–54 where a pastoral Apollo 'burns' with desire) and the beautiful goatherd Branchos (Call. fr. 229).   **Ἀγεάνακτι:** the name is rare, though of regular formation, and both Agenax and Hegesianax are common enough; Bowie (1985) 73 notes the 'frequency of names in -anax or -anaktidas on Lesbos, and particularly in Mytilene'. Lawall (1967) 88–94 connected the name with the ἄναξ of 79: Ageanax was a 'prince' with whom the lowly goatherd had fallen in love. Of itself, however, 'Ageanax' is not necessarily an aristocratic name (cf. G. Giangrande, *JHS* 88 (1968) 170), though Lykidas' song may have contributed something to *Ecl.* 2.1–2 *formosum pastor Corydon ardebat Alexin,* | *delicias domini, nec quid speraret habebat.* The 'object of desire' is, of course, always the lover's 'master', whatever the social situation.   **Μυτιλήναν:** the normal form up to *c.* 300 BC, after which Μιτυλήνη, the form standardly found in MSS, starts to appear (cf. *RE* xvi 1411–12). For T. the matter must be doubtful, but in this song we might have expected the older form with its associations with Lesbian lyric.

53–4 'both when the Kids appear at evening and the south wind harries the waves of the sea, and when Orion sets his feet upon Ocean'. The constellations of the Kids (*Haedi*), obviously of special interest to a goatherd, and Orion, particularly at its setting (cf. Hes. *WD* 614–26), are both associated with stormy weather which is bad for sailing; the lines refer to a time in late October or November, but the point does not lie in chronological specificity: if Ageanax 'saves' Lykidas, he will have a fair voyage *whenever* he sails, even if he sails at the least propitious time of the year. Weingarth (1967) 129 understands the lines as a strategy of Lykidas to delay Ageanax's departure, but this depends on the interpretation of 55–6 (where see n.).   χὦταν: the only example of ἄν in the 'bucolics', perhaps appropriate to Lykidas' high-style song (cf. Hunter (1996a) 42). νότος: a moderate south wind would in fact be useful in sailing from Cos to Mytilene, but poetry associates this wind with dangerous storms, cf. Hes. *WD* 675 νότοιό τε δεινὰς ἀήτας, Hor. *C.* 1.3.14 (in a *propemptikon*), and that is the point here.   ὑγρά: high-style, cf. 22.167, Pind. *Pyth.* 4.40, Friis Johansen–Whittle on Aesch. *Suppl.* 258–9.

55–6 Cf. *Ecl.* 2.68. How is Ageanax to 'rescue' Lykidas: by yielding physically to Lykidas' desire (cf. 2.131–3) or by going far away so that the passion will abate (so Heubeck (1973) 11–13, Seeck (1975a), Furusawa (1980))? Σ52–6h understand the conditional of 55 as the equivalent of a purpose clause, and the second alternative seems both to suit the choice of verb, 'protect from', 'rescue', and the imaginary narrative. The satisfaction of desire normally leads only to increased desire, and it might be thought odd that Lykidas would be happy to see Ageanax sail away once he has begun a physical relationship with him; the menace of stormy weather might be a subtle reminder to Ageanax that he would really be better off staying (cf. Cairns (1972) 164), but that does not seem to fit the tone of the poem. Rather, Ageanax should go far away as soon as possible, even at a time of bad weather, so that Lykidas' pain will lessen; he will not forget the beloved boy (69–70), but the raging fire will give way to calmer passions. Such an interpretation also suits the subject of Simichidas' following song.   τὸν Λυκίδαν: the use of his own name suits the grand, oracular tone of 52–5; the sudden intrusion of the first person in 56 is to be felt as an emotional break in style.   ὀπτεύμενον: cf. 3.18–20n. The imagery is ubiquitous in ancient poetry, but Sappho fr. 38 Voigt ὄπταις ἄμμε (context unknown) may be relevant. While Ageanax is to sail on the water, Lykidas burns with fire: the contrast is heightened by the fact that Aphrodite is connected with the sea as well as with the fire of love, cf. Meleager, Anth. Pal. 5.176.5–6 (= HE 4026–7) θαῦμα δέ μοι πῶς ἄρα διὰ γλαυκοῖο φανεῖσα | κύματος ἐξ ὑγροῦ, Κύπρι, σὺ πῦρ τέτοκας, Nisbet–Hubbard on Hor. C. 1.5.16.

57–8 Cf. Ecl. 9.57–8, a typically Virgilian combination of 2.38–9 and the present lines (can the identity of line numbers be a coincidence?).   χἀλκυόνες: 'halcyons' were believed to bear their young at the winter solstice and, when calm, the fourteen days around the solstice were the 'halcyon days', cf. Arist. HA 5 542b4–17, Thompson, Birds s.v., Bömer on Ovid, Met. 11.410–748. Halcyons were early identified with the kingfisher, and Aristotle was able to give a detailed description of this truly rara avis (HA 8 616a14–18, 'not much bigger than a sparrow; its colour is dark blue and green and purplish ... its beak is on the green side and is long and narrow'). 'The halcyons will calm the waves ...' may simply be a way of saying 'it will be as calm as on the halcyon days', but perhaps there is an idea that halcyons themselves can affect the weather (with their beautiful voices?, cf. Thompson, Birds 47); at Arg. 1.1084–1102 the appearance of a halcyon is an omen of coming good weather. It may be relevant that Demetrius, On style 166 lists the subjects of Sappho's poetry as 'loves and spring and the halcyon'.   τὰ κύματα τάν τε θάλασσαν: cf. 11.49. The phrase amounts to 'the waves of the sea', but the accumulative series of four nouns emphasises the complete stillness which will take over; on 'hendiadys' in Greek cf. D. Sansone, Glotta 62 (1984) 16–25, Laura Rossi, AION 15 (1993) 121–44.   τόν τε νότον τόν τ' εὖρον: storms are often conceived as battles between winds, cf. Il. 16.765 ὡς δ' εὖρός τε νότος τ' ἐριδαίνετον ἀλλήλοιιν, Od. 5.295–6, Prop. 3.15.31–2, Hor. C. 1.3.12–16 (a propemptikon), 1.9.9–11.   ἔσχατα 'in the lowest depths'.

59–60 > Georg. 1.399.   γλαυκαῖς Νηρηίσι ταί τε κτλ. 'who (ταί τε, relative) of birds are most dear to the green Nereids'. Γλαύκη and Γλαυκονόμη are the names of individual Nereids (Hes.

Theog. 244, 256), and Nereids have a prominent rôle in propemptic poetry, as they were believed to have power over the winds (cf. Hes. *Theog.* 252–4, Hdt. 7.191.2) and to protect travellers, cf. J. M. Barringer, *Divine escorts* (Ann Arbor 1995); other Nereids include γλαυκὰ ... Γαλάνεια (Eur. *Hel.* 1457–8) and Εὐπόμπη (Hes. *Theog.* 261). **ὅσοις τέ περ ἐξ ἁλὸς ἄγρα** 'and to all whose catch comes from the sea', i.e. fishermen. The transmitted ὅσαις presumably arose from the feminines of 59.

61–2 Lykidas now imagines that Ageanax has 'got the message' and is indeed about to set sail; he therefore wishes him a fair sailing in the more conventional optative. Those who understand 55–6 as a request to Ageanax for physical intimacy must explain that this has taken place in an imagined gap before these verses. Lykidas' prayer is addressed to no god: perhaps he does not need such assistance. **ὥρια** 'opportune', an extension of the more usual sense 'in due season' (*Od.* 9. 131 ὥρια πάντα at line-end, Hes. *WD* 630 αὐτὸς δ' ὡραῖον μίμνειν πλόον), cf. Arat. *Phaen.* 153–4 ὁ δὲ πλόος οὐκέτι κώπαις | ὥριος. Others prefer ὥρια 'favourable', as a hyper-Doric form of οὔρια, the standard adjective in such a context. **γένοιτο ... ἵκοιτο:** a rhyme of the final two syllables of the verse with the two syllables before the caesura is rare (cf. 15, 1.96, 24.9, Kidd on Aratus, *Phaen.* 360), though very familiar from medieval Latin ('Leonine verses'). Both here and at 24.9 the effect may suggest a (sub-literary) magical incantation: Lykidas' very words work to effect a safe voyage for Ageanax. The style of *Ecl.* 8.80, *limus ut hic durescit, et haec ut cera liquescit* (love magic), is thus suitably 'Theocritean', as well as indebted to the magical spells of the sub-literary tradition (E. Norden, *Die antike Kunstprosa* (Leipzig 1898) II 813–24). **εὔπλοος:** the nominative makes clear that Ageanax is the subject of ἵκοιτο. The transmitted εὔπλοον has been defended as a 'transferred epithet' actually referring to Ageanax (G. Giangrande, *Mnem.* 33 (1980) 356–7) or as a reference to the idea that harbours too are dangerous places (cf. F. Cairns, *Mnem.* 31 (1978) 72–5). For further discussion cf. H. D. Jocelyn, *Mnem.* 34 (1981) 316–21, A. Andrisano, *MCr* 21/2 (1986/7) 267–75. Prayers for εὔπλοια were a standard element of (real and literary) departures (cf. D. Wachsmuth, ΠΟΜΠΙΜΟΣ Ο ΔΑΙΜΩΝ. *Untersuchung zu den antiken Sakralhandlungen bei Seereisen* (Diss. Berlin 1967) 466–79), but the cult of Aphrodite Εὔπλοια at Knidos

(Paus. 1.1.3) adds point here: Aphrodite will save Ageanax, if he saves Lykidas from her.   ὅρμον: 'Mytilene has two harbours, of which the southern can be closed and holds only fifty triremes, but the northern is large and deep, and is sheltered by a mole' (Strabo 13.2.2).

63–4 > *Ecl.* 2.47–50. As often in *propemptika*, Lykidas promises to celebrate Ageanax's safe arrival; here the promised celebration does not involve sacrifice, perhaps because the singer himself is divine. How Lykidas is to receive news all the way from Lesbos on the same day as Ageanax arrives is a question we perhaps should not ask, but if he were divine there would be no problem at all: Apollo needs no messengers (cf. Pind. *Pyth.* 3.28–30, Apollo's 'all-knowing mind'). Although Lykidas will have musicians and others (τις 66) around him, there is no sign that he will have fellow-symposiasts in the full sense (contrast the otherwise similar Ar. *Peace* 1131–9); he therefore drinks alone, an activity which the iconographic tradition particularly associates with gods, cf. M. Steinhart and W. Slater, *JHS* 117 (1997) 203–11.   ἀνήτινον: fragrant dill is often mentioned as a garland flower, cf. 15.119, Alcaeus fr. 362 Voigt, Sappho fr. 81 Voigt, Thphr. *HP* 9.7.3.   λευκοΐων: i.e. ἴον τὸ λευκόν, perhaps 'stock', but the identification is uncertain, cf. Lembach (1970) 158–60. φυλάσσων: cf. 3.21–3n. Poets treat the disintegration of a symposiast's garland as a sign that he is in love (Call. *Epigr.* 43, Ath. 15 670a), so the verb here may indicate Lykidas' release from passion, however that is to be understood (55–6n.).

65 τὸν Πτελεατικὸν οἶνον: the definite article serves the clarity (*enargeia*) of Lykidas' vision: he imagines the party as taking place, 'and I shall take the wine of Ptelea (which lies at my side)…' The reference of the adjective is quite obscure. Σ allege that Ptelea was a place on Cos which, if a guess, is a reasonable one; Ptelea and Pte-leon are not uncommon place-names (a Ptelea was associated with Ephesos, which would be geographically appropriate, and there were Arcadian and Attic Pteleas, the latter a deme of the *phyle* Oineis 'of the wine', cf. *RE* XXIII 1478–9). Wilamowitz (1924) II 138 suggested that the reference was to Πέλη (cf. modern Pyli) in the Haleis deme (see map); it would suit Lykidas' party if he was to drink a very local wine, but that Πτελέα was a dialect form, or transparent distortion, of Πέλη is not clear. Others follow Σb–c in understanding

that the vines have been trained on elm-trees (πτελέαι), an interpretation to which *Ecl.* 2.70, *semiputata tibi frondosa uitis in ulmo est*,
may allude.

66 This line has been taken to show that Lykidas' celebration will
be indoors, and presumably in winter (53–4); by contrast, the song of
the townsman Simichidas will largely be set out of doors. If so, the
difference would mark the wider scope of Lykidas' sense of 'the
bucolic'. στιβάς (67), however, more naturally suggests an outdoor
setting.   **κύαμον:** the collective singular (cf. 1.49, 53, 11.10, 14.17,
K–G 1 13–14) is very common in the food lists of comedy, e.g.
Ephippus frr. 12–13 K–A. 'Beans' of all kinds – here probably
'broad beans' – appear in literature both as the food of the very
poor and, as here, as a τράγημα ('nibble') accompanying the drinking of wine; in the latter case the resonance is of simple pleasures or
even the Golden Age, cf. Xenophanes fr. 13 G–P πὰρ πυρὶ χρὴ
τοιαῦτα λέγειν χειμῶνος ἐν ὥρηι | ἐν κλίνηι μαλακῆι κατακείμενον,
ἔμπλεον ὄντα, | πίνοντα γλυκὺν οἶνον, ὑποτρώγοντ᾽ ἐρεβίνθους
κτλ., Pl. *Rep.* 2 372b–c, Ar. *Peace* 1131–9, Arnott (1996) 486–7.

67–8 His couch of grass or rushes (cf. 133–4, 13.34) will be covered 'cubit-high' with wild plants. The artful 'rising tricolon' of 68
(cf. 13.45n.) converts a botanical list into a lyrical vision.   **κνύζαι**
'fleabane', cf. Lembach (1970) 29–31. Σ ascribe cooling, ant-
aphrodisiac properties to this plant, which would be contextually
appropriate, but there is little other evidence for the belief. It is
included among καλὰ πάντα at 4.24–5.   **σελίνωι:** cf. 3.21–3n.

69 μαλακῶς: the primary sense is 'on my soft couch, in some
luxury' (cf. 15.28, Ar. *Ach.* 70), but there is also a clear suggestion
that the 'burning desire' of 56 has been replaced by calmer emotions; μαλακῶς colours both verb and participle, with which it is
associated by alliteration.   **μεμναμένος Ἀγεάνακτος:** 'remem-
bering A.' suggests 'drinking to the memory of A.' Before drinking,
Lykidas would say (aloud or to himself) Ἀγεάνακτος (the 'genitive
of the toast', K–G 1 376), cf. 14.18–20, Call. *Epigr.* 29 ἔγχει καὶ
πάλιν εἰπὲ "Διοκλέος" κτλ.; inverted commas around Ἀγεάνακτος
would catch the effect.

70 The transmitted αὐταῖσιν κυλίκεσσι makes no sense (*pace* A.
M. Mesturini, *QUCC* 37 (1981) 105–12, who sees the *topos* of lovers
drinking from the same (αὐταῖσιν) cups). Valckenaer's αὐταῖς ἐν

κυλίκεσσι will mean '[remembering A.] while drinking, [and pressing my lips ...]' or (cf. Serrao (1971) 58) '[remembering A.] both while drinking and when I press my lips ...' These are not impossible, but the true reading may be as banal as (e.g.) πάσαις ἐν κ. or πασαῖσι κ., the error arising from αὐλ- immediately beneath. **χεῖλος ἐρείδων:** an obvious image of the kiss. A cup dedicated to the beloved must be drained entirely.

71–2 > *Ecl.* 5.72–3, cf. 10.41.   **αὐλησεῦντι:** the music of αὐλοί was an ordinary accompaniment of the symposium, but here the pipes are likely to be rather more rustic, cf. 6.42–3n. The origin of the pipers remains quite mysterious. If Ἀχαρνεύς refers to the Attic deme of Acharnai, the reasons for the choice are unknown; Wilamowitz (*Hermes* 34 (1899) 616) suggested that 'Acharnian' here was a transparent modification of 'of Halasarna', a Coan deme near the south coast (modern Cardamina), where there was an important cult of Apollo (Sherwin-White (1978) 61–3, 300). Σ claim that Lykopos was the name of a Coan deme (cf. Lykopeus in 4); such names are otherwise only associated with Aetolia.

72–89 The symposium was a traditional site for the performance of poetry, here of a kind appropriate to the setting. Lykidas will listen to the stories of two, or perhaps three (78–89n.), mythical forebears, which have an obvious relevance to his own situation: Daphnis' death was somehow caused by love, and Komatas was saved from torment by the beauty of his own poetry, cf. further Weingarth (1967) 143–5, Macleod (1983) 168–70. Both offer consolation: the story of Daphnis assures the hearer that others have suffered more than he, and the story of Komatas is of triumph over adversity. The heat of Lykidas' passion, already calmed by Ageanax's departure, is further displaced into the aesthetic experience of listening to song; poetry thus acts as a φάρμακον against desire, although rather differently than in Idyll 11.

The narration of a song in indirect speech goes back to Homer's account of the songs of Demodokos in *Od.* 8 (for the lyric tradition cf. Pind. *Nem.* 5.22–39), but Hellenistic poets seized the opportunities offered by this form for the confusion of different poetic voices and the interplay of 'direct' and 'indirect' speech, cf. *Arg.* 1.496–511, 2.703–13 (the songs of Orpheus), Hunter (1993a) 148–51. The direct address to Komatas in 83–9 fuses Tityros' song with a personal intrusion by Lykidas (or Lykidas/Theocritus) into that song. Virgil took over the style, organisation (a mythological catalogue) and experimentation with 'voice' of 7.72–89 for the song of Silenus in Eclogue 6, which incorporates the lament (in direct speech) of Pasiphae; 'Silenos' was one of the ancient explanations for 'Tityros' (cf. Σ 3.2a, 3.1–2n.). Virgil thus produced a mixture of the Dionysiac (Silenus) and the Apolline (*Ecl.* 6.3–12, 82–4) to match that same mixture in Idylls 1 and 7. Particularly noteworthy rewritings are: (i) Virgil's quotation (6.47, 52) of Calvus fr. 9 Büchner–Courtney, *a, uirgo infelix* . . . , reverses the *makarismos* of Komatas in 83. At 6.45, *et fortunatam, si numquam armenta fuissent* produces a similar effect, with its apparent wish that 'bucolic' had never been invented. (ii) Silenus sings of Hylas, a subject of a Theocritean poem, just as Tityros repeats the subject of Idyll 1. (iii) Pasiphae's adored bull, *latus niueum molli fultus hyacintho* (line 53), is an extraordinary rewriting of Lykidas taking his ease in 66–70. See also 77n. (iv) The 'divine Komatas', for Lykidas an irrecoverable model, becomes Virgil's immediate predecessor Gallus (himself *diuinus poeta* at *Ecl.* 10.17), initiated into poetry by the Muses.

73 For the myth of Daphnis cf. Idyll 1, Intro. **Ξενέας:** the name of Daphnis' beloved is very variously given (cf. Hunter (1983b) 108 n. 32), and Xenea occurs only here. Xeneia and Xeino, and the masculines Xeinias, Xeinis and Xenas are all attested names.

74 > *Ecl.* 5.28, 10.13–14. **ὄρος:** quite likely Mt Etna, *the* Sicilian mountain. **ἀμφεπονεῖτο:** the simple πονεῖσθαι may denote 'feel pain', so the meaning may be 'was in distress for [Daphnis]'. More likely, however, there is a particular nuance: the mountains 'lamented in suffering for [Daphnis]', cf. *EA* 31–2 "τὰν Κύπριν αἰαῖ" | ὤρεα πάντα λέγοντι (with Reed's note), *Ecl.* 5.28. The extension of meaning is helped by the parallelism with ἐθρήνευν, by the fact that mountains are the obvious place *around* which song or lamentation of any kind will *echo* (cf. *EB* 23), and because πόνος is closely linked with song in this poem (51, 139). For the 'pathetic fallacy' cf. 1.71–5n.

75 **Ἱμέρα:** genitive of Ἱμέρας, with the regular Doric contraction of -αο, cf. 1.103, 4.1, 13.7 etc. Two rivers of this name rise in Central Sicily, one flowing south, the other north to the coast beside the town of Himera; they were often regarded as branches of the same river (cf. *RE* VIII 1620–1). There is here an allusion to Stesichorus of Himera who sang of Daphnis (above, p. 65), but the context also associates the name with ἵμερος 'desire', thus making it particularly appropriate to Daphnis' suffering. It is not necessary to assume that the Himeras has become the site of Daphnis' death.   φύοντι: the present tense, like the simile which follows, allows us to hear Tityros' song, as well as Lykidas' report of it. The past tense of the papyri probably arose by correction after a false division as αἶτ' ἐφύ-.

76 'when he was wasting, as snow [wastes] ...' For the simile in indirect speech cf. *Od.* 8.518.   χιὼν ὥς τις: 'generalising' τις is common in similes, even with rather unexpected nouns, cf. Eur. *Tr.* 1298 καπνὸς ὥς τις, J. Vahlen, *Opuscula Academica* (Leipzig 1908) II 180–202. For this image cf. *Od.* 19.205–9 (Penelope weeping as she listens to her disguised husband), Call. *h.* 6.91–2 (with Hopkinson's note). That Daphnis melts 'like snow' may be connected with the watery manner of his death and/or the fact that a spring appeared where he died (above, p. 66). Cf. also Berger (1984) 17: 'Daphnis melting in desire ... serves as a harbinger to the spring that blossoms in the story of Comatas.'   κατετάκετο: the evidence suggests that the augmented form is as probable as κατατάκετο, even in the high style of this poem, cf. Molinos Tejada 264 78, K. Mickey, *TPhS* 1981.50–1.   Αἷμον: the Balkan range (Stara Planina) of northern Thrace, which runs east through modern Bulgaria; here it is conceived as the freezing (Virg. *Georg.* 2.488) northern boundary of the Greek world. T. probably has in mind a single mountain believed to be so high that the Euxine and the Adriatic were both visible from its summit (Strabo 7.5.1, Livy 40.21.2).

77 > *Ecl.* 6.30, 42, 8.44, *Georg.* 1.332. Athos is the highest mountain for someone whose horizons are fixed in the Aegean; Rhodope runs south and south-east through modern Bulgaria (Rodopi Planina); Strabo 7.5.1 says that it is second in height only to Haimos. The Caucasus range runs between the Black Sea and the Caspian and formed the north-eastern boundary of the known world. Cf. Rosenmeyer (1969) 114, 'the vast world opens up before us to enhance the fiction that the grief cannot be contained'.

78–89 The subject switches to 'the goatherd' who was placed in a box because of the wickedness of his master and subsequently nurtured by bees. This is a foundation myth for 'aipolic' poetry, as

Daphnis is the founding hero of 'bucolic' song, and it is appropriate
to Lykidas the goatherd that it comes in the climactic position. Σ
summarise a story from Lykos of Rhegion: 'In a cave of the Nymphs
on Mt Thalamos near Thurii ... a shepherd (ποιμήν) regularly
sacrificed his master's (δεσπότου) animals to the Muses; in his anger
at this, the master shut him away in a box (λάρνακα) to see whether
the goddesses would save him. After two months he opened the box
and found the shepherd alive and the box full of honeycombs'
(*FGrHist* 570 F7). T. clearly alludes to this story; his goatherd is a
poet (82), but it is not clear from the summary whether the sacrifices
to the Muses indicate that the same was true of Lykos' herdsman.
This South Italian folktale, like the story of Daphnis, may have
appeared in poetry before T., but there is no other evidence.

In 83–9 Tityros/Lykidas apostrophises a goatherd called Komatas
who '*also* was locked in a box, and *also* laboured through the spring
of the year feeding upon the honeycombs of bees'. If Komatas and
'the goatherd' of 78–82 are identical, then the comparison is presumably with Daphnis who is regularly said to have been exposed as
an infant (perhaps in a λάρναξ), though bees enter the Daphnis
story elsewhere only in texts plainly influenced by T. It seems at
least as natural to understand that Komatas is being likened to, not
identified with, the nameless poet-goatherd of 78–82 (so Radt (1971)
254–5); the verbal parallelisms (φέρβον 80 – φερβόμενος 85, ἄνθεσσι
81 – ἔτος ὥριον 85) support this interpretation. We therefore have
three, not two, founding figures of bucolic and aipolic mythology –
Daphnis, 'the goatherd', and Komatas. Although Komatas is clearly
in some senses a 'self-representation' of Lykidas (cf. 85n., Alpers
(1996) 150–1), 'You Komatas, as well as I (Lykidas)' (so Van
Groningen (1959) 33 n. 1) seems less probable, and 'you Komatas, as
well as Ageanax' entirely improbable (N. Palomar Pérez in *Homenatge
a Josep Alsina* (Tarragona 1992) 1 253–7).

78 εὐρέα: cf. 1.65n.

79 κακαῖσιν ἀτασθαλίαισιν: a variation on a Homeric phrase
(*Od.* 12.300, 24.458) creates a typically grand 'heroisation' of the fate
of the goatherd.   **ἄνακτος:** cf. 52n.

80–1 σιμαὶ ... μέλισσαι: the mannered hyperbaton perhaps
reflects a belief that σιμαί 'blunt-nosed' was an old word for bees,
connected with σίμβλος (cf. Σ, *Et. Mag.* 713.23 Gaisford, Σ Hes.

Theog. 594). For bees and poets cf. 1.146–8n.   **κέδρον ἐς ἀδεῖαν:**
cedar has a distinctive fragrance (cf. *Epigr.* 8.4, *Od.* 5.59–60 etc.), and
its use for coffins (Eur. *Tr.* 1141, *Alc.* 365) is relevant here.
ἄνθεσσι: that bees actually brought 'flowers' back to the hive, not
just 'the products of flowers', is a widely attested ancient view, cf.
Davies–Kathirithamby 56–8, Mynors on Virg. *Georg.* 4.38–41.

82 The bees saved Komatas 'because the Muse poured sweet nec-
tar over his mouth', i.e. the Muses had made Komatas a poet (cf.
Hes. *Theog.* 81–4, 97), so the bees, as the embodiments of poetic
sweetness, kept him alive in an appropriate manner. The *Theogony*
passage is about good kings and poets, not a bad ἄναξ. A οὕνεκεν-
clause not infrequently rounds off a verse-paragraph cf. Call. *h.* 3.45,
Griffiths (1996) 111.

83 μακαριστέ: principally, though not exclusively, used of the
dead (οἱ μακαρῖται).   **Κομᾶτα:** the name of an Italian goatherd
in Idyll 5, and a known historical name from Cyrene and Rhodes
(*LGPN* I s.v.), though not otherwise known as a mythical poet.
τάδε τερπνὰ πεπόνθεις 'these pleasures were your fate [pluperfect]',
a suitable way to refer to the mysterious mixture of sweetness and
toil in 84–5. Gow prefers to understand the verb as perfect in form
and present in sense (cf. 11.1n.).

85 φερβόμενος: for the prosody cf. 11.45–8n.   **ἔτος ὥριον**
ἐξεπόνασας 'laboured through the spring of the year'; *Eλ* 73 ἀνὰ
νύκτα τὸν ἱερὸν ὕπνον ἐμόχθει is a similarly striking locution. T.'s
phrase is hard to parallel, but cf. δείελον ἦμαρ 'evening', *annus hiber-*
nus 'winter' (Hor. *Epod.* 2.29); others understand 'the year with its
seasons'. The flowers of 81 suggest that the goatherd also suffered
during the spring or summer. The verb, glossed by Σ as ἐπλήρωσας,
suggests through echo of 51 (where see n.) that Komatas' 'feeding
upon honeycomb' was metaphorical as well as literal, i.e. he composed poetry, though it is not necessary to suppose (with Radt (1971)
254–5) that a particular poem known to T.'s audience is at issue. The
echo shows how closely Lykidas associates himself with Komatas.

86 > *Ecl.* 10.35. Bing (1988) 60–2 notes the contrast between the
'cocks of the Muses' who try to compete against Homer, and Lykidas
who regrets that he was not lucky enough to have had the privilege
of listening to the great poets of a now irretrievable past; Lykidas'
modesty again contrasts with the more usual agonistic rivalry of

poets, embodied in the attitudes of Simichidas. The fourth-century tragedian Astydamas regretted that he did not live with the great poets of the past so that he could properly be judged against them (*TrGF* I 60 T2a).   ἐπ' ἐμεῦ 'in my time'. The transmitted ἐπ' ἐμοί would most naturally suggest 'would that *it were in my power* for you to be alive ...', which would make excellent sense (particularly if the speaker were a god) but seems syntactically impossible; LSJ offer one dialect example of ἐπ' ἐμοί as 'in my time'. Gallavotti suggested ἔτι μοι.

87 For the syntax cf. 11.55n.   τοι 'for you'. Lykidas imagines filling the rôle that Thyrsis offers at 1.14, and cf. 3.1–2.   καλάς: Lykidas is a connoisseur of goats, but Komatas' goats reflect the divinity (89) of the herdsman; cf. the wonderful condition of the goats herded by Apollo at Call. *h.* 2.50–4.

88 ὑπὸ δρυσὶν ἢ ὑπὸ πεύκαις: not just a *locus amoenus*, but an epic juxtaposition (cf. *Il.* 11.494, 23.328) in keeping with the general style of the song, cf. 1.1n. Oaks which grieved for Daphnis (74) now offer shade for the performance of peaceful bucolic song: thus is Lykidas' own emotional catharsis plotted through the song.

89 ἁδὺ μελισδόμενος: cf. 1.1.n. The participle brings out the meaning of the image of the μέλισσαι.   θεῖε Κομᾶτα closes a ring around the apostrophe begun in 93, cf. 3.6–22, 6.6–19. The epithet does not merely 'mark Comatas as an inspired minstrel' (Gow), like the θεῖοι ἀοιδοί of Homer (*Od.* 4.17, 8.87 etc.); for Lykidas, and all bucolic poets, Komatas is a divine, or at least heroised, presence.

90 ἀπεπαύσατο: cf. 1.138n.

91–2 Λυκίδα φίλε: cf. 27. Simichidas sees 'bucolic' song as essentially a matter of rustic reference. He therefore 'hyper-bucolicises' by echoing Hesiod's investiture as a poet by the Muses, αἵ νυ ποθ' Ἡσίοδον καλὴν ἐδίδαξαν ἀοιδήν, | ἄρνας ποιμαίνονθ' Ἑλικῶνος ὑπὸ ζαθέοιο (*Theog.* 22–3), but changing Hesiod's Muses into the more obviously rustic 'Nymphs' (148n.). He presents himself ἀν' ὤρεα βουκολέων, not because this is (or was) his profession or because the verb may mean 'wander' (Giangrande (1980) 137–9, cf. *Ecl.* 6.52), but because he mistakenly (cf. 1.80n.) sees 'herding on the mountain' as the inevitable setting for the composition of 'bucolic' poetry (cf. Lykidas' ἐν ὄρει, 51), no less inevitable than Pan, who duly appears in his poem. He does not expect Lykidas (or us) to believe that he is a cowherd, but he regards the mere form of words as necessary; perhaps in his (over-)sophistication he regards *Theogony* 23 as also just a metaphor. Moreover, by aligning himself with Daphnis 'the cowherd' against the goatherd alliance of Lykidas–Komatas, he continues the sense of an *agon*, which is so dear to him; cf. the exchange of 'aipolic' and 'bucolic' performances in Idyll 1.

πολλὰ μὲν ἄλλα: a familiar rhetorical strategy, by which the speaker 'selects one choice item from a multitude of possibilities' (W. H. Race, *The classical priamel from Homer to Boethius* (Leiden 1982) 105). It goes without saying that those possibilities may be purely imaginary. **κἠμέ:** primarily 'me as well as you' (cf. ἐν ὄρει 51), but we will also hear 'me as well as Hesiod'.

93 > *Ecl.* 3.73.   **ἐσθλά:** cf. 4n. Simichidas' pride (highlighted rather than concealed by που) contrasts sharply with Lykidas' modesty (μελύδριον 51).   **Ζηνός:** Ζανός may be correct (cf. 18.19, *Epigr.* 22.1, Gallavotti (1984) 8–9), but is by no means limited to Doric, cf. Molinos Tejada 39, and Ζην- occurs on Coan texts (Schwyzer 1 577). The present verse is a version of the Homeric 'heaven-high fame', cf. Ar. *Birds* 216 (bird-song rises) πρὸς Διὸς ἕδρας, *P. Vind. Rainer* 29801 Α60 (Gow, OCT p. 168) πῆι μελέων κλέος εὐρὺ τὸ καὶ Διὸς οὔατ' ἰαίνει;, but it is difficult not to see a reference to Ptolemy Philadelphos, who was born on Cos and whose assimilation to Zeus was a commonplace of contemporary poetry (e.g. 17.131–4). It is characteristic of Simichidas to keep his eye on the *Realpolitik* of patronage. It is very difficult, though entirely reasonable, to draw inferences from this verse about T.'s own relations with Philadelphos.

94 The implication may be that poets should leave it to others to judge the relative merits of their poems, cf. 27–31n.   **γεραίρεν:** infinitive, cf. 1.14n. Simichidas presumably means 'I will pay you the compliment of performing my very best song', but 'honour' is something one standardly does to gods, and we will be tempted to see that nuance here.

95 To be 'dear to the Muses' can mean 'to be a good poet' (1.141, 5.80–1), but this is a wonderfully naïve remark if Simichidas is actually speaking to Apollo.

96–127 Simichidas tries to help his friend Aratos who is suffering

in love, before urging him to join in giving up such pursuits and
leading a quiet life. The theme of the song thus has much in common with Lykidas', as is to be expected in a 'bucolic exchange'; for
Lykidas' lyrical self-absorption, however, Simichidas substitutes a
detached display of poetic fireworks. Like Lykidas, Simichidas' song
experiments with different voices: 103ff. may be taken as a re-
creation of the song of Aristis (so Heubeck (1973) 9–10), or (more
probably) as the voice of the poet himself. On the delivery of the
song cf. 98n.

96–7 A sneeze was always taken as an omen of good or ill, cf. *Od.*
17.541–50, and at 18.16 'a good man sneezed for Menelaos' when he
competed with the other suitors, which – if we ignore the history of
the marriage – was presumably a good omen. Here the basic sense is
'the Loves have affected Simichidas', but whether that is for good
or ill has been debated since antiquity (cf. Σ). In fact, however,
Simichidas is δειλός, as all lovers are, but the contrast between his
passion and that of Aratos is not requited vs unrequited love, as
nearly all *eros* is 'by definition' unrequited; rather, there is a contrast
between *the nature* of Simichidas' love (which he freely confesses) and
the gut-burning desire from which Aratos suffers and which he perhaps seeks to conceal (105). Simichidas distances himself from his
passion with resigned and amused irony, whereas Aratos, as to some
extent Lykidas also, is totally involved in his suffering; as the simile
of 97 makes clear, Simichidas is thus 'happier' than Aratos, though
he too is a victim of the Erotes. It is perhaps tempting to extrapolate
a more general contrast between ideas of the 'emotional investment'
demanded by heterosexual desire and that found in paederasty, but
literature offers no clear evidence for such a contrast at this date; for
general considerations cf. Hunter (1996a) 167–71. On this opening cf.
W. A. Oldfather in *Classical studies presented to Edward Capps* (Princeton
1936) 268–81, Seeck (1975a), Furusawa (1980) 57–61.   **Σιμιχίδαι**
picks up and contrasts with τὸν Λυκίδαν (55).   **Μυρτοῦς:** because
of the myrtle's association with Aphrodite, such names often, though
not always, belong to *hetairai*, cf. Headlam on Herodas 1.89.
εἴαρος: goats 'love the spring' because it offers fresh food and abundant opportunities for mating; the assonance may evoke an 'etymological' connection between *eros* and springtime, cf. K. J. McKay,
AUMLA 44 (1975) 185. The earthy and amused comparison, cf. 4.39

ὅσον αἶγες ἐμὶν φίλαι, ὅσον ἀπέσβης, is used by Simichidas as a marker of what he perceives as appropriate to the 'bucolic'. Σ understand 'as much as goats love *in the springtime*, i.e. wildly' (cf. Furusawa (1980) 58 n. 103), but the balance of the sentiment is against this.   ἔρανται: for the variation of active and middle cf. 29.32; ἐρᾶντι may, however, be correct (cf. 1.90 γελᾶντι).

98 For Aratos cf. Idyll 6, Intro.   τὰ πάντα: cf. 3.3–5n. ἀνέρι τήνωι: the singer emphatically distances himself from the events he is describing. Whereas the singer of Lykidas' song unambiguously identifies himself as Lykidas (55), Simichidas' song could be performed by another singer: μοι in 103 and 118 are inconclusive, and even 'my *xeinos*' in 119 does not *necessarily* pick up 98. Simichidas' song could be performed by others, whereas Lykidas' performance is wholly personal.

99 Aristis – the name is very common all over the Aegean, though not yet attested precisely in this form on Cos – 'knows' of Aratos' passion, and (?) has told Simichidas; hence perhaps the uncertainty over the identity of the beloved (105). Many critics have suggested that Aristis is to be understood as having written a poem on the subject, or at least that his knowledge of Aratos' suffering is a direct result of the special insight poets have, cf. Lawall (1967) 95, Furusawa (1980) 63–5. In either case, he functions as Simichidas' answer to Lykidas' Tityros, who sang of Daphnis' love.

100–1 > *Ecl.* 7.22–3.   ἐσθλός: cf. 12n.   ἄριστος: the pun perhaps echoes one made by 'Aristis' himself, but there is clearly more involved here than we can now recover. Aristis is described not just as good enough to compete as a kitharode at the Pythian musical contests, but as an equal to Apollo himself, the divine φορμιγκτάς (*Il.* 1.603–4, *h. Ap.* 182–8 etc.); Simichidas has clearly not understood the lessons to be drawn from Lykidas' modesty. If Lykidas is Apollo, the verses are notably amusing.   φόρμιγγι: an archaising, high-style word for the kithara which Aristis will have used.

102 The ὡς-clause is probably dependent upon οἶδεν rather than ἀείδειν. The language recalls 56, in the amoebean manner of song-exchange.   ὀστέον: the Doric form is ὀστίον, but in this poem choice is very difficult, cf. above, p. 150.

103–14 Pan's well-known fondness for beautiful boys (and goats) makes him the appropriate god for Simichidas' overtly 'bucolic' prayer. The prayer is an ἀγωγή, a request, familiar in magical texts, to a god to bring the loved one to the lover's door (cf. J. Winkler, *The constraints of desire* (New York/London 1990) 82–98); Simichidas' prayer is, however, of a striking kind. If Pan does what he asks, the god's reward will not be a fat sacrifice or new honours, but merely a wish (not a promise) that Pan's statue not get a whipping in an arcane Arcadian rite; such a reward is clearly not within the suppliant's gift. If, however, Pan fails to do what is asked, his punishment (expressed again as a wish) will be physical torture and a fantastic inversion of the pastoralist pattern: he will spend the winter in the freezing north and the summer in the burning south (contrast Pind. *Isthm.* 2.41–2). These ironic and learned wishes show that Simichidas is striking a witty pose, both literary and personal: such for him is what constitutes the 'bucolic' world, and he is not really interested in whether or not Aratos 'catches' Philinos, an affair whose ultimate insignificance is displayed in the ludicrous exaggeration of the threats to the god. It is, as Aratos is to understand, Simichidas' own relationship with Aratos which matters.

103 Relative clauses giving a god's special sites are a standard feature of prayer and hymnal style, cf. *Il.* 1.37–8 'Hear me, Lord of the silver bow, who rule Chryse and holy Killa ...', Norden (1913) 168–76.   Ὁμόλας: a mountain and town north of Mt Ossa in Thessaly; it is beside Tempe (1.67n.), which may have influenced the adjective ἐρατόν. A special association between Pan and this area is otherwise unattested; it may be an arcane reference on a par with 106–8.   λέλογχας 'received as your portion (λαγχάνειν)', i.e. 'rule over'.

104 ἄκλητον: καλεῖν, 'call', 'invite', is the standard term for asking a lover to visit, cf. 2.101, 116, 3.7, 29.39. Pan is asked to perform a piece of magic on a par with Aphrodite's carrying-off of Paris in *Il.* 3.   κείνοιο: if correct, this is a striking epicism (for τήνοιο), though a complex one, for Homer has only κείνου, not κείνοιο, and T. otherwise only τήνω, not τήνοιο, cf. Gallavotti (1984) 41–2; Coan Doric in fact uses κῆνος (Buck (1955) 101). If κείνοιο is correct, it will mark the elevation (and artificiality?) of the prayer.   ἐρείσαις 'press him into ...'

105 On the reasons for the apparent uncertainty (or feigned ignorance) as to the identity of the beloved cf. 99n. εἴτε τις ἄλλος is necessary both to cover all the options with Pan, in case Philinos is not in fact the *eromenos*, and to tease Aratos with the changeability of his affections and the relative insignificance of the *eromenos* (cf. 103–14n.). In the subsequent prayer to the Erotes the apparent uncertainty disappears, as the gods need a particular target for their arrows.   ἄρα 'indeed', 'in truth', cf. Denniston 37–8.   **Φιλῖνος ὁ μαλθακός:** Philinos (< φιλεῖν) is a very common name all over the Aegean, but particularly at Cos (*LGPN* I s.v. distinguish forty Coans of the name). At 2.115 Delphis claims to have beaten Φιλῖνος ὁ χαρίεις, who has often been identified with a very successful Coan athlete of the first half of the century, Philinos son of Hegepolis (Paus. 6.17.2, *LGPN* I s.v. 46), but the identification is uncertain at best; μαλθακός may, however, be a pejorative way of saying much the same as χαρίεις. 'Softness' characterises 'feminine' men (cf. Ar. *Thesm.* 191–2 of Agathon), and μαλθακός or μαλακός is used of pathics at least as early as [Arist.] *Probl.* 4 880a6; *P. Hib.* 1.54.11 (*c.* 245) refers to a dancer as 'Zenobios ὁ μαλακός' (cf. Plaut. *MG* 668). The adjective is thus part of Simichidas' strategy for weaning Aratos from his love; Philinos is simply not worth so much attention. Some of the more brutal implications of μαλθακός are picked up again in 120–1 (where see n.). Dover (1978) 79 notes a certain shift in poetry after the fourth century towards preferred 'feminine characteristics in eromenoi', but most of the unambiguous literary evidence is rather later than T.

106 Three initial spondees, the only such verse in Idyll 7, mark the (mock) seriousness of the promises.   **ὦ Πὰν φίλε:** cf. Pl. *Phdr.* 279b7, 1.64n.

107–8 The whipping of Pan's statue with squills by 'Arcadian boys' is a rite not otherwise attested, but of a common type, and squills had many magical uses (Hipponax fr. 6 West, Lembach (1970) 63–5, Polunin–Huxley 214); Pythagoras was said to have written a book about them (Pliny, *NH* 19.94). T. presumably had a source in a work on Arcadian history and/or customs, cf. *FGrHist* IIIB, pp. 25–40, but the very obscurity of this practice in Pan's homeland suits Simichidas' conception of 'bucolic'. A tantalising scrap of a scholion in Π⁵ seems to refer to a Spartan custom, perhaps adduced as a parallel to the Arcadian rite. It may be relevant that one type of squill at least was thought to have the same inflammatory effect upon the

skin as nettles (Arist. fr. 223 Rose, Nicander, *Alex.* 254); the whipping
will thus lead 'naturally' to the discomforts of 109–10. The Homeric echo
offers a potent reminder to Pan of his suffering, cf. *Il.* 23.716–17
(Ajax and Odysseus wrestling), πυκναὶ δὲ σμώδιγγες ἀνὰ πλευράς
τε καὶ ὤμους | αἵματι φοινικόεσσαι ἀνέδραμον, which would be
precisely the result of the whipping.   **κρέα:** Munatios (*apud* Σ) saw
here a reference to an Arcadian festival (ἑορτή), not just an occasional practice. He also noted that the Chians whipped Pan when
'the *choregoi*' sacrifice too small an animal, with the result that the
subsequent feast is unsatisfactory; Buecheler deleted the reference to
'the Chians', thus making Munatios' explanation apply to the Arcadian practice. Pan would indeed be the right god to blame for skinny
flocks (from which sacrificial animals would be taken), as well as for a
poor supply of wild game, but it seems more likely that the reference
here is to hunting; κρέα 'carcass' (cf. Call. *h.*3.88) may be 'hunts-
man's language' for 'game', 'meat', cf. the proverb 'a hare running
for its meat (κρεῶν)' (*CPG* I 108). In the absence of other texts, however, we must confess ignorance; for speculation as to the nature and
meaning of the rite cf. Borgeaud (1988) 68–73.

109–14 It is standard magical practice to threaten the god or spirit if he does not do what you want, cf. *PGM* XII 141–4 'If you dis-
obey me and don't go to him, [name of spirit], I will tell the great
god, and after he has speared you through, he will chop you up into
pieces and feed your members to the mangy dog who lies among the
dungheaps. For this reason, listen to me immediately, immediately;
quickly, quickly, so I won't have to tell you again' (trans. Kotansky),
M. Fantuzzi and F. Maltomini, *ZPE* 114 (1996) 27–9. Such threats
may be appropriate to the request: thus in *P. Berol.* 21243, col. ii.26–
30 (W. Brashear, *ZPE* 33 (1979) 261–78) a headache sufferer is to
threaten Osiris, Ammon and Esenephthys with continuous head-
aches until the sufferer's headache stops. So here, the torments with
which Pan is threatened are a wildly exaggerated version of the sufferings of the lover who endures sleepless nights of cold outside the
beloved's door (122–4) and emotional anguish on a par with 'sleeping on nettles' (cf. 13.64–71n.). Such magical practices found literary
expression in the contemporary vogue for 'curse poetry', i.e. catalogues of outlandish punishments which the poet wished upon an
enemy, cf. Call. *Ibis*, Moero, *Curses*, Euphorion, *Curses or The Cup-*

stealer, Watson (1991), M. Huys, *Le poème élégiaque hellénistique P. Brux. Inv. E. 8934 et P. Sorb. 2254* (Brussels 1991). Watson (1991) 135–7 notes that these threats to Pan are marked by the comic 'incongruity between offence and punishment' typical of 'curse poetry'; the 'genre' has deep roots in earlier periods (cf. Hipponax fr. 115 West, a 'reverse *propemptikon*'), but Simichidas here produces a 'bucolicised' version of a contemporary poetic style.

109–10 The initial spondees pick up 105 to mark the other side of the promise. The first threat, enlivened by the harsh alliteration in 110, is that the god will scratch himself all over to relieve the itching of insect bites and sleep in nettles, both not entirely 'unrealistic' misfortunes to befall a countryman.   **νεύσαις:** νεύσεις would be an example of the future used 'when the condition contains a strong appeal to the feelings or a threat or warning' (Goodwin § 447), but it may be a learned correction.   **κατὰ ... κνάσαιο:** tmesis; the verb is an aorist optative passive.

111–14 > *Ecl.* 10.65–8. Simichidas now outdoes Lykidas' catalogue of mountains (76–7).

111–12 The Edoni inhabited the mountains between Macedonia and Thrace, whereas the Hebros (Maritsa), a by-word for cold and ice (Philip, *Anth. Pal.* 9.56.1 (= *GP* 2879), Hor. *C.* 3.25.10, *Epist.* 1.3.3), flows through modern Bulgaria, dividing Haimos from Rhodope (76–7n.), and then turns south towards the Aegean; it now marks the border between Greece and Turkey. Simichidas thus picks up (rather loosely) the geography of Lykidas' song as part of bucolic 'capping'; so too 'the pole star' replaces Lykidas' Orion (54), with which it was actually associated (24.11–12, *Od.* 5.273–4, Krevans (1983) 218).

Interpretation, and perhaps text, of 112 are uncertain. If Pan is 'turned towards the Hebros' the idea will be that he is heading north, i.e. even in this desperate place he is heading in the wrong direction. Pause after ποταμόν would, however, produce a rhythmical structure to match 114, but τετραμμένος ἐγγύθεν Ἄρκτω is very difficult. A participle meaning 'camped' *vel sim.* would suit excellently, but nothing plausible has been suggested; the unmetrical variant κεκλιμένος presumably started life as a gloss.

113–14 πυμάτοισι παρ' Αἰθιόπεσσι: cf. *Od.* 1.23 Αἰθίοπας ... ἔσχατοι ἀνδρῶν. By 'Ethiopia' T. means the desert south of Elephantine (cf. Hdt. 2.29, Strabo 1.2.25); wherever they were placed geographically, however, the Ethiopians ('the burnt ones') were regarded as the nearest neighbours of the sun (Diggle on Eur. *Phaethon* 4), and this is the point of the threat: you can't get hotter than this. Herodotus equates Pan with the Egyptian Mendes, and he was worshipped in southern Egypt (Hdt. 2.46, Strabo 17.2.3, Diod. Sic. 1.18.2). **Βλεμύων:** a tribe which actually lived between Meroe and the Red Sea (cf. Strabo 17.1.2, following Eratosthenes, *RE* III 566–8, F. M. Snowden, *Blacks in antiquity. Ethiopians in the Greco-Roman experience* (Cambridge, Mass. 1970) 116–17), but here imagined to inhabit a desert south of the sources of the Nile. 'The rock of the Blemyes' may well have figured in a contemporary discussion of the Nile's sources. The point of 'from where the Nile is no longer visible' is not merely that the famous problem of the river's sources meant that this is a way of saying 'as far south as you can go', but it is in summer that the Nile flooded and water would be most abundant in its vicinity; this is, therefore, what you would wish to see in the summer, and the fact that Pan will not have this privilege twists the knife, as does 112.

115–19 After 114 the singer may (comically) pause to see whether his prayer is answered; such a performative joke would suit the general tone of his treatment of Aratos' affair and the literary affiliations of the song. As no *eromenos* suddenly materialises in Aratos' embrace, he changes tack to punish the boy: just as Pan was threatened with a version of Aratos' suffering, so now Philinos is to feel the anguish of love.

115–16 Pausanias (7.5.10, 7.24.5) locates 'the spring of Byblis' at Miletos; Hyetis is completely unknown, though the name has an obvious appropriateness for a spring. If this is the spring into which Byblis was metamorphosed after killing herself as a result of an incestuous passion of (or for) her brother Kaunos, there will be a good reason for the Erotes to be there: it is a permanent memorial to their power and hence 'sweet [to the Erotes]'. It is not improbable that these verses allude to particular (Hellenistic) poems: Apollonius wrote a *Foundation of Kaunos*, and cf. Nicaenetus fr. 1 Powell, Krevans (1983) 207–8. This would then be another contemporary poetic manner – and one employed by T. himself – which Simichidas incorporates into his potpourri; for 'ktistic' poetry at this date cf.

Hunter (1989) 10–11. Miletos was under the control of Philadelphos after 279 (*RE* xv 1605–6), and there may be a political element in T.'s choice of cult.   **λιπόντες:** the standard mode for a 'cletic' prayer, cf. 1.125, Sappho fr. 2 Voigt, Nisbet–Hubbard on Hor. *C.* 1.30.   **Οἰκοῦντα:** a Carian town not far from Miletos, said to have been founded by Byblis' father, the eponymous Miletos (Parthenius, *Erot. Path.* 11); Σ Dion. Perieg. 825 reports that Miletos founded a temple of Aphrodite at Oikous, and that the settlement was subsequently moved to the site of 'Miletos' by Miletos' son, Keladon.   **Διώνας:** the mother of Aphrodite, cf. 15.106, 17.36. It is Aphrodite herself who is elsewhere associated with Oikous and Miletos (Posidippus, *Anth. Pal.* 12.131.1 (= *HE* 3082)), and some see here an anticipation of the familiar Latin equation *Dione = Venus* (Bömer on Ovid, *Fasti* 5.309); another possible example at *EA* 93 is disputed. In view, however, of our ignorance of the sources and 'historicity' of the passage, such an assumption seems dangerous; there is nothing intrinsically improbable in a cult of the goddess's mother.

117 The comparison, perhaps to the rosy cheeks of the boy gods, may have a particular point for the Erotes of Miletos, but if so, it is unknown; it may have been purely conventional, cf. 'Plato', *Anth. Plan.* 210.2 πορφυρέοις μήλοισιν ἐοικότα παῖδα Κυθήρης, *Arg.* 3.121–2 (Eros) γλυκερὸν δέ οἱ ἀμφὶ παρειάς | χροιῆς θάλλεν ἔρευθος, but here it provides the required 'bucolic' element in the prayer to the Erotes (cf. 144).

118–19 An *eromenos* was not normally represented as feeling *eros*, so Philinos is to be punished with desire for someone else. The verses could be taken as the standard warning to the beloved that he or she will themselves one day suffer in love, so they should show pity now (23.33–4 etc.); thus in weaning Aratos from his passion, Simichidas does not *openly* reveal his hand until 122.   **ἱμερόεντα:** as Philinos inspires desire, his punishment will be appropriately reciprocal. **δύσμορος:** here used in reproach, cf. Men. *Sam.* 255, δύστηνος at 15.31, 87, τάλας at 2.4 and ὠιζυρέ at 10.1.

120–1 That Philinos is himself to feel desire leads 'naturally' to the idea that he is himself losing the attractiveness of an ideal *eromenos*. Aratos ought therefore to reflect upon whether Philinos is worth the trouble, particularly in view of the harsh imagery (cf. below); on

the surface, however, the verses are a dramatised version of the
standard argument that the beloved should yield now, because soon
no one will ask them (29.27–34, Theognis 1305–10, *Ecl.* 2.17–18 etc.).
Serrao attractively suggests ((1971) 65–6) that the Erotes have heard
the prayer of 117–19 and are already at work, afflicting Philinos with
an unrequited and wasting passion; hence the suddenness in the
deterioration of 'lovely Philinos', matching the speed with which
'ripe' pears become 'over-ripe'. The verses contain a reworking of
Archilochus, *SLG* 478.24–31:

> Νεοβούλη[
> ἄ]λλος ἀνὴρ ἐχέτω·
> αἰαῖ πέπειρα δ.[
>
> ἄν]θος δ' ἀπερρύηκε παρθενήιον
> καὶ χάρις ἣ πρὶν ἐπῆν·
> κόρον γὰρ οὐκ[
>
> ..]ης δὲ μέτρ' ἔφηνε μαινόλις γυνή·
> ἐς] κόρακας ἄπεχε·

Let some other man have Neoboule; alas, she is all too ripe ...
her maiden's bloom has lost its petals; gone is the charm she
once had. She can't get enough ... a crazy woman. No thanks –
let her go to the crows!

'Archilochus' rejects Neoboule as past her best and more than a little
'shop-soiled'; Aratos will not find it hard to apply this to the case of
Philinos. On the reworking of Archilochus cf. esp. Henrichs (1980).
T. may have been drawn to this poem, *inter alia*, by the fact that the
narrative of a seduction 'amidst the flowers' could readily be constructed as a proto-bucolic.   **καὶ δὴ μάν:** if sound, this unparalleled collocation probably suggests 'and indeed ...', rather than 'in
any case ...', i.e. he is already (over-)ripe for a passion of his own,
cf. further Wakker (1996) 259–60.   **ἀπίοιο πεπαίτερος:** 'riper
than a pear' indicates that Philinos is not worth the chase any more.
In Archilochus' πέπειρα δὶς τόση (with West's probable supple-
ment), 'ripeness' is the result of excessive sexual activity (cf. Ar. *Eccl.*
896, Henrichs (1980) 21), and there may be a hint here that 'Philinos
the soft' has been promiscuous. 'Riper than a pear', cf. Aesch. fr.

264 Radt πεπαίτερος μόρων 'riper than mulberries' (of Hector), continues the 'bucolicisation' of erotic *topoi*.   γυναῖκες: married women, who express regret at the fading of male beauty. If Philinos is already suffering from unrequited *eros* (120–1n.), the sudden wasting of his beauty is explained, cf. 2.85–90.   καλὸν ἄνθος: cf. Archilochus loc. cit., Theognis 994 παῖς καλὸν ἄνθος ἔχων, 1305–6 etc.; the image is a very common one.

122 Simichidas finally suggests overtly that Aratos should give up the pursuit of Philinos, and not just Philinos: the plural verbs and, despite 125 (where see n.), the generalising tone of the verses indicate that Simichidas is proposing that they both give up the pursuit of pretty boys and women, of Myrto no less than Philinos. Others interpret the plural verbs as a way of 'softening the blow' (a 'sociative' plural) or an indication that Simichidas has accompanied Aratos on *komoi*; neither idea is impossible, but neither does justice to the final verses of the song. Harder to judge is the tone of the advice: is the wish for a 'quiet life' free from *eros* as impossible as the wish to hear Komatas? Is that what the presence of 'the beautiful Amyntas' (132n.) demonstrates?   φρουρέωμες: there is a hint of the military imagery most familiar from Ovid, *Am.* 1.9, cf. lines 7–8 *peruigilant ambo, terra requiescit uterque:* | *ille fores dominae seruat, at ille ducis* (where see McKeown's notes).

124 The heavily spondaic four-word verse perhaps evokes the stiffness of the wretched lover.   νάρκαισιν 'stiffness', suggestive of death; the komast wakes on his beloved's doorstep and his body can hardly move. Wilamowitz, *Kleine Schriften* II (Berlin 1971) 75 n. 1 understood 'emotional torment', which Aratos might as well suffer in his own bed; this seems less in keeping with the mimetic realism of 'the crowing cock'.

125 A very difficult line: 'Let Molon alone, good friend, be throttled in [lit. from] that wrestling-school.' The imagery of love as a wrestler or boxer is very common (1.97n.), and as the *palaestra* was a central focus for paederastic emotions (as in Idyll 2), a metaphorical use of the noun as 'the torments of love' is not impossible; 'choking' is a common metaphor of emotional distress. Di Marco (1995b) attractively suggests that, as ἄγχειν was a choking hold applied in the pancration to the loser held immobile on the floor (cf. Lucian, *Anacharsis* 1), the image is that of the unsuccessful komast lying prostrate like a defeated wrestler (cf. 3.52–4n.) and being 'throttled' by the *eromenos* Philinos; he notes that ἐπί would in that case be easier than ἀπό.   **φέριστε:** only here in T. (φέρτερον at 1.148). **Μόλων:** presumably a rival for Philinos' affection (and another reason why the pursuit is not worth it). The name was common in Athens and is attested on Chios, Crete and Delos (*LGPN* I, II s.v.). Some critics have preferred μολών.

126–7 *Arg.* 3.640 (Medea) ἄμμι δὲ παρθενίη τε μέλοι καὶ δῶμα τοκήων may have some relation to 126.   **ἀσυχία:** if understood as 'the absence of disturbing passions' this was a widely desired ideal in Hellenistic culture; it was associated with a number of philosophical schools – the Epicureans (*ataraxia*), Pyrrhonist sceptics (Long–Sedley I 18–22), and the Stoics (cf. *SVF* III 111) – but its roots go far back (cf. KRS 429–33 on Democritean ethics), and it had a deep hold outside the technical discussions of the schools, cf. M. Pohlenz in ΧΑΡΙΤΕΣ *Friedrich Leo ... dargebracht* (Berlin 1911) 101–5, Rosenmeyer (1969) *passim*.   **ἐπιφθύζοισα:** cf. 6.39–40n; the preposition might denote 'spit on ...' or 'spit for ...', i.e. 'in protection of', cf. the various uses of ἐπαείδειν. Simichidas' poem closes on a note of 'bucolic' superstition as it had opened with a sneeze; the juxtaposition of this rusticity to the 'intellectual' ideal of ἀσυχία is just the last of the tonal paradoxes in which the poem has abounded. **τὰ μὴ καλά:** the expression is deliberately general, for anything which might disturb *hasychia* is to be turned aside. In the context, however, it is love which is uppermost in our minds: it is not so much that there is a final dig at Philinos as an example of τὸ μὴ καλόν (cf. 6.19), but that the pursuit of 'beautiful' boys and girls brings in its train 'unbeautiful' passions, jealousies and disturbances. For a rather different view cf. Gershenson (1969) 151–5.

128 γελάσσας: cf. 42n.

129 ἐκ Μοισᾶν ξεινήιον 'a mark of *xenia* arising from the Muses'; it is because of the Muses that they have become ξένοι, cf. 12. Others understand simply 'from the Muses', i.e. Lykidas was merely acting as an intermediary, but this hardly accords with Simichidas' perception of the situation. On the reworking of Hesiod cf. above, p. 149.

130 Lykidas turns off 'in the direction of Pyxa' (genitive). Σ name Pyxa as a Coan deme, and this has plausibly been identified with the 'deme of the Phyxiotai' known from Coan inscriptions; the centre of the deme was probably near modern Asphendiou (see map). If this is indeed T.'s Pyxa or Phyxa, then Lykidas here turns south. Σ130–1a claims that there was a temple of Apollo at 'Pyxa' from which the god was called 'Pyxios', whereas Σ130–1c apparently claim the title 'Phyxios' for both Apollo and Pan. 'Phyxios' is indeed found in the same text as Apollo Horomedon (45–6n.), but it is unclear to which god it there applies. There is, however, a strong case for the association of Apollo with Pyxa or Phyxa – both forms may have been known – and this has obvious implications for the interpretation of the poem.

131 ἐγών τε καὶ Εὔκριτος: cf. 1; the repetition, in the same *sedes*, marks the new direction that the poem, as well as its characters, takes.

132 στραφθέντες: the imagined location of Phrasidamos' farm has been much debated; most naturally, we understand that Simichidas and friends leave the main road at the same point as Lykidas. If this is correct, then Phrasidamos' farm is imagined to lie close to the main road near the turn-off to P(h)yxa–Asphendiou; this may, however, extend the boundaries of the Haleis deme too far. **καλὸς Ἀμύντιχος:** diminutives, here presumably affectionate, in -ιχος are a common Doric feature (cf. 4.20, Headlam on Herodas 1.6). The description leaves little doubt that Amyntas is an *eromenos*, whose listening presence can now be seen to colour Simichidas' song at least, cf. Stanzel (1995) 281–2, Bowie (1996) 96–9.

133 A four-word *spondeiazon* (*ssdds*, cf. 13.20n.) perhaps suggests the release of weight as the travellers lie down. There is an echo of *Od.* 5.462–3 (Odysseus reaches the safety of Phaeacia) ὁ δ' ἐκ ποταμοῖο λιασθεὶς | σχοίνῳ ὑπεκλίνθη; Odysseus is the epic traveller *par excellence*, and the echo positions T.'s 'epic journey' against Homer. Cf. further 156n.

134 οἰναρέοισι 'vine leaves'. Vines were stripped in late summer to allow the grapes better to ripen (cf. *Ecl.* 9.61); for the Dionysiac atmosphere cf. 154n. In the time of 'harvest and fruitfulness' (cf. 143n.) Laertes slept on leaves in a vineyard (*Od.* 11.192–4): the assimilation of the Thalysia to mythic experience (cf. 148–55) is thus already starting.

135–47 > *Ecl.* 1.51–8. As the journey began with an evocation of a miraculous spring and pleasance from the legendary past, so it concludes in an idealised *locus amoenus*. The similarities, which extend to clear verbal reminiscence (136), suggest that Phrasidamos and Antigenes repeated, if not in fact outdid, what their ancestor Chalkon achieved in the mythic past; so too the creation of the spring of Bourina is replayed in the 'miraculous' appearance of wine at the ritual (154n.). The technique is similar to that whereby Pindar suggests that the achievements of his victor-patrons recall and replay the achievements of their ancestors. Moreover, both the *locus* which Phrasidamos created and the celebration which he held there are depicted in ways which mythicise them: the legendary past is not merely replayed in the near past of Simichidas' memory, but that near past is already itself mythic.

The 'pleasance' shares many familiar features of such descriptions throughout Greek and Latin literature, cf. G. Schönbeck, *Der Locus Amoenus von Homer bis Horaz* (diss. Heidelberg 1962) 112–27, Elliger (1975) 333–42, but both the detail and the style of the description are remarkable. There is a powerful appeal to the senses: we move from sounds associated with coolness (135–7), to the persistent sounds of animate nature (138–42), to the scents of nature (144–6) and then to the pleasures of taste (the wine). The improbable orchestra of birdsong (139–41) further draws our attention to the 'generic' nature of the description. All such descriptions in ancient literature are, of course, to some extent typical: this is not a matter of whether the description is 'realistic', but of how ancient writers used familiar literary codes to convey meaning. So too, the similarity to the opening *locus* of Bourina draws attention to the difference between 'the literary' and 'the real'. What is important about any such description is its particularity, which may (as here) consist in the very accumulation of familiar detail. The style of the passage is marked by antithesis, chiasmus, parallelism and significant word-order; the 'stilted symmetries' (Griffiths (1979) 37 n. 69) foreshadow the later bucolic mannerism of, say, Longus more closely than anything else in T., and have been very differently interpreted. For some critics, this is the beautiful essence of bucolic poetry, perhaps now available to Simichidas because of his encounter with Lykidas (cf. Pearce (1988)); for others, the description is the absurd romanticism of a city-dweller as he 'settles down comfortably to enjoy a good bottle' (Giangrande (1980) 140–1).

The overt artifice of the passage matches the artifice of the *locus* which Phrasidamos and his family have created; both pleasures are man-made, and as the farm recalls a legendary *locus*, so the description is created from the literary heritage. This passage thus establishes the dialectic of art and nature which was to dominate all subsequent 'pastoral' literature, which claims to describe 'the natural', but does so in overtly artificial ways, cf. Hunter (1983b) 45–6, Zeitlin (1994). So too, the apparent disjunction between the unusual specificity of topographical reference throughout Idyll 7 and the overtly generic *locus amoenus* dramatises the ironic fracture at the heart of the 'literature of nature'. 'Bucolic' is the imposition of (urban) art upon (rural) nature, a process from which 'nature' cannot emerge unchanged. Many of the details of the description are found elsewhere as images for poetic creation (cf., e.g., Lawall (1967) 102–6, P. Kyriakou, *Homeric hapax legomena in the Argonautica of Apollonius Rhodius* (Stuttgart 1995) 216–31), and this reinforces our sense that we are learning about the nature of 'bucolic song'. If we find the 'symmetries' amusingly appropriate to what we have learned of Simichidas, this too is only right: the 'bucolic' vision is inherently ironic because the task it sets itself is impossible. If, however, we sense a change in the narrator, it lies perhaps in his appreciation of that irony: the mannerisms of the description and the appeal to 'bucolic' myth (149–53) reveal a narrator now able to revel in the contradictions of bucolic; Lykidas has, then, achieved something. The paradigmatic (or 'mythic') quality of this passage was recognised by Virgil when he reworked it for Meliboeus' bitterly programmatic description of the pleasures which Tityrus has secured and he has lost, *fortunate senex, hic inter flumina nota* etc. (*Ecl.* 1.51–8).

135 ἄμμιν: cf. 2n.   κατὰ κρατός 'over our heads'; the unusual phrase is influenced by, and perhaps glosses, κατὰ κρῆθεν in Homer's description of Tantalos (*Od.* 11.588 with Σ ad loc.), cf. 145–6n.

136 Cf. 8, and on the meaning of the repetition above 135–47n.

137 κατειβόμενον κελάρυζε: cf. *Il.* 21.261, the simile of a gardener irrigating his orchard. Here too, it is suggested, the pleasantly alliterative spring (1.7–8n.) is the result of human effort in organising nature; so too, the Homeric phrase marks T.'s 'source', but also reads Homer as himself 'bucolic'.

138 αἰθαλίωνες 'soot-coloured', and therefore invisible in the 'shady boughs'; the epithet makes clear the debt of the description to imagination and the literary heritage.

139–41 λαλαγεῦντες: cf. Aristophon fr. 10.6–7 K–A μεσημβρίας λαλεῖν | τέττιξ. The verb λαλεῖν is used of crickets at 5.34 and λαλαγεῖν of birds at 5.48.

139 ἔχον πόνον: the transference of this epic phrase to the aesthetic πόνος of song (51n.) is wittily paradoxical, as cicadas seem to have been notoriously lazy, cf. Petropoulos (1994) 47–68. 'Hard work' perhaps also hints at the mechanism of that song: male cicadas 'sing' by vibrating a membrane in the thorax (Arist. *HA* 4 535b 6–9). The *vox propria* for the sound of the cicada is τερετίζειν with which the noun τέττιξ is associated (cf. *Et. Mag.* 755.4–5 Gaisford, Davies–Kathirithamby 113–14); in view of ὀλολυγών and τρυγών which are named 'from their sound' (Σ139a), we should hear the sound of the τέττιγες also as they are named.   **ὀλολυγών:** cf. Aratus, *Phaen.* 948 (a sign of coming rain) τρύζει ὀρθρινὸν ἐρημαίη ὀλολυγών; an echo of Aratus would suit the overtly literary character of this passage. Wherever an ὀλολυγών ('something which ὀλολύζει') appears in literature it poses problems of identification (bird or frog?), but here it is very likely the nightingale, which 'usually sings unseen in thickets' (Dunbar on Ar. *Birds* 202–4), cf. White (1979) 9–16, Hunter (1983a) 197–8; πυκιναῖσι ... ἀκάνθαις varies πετάλοις ... πυκινοῖσιν of the nightingale's habitat at *Od.* 19.520, and cf. *EB* 9, Cat. 65.13. In a striking effect, the ὀλολυγών is given the verb appropriate to the τρυγών (τρύζειν), whereas the τρυγών has the verb (στένειν) appropriate to the nightingale, the bird of mourning (ἁ στονόεσσα, Soph. *El.* 147).

140 τρύζεσκεν: like the sound of the nightingale, the verb emerges from the centre of thorn-thickets. Note the chiastic order τρύζεσκεν ἀκάνθαις ... ἀκανθίδες ... τρυγών.

141 ἀκανθίδες: a small bird, variously identified as a finch or a linnet (J. Pollard, *Birds in Greek life and myth* (London 1977) 52–3); Arist. *HA* 8 616b 32 describes its voice as λιγυρά. The etymology from ἄκανθαι is commonly attested and alluded to at Virg. *Georg.* 3.338 *litoraque alcyonen resonant, acalanthida dumi.*   **τρυγών** 'turtle-dove', whose 'monotonous croon' (Arnott (1996) 253) was notoriously persistent, cf. 15.88; the verb was picked up by Virgil (*Ecl.* 1.58 *gemere ... turtur*) and cf. Thompson, *Birds* s.v. τρυγών.

142 ξουθαί: frequently used of bees and nightingales (*Epigr.* 4.11), this word seems in different contexts to be used of both sound and colour; here the former seems likely, 'humming'. Cf. Dale and Kannicht on Eur. *Hel.* 1111, G. Reiter, *Die gr. Bezeichnungen der Farben Weiss, Grau und Braun* (Innsbruck 1962) 104–14. This high-style and common poeticism contributes to the overt poeticisation of nature.   **περὶ πίδακας ἀμφί:** this unparalleled use of the double preposition both evokes the apparently random darting of the bees *around* the spring, and again calls attention to its own artifice. Homer and later poets use both ἀμφὶ περί and περί τ' ἀμφί τε (cf. Hunter on *Arg.* 3.633); of particular relevance may be *Il.* 2.305–7 (the Greeks in a *locus amoenus* at Aulis), ἡμεῖς δ' ἀμφὶ περὶ κρήνην ἱερούς κατὰ βωμοὺς κτλ., in a passage containing Homer's only example of ἀμφιποτᾶσθαι (2.315). In some passages (as here) one or other of the prepositions can be explained as in tmesis or 'anastrophic' tmesis with the verb, but this does not illuminate the poetic effect.

143 A further carefully, and overtly, wrought verse. The order 'grain – fruits' is reversed in the subsequent verses, 'fruits (144–6) – grain (155–7)'.   **θέρεος** 'the [time of the] grain-harvest', cf. 25.28, LSJ s.v. II, *Ecl.* 5.70 *ante focum, si frigus erit; si messis, in umbra*   **ὀπώρας** 'the [time of the] fruit-crop', which need not be different from the time of the grain-harvest (cf. Reed (1997) 138), but the conjunction suggests the work of the divine in this 'mythic' spot. Personified Opora is frequently associated with Dionysos and the vintage (cf. Arnott (1996) 497); for the importance of Dionysos in this passage cf. 154n.

144 Cf. *Ecl.* 7.54. Like the characters themselves, the line is framed by fruit; the chiastic structure works against and highlights the unordered bounty of nature. Whether, despite 136, we are to visualise fruit which rolls around after dropping off trees or fruit which rolls off the heaps gathered together for the festival (Furusawa (1980) 143–4) is not perhaps to be asked. Pear-trees and apple-trees are topically abundant (cf. *Od.* 7.115 (Alcinous' orchard), Call. *h.* 6.27–8 (Demeter's grove), Lembach (1970) 137–9); of particular importance (cf. 135, 145–6nn.) is *Od.* 11.589 (Tantalos) ὄγχναι καὶ ῥοιαὶ καὶ μηλέαι ἀγλαόκαρποι κτλ.

145–6 ἐκέχυντο 'bent [to the ground]', a variation on the idea that trees 'pour' their fruit, cf. *Od.* 11.588 (Tantalos) δένδρεα δ' ὑψιπέτηλα κατὰ κρῆθεν χέε καρπόν, *Arg.* 1.1142–3 (another scene of 'miraculous' nature) δένδρεα μὲν καρπὸν χέον ἄσπετον, ἀμφὶ δὲ ποσσὶν | αὐτομάτη φύε γαῖα τερείνης ἄνθεα ποίης. The god against whom Tantalos committed his greatest offence is Demeter, who tasted Pelops' shoulder when Tantalos served his son to the gods (for the sources cf. Gantz (1993) 11 531–6); Simichidas and friends are allowed to enjoy the pleasures of the *locus* because they have come to pay respects to Demeter. Philip Hardie points out that we, like Tantalos, will never enjoy the reality of the pleasures depicted in the bucolic text.   βραβίλοισι '[wild] plums', cf. Lembach (1970) 139–40.

147 'the four-year seal was removed from the necks of the wine jars'.   τετράενον 'four years old'; the transmitted τετράενες may have arisen from assimilation to τετραετές, and forms in -ενος are standard elsewhere, cf. Pfeiffer on Call. fr. 33. The grammatical tradition explains ἔνος as an Attic form of ἔτος. The parallel at 14.16 makes 'four years' more likely than the seven offered by Σ; for an ancient connoisseur, this is not very old, but a special vintage is clearly being served. Coan wine enjoyed an excellent reputation (cf. Strabo 14.1.15, 14.2.19 etc.), and viticulture was at the heart of the island's economy (Sherwin-White (1978) 236–41).   ἄλειφαρ: an adhesive used to seal the stopper in the jar; perhaps pitch (cf. Hor. C. 3.8.10).

148–55 The memory of the drinking causes Simichidas to compare the glorious wine to two famous 'divine' wines of the mythical and literary past; just as Phrasidamos' garden has been 'mythicised' in the manner of its description (135–47n.), so the rustic celebration itself recalls and replays the past, as the questioning of the Nymphs (148n.) 'bucolicises' the epic practice of questioning the Muses (*Il.* 2.484–93 etc.). Simichidas is already seeing his rustic party pass into literature. Both myths have 'bucolic' settings and strong links with Sicily: we are thus now forced to hear the voice of the Sicilian poet, as well as that of his character. T. asks, with amusing hesitancy, whether his poem is worthy of the 'bucolic' past. The irony is intensified by the gap which yawns between Simichidas' jolly party and the centaurs and Cyclopes of myth, whose symposia had notoriously bloody outcomes which Simichidas and his friends would certainly not have wished to imitate (cf. Miles (1977) 158, Fantuzzi (1995b) 27–8).

148 > *Ecl.* 10.11. On a point of information about the mythic and literary past Simichidas invokes the Nymphs, rather than the Muses, because the subject is 'bucolic' (91–2n.), and in particular those Nymphs who most resemble the Muses through association with Apollo: the Nymphs of the Castalian spring, dear to Apollo, below Parnassos at Delphi (*RE* x 2336–8). Castalia is associated with the Muses in Latin poetry, but the distinction between Nymphs and Muses is always important in T.

149–50 When entertaining Herakles in his Arcadian home, the centaur Pholos served a marvellous wine which had been entrusted to him by Dionysos himself; its aroma attracted the other centaurs and a crazed battle, during which (in some versions) Pholos was killed, ensued. According to Apollodorus 2.5.4, the centaurs sought refuge with Chiron at Malea and Herakles accidentally inflicted a mortal wound upon Chiron; Diodorus' account, however, may be read as implying that Chiron was present with Pholos (4.12.8), and this is the natural interpretation of T.'s verses also. Stesichorus of Himera included the entertainment of Herakles in his *Geryonais* (*PMG* 181), which was also the subject of two Sicilian comedies, the 'Herakles *chez* Pholos' of Epicharmus (fr. 78 Kaibel) and the 'Chiron' of uncertain authorship (Epich. fr. 290 Kaibel), and very likely also the Δράματα ἢ Κένταυρος of Aristophanes.   ἆρά γέ παι 'Was it in any way ...?', cf. Denniston 50.

151 τῆνον τὸν ποιμένα 'that famous shepherd'.   Ἀνάπωι: cf. 1.68n. That the Cyclops is now placed at Syracuse rather than Etna may suggest an evocation of Philoxenus rather than Homer (cf. Idyll 11, Intro.), but such mythic 'looseness' is ubiquitous in ancient poetry.

152 κρατερόν: used of Polyphemos at *Od.* 9.407, 446.   ὃς ὤρεσι νᾶας ἔβαλλε 'who used to throw mountains at ships', an amusing exaggeration of *Od.* 9.481–3 (one ship only); the point of the exaggeration is that marvellous wine could turn even this monster into a dancing symposiast.

153 νέκταρ: the wine which confounded the Cyclops in *Od.* 9 (τόδ' ἀμβροσίης καὶ νέκταρος ... ἀπορρώξ 359, cf. 196–205) had been given to Odysseus by Maron, a priest of Apollo. νέκταρ is a common high-style term for wine (Arnott (1996) 351).   χορεῦσαι: dancing, whether orderly or drunken, was a familiar feature of sym-

posia. Philoxenus' citharoedic *Cyclops* very likely included a dance
(cf. Ar. *Plut.* 290–5), and the Cyclops' song at Eur. *Cycl.* 503–10 may
well have been accompanied by dance. A dancing Cyclops seems
also to have entered the pantomime tradition, cf. Hor. *Sat.* 1.5.63,
Epist. 2.2.125.

154 τόκα brings us back to the opening ἧς χρόνος ἀνίκα.
διεκρανάσατε 'caused to spring up [like a fountain]', cf. A.
Barigazzi, *SIFC* 41 (1969) 9. The appearance of the marvellous wine
is a Dionysiac 'miracle' to match Chalkon's creation (ὁ ἄνυε κράναν)
of the water-spring of Bourina (135–47n.), cf. Eur. *Ba.* 707 κρήνην
ἐξανῆκ' οἴνου θεᾶς, Nisbet–Hubbard on Hor. *C.* 2.19.10. The 'Castalian Nymphs' (148n.) are thus cast as the 'source' of bucolic inspi-
ration (cf. *Ecl.* 7.21–2 *nymphae noster amor Libethrides, aut mihi carmen,* |
quale meo Codro, concedite etc.). In Idyll 7, therefore, no less than in
Idyll 1, the production of 'bucolic' is closely linked to Dionysos. Neither διακρανάω nor διακρανόω occurs elsewhere, and various
glosses in Σ show that the verb was already a puzzle in antiquity:
Σ154b ἀποκαλυφθῆναι ἐποιήσατε comes very close to the required
meaning. 'Mixed with water from your spring' is the standard
modern interpretation.

155 ἀλωίδος 'of the threshing-floor'; the variant ἀλωάδος is not
impossible, and there seems to have been ancient variation in the
breathing (cf. ἀλωή, but ἅλως). For the ritual association of Demeter and the 'heaps' on the threshing-floor cf. Adaios, *Anth. Pal.* 6.258
(= *GP* 5–10), *Orph. Hymn* 40.5. The Attic Haloa seems to have been a
festival of Demeter and Dionysos (cf. H. W. Parke, *Festivals of the
Athenians* (London 1977) 98–100), and it is these two gods who are
combined in the celebration with which the poem ends; for their
close association cf. *Ecl.* 5.79, Call. *h.* 6.70–1 with Hopkinson's note,
and for Dionysos' important cult on Cos Sherwin-White (1978) 314–
17, Burkert (1993) 270–5.

156 The wish for a repetition need not *necessarily* be an 'unfulfill-
able' wish, such as 'Would I were young again . . .', despite the tension between αὖτις and ἧς χρόνος (1); the celebration and walk may
be repeated, even if the meeting with Lykidas cannot, cf. Ovid, *Am.*
1.5.26 (after a recollected experience) *proueniant medii sic mihi saepe dies.*
As the songs of Lykidas and Simichidas both finished with wishes for
the kind of 'peace' which the speaker finds most desirable, so the

frame ends with a corresponding prayer in the mimetic world of the narrative. Workers and invited guests would apparently place winnowing-fans in a heap of grain to signal the completion of the harvest; T. too has finished his 'Thalysia'. Similar customs are recorded on a number of Aegean islands (including Cos) in more recent times, cf. Petropoulou (1959) 11, Petropoulos (1994) 25. The 'sense of an ending' is reinforced by an echo of Teiresias' prophecy to Odysseus that, after killing the suitors, he must take up his oar and carry it until he meets 'men who do not know the sea'; when a traveller says that it is a winnowing-shovel he is carrying, he must plant (πήξας) the oar in the earth and sacrifice to Poseidon; this will be the end of his wanderings (*Od.* 11.119–37). Simichidas' *Odyssey* is also over. A rather similar tool, the λίκνον, is found elsewhere in connection with the mysteries of Dionysos and perhaps Demeter (cf. G. E. Mylonas, *Eleusis and the Eleusinian Mysteries* (Princeton 1961) 206).   μέγα perhaps points to the existence of special fans made solely for this ritual purpose.   γελάσσαι: the smile will indicate her favour and approval.

157 μάκωνας 'poppies', a standard attribute of Demeter (Hopkinson on Call. *h.* 6.44), though the significance is unclear. The description implies a statue of Demeter beside the threshing-floor.

V Idyll 10

A conversation and subsequent song-exchange between two reapers: Milon asks why Boukaios is falling behind, and teases him on learning that his friend is in love. At Milon's suggestion, Boukaios sings a love-song for his beloved, which is answered by a work-song from Milon.

Although reapers are a standard part of the country-scene, and 7.29 seems to include them in standard settings for 'rustic music-making', Idyll 10 is clearly distinguished from the 'bucolics', in both theme and style. Love is always a distraction, but for herdsmen the distraction is largely mental, as they have little else to do as they watch their flocks. Love, however, threatens the very livelihood of the reaper, by keeping him from earning his living. The agricultural theme of the poem thus replays the central message of Hesiod's *Works and days*: given the conditions which the gods have imposed, the only sensible policy is one of unremitting work (*WD* 299, 308–16, 397–400 etc.), involving the avoidance of idleness and, in particular, the dangers posed by women (*WD* 66, 373–5, 695–705). Idyll 10 thus thematises an opposition between two views of the countryside: a place of romantic fantasising, as we have seen it in, say, Idylls 3 and 11, and a place of back-breaking labour. Both views are highly stylised, and neither is 'realistic': Milon's homely wisdom is as partial and second-hand as the trite images of Boukaios' love-song. As Idyll 7 explored the ironies involved in writing 'bucolic song', so Idyll 10 suggests that the 'Hesiodic' view is just as limiting; poetry, in fact, can only approach the 'countryside' through traditional schemes which inevitably distort. Moreover, the contrast between the two songs, both represented in (recited) hexameters, displays the distance between such songs and the real exemplars of which they are literary copies; at the heart of the poem lies an acknowledgement of the fiction of such poetry, whose strength derives in fact from the very improbability of the mimetic task it has set itself.

If Boukaios' position recalls that of other Theocritean lovers (1n.), it is natural to ask whether Idyll 10 was written against a background of pre-existing 'bucolic' poetry; if so, Milon's mockery would, in part, be the knowing self-irony of the poet. So too, there are marked stylistic differences from 'the bucolics': very few Homerisms, no unaugmented past tenses (Di Benedetto (1956) 53–4), and significantly more breaches of the Callimachean 'rules' than in the bucolics (Fantuzzi (1995a) 237). T. may have felt that such a rhythmical practice was appropriate to the Hesiodic setting of men at work, but given the particular nature of Boukaios' complaint and the institution of song-exchange, it is at least tempting to see a deliberate guying of the fiction and conventions which T. himself has established in other poems, cf. further 41n., 58n. All of T.'s poems, however, have generic concerns, and there is little basis here upon which to construct a firm relative chronology.

Poems in which one character ascertains that another is in love and then either sympathises or teases the lover are familiar in Hellenistic and Roman poetry, cf. Call. *Epigr.* 30, 43, Asclepiades, *Anth. Pal.* 12.135 (= *HE* 894–7), Hor. *C.* 1.27, Prop. 1.9, Cairns (1972) Index s.v. 'symptoms of love'. T. himself offers another version at 14.1–9 (cf. Hunter (1996a) 111–13). Cairns (1970) argues that the wit of Idyll 10 consists, as in Idyll 3, in the transference to a rural setting of an essentially urban, indeed symposiastic, form. This, however, is to take too narrow a view; instances such as the opening of Menander's *Heros* in which the scene-type is played out between two slaves show that it has no inevitable link with a particular setting. There is no reason to think that the poem exploits '[not] the real rusticity of rustics but ... the literary rusticity of rustics behaving like townsmen'. The 'rusticity' is, of course, not 'real', but its un-reality derives from competing literary images of the countryside, not from a transference from an 'urban' form.

Title. Ἐργατίναι ἢ Θερισταί.

Modern discussions. Cairns (1970); Hopkinson (1988) 166–72; Hutch-inson (1988) 173–8; Ott (1969) 57–66; Reinhardt (1988) 43–9; Strano (1976); Whitehorne (1974).

1 Unlike Idylls 1–8, the opening verse lacks bucolic diaeresis. **ἐργατίνα:** for Milon's Hesiodic stress upon 'work' cf. Intro. above. Of itself, the word implies nothing about Boukaios' social status; it is a reasonable inference from 45 that he is a free man who has hired out his labour. **Βουκαῖε:** Boukaios is not found as a name else-where, but Nicander (*Ther.* 5) uses βουκαῖος as a noun, 'oxherd', and Βουκολίων, Βουκόλος and Βούτας are all real names. The name may have particular point: Boukaios plays the 'Daphnis rôle' – the bucolic hero suffering from love – here mocked by 'Milon', whose famous namesake (7n.), like all athletes, would take a more Priapic view of sexual desire. **τί νῦν ... πεπόνθεις;:** cf. 1.81n.; for the verbal form cf. 11.1n. **ὠιζυρέ:** cf. 7.118–19n. Here the tone is of friendly teasing, but elsewhere it may convey contempt (Ar. *Birds* 1641) or exasperation (Ar. *Clouds* 655, *Lys.* 948).

2 Love puts the lover off his or her usual activities and induces 'idleness', as, for example, the Cyclops (Idyll 11) and Dido (*Aen.* 4.86–9) discovered. Hesiod recommends a well-fed ploughman who can drive a straight furrow and keep his mind on the job (*WD* 441–5); as a reaper, Boukaios fails on all three counts (57n.). **οὔτε τὸν ὄγμον:** οὔθ' ἐὸν ὄ. is the best attested reading, but ἑός with the sense 'your' is a feature of high Hellenistic poetry which would here lack point (cf. 17.50, *Arg.* 3.140, Rengakos (1993) 117). That the reference

is to Boukaios' swathe requires no specifying, cf. 6 τᾶς αὔλακος.
δύναι: a descendant of *δύνα[σ]αι, cf. Soph. *Phil.* 849 (lyric), K–B II
68, W. G. Rutherford, *The New Phrynichus* (London 1881) 463–6.
Some grammarians regarded such forms as Doric (Σ *Il.* 14.199).

3 'nor do you cut the crop at the same pace as your neighbour,
but you fall behind ...'   **τῶι πλατίον:** lit. 'the one near by';
πλατίον (Dor. for πλησίον) is the adverb, cf. 5.28, Pl. *Tht.* 174b2 ὁ
μὲν πλησίον καὶ ὁ γείτων.

4 ὄις ποίμνας: sc. ἀπολείπεται.   **κάκτος:** not modern 'cactus',
but an unidentified plant with edible stems and a 'broad, spiny leaf'
(Thphr. *HP* 6.4.10), cf. Ath. 2 70d–71c, Lembach (1970) 79–80. Theophrastus reports that it only grows in Sicily (cf. Epicharmus frr. 159–
61 Kaibel), but this would be a very uncertain base upon which to
seek a setting for Idyll 10. A fawn is pierced by a 'sharp κάκτος'
in Philitas fr. 16 Powell, but there is no obvious link between the
passages. At one level, Milon speaks more truly than he knows, for
Boukaios has been pierced by the thorns of love (cf. 13.64–71n.).

5 καί 'and even', cf. Denniston 291. For the tripartite division of
the day assumed here cf. 13.10–13n.

6 'seeing that now at the start you don't bite into your row'. The
genitive may be taken with both participle and verb.   **οὐκ
ἀποτρώγεις:** cutting the swathe is likened to taking successive bites
from food, but there is no clear parallel for this colloquialism. As,
however, the verb is properly 'nibble off', we ought perhaps to read
οὐδ' ἀποτρώγεις 'you don't even nibble at your row'.

7 Μίλων: the name recalls the famous athlete of Kroton (4.6n.),
whose legendary strength and appetite embody the 'manliness'
which his latterday namesake values so highly.   **ὀψαμάτα** 'who
mows till late', cf. Hes. *WD* 490 ὀψαρότης 'one who ploughs late in
the season'.   **πέτρας ἀποκομμ' ἀτεράμνω** 'chip off a hard rock'.
The idea that physical and emotional strength go together is over-
turned in the narrative of Herakles' love in Idyll 13.

8–9 These lines evoke proverbial expressions of dangerous fantasy, cf. Hes. fr. 61 M–W νήπιος ὃς τὰ ἑτοῖμα λιπὼν ἀνέτοιμα διώ-
κει, Pind. *Pyth.* 3.19–23 (Koronis) ἀλλά τοι | ἤρατο τῶν ἀπεόντων·
οἷα καὶ πολλοὶ πάθον. | ἔστι δὲ φῦλον ἐν ἀνθρώποισι μαται-
ότατον, | ὅστις αἰσχύνων ἐπιχώρια παπταίνει τὰ πόρσω, | μετα-
μώνια θηρεύων ἀκράντοις ἐλπίσιν, Thucyd. 6.13.1 (Nikias warns the

Athenians) δυσέρωτας ... τῶν ἀπόντων. Again there is a Hesiodic pattern informing the poem: WD 366–7 ἐσθλὸν μὲν παρεόντος ἐλέσθαι, πῆμα δὲ θυμῶι | χρηίζειν ἀπεόντος. **τῶν ἀπεόντων:** Boukaios probably intends this as a generalising masculine, i.e. covering female 'objects of desire' as well, but Milon takes it (or pretends to take it) as neuter (τῶν ἔκτοθεν); Boukaios thus has to be more explicit about the nature of his trouble in 10. For Milon, a man who has to work to feed himself should be interested only in that work, cf. 13. Love, in particular, may be the preserve of those who do not have to work, cf. Theophrastus fr. 558 Fortenbaugh, eros is a πάθος ψυχῆς σχολαζούσης.

11 χαλεπὸν χορίω κύνα γεῦσαι 'it's a bad thing to give a dog a taste of guts'. The proverbial expression takes the standard proverbial rhythm, the paroemiac (a catalectic anapaestic dimeter), cf. 15.62, 95, 26.38. The point of the proverb is, presumably, that once a dog has eaten something as attractive as guts, it will go on eating or trying to find them, and neglect all other duties, perhaps even killing to find the taste again, cf. Hor. Sat. 2.5.83, G. Williams, CR 9 (1959) 97–100. Some grammarians explained χορίον as 'afterbirth'.

12 σχεδὸν ἐνδεκαταῖος 'for nearly ten days now', cf. 14n.

13 'You clearly draw your wine from the cask; I have only drink gone sour, and not enough of that.' For ὄξος of sour wine cf. Et. Mag. 626.51 Gaisford, Hunter (1983a) 150–1. Another proverb ironically (note δῆλον) contrasts Boukaios' 'wealth', which affords him time for love, with Milon's more mundane concerns, cf. Eur. fr. 895 Nauck ἐν πλησμονῆι τοι Κύπρις, ἐν πεινῶντι δ' οὔ, Men. Heros 16–17 (to a slave in love) πλέον δυοῖν σοι χοινίκων ὁ δεσπότης | παρέχει. πονηρόν, Δᾶ'· ὑπερδειπνεῖς ἴσως.

14 'For this reason all the ground in front of my door has not been hoed since the sowing.' If Boukaios is referring to the crop currently being harvested, the verse is hard to reconcile with his assertion that he has been in love 'for nearly ten days'. Most probably, therefore, he is referring to his own plot near his home, which might have been sown with, say, pulses or vegetables not long before the main grain harvest in May–June, but which has since been neglected as he languishes in love, cf. 11.73–4, Ecl. 2.70–2, Whitehorne (1974) 35–8. Other proposals have been made. Some take the expression as purely proverbial – Boukaios is in a bad way – but there is no other evidence for such a proverb, and this explanation does not account for the strongly inferential τοίγαρ. Serrao (1971) 93–108 saw the apparent inconsistency arising from a learned use of ἐνδεκαταῖος to mean not 'on the tenth day', but 'on a critical day', i.e. 12 will mean 'I am in love, and it's now at crisis point'. Homer may use the 'eleventh or twelfth day' to denote a critical time, regardless of strict chronology (cf., e.g., *Il.* 21.156), but the alleged *doctrina* is not convincing. H. White, *Corolla Londiniensis* 1 (1981) 129–35 understands 12 as 'I am in love [with a fever] which recurs roughly every eleven days', but the Greek can hardly bear that sense; contrast 30.2.

15 For the division of the verse between speakers cf. 4.45n. λυμαίνεται 'ravages': love's effects are not gentle, cf. Ar. *Frogs* 59 ἵμερός με διαλυμαίνεται.   ἁ Πολυβώτα: 'Polybotas' girl' might be his daughter or his slave; if we are to infer that 'Mr Many Cattle' is rich, then the latter is perhaps more likely, cf. 26–7n. 'Polybotas' occurs elsewhere only as the name of a giant in Coan myth (Apollod. 1.6.2, Strabo 10.5.16), but this too is a fragile basis for inferences about the poem's setting.

16 Cf. 6.41n. Hippokion is not otherwise attested, though Hipp-names are very common; it may be intended to sound like a hypocoristic for, say, Hippokles. The reaping tune *par excellence* was the 'Lityerses' (cf. *Suda* λ 626, 41n.), and it is tempting to think that this is what the girl was playing: Boukaios, however, was fixated on the player, not the tune.

17 εὗρε θεὸς τὸν ἀλιτρόν 'god finds [gnomic aorist] the wicked', a semi-proverbial jest at the amusing appropriateness of Boukaios' beloved; in Milon's view, Boukaios has taken his mind off his proper task and been suitably rewarded: 'you have got what you have long wanted', i.e. the punishment fits the crime. Milon's jesting response finds a close parallel in the response of Horace in a similar situation at *C.* 1.27.18–24.

18 'A praying mantis [cf. Davies–Kathirithamby 176–80] will embrace you all night.' The girl in question is in Milon's judgement thin and ugly (24–8); whether the Greeks knew of the tendency of the female praying mantis to devour the male during mating is unclear. Strano (1976) 457–8 understands the verse quite differently. Noting that people around Etna regard the praying mantis as a bringer of good luck, he suggests that Milon is simply congratulating Boukaios on his good fortune: to have such an insect in your bed would be really fortunate.   **χροϊξεῖται** 'embrace', lit. 'place her skin (χρώς) on yours', cf. Call. fr. 21.4 (= 23.4 Massimilla) χροισσα-μένη; a related verb χρωτίζεσθαι is used at *Frag. Gren.* 36.

19–20 'Wealth is not alone (αὐτός) in being blind, but heedless Eros is also blind.' The reference to Wealth, proverbially blind as early as Hipponax fr. 36 West (ἔστι γὰρ λίην τυφλός, cf. Diggle on Eur. *Phaethon* 166), itself has point for these relatively poor labourers; both gods have been truly 'blind' for Boukaios. He acknowledges the girl's imperfections by appealing to the proverbial truth that the lover is 'blind' as far as the beloved is concerned, cf. Pl. *Laws* 5 731e 5–6 τυφλοῦται γὰρ περὶ τὸ φιλούμενον ὁ φιλῶν, Hor. *Sat.* 1.3.38–9 etc. As often, a characteristic of the lover is transferred to Love himself (cf. 6.18–19n.): 'blind Love' is a very rare image throughout antiquity, cf. *Orph. fr.* 82 Kern, *Anth. Lat.* 812.6 Riese (where, however, *caecus* may be 'blinding' or 'invisible', cf. *Arg.* 3.275, Prop. 2.12.11 etc.), V. Buchheit, *C&M* 25 (1964) 129–37. The form of the expression may have been influenced by a saying attributed to Demetrius of Phaleron (fr. 121 Wehrli), οὐ μόνον τὸν πλοῦτον ἔφη τυφλόν, ἀλλὰ καὶ τὴν ὁδηγοῦσαν αὐτὸν τύχην.   **μὴ δὴ μέγα μυθεῦ:** the implicit warning in the previous words is now made explicit. 'Big talk' can incur divine anger and suitable punishment, cf. Eur. *HF* 1244, Pl. *Phaedo* 95b5–6 etc. For the *irrisor amoris* caught by love cf. Prop. 1.9 (with Fedeli's commentary).

21 μόνον 'just'.

22 τι κόρας φιλικὸν μέλος ἀμβάλευ 'strike up a love song for your girl [objective genitive]'. Milon's friendly advice reverberates with T.'s favourite theme of the power of song to assist in the pain of love.   **ἀμβάλευ:** cf. 4.31 ἀγκρούομαι. ἀμβάλευ (< ἀνάβαλευ) is in pointed opposition with κατάβαλλε.

24–37 Boukaios' song falls into seven couplets, imitative of the small verse-groupings of popular song; the 'real life' equivalents of such a song would presumably have been in lyric lengths, cf. 39n., Pretagostini (1992) 82–3, Hunter (1996a) 125–7.

24–5 > *Ecl.* 10.72. A formal prayer to the Muses, rather too ambitious for the context, precedes the song proper, which is demarcated in ring composition by the opening and closing addresses to Bombyka (cf. 3.6–23).   **Μοῖσαι Πιερίδες** 'Muses of Pieria' (cf. 11.3n.), a near echo of the opening of Hes. *WD* Μοῦσαι Πιερίηθεν, suggests the mental distraction which has turned Boukaios from hard work to what Hesiod warns against most vehemently, the attractions of the female.   **συναείσατε** 'join me in singing'; for such a hymnal invocation to the Muses cf. *IG* iv (*ed. min.*) 1.131.3 καί μοι συναείσατε | τὰν Ματέρα τῶν θεῶν, Posidippus, *SH* 705.5, Pl. *Phdr.* 237a 7–10 ἄγετε δή, ὦ Μοῦσαι ... "ξύμ μοι λάβεσθε" τοῦ μύθου, ὅν με ἀναγκάζει ὁ βέλτιστος οὑτοσὶ λέγειν. Without the 'present help' of the Muses, no song can be lovely or successful (cf. Bion fr. 9.3–4). **ῥαδινάν:** an epithet of Aphrodite (cf. 17.37, Hes. *Theog.* 195, Sappho fr. 102.2 Voigt etc.) throws the best possible light on the girl's thinness. For the euphemism cf. Lucr. 4.1166–7 *ischnon eromenion tum fit, cum uiuere non quit | prae macie; rhadine uerost iam mortua tussi* (with Brown (1987) 290–1), Ovid, *AA* 2.660 *sit gracilis, macie quae male uiua sua est*, below 26–7n.   **ἄψησθε:** the Muses' help will be 'tangible'. The hands of gods traditionally bestow beauty (cf. Hdt. 6.61.5) or other blessings (cf. 17.36–7), but the present case is particularly close to Callimachus' request to the Graces to wipe the unguent from their hands on to his elegies (fr. 7.13–14 = fr. 9.13–14 Massimilla). Here it is not merely the 'Bombyka' song which needs to be made beautiful, but Bombyka herself.

26–7 The lover's propensity to euphemism is celebrated in a famous passage of Plato's *Republic*: 'Isn't this how you and others like you behave towards good-looking young men? Don't you compliment a snub nose by calling it "pert" (ἐπίχαρις), describe a hooked nose as "regal", and call one which falls between these two extremes "perfectly proportioned"? Don't you call swarthy young men "virile" (ἀνδρικούς) and pallid ones "children of the gods"? And who do you think invented the term "honey-coloured" (μελίχλωρος)? It could only have been some lover glossing over and making light of a sallow complexion (τὴν ὠχρότητα), because its possessor was in the alluring period of adolescence' (5 474d7–e5, trans. Waterfield). For further examples cf. Lucr. 4.1153–70, Hor. *Sat.* 1.3.38–54, Ovid, *AA* 2.657–62, Brown (1987) 128–31, 280–94.   **Βομβύκα χαρίεσσα:** cf. the opening of the 'Amaryllis song' 3.6, 13.7n. The girl is named for her art: βόμβυξ is variously the *aulos* itself, a part of an *aulos*, or one of the sounds it produces, cf. Michaelides (1978) 52–3. In view of

what follows it is to be noted that Βαμβύκη was a major Syrian city,
cf. R. Verdière, *RSC* 13 (1965) 174–7.   **Σύραν:** to Greeks Syrians
were dark-skinned, whereas white was the privileged colour for
women. The nickname may have been just that, or (perhaps more
likely) we are to understand Bombyke really was Syrian. If so – we
are perhaps even to understand that most people 'called' Bombyke
Σύρα, which is a very common slave name – the fatuousness of
Boukaios' compliment is starkly revealed.   **ἰσχνάν:** cf. Lucr.
4.1166 (cited in 24–5n.), where, however, this word itself is euphe-
mistic; here it is pejorative.   **ἀλιόκαυστον:** cf. Song of Songs
1.5–6 μέλαινά εἰμι καὶ καλή ... μὴ βλέψητέ με, ὅτι ἐγώ εἰμι με-
μελανωμένη, | ὅτι παρέβλεψέν με ὁ ἥλιος κτλ.   **ἐγὼ δὲ μόνος**
breaches 'Hermann's bridge' whereby word-end is avoided after the
first short of the fourth biceps, cf. 8.10 (with Gow's note), 14.64, 70,
15.25, 18.15 (the most marked infringement), 24.102; on such features
in general cf. Intro. Section 4.   **μελίχλωρον** 'honey-coloured', in
Plato a euphemism for 'pale' or 'sallow', but here used instead of
'dark', cf. Lucr. 4.1160 *nigra melichrus est*; honey itself comes in many
shades. In Egypt μελίχρως was a standard term to denote ordinary
Egyptian skin colour, i.e. neither μελάγχρως nor λευκόχρως, cf.
Hasebroek (1921) 30, Cameron (1995) 234.

28–9 > *Ecl.* 2.18, 10.38–9. Bombyka's dark complexion is mitigated by the example of dark but beautiful flowers, cf. Asclepiades,
Anth. Pal. 5.210.3–4 (= *HE* 830–1) εἰ δὲ μέλαινα, τί τοῦτο; καὶ
ἄνθρακες· ἀλλ' ὅτε κείνους | θάλψωμεν λάμπουσ' ὡς ῥόδεαι κάλυκες.
No connection between the two passages is necessary (*pace* E. Courtney, *LCM* 15 (1990) 117–18, Cameron (1995) 235–6), but any borrowing is more likely to be from Asclepiades to T. than vice versa,
because of Boukaios' obvious aping of high poetry.   **καὶ ... καί**
'both ... and'.   **ἁ γραπτὰ ὑάκινθος:** cf. 18.2 ('hyacinth' garlands),
11.25–7n. The flower is 'inscribed' with markings which were interpreted as ΑΙ, i.e. Αἴας or αἰαῖ, depending on the myth being followed, cf. Euphorion fr. 40 Powell, *EB* 6–7; the letters were most
commonly thought to commemorate the death either of Ajax or
the eponymous Hyakinthos, an *eromenos* of Apollo. With this touch,
Boukaios hopes to raise the level of his poem by borrowing from the
tragic pathos of myth.   **ἀλλ' ἔμπας κτλ.** 'But nevertheless they
are chosen first (τὰ πρᾶτα adverbial) among garlands.' The exact

sense is uncertain; others understand 'are collected [as] the first [things] among garlands' or 'are reckoned [cf. LSJ s.v. λέγω II 1] in the first place among garlands'. *Ecl.* 2.18, *uaccinia nigra leguntur*, offers a brilliant aural echo of this verse, not necessarily an interpretation of it.   **τοῖς στεφάνοις:** for the rhythm cf. 3.1–2n.

30–1 > *Ecl.* 2.63–5. Climactic sequences such as this, which have clear links with priamel form, are a familiar feature of 'pastoral' poetry, cf. 8.57–9, 79–80, Pl. *Phdr.* 241d1 ὡς λύκοι ἄρνας ἀγαπῶσιν, ὡς παῖδα φιλοῦσιν ἐρασταί, Rosenmeyer (1969) 257–61. The break in the sequence caused by 'the crane [follows] the plough' (cf. below) is presumably a further sign that Boukaios has over-stretched his poetic gifts.   **τὰν κύτισον:** named as goat food also at 5.128 and Eupolis fr. 13.3 K–A; Aristotle includes it among plants which bring an increase in milk production (*HA* 3 522b27). It has regularly been identified with 'tree-medick', *Medicago arborea*, Polunin–Huxley (1965) 96.   **λύκος:** lovers, particularly admirers of young boys, were proverbially likened to wolves, cf. Pl. *Phdr.* 241d1 (cited above), G. Luck, *CQ* 9 (1959) 34–7, 13.62–3n. This idea resonates within the sequence, without ever being made explicit.   **ἀ γέρανος:** the southerly migration of the crane was used as signal of the ploughing-season, cf. Hes. *WD* 448–50, Ar. *Birds* 710. The crane 'follows' the plough, not – as the preceding sequence may have suggested – to eat it, but to eat the worms it turns up or perhaps the seed which is scattered (cf. Antipater of Sidon, *Anth. Pal.* 7.172). The shift in the sequence is mildly comic, and would be more so if we are to understand that, from the point of view of weather-signs, it should really be 'the plough follows the crane'.   **ἐπὶ τίν:** cf. 13.49n.

32 Croesus of Lydia was a king whose great wealth (Hdt. 1.30–3) passed into legend, cf. 8.53, Philemon fr. 159 K–A, Cat. 115.3, Otto 98–9.

33 > *Ecl.* 7.35–6. 'We would both be gold statues dedicated to Aphrodite.' Boukaios imagines himself as a Hellenistic monarch erecting statues of himself and his wife, perhaps on their wedding day; the statues will, in his fantasy, ensure the *kleos* of their love, cf. 12.17–21. Philadelphos himself erected many lavish statues of members of the royal house and of other favourites, including his female cup-bearer Kleino, who was represented holding a cup (as Bombyka will have her pipes), cf. Ath. 10 425e–f citing Polybius 14.11; some 'Ptolemaic' reference has been suspected in these verses, perhaps rightly, cf. Whitehorne (1974) 39–40, Burton (1995) 131–2. The absurdity of the fantasy recalls Plato's image of the 'small, bald metalworker who's come into some money. He's just got himself out of debtors' prison, he's had a bath and is wearing brand-new clothes [cf. line 35] and a bridegroom's outfit, and he's about to marry his master's daughter ...' (*Rep.* 6 495e5–8, trans. Waterfield).

34 Bombyka would be represented with her tools of trade and symbols of Boukaios' love (cf. 3.10–11n., 11.10). The fussiness of ἤ ... ἤ recalls the literal-mindedness of the Cyclops, cf. 11.58–9n. **αὐλώς:** perhaps, despite the definite article, rather grander than what she plays now, cf. 6.42–3n. The 'wealth of Croesus' will be used to buy Bombyka a new instrument and Boukaios new shoes. For such a statue of a musician cf. *CEG* 2.509.

35 σχῆμα '[new] clothes'; καινάς also colours the preceding noun, by the figure known, presumably by coincidence, as the σχῆμα ἀπὸ κοινοῦ. The word σχῆμα for 'clothes' is well attested only in later Greek, but Boukaios' language can be as strained as his imagery. **ἀμύκλας** 'shoes of Amyklai [in Laconia]', a well known, and rather posh, type, cf. Ar. fr. 769 K–A, Hesychius α3838 etc.; 'on both feet' is amusingly naïve. Theocritean countrymen are often concerned with footwear, cf. 4.56, 7.26, and here the idea leads into Boukaios' praise of Bombyka's feet.

36–7 These lines are Boukaios' version of the 'catalogues' of the beloved's charms familiar from Hellenistic and Roman poetry, as well as the poetry of other cultures, cf. Dioscorides, *Anth. Pal.* 5.56 (= *HE* 1463–8), Philodemus, *Anth. Pal.* 5.132 (= *GP* 3228–35), Ovid, *Am.* 1.5.19–22 (with McKeown's notes), Song of Songs 5.10–16, 7.2–6. Such catalogues regularly move from head to foot or vice versa; Boukaios cuts the form to its bare essentials by mentioning only the two extremities; it is tempting to think that, unlike Dioscorides, Philodemus and Ovid, T.'s readers are to understand that feet and head are the only part of the beloved's body which Boukaios has seen. **Βομβύκα χαρίεσσα:** cf. 24–5n. **ἀστράγαλοι:** why Bombyka's feet are compared to 'knucklebones' has long been a puzzle. It may be a rather strained image marking the smooth 'moulding' of her feet, and from the side some preserved examples of *astragaloi* can indeed vaguely resemble human feet. More probably, however, Boukaios incompetently applies to the feet an image which, if it has any meaning at all, should apply only to the ankles, which roughly correspond to the animal knuckle from which *astragaloi* were made. Ankles were a marked point of beauty: καλλίσφυρος, τανίσφυρος, τανύσφυρος and εὔσφυρος are all terms of praise in high, archaic poetry, and T. himself calls Hebe 'white-ankled' (17.32).   **τευ:** this genitive form is a regular variant of τευς in the MSS, and was associated by ancient grammarians with Laconia (cf. *GG* II 1.75, K–B I 583); the form in -ς is guaranteed at 2.126 and 11.55.   **ἁ φωνὰ δὲ τρύχνος:** τρύχνος or στρύχνος are various edible and inedible plants of the nightshade family (Lembach (1970) 68–71). 'Your voice is a narcotic plant' is a possible, if rather extreme, absurdity for Boukaios (cf. the Homeric 'lily-like voice' *Il.* 3.152 etc.), but some plants of this family were also believed to possess aphrodisiac qualities (cf. Thphr. *HP* 9.9.1 on μανδραγόρας), and this may be thought a more likely compliment. Σ however refer to the plant's softness, and late grammarians cite a proverb ἁπαλώτερος τρύχνου together with a 'parody' in Aristophanes μουσικώτερος τρύχνου (fr. 964 K–A); the word may therefore have had a meaning which we can no longer recover. The voice is a familiar feature of catalogues of beauty and ugliness, cf. 20.6, 26–7, but Boukaios may have transferred to the voice an image more appropriate to the mouth, which is often compared to a flower, usually a rose (*EA* 11, Dioscorides, *Anth. Pal.* 5.56 (= *HE* 1463) etc.).   **τὸν ... τρόπον** 'your character', cf. *CEG* II 590.4–5 τοὺς δὲ τρόπους καὶ σωφροσύνην ἣν εἴχομεν ἡμεῖς | ἡμέτερος πόσις οἶδεν ἄριστ' εἰπεῖν περὶ τούτων. For Boukaios it surpasses description, for us it is *his* powers of description which fail; if he has only ever worshipped Bombyka from afar, he in fact knows nothing of her character.

38–40 Milon's ironic response, marked by ἦ, passes judgement on the poem we have just heard or read. Line 38 praises the text of the poem (ποῶν ... ἀοιδάς) and 39 its performance; such a disjunction is more 'natural' in a Hellenistic than a classical context.

38 Βοῦκος: presumably a familiar shortening of Βουκαῖος.

39 'How well he measured out the style of the harmony.' Milon's teasing use of the 'technical' language of music calls our attention to the gap between the written text and the song, represented in hexameters but to be imagined in a quite different mode, cf. 24–37n. ἐμέτρησεν does not therefore necessarily refer to dactylic form. Milon seems to mean that Boukaios' choice of ἁρμονία was entirely appropriate to the words of the song, cf. Pl. *Rep.* 3 398d9; Boukaios is thus mocked as μουσικός (23) in a semi-technical sense, cf. Pl. *Rep.* 3 398e1 (Socrates to Glaucon) τίνες οὖν θρηνώδεις ἁρμονίαι; λέγε μοι· σὺ γὰρ μουσικός. Marco Fantuzzi suggests that, with this verse, T. also comments ironically on the relatively poor hexameter structure ('*Gliederung*') of the song. It is a persistent theme of Greek musical discussion that the various 'modes' had moral implications; for Milon, Boukaios' 'mode', as well as the words of the song, will have been redolent of 'softness and idleness' (Pl. *Rep.* 3 398e6–7), and therefore quite inappropriate to 'real men' (56).   **τὰν ἰδέαν:** cf. Ar. *Frogs* 384 ἑτέραν ὕμνων ἰδέαν.   **τᾶς ἁρμονίας:** the *harmoniai* were the different musical 'modes' (Dorian, Phrygian etc.), as determined by different melodic scales, cf. Pl. *Rep.* 3 398d1–9c6, Ath. 14 624c–5a, R. P. Winnington-Ingram, *Mode in ancient Greek music* (Cambridge 1936), Michaelides (1978) 127–9, West (1992) 177–9.

40 A beard should be a sign of wisdom and maturity (cf. 14.28), but Milon ironically claims to have been shown up by Boukaios' musical skill; it is a reasonable inference that Milon is somewhat older than Boukaios.

41 Without explanation Milon now offers a song in return, thus creating the typical song-exchange. His song, however, is presented as a traditional work-song applicable to all reapers and 'composed' by none, and therefore devoid of the maudlin self-absorption of Boukaios' offering.   **θᾶσαι δή:** the illogicality of 'look at this song' is scarcely felt in colloquial language, cf. 1.149, 7.50–1, but the verb suggests the 'admiration' associated with the contemplation of works of (visual) art, cf. *Epigr.* 17.1 θᾶσαι τὸν ἀνδριάντα κτλ.; just how 'artistic' the song is may be debated.   **τῶ θείω Λιτυέρσα:** for Milon Lityerses is 'divine', as Komatas is for Lykidas (7.89) and Simonides for a poet seeking patronage (16.44). Lityerses, son of Midas, was a Phrygian culture-hero and inventor of agriculture after whom a reaping-song was named, cf. Apollodorus, *FGrHist* 244 F149. No other source ascribes traditional songs to him, but the idea is in keeping with the tendency to ascribe all institutions to single 'inventors'. Stories told how he challenged visitors to reaping contests and cut off the heads of his victims; he himself was finally killed by Herakles. Such a manly figure is an obvious rôle model for the 'unbreakable' (7) Milon, and carries an amusing threat to Boukaios. The contemporary poet Sositheos wrote a satyr-drama *Daphnis or Lityerses* (*TrGF* 99 F1a–3) in which, after roaming the world in search of his beloved, Daphnis found her in servitude to Lityerses; they were both released by Herakles. A surviving fragment (fr. 2) paints the Phrygian king as himself something of a Herakles: a big eater who accomplished hard, physical tasks. In associating Milon with such a figure and condemning Boukaios' 'starving' love (57), the poem replays the myth of Sositheos' play in a quite different mode: Boukaios becomes a comically lovesick Daphnis whose 'bucolic' sufferings find no pity in Milon's harsh, Hesiodic conception of the world.

42–55 Milon's song matches that of Boukaios in length and like it is arranged in couplets. In this case, however, the couplets do not evoke the lyric snatches of a love-song, but rather the short phrases of real work-songs (cf. *PMG* 849, 869) and the gnomic wisdom of the Hesiodic tradition.

42–3 Demeter is the proper divinity to whom working men should pay heed, not Boukaios' Muses. The repetition of πολυ-compounds in prayers is a common feature, but it is likely that there is traditional 'Demeter' poetry behind these verses, as there will be behind Call. *h.* 6.2 Δάματερ, μέγα χαῖρε, πολυτρόφε πουλυμέδιμνε, 136–7 φέρβε βόας, φέρε μᾶλα, φέρε στάχυν, οἶσε θερισμόν, | φέρβε καὶ εἰράναν, ἵν' ὃς ἄροσε τῆνος ἀμάσηι.   **εὔεργον** 'easy to work', an important quality for a task as back-breaking as reaping. This verse opposes solid, material advantages to the aesthetic wishes of Boukaios' second verse.

44–5 The δράγματα are the 'handfuls' of the crop which are mown at one time and then bound together into ἄμιλλαι, cf. *Il.* 18.550–7.   **παριών τις:** sensitivity to criticism by outsiders is characteristic of Greek society at all periods.   **σύκινοι:** figwood was proverbially weak, cracking under the least strain; among many relevant proverbs is συκίνη ἐπικουρία 'as much assistance as figwood', cf. further *CPG* II 210–11, Hor. *Sat.* 1.8.1, LSJ s.v. I 2. Strano (1976) 456 says that 'figwood' is still a common pejorative term in

Sicily. σύκινοι ὤνδρες (Edmonds), 'the men are figwood', is possible, but not necessary.   μισθός: cf. 1n.

46–7 'The cut end of your sheaf should face the north or west wind; that way the ear grows fat.' A κόρθυς was a sheaf cut roughly half-way up the stem rather than at the base; such grain would be cut before it was ripe and these verses give instruction either for how it is to be stored under cover while ripening (cf. *Geopon.* 2.27.1) or how it is to lie in the fields until collected. Theophrastus also notes that it is the North Wind which is best for the ears of grain (*CP* 4.13.4).

48 A rule for threshing is introduced to contrast (δέ in 50) with what is necessary when reaping.   τὸ μεσαμβρινόν: adverbial 'during the middle part of the day', cf. 1.15.

49 'At that time [i.e. when it is hottest] the grain and chaff are most easily separated from the straw.' As, however, ἄχυρον is usually just the chaff, not grain and chaff together, there is some uncertainty about the meaning. Others understand (with a more regular sense of the verb) 'the grain and chaff are produced from the stalk and ear'.

50–1 Reapers traditionally keep very long hours (cf. Hes. *WD* 571–81). The Hesiodic structure of these verses may be seen from a comparison with *WD* 368–9 ἀρχομένου δὲ πίθου καὶ λήγοντος κορέσασθαι, | μεσσόθι φείδεσθαι.   κορυδαλλῶ: 'up with the lark' is as common in English as it seems to be unparalleled in Greek. ἐλινῦσαι δὲ τὸ καῦμα 'rest during the heat [of midday]'. Reapers should avoid the blazing sun and also, by implication, the furnace of love's heat.

52–3 Mention of the heat leads into the pleasures of a cool drink.   παῖδες: cf. 13.52n.   τὸ πιεῖν: an epexegetic infinitive is common after verbs of giving etc., i.e. 'give someone [something] to drink'; cases such as this where the article is added to the infinitive are much rarer, but well established, cf. Goodwin §795.   πάρεστι: sc. τὸ πιεῖν.

54–5 'Better, stingy overseer, to boil the beans, so that you don't cut your hand with cumin-splitting.' The overseer is told to get on with preparing the men's food, rather than devoting himself to stingy savings. 'Cumin-splitting' was a proverbial expression for stinginess (our 'cheese-paring'), cf. Sophron fr. 110 Kaibel, Ar. *Wasps* 1357 etc., but as cumin was used to flavour soups, there is a literal sense also: 'Stop trying to cut the ingredients as small as possible and start cooking!' Others prefer to take κάλλιον as an adverb modifying an imperatival infinitive: 'Boil the beans better …' τὸν φακὸν 'lentils', used to make lentil-soup, φακῆ. χεῖρα: χῆρα may be correct – it occurs, for example, in the Sophron papyrus and the text of Alcman – but Π⁹ is strongly Doricising, and there can be no certainty.

56 μοχθεῦντας: μοχθέντας (Π³) might be an athematic form of a contracted verb (1.36n.), or a specifically Cyrenean feature, εον > ευν > εν, cf. Ruijgh (1984) 74–5. This *lectio difficilior* has a good chance of being right, but a simple slip by the scribe of the papyrus cannot be ruled out. ἄνδρας carries emphasis: 'real men', rather than the infantilised weaklings (58) represented by Boukaios.

57 πρέπει: sc. σε. λιμηρόν: the lover is traditionally thin with wasting, whereas Milon values a hearty appetite. No firm distinction can be drawn between this interpretation and the implication that, unless Boukaios pulls himself together, he will starve because no one will pay his wages. The passage is informed by the Hesiodic opposition between Λιμός 'Hunger' and Demeter (*WD* 298–302 and *passim*); already in Hesiod, the torment caused by a beautiful woman is 'limb-ravaging' (*WD* 66). It is less probable that there is a further reference to Bombyka's thinness.

58 This line is an example of a very rare verse-form. Spondees in both fourth and fifth feet are nowhere attested in the 'bucolics' and are rare elsewhere (cf. 15.48, 83, 143, 16.56, 22.216, 25.30, 98–9, 154, Philitas fr. 7.3 Powell); the pattern *ssdss* is paralleled only at 25.98, and is entirely absent from Callimachus and Apollonius. This harsh form, which closes the poem with its only *spondeiazon* (if τύγε μᾶλον is correctly read in 34) and a strong breach of Naeke's Law (1.130n.), is expressive of Milon's contempt; he negates dactylic rhythm as far as possible in order to negate the sentimental nonsense which, in his view, accompanies it. μυθίσδεν: cf. 1.14n. τᾶι ματρὶ … ὀρθρευοίσαι 'to your mother when she stirs in bed in the early morning'. Men should be out reaping at the crack of dawn; women (cf. Hes. *WD* 519–21) and children and any 'men' who resemble them stay at home and talk about such nonsense as *eros*. The infantilised Cyclops too involves his mother in his passion (11.67–71), but we need not infer that Boukaios actually lives with his mother; this is merely Milon's way of expressing contempt. Revealing their passions to parents and other relations was in fact to become a characteristic of the heroes and heroines of the later novel, but these pampered figures did not have to work for a living, cf. Ninos to his aunt (Stephens–Winkler p. 36), Chaireas to his parents (Chariton 1.1.8).

VI Idyll 11

The love of the young Cyclops, Polyphemos, for the sea nymph Galateia illustrates the truth that there is no alleviation for the pain of love other than 'the Muses'. Polyphemos' song (19–79) is preceded by a gnomic opening and address to Nikias (1–6) and the introduction to the narrative *exemplum* (7–18); the poem closes with a two-verse confirmation of the lesson to be drawn from the paradigm. Idyll 11 has important similarities to Idyll 3, the song of another 'locked-out' herdsman, and to Idyll 13, another poem on *eros* addressed to Nikias; with the latter it shares a structure, familiar from archaic poetry, of gnomic opening followed by 'mythical' exemplification.

Nikias (and his wife) are also honoured in Idyll 28 and Epigram 8, which depict him as living in Miletos. He was a doctor (11.5, 28.19–20, Epigram 8), and the *Hypothesis* to Idyll 11 cites Dionysios of Ephesos (perhaps roughly contemporary with T.) for an association between Nikias and the famous doctor Erasistratos of Keos, cf. 1–6n., above, p. 2. It has often been guessed that Nikias and Erasistratos met each other (? and T.) on Cos, cf. *RE* vi 334, but there is no evidence to support the guess, and Alexandria, where Erasistratos studied, seems as likely. Nikias was also a poet (11.6, 28.7), and very likely the 'Nikias' to whom eight extant epigrams are ascribed (*HE* 2755–86) and who was included in Meleager's *Garland* (*Anth. Pal.* 4.1.19–20 = *HE* 3944–5, cf. A. Lai, *QUCC* 51 (1995) 125–31). For his 'reply' to Idyll 11 cf. below, p. 221.

Galateia appears in early catalogues of Nereids (*Il.* 18.45, Hes. *Theog.* 250), but no stories are told of her; later antiquity connected her with γαλήνη 'calm weather' (6.34–8n.), as well as with γάλα. A connection with the 'milk-white foam' of the sea is not in fact improbable; Callimachus uses milk and sea-foam together as examples of pure whiteness (fr. 260.57 = *Hecale* fr. 74.16 Hollis). The historian Douris (*c.* 340–260 BC) recounted that Polyphemos had set up a shrine to Galateia, as a kind of tutelary dairy spirit, and that this was the origin of Philoxenus' famous poem (*FGrHist* 76 F58 = *PMG* 817); Douris may be simply applying rationalising techniques to a recent *cause célèbre* (i.e. Philoxenus' poem), but an ancient cult of the Nereid on Sicily is not *per se* unlikely. Timaeus already knew of a son of Galateia by the Cyclops (Idyll 6, Intro.). In Euripides' *Cyclops* of (?) 408 BC Silenos swears to the Cyclops by 'the daughters of Nereus' (*Cycl.* 264), but whether this is a pointed dig at Polyphemos' love or evidence that the story of Polyphemos and Galateia was not yet common currency we cannot know. Be that as it may, it was certainly the 'new dithyramb' of the late fifth / early fourth century which took up the story of Polyphemos with enthusiasm (cf. Didymus, *Dem.* 12.57–62, p. 46 Pearson–Stephens). From the *Cyclops* of Timotheus survives one fragment (*PMG* 780) which refers to the wine which destroyed Polyphemos, and there is no reference to Galateia. Timotheus' poem was probably close in time to the famous *Cyclops or Galateia* of Philoxenus of Kythera, but priority cannot be established.

Our main source for this latter poem, a report by Phaenias (second half of the fourth century) preserved in Athenaeus (*PMG* 816 = Phaenias fr. 13 Wehrli), records that Philoxenus was a favoured poet at the court of Dionysios I of Syracuse (ruled *c.* 404–367 BC), but that when he was caught trying to seduce a mistress of Dionysios called Galateia, he was dispatched to the stone quarries where he wrote an 'allegorical' poem on his adventures, casting Dionysios as the Cyclops, Galateia as the nymph of the same name, and himself as Odysseus. Unlike T., therefore, Philoxenus set the love of Polyphemos for Galateia at the time of Odysseus' visit, and Odysseus may have tried to persuade the Cyclops to let him go with promises to win Galateia over (cf. *PMG* 818). It is clear that a centre-piece of the dithyramb was a love-song by the Cyclops to the accompaniment of the lyre (cf. *PMG* 819), and it was very likely during this that 'Polyphemos told the dolphins to tell Galateia that he was healing his love through the Muses' (*PMG* 822), the theme that becomes central to T.'s poem. Philoxenus' dithyramb is parodied in the *Plutus* of Aristophanes (388 BC), and it is a reasonable hypothesis that Philox-

enus had performed it in Athens shortly before this date. It clearly
achieved a remarkable notoriety within a brief space of time, probably both for the virtuosity of Philoxenus' musicianship and the brilliant conceit of a lovesick Cyclops. How much truth there is in
Phaenias' account must remain open; at the very least, the story of
kitharodic composition while detained in the quarries looks fictional.
While it is quite possible that the poem contained political satire, it
may also be the case that some at least of the biographical tradition
is owed to Middle Comedy plays inspired by Philoxenus (cf. Antiphanes, *Cyclops*, Nicochares, *Galateia*, ?Eubulus, *Dionysios*, cf. Arnott
(1996) 139–40). For the myth of Galateia and the dithyramb of
Philoxenus cf. Holland (1884); Pickard-Cambridge (1962) 45–8;
H. Dörrie, *Die schöne Galatea* (Munich 1968); F. Bömer, *P. Ovidius
Naso, Metamorphosen Buch XII–XIII* (Heidelberg 1982) 406–9; D. F.
Sutton, *QUCC* 42 (1983) 37–43.

The 'bucolic' elements of the Homeric Cyclopes – idealised pas-
toralists ignorant of agriculture, *polis* institutions and colonialist and
commercial imperatives (*Od.* 9.107–15, 125–30) – had already been
given a prominent place in Euripides' *Cyclops* (even if his Polyphemos is as much sophist as primitive), and, to judge from Aristophanes' parody, were important also in Philoxenus' dithyramb. Polyphemos was one obvious epic model for T.'s herdsmen. Σ *Od.* 9.456
observes that οἱ νεώτεροι consider it βουκολικόν for Polyphemos to
converse with his ram; this is of a piece with the rhetorical tradition
that saw T.'s poetry as a primary example of 'simplicity' (ἀφέλεια)
and 'sweetness' (γλυκύτης), one source of which was to ascribe
human emotions and motivations to animals (Hermogenes 335.8–23
Rabe), but it also suggests some of the Homeric interpretation which
may lie behind T.'s exploitation of the Cyclops figure. It would be
nice to know whether Idyll 11 was written against a background of
an already existing set of hexameter bucolic conventions: does the
Idyll exploit a world which was familiar to T.'s readers from T.'s
own poems? The idea is a tempting one: there is no really good evidence (certainly not in 7) for the common assumption that Idyll 11
was written in Sicily, and no good reason to date all 'Sicilian' poems
early in T.'s career (Intro. Section 1). Nevertheless, the evidence is at
best equivocal.

Idyll 11 stands outside the 'bucolics' in all the main branches of the transmission. Moreover, despite the obvious similarities with the *paraklausithyron* of Idyll 3, the framing addresses to Nikias provide a quite different structure from the 'bucolic' mimes of Idylls 1, 3, 4, 5 and 7, although Idyll 6, the other Cyclops poem, offers a partial parallel. Nevertheless, many aspects of the poem (e.g. the claim to skill on the syrinx in 38, the remarkable mixture of animals in 40–1) gain added point if viewed in the light of 'bucolic conventions', and Damoitas and Daphnis in Idyll 6 treat Polyphemos and Galateia as a mythical story with parallels to their own situation. In the absence of clear criteria for 'the bucolic' (as opposed to βουκολικὰ ἀοιδά), there seems little point in drawing other than formal distinctions between this poem and the non-mythological mimes, particularly as the Polyphemos of Idyll 11 has so much in common with other bucolic lovers; the great importance of this poem for Virgil's *Eclogues* ought also to count for something.

One formal consideration of great importance is stylistic. Idyll 11 differs markedly from 'the bucolics', both linguistically and (even more) metrically. It contains a number of rare Doricisms (cf. 25–7, 39, 42–3, 52, 60nn.) and very few guaranteed Homeric forms (Di Benedetto (1956) 53). It has many more infractions of the 'Callimachean' metrical rules (Intro. Section 4, 1.130n.) than any other poem with a bucolic setting, differs markedly from the 'bucolics' in regard to 'bucolic diaeresis' (56% as opposed to 80%, cf. above, p. 20), and also stands out for the sheer number of hexameter patterns it deploys (17 in 81 verses); the whole metrical impression is one of roughness, in comparison with the bucolic mimes, cf. 1n., Legrand (1898) 341–2, Stark (1963) 373–4, Fantuzzi 1995a. Thus, for example, 41–2 offer successive breaches of 'Naeke's Law' (1.130n.) and 45–6 show hiatus at the central caesura and metrical lengthening in the same position in successive verses. The two most obvious explanations are either that Idyll 11 is an 'early' poem, i.e. that T.'s style became more refined as time went on, or that the Cyclops is given a style appropriate to his lack of sophistication. Against the latter view it has been argued that there is no strongly marked metrical (as opposed to verbal) difference between the frame and the song of the Cyclops, but the association of the poet and his Sicilian forebear is central to the poem's design (cf. below). If the style of Idyll 11 was indeed set against a body of pre-existing bucolic, then it would be legitimate to see a form of self-parody by T., but some parodic effect is not in fact dependent upon the relative chronology of the corpus, as the 'Callimachean rules' represent a standardisation of general tendencies in all sophisticated poetry; the style of Idyll 11 is thus highly marked, whether or not it should be judged against 'the bucolics'. In other words, the style *may* be both early and parodic.

The strong identification between the poetic voice and that of the Cyclops, who was 'one of us' (line 7), establishes Polyphemos as an aetiological paradigm for all subsequent (Sicilian) lovers and poets. This association is usually read in biographical terms – T. or Nikias or both are in love, or have recently recovered from it – but the literary meaning of the paradigm is at least recoverable. A central irony, both comic and tragic, of Idyll 11 lies in our knowledge of what is to come: some of what the Cyclops sings (the arrival of a stranger, the loss of his eye etc.) was indeed to prove all too true. Such an irony, which arises from the writing of a 'prequel' to a famous myth or literary work, is a familiar phenomenon in Hellenistic and Roman poetry (cf. A. Barchiesi, *HSCP* 95 (1993) 333–65); we may compare the dark ironies of Apollonius' description of the early relations of Jason and Medea, to be read against our knowledge of Euripides' tragedy. It has been attractively suggested that the young Cyclops draws disaster upon himself, because quotations from poetry (particularly Homer) were used in magical spells to effect particular emotional and physical states (Fantuzzi (1995b) 17–18); in referring to Homeric events of which he has no knowledge, Polyphemos unwittingly ensures their occurrence. More generally, however, the Cyclops is trapped in the language, not just of Homer, but of Odysseus. T.'s creation is forced to express himself with words and phrases which prove already loaded against him, even where they do not refer specifically to *Odyssey* 9, cf. nn. on 25–7, 34–7, 45–8, 53. He is a pathetic victim of poetic tradition, who functions as a (comic) paradigm for the position of the dactylic poet in a post-Homeric world; T. too is 'trapped' by the weight of tradition which accompanies his verse, and he too is bound to 'lose' to Homer, as Polyphemos does to Odysseus. Not only Homer, of course: both T. and the Cyclops must also recycle the love poetry of Sappho (19–23), and doubtless other poets also. Poetic success, of any kind, is 'not easy to find' (4).

Discussion of Idyll 11 has been bedevilled by two related issues: How can singing be a *pharmakon* for love when it is also plainly a symptom of this 'disease' (lines 13, 39)? Is the Cyclops actually 'cured' of his love at the end of his song? To take the second issue first, ἐποίμαινεν τὸν ἔρωτα (80), particularly when used of a master herdsman (cf. 65), ought to mean 'shepherded, looked after, controlled his *eros*' rather than 'got rid of it'. So too ῥᾶιον διᾶγ' (81) is not 'was cured more easily', but 'felt less pain'. There is in fact nothing in 80-1 to suggest a final 'curing' or *katharsis*, in which despair is replaced by whole-heartedness. Rather, Polyphemos' reverie is broken by the realisation of his deluded situation (72-4), and, (we must suppose) he gets back to his work, having survived another day; he lives to love again. Certainly, 75-9 offer very precarious support to those who wish to see a 'cured' Cyclops (cf. nn. ad loc.). There is a suggestive parallel for the end of the poem in 10.22-37: Milon tells the lovesick Boukaios that he should sing 'some lovesong' (τι κόρας φιλικὸν μέλος) because in that way 'you will find the work easier' (ἅδιον οὕτως | ἐργαξῆι).

The first problem has proved more intractable. The temptation to emend τὰν Γαλάτειαν ἀείδων in 13 (cf. Ovid, *Met.* 13.776-7, where there is no suggestion of singing) has so far not led to any remotely plausible suggestion; cf. also [Bion] fr. 2.3 ἄεισεν Πολύφαμος ἐπ' ἠιόνι τᾶι Γαλατείαι, *EB* 58-9. Crucial is the meaning of *pharmakon*. Although allegedly final cures for *eros* through magical songs were a familiar aspect of 'real life', a familiar literary *topos* saw in music and song a source of 'alleviation' for emotional pain (1-4n.), and the basic sense of *pharmakon* in 1 and 17 is thus most likely 'palliative', cf., e.g., Köhnken (1996a) 181-3: singing will no more make love go away *for good* than one act of love-making, which Longus' Philetas recommends as *pharmakon* (*D&C* 2.7.7), will bring permanent relief from desire (cf. Lucr. 4.1117-20). Lovers are prone to sing of their love (cf. Bion fr. 3), but not every song will offer (temporary) relief ('it is not easy to find ...'), as Idyll 3 plainly illustrates. Like the Homeric *moly* (4n.), however, a *successful* song prevents contact with a destructive force (in this case *eros*) from being completely catastrophic. Stylistically, Polyphemos found a song which suited him, a song which may be viewed as an aesthetic triumph for a Cyclops rather than as laughably pedestrian. Song, therefore, *is* both symptom and *pharmakon*, a word whose notorious doubleness (cf. Goldhill (1991) 249–61) points to a further irony of the Cyclops' position. His song 'relieves' his love, but in 'shepherding' it he keeps it alive; every song rehearses the attractions of Galateia and the course of his passion – there is no ultimate escape.

Σ quote two hexameters which are said to be the opening of a response (ποιημάτιον ... ἀντιγεγραμμένον) to Idyll 11 by Nikias:

> ἦν ἄρ' ἀληθὲς τοῦτο, Θεόκριτε· οἱ γὰρ Ἔρωτες
> ποιητὰς πολλοὺς ἐδίδαξαν τοὺς πρὶν ἀμούσους.

> (SH 566)

This then was true indeed, Theocritus: the instruction of the Loves turns many, who knew not the Muses before, into poets.

Nikias uses a famous quotation from Euripides' *Stheneboia* (fr. 663 Nauck): 'the instruction of Love, then, turns a man into a poet, even if he did not know the Muses before'. In the absence of the rest of the 'response', speculation as to the point of the verses must be brief. Nikias may be teasing T. with the sudden awakening of the latter's own poetic talent, or perhaps even acknowledging the rightness of T.'s advice: 'Yes, I tried writing poetry and it does help.' Nevertheless, the most obvious reference is to the Cyclops, the ἄμουσος *par excellence*, cf. Eur. *Cycl.* 173, 425–6 (ἄιδει ... ἄμουσα), 489–90, Nicochares frr. 4, 5 K–A; perhaps, then, 'many' deliberately includes both T. and his creation. Nikias' response has something of the flavour of Milon's response to Boukaios' song, ἦ καλὰς ἄμμε ποῶν ἐλελάθει Βοῦκος ἀοιδάς (10.38). The Euripidean verses do not actually assert the opposite of 11.1–4, but they do make a quite different point about the relation of poetry and *eros*; it is noteworthy that Plutarch also brings this quotation into juxtaposition with the Cyclops of Philoxenus 'healing his love' (*Mor.* 622c, cf. *PMG* 822), and it may be that Nikias is 'capping' T.'s poem by reflecting an allusion to Euripides in Philoxenus. For a further use of Euripides between T. and Nikias cf. 13.3–4n.

If *eros* is 'by definition' the pursuit of the one who flees (75), a longing for what is absent, then it is bound to hit particularly hard upon a Cyclops. The hallmark of the Homeric and Euripidean Polyphemos (and of the Cyclopes generally) is 'self-sufficiency',

αὐτάρκεια, marked by their ignorance of ships (the vehicles of com-
munication and commercial exchange), agriculture, political systems
and, at least in Polyphemos' case, a contempt for the divine; Polyphemos, moreover, has no wife (76n.), and is isolated and 'self-
sufficient' even within the context of Cyclops society. Menander's
would-be αὐτάρκης, Knemon of the *Dyskolos*, is also characterised
with Cyclopean traits (cf. Hunter (1985) 173 n.9). Desperate desire is
the negation of self-sufficiency, the painful acknowledgement of
'otherness', and so the Cyclops is a limit-case of general experience.
Here too T. has developed a Homeric picture. The Homeric monster channelled his affections towards a ram, but a ram that ultimately played him false (*Od.* 9.447–60); in the *Odyssey*, as in Idyll 11
(54–5), he uttered an impossible wish for a *contra naturam* sympathy
between different species, as the only way out of his grief: 'Would
that you could become *homophron* with me and endowed with speech
so that you could tell me ...' (*Od.* 9.455–6). Lines 54–5 of Idyll 11
mark Polyphemos' love as (comically) bucolic (cf. 1.85–91n.), but also
universalise his experience. 'Self-sufficiency' is both the Cyclops'
boast and his undoing. So too, Galateia, 'the Lady of the Milk', is a
fantasised projection of Polyphemos' usual pursuits; she is his Muse,
just as Amaryllis inspires the goatherd of Idyll 3. Those who live
alone are compelled to create their own 'other' to answer a universal
need; 'self-sufficiency' is a slogan with which we try (unsuccessfully)
to cheat our nature.

    Idyll 11 was a famous and much imitated poem in antiquity. It is
probably alluded to already in an epigram of Posidippus (cf. 6on.,
6.6–7n.), and an epigram of Callimachus (46 = *HE* 1047–56) has not
implausibly been understood as referring to it. The opening verses
are:

        ὡς ἀγαθὰν Πολύφαμος ἀνεύρατο τὰν ἐπαοιδάν
        τὠραμένωι· ναὶ Γᾶν, οὐκ ἀμαθὴς ὁ Κύκλωψ.
      αἱ Μοῖσαι τὸν ἔρωτα κατισχναίνοντι, Φίλιππε·
      ἦ πανακὲς πάντων φάρμακον ἁ σοφία.
      τοῦτο, δοκέω, χἁ λιμὸς μόνον ἐς τὰ πονηρά
      τὠγαθόν· ἐκκόπτει τὰν φιλόπαιδα νόσον.

What a good incantation Polyphemus discovered for the lover;
by Earth, the Cyclops was not a fool! The Muses, Philip, take

the swelling out of love; poetry is the universal *pharmakon* for everything. This too is the only advantage which hunger brings in bad circumstances: it makes you forget the disease of desire for boys.

The Doric dialect, the medical language and the possibility that Philip, like Nikias, was a doctor (cf. Gow–Page ad loc.) all suggest allusion to T.; οὐκ ἀμαθής ὁ Κύκλωψ may also allude to Nikias' reply to T. In addition to echoes in Longus and later bucolic, Idyll 11 is the primary model for one of Lucian's *Dialogues of sea gods* (78.1 Macleod) and was echoed by Nonnus (cf., e.g., 6.303); a paraphrase of the Idyll is found at 6.502–34 of the twelfth-century iambic 'romance', *Drosilla and Charikles*, by Niketas Eugenianos (ed. F. Conca, Amsterdam 1990). In Latin poetry, Idyll 11 is the primary model for Eclogue 2 (cf. DuQuesnay (1979)), and was rewritten in a completely different mode by Ovid, whose Galatea tells the story herself and who has her own lover, the handsome Acis (*Met.* 13.738–897, cf. J. Farrell, *AJP* 113 (1992) 235–68). T.'s poem was also clearly influential on the rich artistic tradition for the story, cf. Philostratus, *Imag.* 2.18, Nicosia (1968) 70–8, M. Guarducci, *Mem. Acc. Lincei* 23 (1979) 280–3.

Title. Κύκλωψ (Σ) or Κύκλωψ καὶ Γαλάτεια (MSS).

Modern discussions. Barigazzi (1975); Brooke (1971); Cozzoli (1994); Deuse (1990); Elliger (1975) 344–50; Erbse (1965); Goldhill (1991) 249–61; Gutzwiller (1991) 105–15; Hopkinson (1988) 148–54; Horstmann (1976) 80–105; Manuwald (1990); Ott (1969) 190–206; Schmiel (1993); Schmitt (1981); Spofford (1969); Stanzel (1995) 149–76; Stark (1963) 368–75; Walker (1980) 70–8.

1–6 These lines fall into three couplets, but this opening effect is not as strongly marked as in, say, Idyll 13. The gnomic utterance is of conventional form (cf. Men. fr. 518 K–T οὐκ ἔστιν ὀργῆς, ὡς ἔοικε, φάρμακον | ἀλλ' ἢ λόγος σπουδαῖος ἀνθρώπου φίλου), although the more usual claim – at least in the novels and amatory poetry of later antiquity – is that the only *pharmaka* for love are possession of the beloved (cf. Longus 2.7.7, 'correcting' T., Chariton 6.3.7, *P. Mich. Inv.* 5 (Stephens–Winkler p. 176), Heliodorus 4.7.7, Prop.

1.5.27–8 (with Fedeli's note)) and death (23.24). Lines 1–6 were much imitated, and their assertion is explicitly denied by Plutarch, *Mor.* 759b. The 'real world' was in fact full of people who claimed to be able to put an end to love by magical means, including 'sung spells' (cf. 2.90–2).

That song offers alleviation for the pain of love is a particular instance of the widespread belief that song and music offer relief from emotional distress of all kinds (cf. W. Stroh, *ANRW* II 31.4 (1981) 2648–58, Meillier (1982)); already in Hesiod, the song of 'the servant of the Muses' brings forgetfulness of trouble to the man 'who is pained and grieving in his heart' (*Theog.* 98–103, cf. 15 ὑπο-κάρδιον ἕλκος). Music may be viewed as a 'doctor' (cf. Pind. *Nem.* 4.1–4, Nisbet–Hubbard on Hor. *C.* 1.32.15), and T. here teases Nikias with the uselessness of one of his own *technai* when faced with *eros*. In antiquity, professional medical men had in fact more to do with 'lovesickness' than is common now, and a symptomatology of love (weight loss, fever etc.) became familiar in medical, as in literary, texts, cf. 2.85–90, P. Toohey, *ICS* 17 (1992) 265–86. Erasistratos of Keos, with whom Σ associate Nikias (above, p. 215), is said by later texts to have performed a famous diagnosis of lovesickness from variations in the pulse, and 1–6 must be seen against a background of genuine medical practice and/or anecdote, cf. Galen xiv 630–5 Kühn, Heliodorus 4.7, J. Mesk, *RhM* 68 (1913) 366–94. Moreover, the healing effect of (instrumental) music on the passions is a common idea in ancient musical writing; it is particularly associated with the Pythagoreans (cf. Aristoxenus fr. 26 Wehrli, 'the Pythagoreans produced a *katharsis* of the body through medicine and of the soul through music'), and was fiercely rejected by Epicureans (cf. Philo-demus, *De musica* iv pp. 55–9 Neubecker, a discussion which admits the possible efficaciousness of *poetry*, as opposed to music, and refers to Philoxenus on the Cyclops). There is perhaps a contrast between the 'doctoring' of the Muses associated with the Greek West and the powerlessness of the medicine of the eastern Aegean.

1 πὸτ τὸν ἔρωτα: for the apocope of the preposition cf. πὸτ τῶ Διός (4.50, 5.74, 15.70), in the mouths of 'low' characters from the Greek West, and πὸτ τὰν ζόαν (*Epigr.* 18.9) in a celebratory inscription for Epicharmus; this is a common feature of West Greek inscriptions (cf. R. Günther, *IF* 20 (1906/7) 25–31), and is a 'marked'

form which, like πεφύκει which follows, establishes a voice shared by both poet and Cyclops, cf. Molinos Tejada 330–1.   **πεφύκει:** a perfect with present ending (cf. 1.102, 4.7, 5.28, 33, 15.58 etc.). This is a widespread phenomenon in Doric (cf. P. Chantraine, *Histoire du parfait grec* (Paris 1927) 192–4, Buck (1955) 118, Molinos Tejada 302–5), but the grammatical tradition associated it with Syracuse (cf. Epicharmus fr. 190 Kaibel), and its appearance here, in a word which also creates a breach of 'Naeke's Law' (1.130n.), is stylistically programmatic. The author of Idyll 9 also begins his poem with a breach of 'Naeke's Law'.

2 ἔγχριστον ... ἐπίπαστον 'to be applied by smearing (χρίειν) or sprinkling (πάσσειν)'; the former is appropriate to 'wet' remedies such as oil or creams, the latter to 'dry' ones, such as ground herbs. Both suggest that *eros* is a 'flesh wound' to which external remedies might be applied, cf. 15–16. For the *topos* of different kinds of φάρμακα cf. Aesch. *PV* 479–80, Eur. *Hipp.* 516 (love magic).   **ἐμὶν δοκεῖ:** T. either opposes his view *qua* poet to that of Nikias *qua* doctor or (with mock modesty) acknowledges that he is encroaching into the field of medicine where Nikias is an expert. By themselves, the words carry no implication that the truth of the assertion has recently dawned on T. as a result of some personal love-experience. There may be some point in the contrast with ὡς ἐδοκεῦμες in 13.1.

3 ἢ ταὶ Πιερίδες is emphatically enjambed at the head of the hexameter. The Muses are given a grand title, 'daughters of Pieria' (cf. 10.24, Hes. *WD* 1), to accord with their importance; Pieria is the mountainous region north of Mt Olympus where the Muses were born.   **κοῦφον** 'light', 'painless', i.e. a remedy which will not hurt, cf. 17.52; as *eros* is βαρύς 'heavy' (3.15–17n.), so its remedy is as 'light' as the dance of the Muses. An active sense, 'alleviating' (as Σ3b, 7a), would suit very well, cf. 23.9 φίλαμα, τὸ κουφίζει τὸν ἔρωτα, Plut. *Mor.* 455b 'the practices of lovers, such as *komoi* and singing and garlanding [the beloved's] door, bring in some way an alleviation which is not without grace and harmony (κουφισμὸν οὐκ ἄχαριν οὐδ' ἄμουσον)', Arist. *Pol.* 8 1342a14 etc. Nowhere, however, does κοῦφος certainly have the meaning of κουφιστικός, though both seem to resonate here. Moreover, both κοῦφον (cf. Lat. *leuis*) and ἁδύ (1.1n.) have an important place in Hellenistic poetics, cf. Pl. *Ion* 534b3 'for a poet is a light (κοῦφον) and winged and holy thing';

'light Muses' are not far from the Μοῦσα λεπταλέη of Callimachus fr. 1, which is structured around an opposition between heavy and light, big and small. Thus the adjectives are chosen to carry both medical and poetic significance.

4 ἐπ' ἀνθρώποις: perhaps 'in men's power', 'available to men [not just to the gods]', cf. Pind. *Pyth.* 8.76 τὰ δ' οὐκ ἐπ' ἀνδράσι κεῖται, LSJ s.v. ἐπί BI 1g, or '[a remedy to be used] in the case of men', cf. Holland (1884) 241. The apparent paradox of using the Cyclops to illustrate a truth of 'human' life is one of the ways in which the difference between poet and Cyclops is broken down. **εὑρεῖν δ' οὐ ῥᾴδιον:** the right song is as hard to find as a rare herb; it too requires effort (cf. 7.51), cf. Homer's description of the φάρμακον which Hermes gives to Odysseus to protect him from Circe, μῶλυ δέ μιν καλέουσι θεοί· χαλεπὸν δέ τ' ὀρύσσειν | ἀνδράσι γε θνητοῖσι· θεοὶ δέ τε πάντα δύνανται (*Od.* 10.305–6). Song, like *moly*, protects men from the dangerous female (cf. E. Kaiser, *MH* 21 (1964) 200–13). The language again looks both to poetry – εὑρίσκειν suggests poetic or rhetorical *inuentio* – and to medicine: finding the right *pharmakon*, like diagnosis itself, is the job of the skilled doctor.

5–6 Nikias is both a doctor and a poet. Line 6 teasingly exaggerates *Od.* 8.63 (Demodokos) τὸν πέρι Μοῦσ' ἐφίλησε, cf. 28.7 Νικίαν, Χαρίτων ἱμεροφώνων ἵερον φύτον. The standardised division of the nine Muses (*Od.* 24.60, Hes. *Theog.* 75–9) post-dates T., and it was only in later antiquity that their influence was widened to cover the various human *technai* (*RE* XVI 685); nevertheless, as early as *Arg.* 2.512 the Muses teach Aristaios 'healing and divination', and given Apollo's rôle in both medicine and song and the theme of 'healing song', it is clear that the Muses watch over all Nikias' skills.

7 γοῦν introduces a proof of the preceding assertion (Denniston 451–3).   **ῥᾷστα διᾶγ'** 'did as well as possible', i.e. 'suffered as little as possible', cf. Philippides fr. 18 K–A 'whenever a misfortune strikes you, master, think of Euripides, and you will feel better (ῥᾴων ἔσηι)'. The phrase has a medical flavour (LSJ s.v. ῥᾴδιος II 2).   **ὁ παρ' ἁμῖν** 'our [Cyclops]', cf. LSJ s.v. παρά B II 2. The identification of the home of the Cyclopes as Sicily was already 'very ancient' for Thucydides (6.2.1), cf. Eur. *Cycl.*, and Epicharmus had dramatised the Homeric story. T. adduces a local example to strengthen his case: 'you are a doctor and thus know this, whereas I know it because of the example of my countryman'. The phrase need not imply that T. is writing in Sicily. ὁ παρ' ἀμῖν ... ὡρχαῖος suggests both the distance in time of the Cyclops and the modern relevance of his example.

8 It is common to put the names of lovers together in one sentence at the head of a narrative, cf. 6.6n., Call. fr. 67.1–2 αὐτὸς ῎Ερως ἐδίδαξεν ᾿Ακόντιον, ὁππότε καλῆι | ἤιθετο Κυδίππηι παῖς ἐπὶ παρθενικῆι, DuQuesnay (1979) 48–9. **ὡρχαῖος:** i.e. belonging to the heroic age and the subject of 'archaic' poetry. **τᾶς Γαλατείας** 'his Galateia' or 'the well known Galateia', cf. 13, 3.1–2n.

9 The 'first beard' conventionally marks the transition to young manhood or from *eromenos* to *erastes*, when thoughts may turn to marriage, cf. Xen. *Cyr.* 4.6.5 ἄρτι γενειάσκοντα of a young man ready for marriage, *Od.* 11.318–20, Aesch. *Sept.* 534–5 (Parthenopaios, the ἀνδρόπαις ἀνήρ), Pl. *Prt.* 309a–b, Call. fr. 274 (= *Hecale* fr. 45 Hollis), *Arg.* 1.972.

10–11 The slight zeugma, 'he pursued his love not through conventional love tokens but with madness', emphasises the strength of his passion. **μάλοις:** cf. 3.10–11n. **οὐδὲ ῥόδωι:** initial ῥ- lengthens the preceding syllable, in imitation of epic practice, cf. 45, 15.128 (the Adonis hymn), 22.118; there is no example in 'the bucolics' proper. For roses as love-tokens cf. 3.23, 10.34, and for the mixture of (collective) singular and plural Call. *h.* 6.27 ἐν πίτυς, ἐν μεγάλαι πτελέαι κτλ. **κικίννοις:** lovers may have exchanged locks of hair, or perhaps a young man grew a special lock for his beloved as for dedication to a god (Eur. *Ba.* 494, Garvie on Aesch. *Ch.* 6), or presented his beloved with the hair he cut to mark transition to manhood (13.7n.). **ὀρθαῖς μανίαις** 'outright madness', i.e. madness in the 'true' sense of the word; contrast Plato's philosophic lover who is ὀρθῶς μανείς 'mad in the right way' (*Phdr.* 244e4). As ὀρθῶς φρονεῖν is 'to be of sound mind', there is a slight oxymoron in the phrase, which prepares for 72–4 where Polyphemos seeks to recall his φρένες and νοῦς. The description of *eros* as a madness is standard (3.42, 10.31, 13.64–71n.), but it is a different kind of madness which is usually associated with Polyphemos, cf. *Od.* 9.350 (Odysseus to the Cyclops) σὺ δὲ μαίνεαι οὐκέτ' ἀνεκτῶς. In the *Republic* Plato contrasts ὀρθὸς ἔρως with μανία: the former is σωφρόνως τε καὶ μουσικῶς ἐρᾶν (*Rep.* 3 403a–b). T. inverts this pat-

tern and assigns a different place to μουσική.   ἀγεῖτο δὲ πάντα
πάρεργα 'he regarded everything [else] as unimportant'; for such
erotic 'forgetfulness' cf. 13.64–71n.

12 > *Ecl.* 4.21–2.   ὄιες: cf. 6.6–7n.   αὐταί 'without being
told to', 'of their own accord', *ipsae* (*Ecl.* 4.21), cf. Diotimus, *Anth.
Pal.* 7.173.1–2 (= *HE* 1769–70), of cattle whose herdsman has been
killed, αὐτομάται δείληι ποτὶ ταΰλιον αἱ βόες ἦλθον | ἐξ ὄρεος κτλ.,
Ovid, *Met.* 13.781 *pecudes nullo ducente secutae.* The sheep act as they
have always acted (cf. *Od.* 9.451–2); *their* daily routine is not dis-
turbed by erotic passion. Others understand 'alone' (cf. 14, LSJ s.v.
I 3), which is not very different in sense, but misses the nice observation of animal behaviour.

13–15 Cf. above, p. 220. Like Odysseus on Calypso's island, Polyphemos sleeps at night in a cave and spends all day (12–13 evening,
15 dawn) in sad reverie on the shore, 'uncomfortably suspended
somewhere between his own world and that of the nymph' (Brooke
(1971) 74), cf. 17–18n., *Od.* 5.82–4, 151–8. The 'heroic' isolation of
the Cyclops, emphasised by the Homeric *hapax* φυκιοέσσας (*Il.*
23.693), suggests also Achilles in his grief for Patroclus, δινεύεσκ'
ἀλύων παρὰ θῖν' ἁλός (*Il.* 24.12).

14 αὐτός 'alone', cf. *Ecl.* 2.4, and Orpheus at *Georg.* 4.464–6 *ipse
caua solans aegrum testudine amorem* | *te, dulcis coniunx, te solo in litore secum,*
| *te ueniente die, te decedente canebat.* The better attested αὐτῷ, 'there [on
the shore]', lacks point.   κατετάκετο: Polyphemos again resembles Odysseus, κατείβετο δὲ γλυκὺς αἰών (*Od.* 5.152), or T.'s own
Daphnis (Idyll 1, Idyll 7.76); for Lucretius, lovers *tabescunt uulnere caeco*
(4.1120). *Eros* is commonly conceived in 'liquid' terms (M. Davies,
Hermes 111 (1983) 496–7, Campbell on *Arg.* 3.290); on the seashore,
the Cyclops can blend emotionally with the sea, but is for ever bar-
red from physical union.   ἔχθιστον: the Cyclops wishes to be rid
of the terrible pain.

16 '[a wound] which a dart from great Kypris had fixed in his
liver'. To construe Κύπριδος ἐκ μεγάλας only with ἕλκος leaves
βέλεμνον bare; for the late position of the relative cf. 7.103, and for
'fixing a wound', rather than 'fixing an arrow', cf. Pind. *Pyth.* 2.91,
Arg. 3.764–5 ἀνίας ... ἐνισκίμψωσιν ἔρωτες. The Cyclops' all-
consuming passion (ὑποκάρδιον ... ἥπατι, cf. 13.71n.) is described
in an echo of Odysseus' killing of Eurymachos, ἐν δέ οἱ ἥπατι πῆξε

θοὸν βέλος (*Od.* 22.83); even when Kypris tortures Polyphemos, the real enemy is in the background. πᾶξε is the only unaugmented past tense in the poem, and this heightens the sense of quotation.

17–18 Cf. above, p. 220. Lovers standardly gaze out to sea when the beloved is away (Ariadne; Meleager, *Anth. Pal.* 12.53.4 (= *HE* 4331) Φανίον εἰς χαροπὸν δερκομέναν πέλαγος), but the primary model is the unhappy Odysseus on Calypso's island (*Od.* 5.84, 158). At 6.27–8 Damoitas' Polyphemos claims that Galateia inverts the motif by gazing from the sea towards his cave. Hermesianax fr. 1 Powell, δερκόμενος πρὸς κῦμα, μόνη δέ οἱ ἐφλέγετο γλήν, suggests that T. had at least one Hellenistic model for this image of the Cyclops, cf. 5 1n. The move from the seashore (14) to a 'lofty rock' denotes a partial withdrawal from his pain and prepares for the 'success' of the song. At another level, the verses may allude to a rationalising interpretation of a high mountain (?Etna) as the Cyclops gazing out to sea after Galateia, cf. *Od.* 9.190–2 (Polyphemos like a solitary mountain peak). **ἄειδε:** imperfect, thus suggesting that this was not a one-time performance.

19–79 The Cyclops' song is a kind of *paraklausithyron* (Idyll 3, Intro., Cairns (1972) 144–7, DuQuesnay (1979) 46–7) in which, despite his fantasies (54–7), the lover is compelled to seek to entice his beloved out rather than to gain entry himself. It may be divided into four unequal sections, each introduced by an address to Galateia or a self-address: 19–29 (his love), 30–53 (what he can offer), 54–71 (their total separation), 72–9 (resolution). The song lacks the clear paragraphing of the parallel performance in Idyll 3, and this is important in judging its overall effect, cf. *Ecl.* 2.4 *haec incondita*.

19–21 > *Ecl.* 7.37–8. In form, this question is a Cyclopean version of lyrics such as Anacreon, *PMG* 417 πῶλε Θρηικίη, τί δή με | λοξὸν ὄμμασι βλέπουσα | νηλέως φεύγεις ... νῦν δὲ λειμῶνάς τε βόσκεαι | κοῦφά τε σκιρτῶσα παίζεις (cf. 11.21), but there may be a specific model as well. Philoxenus' Cyclops had addressed Galateia as ὦ καλλιπρόσωπε χρυσεοβόστρυχε | χαριτόφωνε θάλος Ἐρώτων (*PMG* 821), but Demetrius, *On style* 162 cites the phrases πολὺ πάκτιδος ἀδυμελεστέρα and χρύσω χρυσοτέρα from Sappho (fr. 156 Voigt), and a probably corrupt notice in a late rhetorician provides a much longer list: οἷον τὰ Ἀνακρέοντος [*PMG* 488], τὰ Σαπφοῦς· οἷον γάλακτος λευκοτέρα, ὕδατος ἁπαλωτέρα, πηκτίδων ἐμμελεσ-

τέρα, ἵππου γαυροτέρα, ῥόδων ἀβροτέρα, ἱματίου ἑανοῦ μαλακω-
τέρα, χρυσοῦ τιμιωτέρα. Which phrases belong to Anacreon or
Sappho or neither is far from clear (cf M. Treu, *Von Homer zur Lyrik*
(2nd ed., Munich 1968) 183–6), but as Sappho is important for 22–3,
it seems that, like Simaitha at 2.106–10, the lovesick Cyclops here
reaches for *the* poet of *eros* to express his complaint. The transformation of Sappho's πάκτιδος ἀδυμελεστέρα ('more sweet-singing
than a harp') into λευκοτέρα πακτᾶς ('whiter than cream cheese') is
a particularly brilliant effect. The 3–2–2–3 arrangement of phrases,
coupled with a chiastic adj.–noun–noun–adj. organisation of the
central terms, confirms the Cyclops' stylistic pretensions. These
verses gave rise to Ovid's truly 'Cyclopean' imitation at *Met.* 13.789–
807. Demetrius, *On style* 123–7 criticises 'hyperboles' such as 'whiter
than snow' as 'particularly frigid because they suggest impossibi-
lities', and he notes that comic poets are fond of such phrases
because the impossible soon turns into the laughable (τὸ γελοῖον).
Comedy is certainly relevant here.

20 λευκοτέρα πακτᾶς: 'Miss Milky' is bound to be very white, the
desirable colour in women, but her name rules out the more obvious
'whiter than milk'. Whether we are to understand that Polyphemos
did not realise the meaning of Galateia's name (as he did not understand Odysseus' disguise as *Outis*) is uncertain. Cheese itself was
proverbially white (cf. Tyro, so named 'for her whiteness', Diod. Sic.
6.7.2 etc.), and the Cyclops, being an expert in such matters (cf. *Od.*
9.246–7), specifically chooses πακτή (?cream cheese or a kind of
thick yogurt, from πήγνυμι 'to set', cf. 66, Antiphanes fr. 131.9 K–A)
as a way of enhancing the compliment. 'The language of love' is,
however, not concerned with realism or truth, and in revealing his
dairy expertise the Cyclops proves a bathetic lover. In the same section where he cites Sappho's comparisons, Demetrius contrasts the
charis arising from the use of 'beautiful nouns' (as in Sappho) with
the laughable effect of 'nouns which are ordinary and common'
(*On style* 163–6); he might well have been describing this verse.

ποτιδεῖν: Polyphemos has certainly seen cream cheese, but (we are
to understand) it is an open question whether he has ever seen Galateia.

21 γαυροτέρα 'more skittish', with the further nuance of 'proud',
'stand-offish'; Galateia is 'playing hard to get', cf. *Ecl.* 3.64 *malo me*

Galatea petit, lasciua puella, Ovid, *Met.* 13.791 *tenero lasciuior haedo*. μόσ-
χος may be a calf of either sex, but there is a clear implication that
Polyphemos would like to 'yoke' her. Cf. Hor. *C.* 2.5, the *iuuenca*
who is not ready for marriage is characterised as *ludere praegestiens*
(8–9, cf. γαυροτέρα) and an *inmitis uua* (10, cf. ὄμφακος ὠμᾶς).
φιαρωτέρα 'brighter', 'glossier', though the exact sense is uncertain.
Young grapes are firm to the touch and Dover saw a reference to
'smooth, sleek skin free from wrinkles' (which might be hard to pre-
serve when living at the bottom of the sea); there may be a specific
reference to the developing breasts of a young girl (made more
obvious by the variant σφριγανωτέρα). For the image of a girl as a
grape, ripening for the inevitable 'pressing', cf. Ar. *Peace* 1338–9
(τρυγᾶν), *GP* 2402, 3218–19, Nisbet–Hubbard on Hor. *C.* 2.5.10, and
perhaps already Alcaeus fr. 119.15–16 Voigt.   ὠμᾶς: as ὄμφαξ
by itself denotes 'an unripe grape', the epithet is not merely indicative of the Cyclops' poetic style (45–8n.), but perhaps also hints at
Galateia's cruelty, her ὠμότης, a characteristic that, later in life,
Polyphemos himself was to display in superabundance.

22–3 The Cyclops' dreams are full of Galateia, but he does
not understand dreaming, and imagines that she comes ashore the
moment he falls asleep and retreats to the water as soon as he wakes
up. The repeated half-line re-works *Od.* 9.333, ὅτε τὸν γλυκὺς ὕπνος
ἱκάνοι, of the time at which Odysseus will put out his eye, to show
the depth of the Cyclops' pain; this sleep *is*, however, 'sweet'
because it brings visions of Galateia, and hence release from suffering. As in the previous verses, echoes of Sappho mark the lover's
poetry, cf. fr. 63.1–3 Voigt Ὄνοιρε μελαινα[... | φοίταις, ὄτα τ'
ὔπνος[... | γλύκυς θέος, ἦ δεῖν' ὀνίας μ[... For such dreams cf.
Aesch. *Ag.* 420–6, Hor. *C.* 4.1.37–8 *nocturnis ego somniis | iam captum
teneo, iam uolucrem sequor*, Ovid, *Her.* 15.123–34 (Sappho to Phaon),
Hunter on *Arg.* 3.616–32. The Cyclops' failure to distinguish dreaming from 'reality' speaks to the very nature of *eros*, which is standardly constructed as desire for something which is *both* real and
insubstantial; Lucretius 4.1097–1104 draws close parallels between
dreaming and sexual desire, as both involve *simulacra* (cf. Brown
(1987) 82–7, Nussbaum (1994) 164–72). Cf. *Ecl.* 8.108 *credimus? an, qui
amant, ipsi sibi somnia fingunt?* The almost repeated half-line perhaps
suggests the simple patterns of the lullaby (cf. 24.7–9, Dover xlvii–l),

appropriate for the childlike Cyclops, and indicates the ceaseless repetition of the dreaming experience.   φοιτῆις δ' αὖθ' οὕτως 'and (continuative δέ) you appear at once just like that [cf. *LSJ* s.v. οὕτως ιν] …' There is doubt over the text, but if αὖθι is used, as in Homer, with the sense of αὐτίκα, then the Cyclops refers to the familiar impression that dreams begin and end precisely when sleep does; others prefer to take αὖθι as 'here'.

24 A *spondeiazon* (cf. 58, 69) closes the opening plea. The simile says more than the Cyclops intends: as wolves eat sheep, so the Cyclops was to be best known for eating those with whom he came into contact, cf. further 13.62–3n.

25–7 > *Ecl.* 8.37–8. Perhaps a further Sapphic echo, cf. fr. 49.1 Voigt ἠράμαν μὲν ἔγω σέθεν, Ἄτθι, πάλαι ποτά. Flower-picking is the almost inevitable setting in myth and literature for rape, but here the girl is chaperoned, and the result is unrequited love; to what extent this incident is a figment of the fantasy of a lonely shepherd is left deliberately unclear. ὑάκινθος is a mountain flower (wild orchid?) which has not been securely identified (cf. Sappho fr. 105b Voigt, Thphr. *HP* 6.8.1–2, Gow on 10.28, Lembach (1970) 174–9); it occurs frequently in connection with Aphrodite or scenes of *eros* (cf. *PMG* 346.7–9).

25 τεοῦς: for this genitive cf. 18.41, Sophron fr. 59 Kaibel, Corinna, *PMG* 654 iv 6, 666; it may be one of the 'broader' features of the Doric of this poem, cf. above, p. 218.

26 ματρί: Thoosa, daughter of Phorkys (*Od.* 1.71–3). It is central to his tragedy that Polyphemos cannot even swim (60n.), though he is the child of Poseidon and a sea-nymph. There is probably an allusion to a 'Homeric problem': Aristotle had discussed how Polyphemos could be a Cyclops when neither of his parents were (fr. 172 Rose).

27 ἐγὼ δ' ὁδὸν ἀγεμόνευον: a Homeric collocation particularly associated with Odysseus (*Od.* 6.261, 7.30, 10.501); even at this moment of tender memory, Polyphemos is trapped in the language of the enemy.

28–9 'Having seen you, from that time forth (ἐκ τήνω) [I was unable] afterwards, and even now am still unable, at all (πᾱι) to cease [from love]' (cf. Hopkinson (1988) 152). The somewhat clumsy redundancy, which suggests a distinction between the time after 'the first sighting' and the present (so Σ), suggests the Cyclops' struggle for words. Others prefer to take ὕστερον with ἐσιδών, but ἐκ τήνω would then lose its force, and the situation is more pathetic if he has seen (or thinks he has seen) Galateia only once. Stark (1963) 361–2 suggested ὕστερον οὐκέτι πάγχυ.   τὶν δ' οὐ μέλει: cf. 3.52.

μὰ Δί': when older, this Cyclops was to be openly contemptuous of Zeus (*Od.* 9.275–8, Eur. *Cycl.* 320–1).

30 χαρίεσσα: cf. 13.7n.   **οὕνεκα:** the only example in T. of prepositional οὕνεκα, perhaps chosen for the rhetorical matching with οὕνεκα as a causal conjunction in 31. In the Hellenistic period the Attic preposition is largely replaced by εἵνεκα, cf. Wackernagel (1953) 591–612, Barrett on Eur. *Hipp.* 453–6.

31–3 > *Ecl.* 8.34. Cf. Hes. *Theog.* 143–5 (of the other group of Kyklopes known to mythology) μοῦνος δ' ὀφθαλμὸς μέσσωι ἐνέκειτο μετώπωι· | Κύκλωπες δ' ὄνομ' ἦσαν ἐπώνυμον, οὕνεκ' ἄρα σφέων | κυκλοτερὴς ὀφθαλμὸς ἔεις ἐνέκειτο μετώπωι. The Cyclops' precise pedantry spares no effort in making us visualise his ugliness. Homer's failure to state *explicitly* (cf. *Od.* 9.453, 503) that Polyphemos had only one eye much exercised ancient scholarship, and some held that he had in fact originally had two, as indeed he does in some ancient representations, cf. Σ *Od.* 9.106, 383; T.'s Cyclops is intent on proving, even to the satisfaction of finicky philologists, that he really is one-eyed. On this problem in general cf. Heubeck on *Od.* 9.105–566 and R. Mondi, *TAPA* 113 (1983) 17–38. Like the komast of Idyll 3 (3.8–9n.), the Cyclops is given the shagginess and broad nose of a silenos; for examples of just such a representation of Polyphemos cf. Fellmann (1972) figs. 11 and 20.

33 ὕπεστι: the transmitted ἔπεστι (sc. τῶι μετώπωι) may have arisen from 31 or as an anticipation of ἐπὶ χείλει. Cf. Call. *h.* 3.52–3 (the other Kyklopes) πᾶσι δ' ὑπ' ὀφρὺν | φάεα μουνόγληνα κτλ.

34–7 > *Ecl.* 2.19–22. The Cyclops' pride in his possessions reworks Odysseus' description of the cave (*Od.* 9.218–23), but may well owe something to Attic comedy, cf. Antiphanes fr. 131 K–A.

34 οὗτος τοιοῦτος ἐών 'though I am such as I have described'. **βοτὰ χίλια βόσκω:** like a good herdsman, the Cyclops knows how many animals he has, though Ovid's Cyclops goes one better, *nec, si forte roges, possim tibi dicere quot sint;* | *pauperis est numerare pecus* (*Met.* 13.823–4). The *figura etymologica* βοτὰ ... βόσκω (cf. *Etym. Mag.*

205.50 Gaisford) adds to the impressiveness of the claim; as βοτά is regularly used of cattle, Polyphemos may be hinting at a higher status than his sheep would normally accord him.

35 τὸ κράτιστον 'the finest' (cf. LSJ s.v. 2). The Cyclops is a connoisseur – of milk; before too long he will drink wine which is both 'finest' (cf. Amphis fr. 36.2 K–A) and 'strongest'.

36–7 οὔτ' ... οὔτ' ... οὐ: the asyndeton throws emphasis upon the final member, cf. 15.137–42, Denniston 510. Polyphemos' boast is expressed in a verbatim quotation of Circe's description of the man-destroying Skylla's cave (*Od.* 12.76), which suggests to us that its 'pleasures' are far from unalloyed; cf. also the wonders of Alkinous' orchard, τάων οὔ ποτε καρπὸς ἀπόλλυται οὐδ' ἀπολείπει | χείματος οὐδὲ θέρευς, ἐπετήσιος (*Od.* 7.117–18). χειμῶνος ἄκρω 'the end of winter', when a shortage of (fresh) cheese might have been expected; Servius (on *Ecl.* 2.22) amusingly observes that cheese can be stored, so that the Cyclops' boast is no great thing. ἄκρος may denote 'the middle of' a period of time (cf. Soph. *Aj.* 285 with Jebb's note), but it more usually refers to the beginning or the end, cf. Hipp. *Aphor.* 3.18 ἄκρον θέρος 'the beginning of summer' (*pace* LSJ), Arat. *Phaen.* 308 ἀκρόθι νυκτός 'at the end of night'. ταρσοί 'wicker racks', for stacking cheeses, cf. *Od.* 9.219 with Σ. ὑπεραχθέες 'full to bursting', not just 'heavy'; the Cyclops presents his cave as a kind of dairy wonderland.

38 > *Ecl.* 2.23–4. Homer does not say explicitly that his Cyclopes play the syrinx (contrast *Il.* 18.525–6), but the ῥοῖζος with which Polyphemos drove his animals was a subject for scholarly discussion (Σ *Od.* 9.315): T.'s Cyclops thus settles a matter of academic contention, and the Cyclops of Idyll 6 is also a syrinx-player (6.9). The Homeric scholia distinguish the ῥοῖζος from syrinx-playing, 'because use of the syrinx is the mark of a civilised (ἥμερος) shepherd'. The use of the syrinx at night to accompany his song (cf. 7.27–31n.), rather than during the day to control sheep or while away the midday hours, is a clear sign of the Cyclops' abandonment of his bucolic rôle. For the sleeplessness of the lover cf., e.g., *Arg.* 3.744–54, McKeown on Ovid, *Am.* 1.2.3. οὖτις: Odysseus' pseudonym creates an obvious irony, cf. 61, 79.

39 The kind of song he has in mind may be like Boukaios' love-song at 10.24–37. τίν: accusative, cf. 55, 68, Corinna, *PMG* 663,

Cercidas, fr. 7.6 Powell (= 3.5 Livrea/Lomiento).   γλυκύμαλον:
lit. 'an apple grafted onto a quince', but 'sweet-apple' well catches
the Cyclops' feelings for Galateia, cf. Sappho fr. 105a.1 Voigt, Lembach (1970) 134, Hopkinson on Call. *h.* 6.28.   ἀμᾶι: Doric form of
ἅμα; 'In the *koine* ἅμα had become a general equivalent of σύν'
(Bulloch on Call. *h.* 5.75).

40–1 > *Ecl.* 2.40–2. This is a Cyclopean version of the goat which
the komast offers to Amaryllis at 3.34–6.   τράφω: this Doric
form, probably occurring also in Pindar, is very poorly attested here,
but cf. 3.16, the form τράχω (2.115, 147), and Molinos Tejada 110–
11.   μαννοφόρως: perhaps 'with neck-markings', hence rare and
prized, rather than (as Σ) 'with ornaments around the neck' (for
which cf. Ovid, *Met.* 10.113), but the meaning (like the text) is uncertain; Pollux 5.99 asserts that μάννος or μόννος is a Doric word for
women's necklaces. Virgil may have understood the word to refer to
markings on the coat, cf. *Ecl.* 2.41.   ἄρκτων: the plural does not
necessarily mean that T. (or his Cyclops) is showing that he knows
bears usually have only one or two cubs at a time (so Arist. *HA* 6
579a20, a passage misunderstood by Gow and DuQuesnay (1979)
68).

42–3 > *Ecl.* 9.39–43.   ἀφίκευσο: Σ asserts that this 'hyper-
imperative' form is Syracusan, and T. may, therefore, have had a
model in Epicharmus or Sophron, cf. Ruijgh (1984) 80; Wackernagel
(1953) 864, however, sees a Hellenistic development.   γλαυκὰν
. . . θάλασσαν: this phrase occurs in Homer only at *Il.* 16.34 (Patro-
klos' reproaches to the pitiless Achilles), and some of the harshness
of that passage carries over into this: who would want to live there?
Σ (bT) notes that it is because of the cruel harshness of the sea that
the Cyclopes and the Laestrygonians were made children of Poseidon, and Polyphemos a child of Thoosa; here again (cf. 38n.) the
Cyclops may reject contemporary academic discussion of his
Homeric model.   ὀρεχθεῖν 'beat angrily' = ῥοχθεῖν, cf. Rengakos
(1994) 122–3, M. P. Cuypers, *Apollonius Rhodius, Argonautica 2.1–310. A
commentary* (diss. Leiden 1997) 312–14.

44 > *Ecl.* 1.79.

45–8 In an attempt to entice Galateia out, the Cyclops performs a
version of the bucolic *locus amoenus*, complete with anaphora, rhyme
and chiasmus, to describe the delights of his cave's setting, cf. 5.31–

4, 45–9, *Ecl.* 10.42–3; he has already dealt with the interior decoration (cheese-racks). Some details are taken from the cave of the Homeric Cyclops (*Od.* 9.183 laurels), but Calypso's cave in which the hated Odysseus 'spent [many] nights' is also recalled: cypresses (*Od.* 5.64), vines (*Od.* 5.69), cool water (*Od.* 5.70). This invitation to the beloved recalls the eroticism of Sappho's 'invitation' to Aphrodite in fr. 2 Voigt to come to a party in a 'lovely apple-grove' filled with incense, cool water and flowers; so here, the combination of phallic cypresses (cf. 27.46), Dionysiac ivy, good wine and refreshing water make clear what the Cyclops has in mind (cf. 44). Hopkinson (1988) 153 suggests that the water may be intended for mixing or cooling the wine of 46, but it is perhaps more likely that the Cyclops uses a standard element of the *locus amoenus*, without considering whether cold, fresh water would be very attractive to a sea-nymph.

The pairing of virtually every noun with an adjective (including 'white snow', perhaps in imitation of the Homeric 'white milk', *Il.* 4.434, 5.902; cf. *Il.* 10.437 λευκότεροι χιόνος) suggests the effort which goes into this set piece. Cyclopean poetry knows nothing of scholarly discussions of the verbal (particularly adjectival) style appropriate to poetry, cf. Arist. *Rhet.* 3 1406a, Elliger (1975) 345–8, and yet its effect depends upon *our* knowledge of them.

45 τηνεί 'there'. For hiatus at the central caesura cf. 3.39, 42, 18.28–9, 22.39. **κυπάρισσοι:** Lindsell (1937) 86 claims that cypresses would, at best, have been rare in the Sicily of T.'s day.

46 ἔστι: cf. 3.39n. **κισσός:** the second syllable is lengthened in arsis at the central caesura, cf. 1.115, 7.85, Gow on 18.5. **γλυκύκαρπος:** in the *Odyssey*, wine was to prove anything but 'sweet' for Polyphemos; for the vines of the Cyclopes cf. *Od.* 9.110–11, 357–8, but the young Cyclops probably simply eats the 'sweet grapes', and urges Galateia to do likewise. Strabo 6.2.3 reports that the volcanic soil of Etna's lower slopes is good for vines. Wine-drinking is largely absent from T.'s 'contemporary' bucolic world, cf. 7.65 (a fantasy party), 147–55 (urban characters in a rustic setting).

47 πολυδένδρεος: in Homer only of Odysseus' estate on Ithaca (*Od.* 4.737, 23.139, 359); again the Cyclops is compelled to imitate that hero. For the thick vegetation on Etna (not, of course, near the summit) cf. Pind. *Pyth.* 1.28, Strabo 6.2.8.

48 χιόνος: cf. Pind. *Pyth.* 1.20 νιφόεσσ' Αἴτνα, πάνετες χιόνος

COMMENTARY: 11.49–53   237

ὀξείας τιθήνα, Strabo 6.2.8.   **ποτὸν ἀμβρόσιον:** the θεῖον ποτόν
(*Od.* 9.205) which will destroy the Cyclops is ἀμβροσίης καὶ νέκταρος
... ἀπορρώξ (*Od.* 9.359).

49 Cf. 7.57–8n.   **τῶνδε** '[in preference to] these things', cf. the
genitive after προτιμᾶν, προτιθέναι etc.

50 The argument moves on: 'if you realise the advantages of
the setting, but still think I'm an unattractive partner, there are
compensations *inside* the cave ...'   **λασιώτερος:** as the following
verses refer to his most prominent feature, it is preferable to see here
a return to the 'shaggy brow' of 31, rather than a reference to body
hair, for which cf. Fellmann (1972) fig. 8 (though other interpretations of that painting have been canvassed) and which would
be another feature shared with satyrs and silenoi (33n.). Homer
draws particular attention to the burning of the Cyclops' brow (*Od.*
9.389). Ovid's Cyclops is a mass of hair all over (*Met.* 13.844–50).

51 > *Ecl.* 7.49–51. Nicetas Eugen. 6.511 rightly understood the
Cyclops to be offering to singe away his shagginess, or allow Galateia to do so. In such a context, however, any reference to fire is
bound to hover between the literal and the metaphorical, as already
perhaps in Hermesianax (cf. 17–18n.). Thus here the cave is both literally and emotionally 'warm' (in comparison to the cold and nasty
sea); for the image of 'fire under the ash' cf. Call. *Epigr.* 44.2 (= *HE*
1082), Meleager, *Anth. Pal.* 12.80.4 (= *HE* 4085). Following the sex-
ualised invitation of 45–8, the Cyclops' 'undying fire' may hint at a
physical, as well as emotional, 'staying power'. The presence of
'undying fire' and (olive) logs in the cave was of course to allow
Odysseus to produce the very tragedy to which the Cyclops alludes
in 53, cf. Fantuzzi (1995b) 17–18.   **δρυός:** oaks are a familiar element of the bucolic landscape (Lembach (1970) 109–11), and make
excellent firewood (cf. 9.19).   **σποδῶ:** the genitive is suggested by
ὑπὸ σποδοῦ in the same *sedes* at *Od.* 9.375 (Odysseus tempering the
stake), and is somewhat more poetic than the dative. With either
reading the tragic irony is apparent.

52 **καιόμενος:** cf. *Od.* 9.390 γλήνης καιομένης 'as the eyeball
burned'.   **τεῦς:** this genitive form is metrically guaranteed at 55
and 2.126.

53 **γλυκερώτερον:** the only instance of this comparative in early
epic is *Od.* 9.28, Odysseus on the pleasure of *seeing* Ithaca; again, the

Cyclops unwittingly echoes the man who is to destroy him. The conceit is a way of saying that Galateia is in fact dearer to him than his eye, cf. *Megara* 9 ('equal to the eyes'), Cat. 3.5, 14.1 ('more than the eyes'), Otto s.v. *oculus*. The present passage seems to foreshadow a later rationalising version in which Odysseus, 'burning' with love, carried off Polyphemos' one daughter (his 'eye'), cf. W. Dindorf, *Scholia Graeca in Homeri Odysseam* (Oxford 1855) I 4–5.

54 After the 'sweet dream' of 44–53, some realisation of the impossibility of his situation dawns; this he expresses in a version of the 'metamorphosis' wish of the lover, cf. 3.12–14n., above, p. 222. Instead, however, of saying 'I wish I were a fish ...', he laments that it can never be. The verse foreshadows his later reproaches against his mother and draws attention to their biological difference (25–7n.). Does he believe that Galateia and his mother breathe with gills? **ὅτ':** probably ὅτι (cf. 79, 16.9), rather than causal ὅτε (LSJ s.v. B). **βράγχι'** 'gills', to enable him to descend (κατέδυν) to the depths.

55 A final clause may take a simple past indicative when it depends upon an impossible wish or a hypothesis contrary to known fact, cf. 4.49, 7.86–9, Goodwin §333.   **τίν:** cf. 39n.   **χέρα:** Polyphemos' *politesse* goes one better than another Theocritean komast: Delphis claims that he too would have come with flowers and been content to kiss Simaitha's mouth (2.118–28). A kiss on the hand is normally a mark of (non-erotic) friendship (*Od.* 21.225, 24.398, [Bion] 2.23), but here we may see a gesture of pleading supplication (cf. *Il.* 24.478).

56–7 For the gift of flowers, perhaps in a garland rather than a bouquet, cf. 2.121–2, 3.21–3n.; despite Galateia's apparent fondness for flowers (26–7), one may wonder how successful they would be as an underwater gift. Once again (cf. 45–8n.), every noun is paired with a (rather simple) adjective.   **κρίνα:** not certainly identified; lilies do not flower in the winter (58), so perhaps 'narcissus', cf. Lembach (1970) 165–6.   **μάκων** 'poppies' (which flower in summer), cf. Lembach (1970) 161–5.

58–9 The ἀλλά covers a piece of Cyclopean reasoning (cf. Radt (1971) 256): having used ἤ ... ἤ in 56–7, he answers the possible objection that it would have been better (and perhaps Galateia would have expected him) to bring both, by explaining why that would not have been possible. His naïve pedantry (cf. 36–7) is obviously amusing, but it also lays bare the artificially conventional nature of 'love-poetry', which has no place for simple ideas of 'realism'.   ταῦτα ... ἄμα πάντ': amusingly exaggerated for two kinds of flower.

60 The text is very uncertain. If the transmitted μαθεῦμαι is correct, it will be an alternative (perhaps a 'back formation' from the aorist) to μαθησεῦμαι, which would follow a regular Doric pattern of marking the future by both -σ- and -ε-, cf. 2.8 βασεῦμαι, Buck (1955) 115; δεούμεθα (ἀντὶ τοῦ δεηθησόμεθα) is, however, cited for Epicharmus (fr. 120 Kaibel).   νῦν μάν 'but as things are', i.e. 'as I don't have gills ...'   νεῖν γε: swimming will at least (γε) give him some taste of life in the water, even if descent to the depths is ruled out. Not knowing how to swim was a mark of the proverbially ignorant (on a par with not knowing the alphabet), cf. Pl. *Laws* 3 689d 3, *CPG* II 39; the Cyclops again reveals himself all too plainly. Posidippus' Cyclops 'often went diving with Galateia', thus reversing T.'s motif (*P. Mil. Vogl.* 1295, col. 3.28–41 Bastianini–Gallazzi). On classical attitudes to swimming cf. E. Hall in H. A. Khan (ed.), *The birth of the European identity: the Europe–Asia contrast in Greek thought 490–322 BC* (Nottingham 1994) 44–80, J. Auberger, *Latomus* 55 (1996) 48–62.

61 With his usual literalism, the Cyclops notes that he will need a teacher to learn to swim, thus rather undermining the resolution of the previous verse. The reference to τις ... ξένος arriving by ship evokes Odysseus–Οὖτις and the theme of *xenia* which is central to the Homeric Cyclops episode; the redundancy of σὺν ναῖ πλέων recalls both the fact that Cyclopes have no ships (*Od.* 9.125–9) and Polyphemos' interest in Odysseus' ship (*Od.* 9.279–80). The Cyclops chooses (unwittingly) an expert swimmer as his teacher, perhaps in fact the *protos heuretes* of the art: cf. esp. *Od.* 5.291–493 where the shipwrecked Odysseus is carried by a storm to Scheria; that episode is full of 'swimming' words.   ὧδ' 'to this place'. Contrast 'here' in 64.

62 ὕμμιν 'you [Nereids]'.

63 Subsequent poetry fulfilled the Cyclops' prayer, but for Bion, not for him, cf. *EB* 62–3 καὶ νῦν λασαμένα τῶ κύματος ἐν ψαμάθοισιν | ἕζετ' ἐρημαίοισι κτλ.

64 Consciousness of his situation foreshadows the return to 'common sense' of 72–9. ἐγών: cf. 3.24n. Choice between ἐγών and ἐγώ is particularly difficult before a following initial ν-. ἀπενθεῖν: apparently a unique example of λαθέσθαι plus infinitive meaning 'forget to ...'

65–6 > *Ecl.* 2.28–30. As we would expect, the Cyclops lists his activities in their proper order: a day in the fields, then milking and cheese-making (cf. *Od.* 9.244–7). τάμισον: curdled milk taken from the stomach of a young animal was used to set cheese, cf. Σ Nicander, *Ther.* 577, Gow on 7.16. 'Miss Milky' is unlikely to be attracted by this occupation. δριμεῖαν 'pungent' (cf. 7.16) rather than 'sharp to the taste'.

67–9 Lest Galateia should object to his implied reproaches, Polyphemos makes clear, with the familiar petulance of the child, that his mother carries sole responsibility for his plight.

67 ἀδικεῖ: this verb is standardly used of 'bad behaviour' by one lover to another (Sappho fr. 1.20 Voigt, Call. *Epigr.* 42.6, L. Belloni, *Aev. Ant.* 2 (1989) 223–33), so its use of the Cyclops' mother emphasises Galateia's guiltlessness.

68 οὐδὲν ... ὅλως 'absolutely none', cf. LSJ s.v. ὅλος III 3. τίν: cf. 39n.

69 ἆμαρ ἐπ' ἆμαρ ... λεπτύνοντα 'growing thinner day by day', an unusual intransitive use of λεπτύνειν (with Meineke's certain emendation); the verb is at home in medical contexts. For the lover's conventional thinness cf. 2.89–90, 14.3, McKeown on Ovid, *Am.* 1.6.5–6.

70–1 For the lover's (conventional) headache cf. 3.52n.; the Cyclops absurdly adds his feet, just for good measure, and '*both* feet' is a further touch which betrays the cunning of the child in appealing for pity. σφύσδειν 'throb', a further medical term which will appeal to Nikias. ἀνιαθῆι ... ἀνιῶμαι: with a touching faith in Thoosa's maternal instincts, the Cyclops threatens to make her feel emotional pain at his (pretended) physical pain, since she feels no pain at his (real) emotional pain.

72–4 > *Ecl.* 2.69–72.

72 Κύκλωψ: his name is Polyphemos (8), but he is also known throughout literature as 'the Cyclops' (cf. 7), although one would not expect him to use this form; as Σ *Od.* 9.403 points out, Odysseus, *qua* character in the story, only uses the proper name after the other

Cyclopes have revealed it, although he continues (as also in Eur. *Cycl.*) to address him as 'Cyclops'. Polyphemos' use of Κύκλωψ here thus activates a sense of his own literary future. Self-address of this kind is particularly common in New Comedy, and this may be part of the flavour here, cf. F. Leo, *Der Monolog im Drama* (Berlin 1908) 94–113, W. Schadewaldt, *Monolog und Selbstgespräch* (Berlin 1926). **τὰς φρένας ἐκπεπότασαι:** cf. 2.19; the verb is a Doric perfect of the frequentative ἐκποτάομαι. Eros has wings and lovers conventionally 'fly' (Anacreon, *PMG* 378 etc.), but here the metaphor marks distraction of mind.

73 αἴ κ': if sound, this will be a Doric version of Homeric εἴ κε plus the optative in the protasis of a conditional, cf. Goodwin §460. Some editors, however, prefer αἴκ, i.e. αἰ plus the κ seen in οὐκ, both here and in other passages of literary Doric (Epicharmus fr. 21 Kaibel, Ar. *Lys.* 1099). **ταλάρως:** wicker bowls in which milk is placed prior to cheese-making, cf. Gow on 5.86; T. is thinking of *Od.* 9.247 πλεκτοῖς ἐν ταλάροισιν. For a long list of 'country work' which can take your mind off love cf. Ovid, *RA* 169–212.

73–4 θαλλὸν ... φέροις: perhaps a memory of *Od.* 17.224 (Melantheus abusing the disguised Odysseus) θαλλὸν τ' ἐρίφοισι φορῆναι; this is not just a matter of the Cyclops 'trapped' in Odyssean language (above, p. 219), for the echo reveals the hopelessness of his wish to 'show more sense': he can no more do this than escape his own future.

75 τὰν παρεοῖσαν ἄμελγε: a dairy version, particularly appropriate to *Gala*teia, of 'a bird in the hand', cf. 10.8–9n. and the corresponding 'fish' version at 21.66 ζάτει τὸν σάρκινον ἰχθύν. Σ cite a proverb τὸν θέλοντα βοῦν ἔλαυνε. Polyphemos seeks comfort in the language and conventional wisdom of his own *techne*, showing that his mind is now moving back to its own sphere. ὁ παρεών 'the current one' may have been a standard term in the language of sexual relationships, cf. Theognis 1270 (horses happily accept one rider after another) ὣς δ' αὔτως καὶ παῖς τὸν παρέοντα φιλεῖ. **τί τὸν φεύγοντα διώκεις;:** the question picks up τί τὸν φιλέοντ' ἀποβάλληι; of 19 to mark the shift of attitude; the masculine is generalising, as regularly in proverbial utterance.

76 > *Ecl.* 2.73. The Cyclops resorts to the familiar consolation of the rejected, cf. 3.35–6; like 77–9 (note 'on the land'), this is for Galateia's ears as much as for himself. ἴσως is thus intended by the Cyclops with καὶ καλλίονα, but we will extend the doubt to εὑρησεῖς. Homer makes it clear that, unlike the other Cyclopes, Polyphemos never married (*Od.* 9.115, 188). From later antiquity, however, there is evidence in both art and literature for a version in which Galateia did succumb and set up house with Polyphemos, cf. Holland (1884) 276–88, Fedeli on Prop. 3.2.7–8, Idyll 6, Intro.

77–8 If these girls are not entirely imaginary, we are perhaps to think of the daughters of other Cyclopes, rather than other Nereids. This laughter marks the Cyclops, like all bucolic lovers, as in some respects a (comic) Daphnis, cf. 1.90–1.   **συμπαίσδεν:** verbs of 'playing' often carry a sexual sense (cf. Asclepiades, *Anth. Pal.* 5.158.1 (= *HE* 824) Ἑρμιόνηι πιθανῆι ποτ' ἐγὼ συνέπαιζον κτλ., Henderson (1975) 157), but the choice of word is appropriate for the infantilised Cyclops.   **κιχλίζοντι:** in the scenario he creates to provoke Galateia and console himself, the 'girls' laugh when he responds to their sexual invitations (cf. 6.15–19), and *he* sees the laughter of pleasure and invitation, but we will see the laughter of mockery, no less cruelly teasing than the invitations themselves, cf. Σ 'perhaps they are laughing at him', Headlam on Herodas 7.123. The lexicographers associate κιχλισμός with πόρναι and gloss the word as καγχασμός 'mocking laughter'.

79 ὅτ': cf. 54n.   **κἠγών τις φαίνομαι ἦμεν** 'I too seem to be someone [important]'; for this use of τις cf. Eur. *El.* 939 ηὔχεις τις εἶναι τοῖσι χρήμασι σθένων, Headlam on Herodas 6.54. 'I *too*', as well, alas, as Οὖτις himself (whose success with females in the course of his travels was notorious). Marco Fantuzzi suggests that there is a contrast between the land, where the Cyclops claims to be 'someone', and the sea, which is Odysseus' realm and completely closed to Polyphemos.

80 οὕτω: a mark of closure, bringing the poem back to the opening 'moral', cf. 13.72, 25.280.   **ἐποίμαινεν τὸν ἔρωτα** 'shepherded his love' (rather than his sheep), i.e. he kept his love under control, 'managed' it, and stopped it from running destructively wild, cf. above, p. 220. βουκολεῖν can mean 'cheat', 'beguile' and such a nuance for ποιμαίνειν is found in a late text (Lucian, *Am.* 54), but 'control', 'look after' is appropriate here. The exact nuance of the participle in *Orph. fr.* 82 Kern ποιμαίνων πραπίδεσσιν ἀνόμματον ὠκὺν ἔρωτα is uncertain.

81 ἢ εἰ: scanned, by 'synizesis', as a single syllable, cf. Ariphron, *PMG* 813.6, Arnott (1996) 592–3.   **ῥᾶιον ... διᾶγ':** cf. 7n. The 'ring composition' acts as a closural 'QED' for the narrative. **χρυσὸν ἔδωκεν:** i.e. to a doctor (like Nikias), not (as Σ) as a bribe to Galateia. Asklepios, the divine model for human doctors, was, according to Pindar (*Pyth.* 3.54–7, cf. Pl. *Rep.* 3 408b–c), bribed with gold to raise a man from the dead, and T. here gently teases Nikias with the high fees doctors could earn.

VII Idyll 6

The poem begins as a third-person address to Aratos: Damoitas and Daphnis 'the oxherd' came together for a song-contest (ἔρισδεν, 5). The songs are quoted directly, separated only by a single narrative verse of transition (20). Daphnis tells Polyphemos how Galateia is doing everything in her power to attract him, but he does not seem to notice. In reply, Damoitas adopts the rôle of Polyphemos and asserts that he knows precisely what Galateia is doing, but he is 'playing hard to get' as part of deliberate strategy to make Galateia capitulate. A closing narrative passage announces that the contest had no winner, but ended in perfect harmony.

The addressee of the poem may reasonably be identified with the Aratos named as Simichidas' 'great friend' and ξεῖνος in Simichidas' song in Idyll 7 (98, 119): both poems have erotic themes, and in Idyll 7 Simichidas seeks to persuade 'Aratos' to abandon his fierce love for a boy. The Aratos of Idyll 7 is most naturally understood to be a Coan or at least resident on Cos; the name is found throughout the Aegean, but is particularly common on Cos (*LGPN* I s.v.). In or before 279 an Aratos served as ἀρχεθέωρος of the Coans to Delos (*IG* XI 2.161b.66), and T.'s friend too presumably moved in high social circles (for T. and 'Simichidas' cf. Idyll 7, Intro.). Although T. else-where (17.1, 22.8–22, perhaps 7.139–40) seems to know the *Phaeno-mena* of Aratus of Soli (cf. M. Pendergraft, *QUCC* 24 (1986) 47–54, A. Sens, *CQ* 44 (1994) 66–9), there are no good grounds for an identi-fication of the poet with this 'Aratos', cf. Wilamowitz, *Kleine Schriften* II (Berlin 1971) 74–85.

The existence of an addressee gives the poem a paraenetic or exemplary flavour, cf. Idylls 11 and 13, where, however, the 'mes-sage' is made explicit. Aratos is clearly invited to apply to himself

(?and his relationship with the poet) lessons gained from the behaviour both of Daphnis and Damoitas and of Polyphemos and Galateia, just as the 'message' of Idyll 11 has clear reference to the fact that the addressee is a poet and doctor; nevertheless, the very uncertainty which surrounds the relationship of (at least) Polyphemos and Galateia suggests that we should be wary of dogmatism about what those lessons might be. The poem *may* be a shy declaration of affection to Aratos (cf. Bowie (1996) 94–5), but it is also a poem very much concerned with the difficulty of interpreting motive and action, and the subjectivity of aesthetic and emotional decisions (note the marked repetition of καλόν, 11, 14, 16, 19, 33, 36).

For the myth of Galateia and the Cyclops cf. Idyll 11, Intro. Timaeus, an older contemporary of T., recorded that Polyphemos and Galateia had a son called Galates (*FGrHist* 566 F69), and so the version, found in late sources, in which Galateia returned Polyphemos' love or was at least reconciled to him (11.76n.) might have been available to T. In one late prose source which may have links with Philoxenus' dithyramb or a drama based upon it (*PMG* 818, cf. Holland (1884) 196–7), Odysseus advises the Cyclops to feign indifference once he (Odysseus) has used his magical skills to send Galateia crazy with love, and if this is not itself derived from Idyll 6, it may again suggest a quite diverse early tradition. Nevertheless, Daphnis' Galateia is at best ambiguous. Is she really crazy with love, or – as 15–17 strongly suggest – is she just teasing the Cyclops, like the giggling girls of 11.77–8? Her behaviour and her motives both demand and defy interpretation, and for this reason Daphnis cannot impersonate her, but must remain as a third-party observer and interpreter. His song makes clear, moreover, that Galateia's very existence is at least as ephemeral as that of her namesake of Idyll 11 (or indeed of those giggling girls); when the dog looks for her, all it sees is the sea (10–12), and cf. 34–8n. 'You don't see her' sings Daphnis, and one reason may be that no one can see her.

Idyll 6 presupposes Idyll 11 both in terms of setting – Polyphemos is now older than he was 'then' (36) – and because the text is replete with allusions to and reversals of Idyll 11 (cf. Ott (1969) 72–6, Köhnken (1996a)); these are noted as appropriate in the commentary. It is hard to resist the inference that Idyll 6 was written later than Idyll 11, and for an audience that knew Idyll 11; there is,

however, no reason to assume that they were written very close in
time to each other or 'circulated' as a pair. If Aratos has been correctly identified (cf. above), Idyll 6 may have been composed on Cos,
but this is no more necessary than that Idylls 11 and 13 were composed at Miletos. Unlike Idyll 11 (above, p. 218), the metrical and
verbal style of Idyll 6 is that of T.'s bucolics.

If Galateia's rôle is ambiguous, so is Daphnis'. His words are as
teasing and shifting as her behaviour (cf. 6–7n., 15–17n., 18–19n.). In
particular, his stress on sight and seeming (8, 9, 11, 19) hints at the
future blindness of the Cyclops, and is part of the challenge he
utters, a challenge instantly met and refuted by Polyphemos in 21–5
(and cf. 35). Daphnis describes things, such as the barking dog, as
though the Cyclops was already literally blind, and not just 'blind' to
what Galateia is doing (for the metaphor cf. Soph. *OT* 371). We are
also challenged to identify the character behind this voice. Although
the goatherd Komatas of Idyll 5 is most naturally understood to be a
latter-day namesake of the legendary goatherd of Idyll 7, it is reasonable to understand Δάφνις ὁ βουκόλος here as *the* legendary
Daphnis of Idyll 1, as the poet of Idyll 8 seems to have done (and cf.
Hypoth. Idyll 1, p. 23 Wendel); no other 'bucolic' poem is clearly set
in the distant past, but the two other poems with addressees, Idylls 11
and 13, also relate myths from the past. Idyll 6 may thus be seen as a
mimetic version of Idyll 11, as well as a complement to it. Daphnis
may be imagined to share an ancient Sicily with the Cyclops, and
this would suit the similarities between the two; T. would thus have
synchronised the two primary models for his bucolic characters, and
in 6–19 Daphnis would be 'playing himself', as he teases his 'friend'
Polyphemos. Nevertheless the structure of frame and included song
suggests that the question of rôle is important in both songs. Against
the 'contest' of Polyphemos and Galateia is set the non-contest of
Daphnis and Damoitas, a couple whose harmony seems to reverse
the bitter rivalry of the herdsmen of Idyll 5 (45n.). For them such
disputes and harsh emotions belong to the world of story and song;
theirs is rather a kind of 'golden-age' equality in which the striving
for advantage has no place. So too the lack of topographical specificity in the setting of the frame serves to set them apart from both
Galateia and Polyphemos and the characters of the other bucolics.

If Daphnis himself is playing a rôle, three possibilities for that rôle deserve consideration. Daphnis may impersonate another teasing friend of the Cyclops, both *praeceptor* and *irrisor amoris* (like Priapos in Idyll 1). Secondly, a late Hellenistic relief in the Villa Albani shows Polyphemos seated on a rock under an oak tree; he holds a lyre and is being watched by a sheep. At his shoulder is a Cupid who is pointing into the distance and Polyphemos turns to follow the direction indicated, cf. G. Rodenwaldt, *Das Relief bei den Griechen* (Berlin 1923) 99 with fig. 120. It is an obvious inference that the Cupid is pointing to Galateia (cf. 6.9), and the voice which tries to interest Polyphemos in Galateia is obviously a voice of desire; could it be Eros himself? Finally – and perhaps most temptingly – the character with most to gain by distracting Polyphemos with the attractions of a beautiful woman is Odysseus; Daphnis places Polyphemos and his interlocutor outside, rather than inside, the cave, but in post-Homeric texts (cf. Euripides' *Cyclops*) the interaction of Odysseus and the Cyclops is not necessarily limited to the interior of the cave. Does Daphnis take the rôle of Odysseus? This would certainly fit his shifting mode of speech and his anonymity (Odysseus was after all 'No Man'), and give particular point to Polyphemos' dismissal of the prophecies of Telemos. For a possible model in Philoxenus cf. above, p. 216.

The brilliant response which Damoitas places in the Cyclops' mouth answers Daphnis' song point for point, and meets all the possibilities created by Daphnis' challenge. We are amused when the Cyclops takes the teasing of Daphnis and Galateia seriously, but his answer also allows for the possibility that he knows that he is being teased: either way, he is not going to fall for it by becoming emotionally upset, i.e. by reliving the agonies of Idyll 11; if Galateia really is crazy about him, she is just going to have to capitulate without further ado. 'I saw her' he says: are these the words of a deluded buffoon, or a neat riposte to Daphnis' challenge from a Cyclops 'in control'? The uncertainties of the game which Galateia and the Cyclops are playing are reflected in the continued vocabulary of seeing, seeming and appearance with which the songs abound (8, 11, 19, 21–2, 25, 28, 31), culminating in the Cyclops' vision of himself in the glassy water, a vision which itself suggests the horrible deceptiveness of sight (cf. n. ad loc.). It is against these 'uncertain appearances' that the apparent harmony of Damoitas and Daphnis is to be judged.

Whereas Daphnis' song had foreshadowed Polyphemos' future, Polyphemos himself has not forgotten about Telemos, and threatens to shut Galateia out (rather than shutting the Greeks in). The Cyclops of Idyll 6 responds almost as though *Od.* 9 did not exist: the rarity of verbal echo of that book is remarkable – even when Telemos is explicitly mentioned, it is *another* book of the *Odyssey* which is reworked. Whereas the young Cyclops of Idyll 11 exists in a timeless dairy wonderland, the Polyphemos of Idyll 6 swears by Pan and Paian, keeps a pet sheepdog, receives lessons in rustic superstition from an old woman and knows of Parian marble; he is, in short, not unlike the 'non-mythical', contemporary characters of the other bucolics. Such 'anachronisms' serve the erasure of *Od.* 9 as a model text; if Idyll 11 showed how Homer had placed all subsequent poets in the hopeless position of young Polyphemos (above, p. 219), Idyll 6 reasserts the power of the present over tradition. The existence of a famous literary model need not (need it?) determine the poetry of the present: T.'s Cyclops can show bravado in the face of the Homeric pattern, no less than T. himself can demand a place for his bucolic poems in a world which already has *Odyssey* 9. The fact that both Telemos and Homer have spoken does not mean that new directions are not possible. The fates of both poet and character lie with us.

The similarities between the story of Daphnis in Idyll 1 and that of Polyphemos and Galateia in Idyll 6 are striking: a girl frantically pursuing a man who apparently takes no notice, thereby earning the titles δύσερως and αἰπόλος; Galateia comes from the sea, as the 'girl' of Idyll 1 may be a water-nymph. The Daphnis of Idyll 6 seems to play the part of the Priapos of Idyll 1 who precisely advised 'Daphnis' in matters of love, whereas Polyphemos finds himself in the rôle of the Daphnis of Idyll 1. These similarities have been interpreted in various ways. The Cyclops may simply show the 'less serious', less dangerous type of *eros*, the comic version of the tragic myth. Bernsdorff (1994) stresses rather that the young Daphnis did not himself learn the lessons of his own song, which foreshadows his fate, as the Cyclops' song in 11 foreshadows his; Fantuzzi (1995b) 18–19 prefers to see here a joke about the supposedly paradigmatic status of myth – myths in Hellenistic poetry are in fact so unstable and 'non-exemplary' that both a Daphnis and a Cyclops can fit the same pattern. What is, however, most important is that (on one level) Idyll 6 is a comic 'reading' of Idyll 1; Polyphemos claims that his behaviour is merely a strategy to get what he wants, but in fact he is imitating what he believes (surely wrongly) to have been Daphnis' strategy. The Daphnis of Idyll 1 was not playing hard to get, but he could well have appeared so: the comic version of bucolic is thus shown to be secondary and parasitic upon the tragic, as Attic comedy was secondary and parasitic upon tragedy. So too, the Cyclops of Idyll 6 suggests a comic version of the Epicurean αὐτάρκης καὶ ἀτάρακτος, set off against the alleged behaviour of Galateia, which is described (by Polyphemos!) as a disturbance to match that which Epicureans saw in *eros* (28n.). As so often, therefore, myth in T. replays, in its own mode, the authorising 'bucolic' myth of Daphnis.

Title. Βουκολιασταί Δαμοίτας καὶ Δάφνις.

Modern discussions. Bernsdorff (1994); Bowie (1996); Fantuzzi (1998a); Gershenson (1969); Gutzwiller (1991) 123–33; Hutchinson (1988) 183–7; Köhnken (1996a); Lawall (1967) 66–73; Ott (1969) 67–84; Stanzel (1995) 177–90; Walker (1980) 60–5.

1–2 > *Ecl.* 7.2.   Δαμοίτας: the name is not uncommon on the Greek mainland, but the majority of attestations come from Thessaly; Bowie (1996) 93–4 makes the attractive guess that T. took the name from Simonides' poems for Thessalian patrons.   **χὡ:** i.e. καὶ ὁ. When the article accompanies only the second of a pair or the last of a series of names, that name is usually also modified by an adjective (7.131–2, 22.34, 140, 26.1); ὁ βουκόλος performs that function here.   **ὁ βουκόλος** 'the famous oxherd', cf. 7.73 Δάφνις ὁ βούτας, Leutner (1907) 40–4.   **τὰν ἀγέλαν:** despite the separate flocks of sheep and goats in Virgil's imitation, the singular most naturally implies that the two boys looked after a single, often scattered, herd; this will be a further indication of their non-eristic harmony. Elsewhere, song contests take place between herdsmen of different flocks (goats vs lambs in Idyll 5, cattle vs sheep in Idyll 8 and perhaps Idyll 9), but only cattle are mentioned in the frame of this poem (45).   **ποκ'** 'once upon a time' regularly introduces mythical narrative in Hellenistic poetry (cf. 7.73, 78, 18.1, 24.1, Call. fr. 230 (= *Hecale* fr. 1 Hollis), Cat. 64.1): T. treats his newly created bucolic fiction as part of the inherited 'sea of myth'. ὡς φαντί at

8.2 imitates and varies this effect.   Ἄρατε: cf. above, p. 243.
συνάγαγον: for the *figura etymologica* with ἀγέλαν cf. 3.43–5n.

2–3 ὁ μὲν ... ὁ δ' 'the latter ... the former'. ὁ μέν could, in prin-
ciple, be either 'the former' (5.94, 11.58) or 'the latter' (cf. K–G
II 264, Denniston 370–1); in 43 it is 'the latter', but in view of that
mannered replay of these opening verses (42–3n.), we cannot be sure
that T. has there repeated rather than varied the initial usage. πυρρός 'golden' refers to the colour of the first 'fuzz' of facial hair (cf.
15.130 of Adonis, who resembles Daphnis in other significant ways,
above, p. 68), whereas ἡμιγένειος 'with beard half-grown' will denote
a somewhat older young man. The difference in age in the context
of the general similarity of the two is a manifestation of an important theme of the poem, cf. above, p. 244. If we are to imagine a relationship between Daphnis and Damoitas on the classical paederastic
model, then the 'half-bearded' one will be the *erastes*, though still
himself young (cf. Pl. *Charm.* 154a, *Euthyd.* 273a7), and the kissing of
42 makes Damoitas the more likely for this rôle; for Daphnis as an
eromenos cf. Epigrams 2 (Δάφνις ὁ λευκόχρως) and 3. Idyll 6, however, seems to foreshadow the less hierarchical homosexual relationships of later erotic literature. In imitating these verses, the poet of
Idyll 8 made Daphnis and Menalcas identical in age (8.3), but also
called Daphnis ὁ χαρίεις (8.1), the standard description of an *eromenos*
(cf. 13.7n.).   ἄμφω stresses the 'togetherness' of the young men.

4 θέρεος μέσωι ἄματι 'in summer, in the middle of the day'.
Whereas elsewhere the burning midday is a time of potential threat
(1.15–18n.), here it marks a moment of repose which matches the
(real or feigned) calm of Polyphemos' mood.

5 It is very unusual to separate τοιάδε (τοῖα, τοιαῦτα, τάδε etc.)
from the speech which it introduces, but the harshness is mitigated
by the change of subject and the need for the (reciting) poet to indicate who is speaking. The intercalated verse, nevertheless, carries
particular stress – Daphnis goes first because he was 'first keen for /
proposed a contest' (ἔρισδεν), not out of any spirit of contention. It
might be thought that the harder job in such a 'contest' was to sing
second and have to adapt to the lead of the first singer, and that
therefore the proposer of the contest should have that task; so in
Idyll 5, Lakon proposes and Komatas eventually begins (ἔρισδε at
5.30 may not mean precisely 'begin the contest'). In Idyll 8, however,

the order is decided by lot. Whether or not there was a 'normal' pattern, it is clear that in Idyll 6 the emphasis is on the absence of disruptive contention. So too, the fact that no prizes or wagers are mentioned before the singing (contrast the wrangling of 5.21–30) removes all sense of an *agon* from the 'contest'; cf. further 42–3n. What is striking is the absence before 5 of any explicit reference to a contest; it is as though the poet here operates with a convention in which the mere fact that herdsmen sit together in the heat of the day signals that a song-exchange will follow. The technique foreshadows that of later pastoral, cf. Alpers (1996) 80–2.

6–7 > *Ecl.* 3.64. The names of the 'lovers' stand, as often, in the first verse (cf. 11.8n.), despite the fact that this is a mimetic 'drama' rather than a narrative.   ἁ Γαλάτεια 'Galateia, whom you know / in whom you are interested', cf. 3.1–5n.   μάλοισιν: cf. 3.10n. Unlike the flirtatious Galateia, Polyphemos himself 'did not love with apples …' (11.10). ποίμνιον … μάλοισιν allows a play on μᾶλον 'apple' and μῆλον/μᾶλον 'sheep', cf. 1.109–10n. Daphnis' style is as shifting and ambiguous as the behaviour he describes.   δυσέρωτα καὶ αἰπόλον ἄνδρα καλεῦσα 'calling [you] backward in love and a goat-keeping man'; the striking parallel with 1.85–6 (where see nn.) is a foreshadowing of Polyphemos' pose as a Daphnis. As Σ notes, the Homeric Cyclops had both sheep and goats (*Od.* 9.184, 220 etc.), but in T. there is no sign of the latter. T.'s herdsmen standardly look after one kind of animal only (cf. 1.80n.), but the pattern seems to be broken by the poet of 9.15–21 (?in the voice of the Cyclops). The transmitted τὸν αἰπόλον might represent the direct speech of Galateia as 'Goatherd, you are backward in love' or 'the goatherd is backward in love' (so Dover), but Meineke's καί seems a significant improvement; τόν may have arisen from 5.88 βάλλει καὶ μάλοισι τὸν αἰπόλον ἁ Κλεαρίστα. Posidippus' αἰπολικὸς δύσερως of Polyphemos (*P. Mil. Vogl.* 1295, col. 3.28–41 Bastianini–Gallazzi) is very likely a near contemporary allusion to this verse, cf. 11.60n.

8 ποθόρησθα: probably 'see', as in 22, rather than 'look at', as in 25. For this form cf. 1.36n.   τάλαν τάλαν 'you poor wretch', an exclamation of (here feigned?) compassion, cf. Call. *Epigr.* 30.1–2 Θεσσαλικὲ Κλεόνικε τάλαν τάλαν, οὐ μὰ τὸν ὀξὺν | ἥλιον, οὐκ ἔγνων, 1.82–3n.   κάθησαι: cf. 11.17; here, by contrast, the Cyclops does not sing of Galateia, but plays the syrinx for his own amusement and as part of his comic rôle-playing as Daphnis, the greatest of all mortal syrinx-players.

9 ἀδέα: cf. 1.1n.; the Cyclops pipes 'without a care in the world'. We might, however, well ask whether Cyclopean syrinx-playing (11.38n.) is likely to have sounded 'sweet'; the Cyclops' adviser is a tease like Galateia.   **τὰν κύνα:** Philippus, *Anth. Pal.* 11.321 (= *GP* 3033–40), treats 'whether the Cyclops had dogs' as the typical *zetema* of stupid grammarians, and the absence of dogs from *Od.* 9 does indeed seem to have been of interest to Homeric scholars (cf. Σ *Od.* 9.221, Eustath. *Hom.* 1622.12–30). Homer in fact uses dogs as markers of civilisation (cf. S. Goldhill, *Ramus* 17 (1988) 9–19), and their absence brands Polyphemos as particularly savage; the Cyclops of Idyll 6, however, is a more ambiguous figure, closer to bucolic norms (for dogs in the bucolic world cf. 5.106, 8.27, 65–6). Cf. further 29–30n., above, p. 247. The Euripidean Polyphemos has hunting-dogs (*Cycl.* 130), as does Daphnis in Aelian's version of the legend (*NA* 11.13).

10–12 If we take 'Daphnis' seriously, we will say that the dog senses the direction from which the apple was thrown and barks at the sea. If, however, we stress the teasing manner of 'Daphnis' and the likely insubstantiality of Galateia, we can explain that dogs just 'naturally' run along beaches and bark at splashing waves; as 11–12 and 35–8 make clear, there is nothing beneath the surface of the sea except one's own images. 'Daphnis' suggests, however, that Polyphemos should react to Galateia's advances with the same vigour as his dog. Somewhere behind 9–14 (the pelting of the dog, the threat to Galateia's legs) lies Odysseus' confrontation with Eumaios' dogs (κύνες ὑλακόμωροι) at *Od.* 14.29–47; surely Polyphemos is not going to allow Galateia to be treated like Odysseus? The -κ- sounds of 11–12 mimic the sound of the waves rippling on the shore.

11 νιν i.e. 'the dog'.   **φαίνει** 'reflects'; more usual in this sense is ἐμφαίνειν.

12 ἄσυχα καχλάζοντος 'gently sounding', here of the shore itself (cf. Pind. *Ol.* 7.2, Dionysius 'Periegetes' 838 perhaps in imitation of this verse) rather than the waves. The better attested καχλάζοντα leaves αἰγιαλοῖο rather exposed and produces hiatus at the feminine caesura (elsewhere in the bucolics only 7.8, cf. 13.23–4n.).

14 κατὰ ... ἀμύξηι: tmesis.   **καλόν:** the first syllable is long, in contrast to καλά in 11, cf. 18–19n.

15 ἃ δὲ has a quasi-deictic force, trying to draw Polyphemos' attention to Galateia.   καὶ αὐτόθε 'even from there', i.e. from the sea.   διαθρύπτεται: Polyphemos is to understand 'makes sexual advances' (cf. 11.77), but we may rather put the stress on the teasing and 'flirting' involved, cf. 17, 3.34–6n.

15–17 Apparently irrational behaviour is compared to the random flight of blown thistledown (elsewhere called πάππος), which is very difficult to grasp but seems to follow us when we move away, cf. W. B. Stanford, *Hermathena* 24 (1935) 101, J. H. Betts, *CP* 66 (1971) 252–3. Galateia's 'suffering', reinforced by the 'burning summer' which evokes the fire of love inside her, is well compared to the almost insubstantial plant, cf. Soph. fr. 868 Radt, Eubulus fr. 106.16–20 K–A (πέτεται κοῦφος ὤν). Σ and some editors take the simile with διαθρύπτεται, but it is hard to see the resulting sense.

'To pursue the one who flees' is a way of saying 'suffer from [unrequited] love', cf. Sappho fr. 1.21–2 Voigt, Call. *Epigr.* 31, and 'Daphnis' here exploits the Greek fondness for 'polar' expressions to produce a verse which Polyphemos is to understand to mean simply 'she is desperately in love [with you]', or perhaps 'when you loved her she avoided you [cf. 11.75], but now that you avoid her she pursues you'. We, however, will also relate the verses to Galateia's present 'teasing' behaviour; Macedonius, *Anth. Pal.* 5.247.3 uses the paradox to describe a fickle lover.

18 'To move the stone from the line' is a proverb taken from a board game (πεσσεία), in which the board was marked by five lines and the moving of a counter from 'the sacred line' was a mark of desperation or near-defeat, cf. Alcaeus fr. 351 Voigt, Sophron fr. 127 Kaibel, *CPG* I 259–60, *RE* XIII 1970–3, R. G. Austin, *Antiquity* 14 (1940) 267–71; thus here Daphnis tells Polyphemos that Galateia would do anything to attract him, she 'leaves no stone unturned'. πεσσεία was supposedly an invention of Odysseus' bitter enemy Palamedes (Radt on Soph. fr. 479), and so this image would be particularly pointed if Daphnis was impersonating Odysseus (above, p. 246).

18–19 ἔρωτι 'to love', a more generalising form of expression than 'to a lover'; *eros* is often given the attributes of someone suffering from *eros*, cf. Men. fr. 53 K–T φύσει γάρ ἐστ' ἔρως | τοῦ νουθε-τοῦντος κωφόν, Pl. *Symp. passim.* '*Through* love' would make more explicit the fact that love is said to warp perceptions (cf. Σ (l) ad loc.,

10.19–20, Di Marco (1995a) 136–9), as though there was such a thing as objective 'beauty' and 'ugliness' (here embodied by the Cyclops), but this seems a less natural way to take the dative with πέφανται. 'The fair seems fair' is a way of saying 'be in love with the fair' (cf. 13.3–4n.); thus 'Daphnis' is telling Polyphemos that Galateia loves him, 'the not fair', despite his ugliness, which is admitted by the Cyclops himself in 11.31–3. The Cyclops of this poem will, however, take a different tack (34–8). At one level, the assertion (ἦ γάρ) of 'Daphnis' is true to human experience, but his description of Galateia has left us with grave doubts about whether true *eros* is involved on her side at all.   **Πολύφαμε:** the repetition from the first verse does not merely close a ring around the speech, but also marks the shift from narrative to didactic moral. The jingle πολλάκις … Πολυφάμε serves the memorable rhetoric of that moral.   **καλὰ καλά:** the variation in vowel length, reflecting two different treatments of original καλϝός, is a very common effect, cf. Call. *h.* 1.55, *Epigr.* 29.3, N. Hopkinson, *Glotta* 60 (1982) 166–7. Only at 2.125, however, does καλ- form the second element of a spondee. Like πολλάκις … Πολυφάμε this effect increases the proverbial and mnemonic flavour of the phrase.

20 ἀνεβάλλετο 'played a prelude', presumably on a syrinx (cf. 43).

21–2 Polyphemos first answers the charge of 8 ('you don't see her').   **Πᾶνα:** this Cyclops is so 'bucolicised' that he can swear by the herdsman god, cf. 4.47, 5.14, 141; contrast the blasphemy of *Od.* 9.273–6. At 11.29 the young Cyclops swears by Zeus. Pan does not appear in Homer, and in Athens at least his worship was acknowledged to be a late historical development (Hdt. 6.105); despite Pan's important rôle in the 'timeless' story of Daphnis (1.122–30), there is some 'anachronism' in this oath, cf. above, p. 247.   **οὐ τὸν ἐμὸν τὸν ἕνα γλυκύν** 'no, by my one sweet [eye]', cf. 24.75 (Teiresias) ναὶ γὰρ ἐμῶν γλυκὺ φέγγος ἀποιχόμενον πάλαι ὄσσων; for the ellipse of μά, regular in Doric, cf. 4.17, 29, 5.17, Headlam on Herodas 5.77; for the ellipse of a word for 'eye' cf. Herodas 5.59–60, 6.23, Call. *Epigr.* 30.6.

22–3 ὧι ποθορῶιμι | ἐς τέλος 'with which I pray to see to the end'; for this form of the optative cf. K–B II 72. Whereas at 11.53 the Cyclops offered to give up his eye, 'than which I have nothing sweeter (γλυκερώτερον)', if Galateia yielded to him, here there is no thought of such bravado. The text is, however, uncertain. Here and in 25 the transmitted present ποθόρημαι (cf. ὅρηαι at *Od.* 14.343, *Oichaliae Halosis* fr. 1 Davies) could be explained, rather awkwardly, as a statement of Polyphemos' (misplaced) confidence; even so, a future tense might have been expected. Secondly, ποτ- is unexpected, and Fritzsche proposed ὥιπερ ὅρημι; but the compound picks up and answers ποθόρησθα of 8.

23–4 Cf. *Od.* 9.507–12 (the Cyclops), 'Ah, it comes home to me at last, that oracle uttered long ago. We once had a prophet in our country, a truly great man called Telemos son of Eurymos, skilled in divining, living among the Cyclops race as an aged seer. He told me all this as a thing that would later come to pass – that I was to lose my sight at the hands of one Odysseus ...' (trans. Shewring). The Theocritean Cyclops' scorn for the prophet reminds us of how, all too late, he was to acknowledge his skill; nevertheless, the fact that Polyphemos, unlike his Homeric model, is fully conscious of the prophecy is part of the presentation of a Cyclops who believes himself 'in control'. So too the verses are a mannered reworking, not of the *Od.* 9 passage, but of Eurymachos' scornful words to another prophet, Halitherses, after the latter has prophesied the return of Odysseus, ὦ γέρον, εἰ δ' ἄγε δὴ μαντεύεο σοῖσι τέκεσσιν | οἴκαδ' ἰών, μή πού τι κακὸν πάσχωσιν ὀπίσσω (*Od.* 2.178–9). The echo bodes ill for Polyphemos (cf. *Od.* 22.79–88, the death of Eurymachos at Odysseus' hands), but it distances him from Homer's Cyclops, cf. above, p. 247.   **φέροι ποτί:** the active is preferable to the middle, and for the hiatus after ποτί cf. 24.22 ἀνὰ οἶκον.

25 πάλιν οὐ ποθόρημι 'I do not return her glance', cf. 8n., 22n.

26 The Cyclops puts into practice the forlorn wish of 11.76; whereas Homer's Polyphemos never married (cf. 11.76n.), the other Cyclopes did (*Od.* 9.115). If 33 means that Polyphemos demands that Galateia be his wife (cf. n. ad loc.), then γυνή in 26 either means something like 'girlfriend' or Polyphemos exploits a tradition that the Cyclopes were polygamous; in *Od.* 9.114–15 θεμιστεύει δὲ ἕκαστος | παίδων ἠδ' ἀλόχων, οὐδ' ἀλλήλων ἀλέγουσι, the plural ἀλόχων avoids the awkward collocation ἀλόχου, οὐδ', but later Greeks may have felt some sensitivity on the matter (cf. Arist. *EN* 10 1180a28–9 paraphrasing the verses with the singular ἀλόχου). Polygamy or a community of wives would suit the primitivism which later Greeks imputed to Cyclops society. If, however, 33 means merely 'sleep with me' or 'be my slave', 26 may refer to 'a wife', without the implication of polygamy. To understand 26 as 'I say that I have another [in mind to be my] wife' would solve the difficulty, but seems hard to get out of the Greek.   ἔχεν: infinitive, cf. 1.14n.

27 ζαλοῖ μ' 'is jealous of me [or of my happiness]', a sense in which ζηλοτυπεῖν is more regular. What is meant is a combination of envy, anger and ill-will, cf. P. Walcot, *Envy and the Greeks* (Warminster 1978), Chadwick (1996) 121–2; that such φθόνος or ζηλοτυπία leads to physical, as well as emotional, 'wasting' is a common idea, cf. 5.12–13, Zimmerman (1994) 44–6. In Idyll 11 it was Polyphemos who 'wasted away' (11.14).   ὦ Παιάν: probably a cry of triumph, 'at the pain he can inflict on her who once pained him' (Hutchinson (1988) 185), rather than an appeal for Paian's protection (cf. 5.79) from the physical effects of Galateia's ill-will. Paian was originally a healing divinity (*Il.* 5.401 etc.), who later came to be identified as a particular manifestation of Apollo; this verse and 5.79 suggest the rusticity of an appeal to Paian, cf. *RE* XVIII 2340–5.

28 The Cyclops offers his own interpretation of the behaviour described in 15–18: Galateia is not flirting, she is in real pain. οἰστρεῖν may refer to purely emotional suffering, but with 'from the sea' there is also a clear implication of movement, 'rushes wildly', cf. Aesch. *PV* 836–7 οἰστρήσασα τὴν παρακτίαν | κέλευθον, Eur. *IA* 77. The οἶστρος, 'frenzy' of love, is a familiar image of high literature (Simonides, *PMG* 541.10, Pl. *Phdr.* 240d1, 13.64–71n.); Epicurus defined *eros* as σύντονος ὄρεξις ἀφροδισίων μετὰ οἴστρου καὶ ἀδημονίας 'a taut craving for love-making accompanied by frenzy and distress' (cf. Lucr. 4.1055 *unde feritur, eo tendit gestitque coire*), which is not a bad description of Galateia's condition as Polyphemos describes it.

29 'And I also urged (< σίζειν) the dog to bark at her ...' As the confusion in Σ suggests, the transmitted variants make no sense (*pace* H. White, *LCM* 1 (1976) 35, 2 (1977) 3), and Ruhnken's emendation seems certain. Polyphemos claims credit for the barking described in 10–14: far from being worried that the dog will hurt Galateia, it was he who orchestrated the whole thing. νιν was probably omitted from the main part of the tradition by haplography after ὑλακτεῖν.

30 The reason (γάρ) why Polyphemos has set the dog at Galateia is to mark the change in circumstances; when Galateia had the upper hand (cf. 11.8 Πολυφάμος, ὅκ' ἤρατο τᾶς Γαλατείας), the dog was entirely passive. Two interpretations of 30 are current: (i) 'For when I was in love with her (αὐτᾶς with ἤρων), the dog would whimper, holding its snout pressed against its flank.' For this as the behaviour of a dog at rest, cf. Σ ad loc., Thphr. fr. 6.54, and for the opposition of ὑλακτεῖν and κνυζεῖσθαι cf. *Od.* 16.162–3. When the Cyclops was looking out to sea and singing his lovesick songs (11.17–18), the dog lay beside him, making the noises that resting dogs make; now all that has changed. (ii) 'For when I was in love, the dog would whimper, placing its snout in her lap (αὐτᾶς with ἰσχία).' Against (ii) it may be objected that the Cyclops' past 'love' was unrequited and so Galateia is hardly likely to have been present, let alone playing with his dog; though we we can hardly rule out a boastful fantasy of the Cyclops, this seems to tell in favour of (i), however attractive the reversal of circumstances and pointed 'whimpering' of (ii). Köhnken (1996a) 181 notes that the dog is 'retrospectively written into the scenery of Idyll 11' because 'only in the changed circumstances of Idyll 6 can the dog take an active part in the Cyclops' new strategy'.

31 ἐσορεῦσα: cf. 3.18–20n.

32 ἄγγελον 'a go-between' (cf. Thestylis' rôle at 2.94–103), or perhaps 'matchmaker' (cf. next note).

32–3 Polyphemos will not entertain any proposal – both Galateia and her messengers will be as *exclusae* as he was in Idyll 11 – until Galateia *herself* swears to yield; αὐτά is to be taken both with ὁμόσσῃ and with στορεσεῖν. **θύρας:** cf. 1.82–3n. We may be surprised that the Cyclops' cave has a door; in Homer it is sealed with a great rock, although θύρῃσιν etc. is used to mean 'at the entrance' (*Od.* 9.238, 243). This may be part of the 'civilised' Polyphemos, but it is at least amusing that he threatens to lock someone *out*, when the most famous story about him was how he locked Greeks *in*. Here again the *Odyssey* is recalled by reversal. **στορεσεῖν καλὰ δέμνια:** 'to make *X*'s bed' is a standard epic way of saying 'be *X*'s wife', cf. *Od.* 3.403, *Arg.* 3.1128–9, and Polyphemos is here demanding, in suitably epic language, a promise of marriage from Galateia, on *his* terms ('on this island'). In imagining Galateia as a komast driven by desire for him, he also uses against her a komastic strategy: a male komast may hold out to the lady he pursues the promise of marriage (cf. 2.132, where Delphis addresses Simaitha as ὦ γύναι), but this 'object of desire' will absolutely insist on a permanent arrangement before yielding to Galateia's desire. Others understand that he merely wants Galateia to be his servant (as well as a sexual partner), cf. 17.133–4 ἐν δὲ λέχος στόρνυσιν ἰαύειν Ζηνὶ καὶ Ἥρηι | . . . Ἴρις. The Homeric Cyclops did not even have a bed, let alone a καλόν one (Od. 9.298).

34–8 > *Ecl.* 2.25–7. Polyphemos now turns to answer the final, and potentially most potent (note οὐδέ 'not even'), allegation made by 'Daphnis', namely that he falls within the class of τὰ μὴ καλά. Galateia has no reason to refuse marriage because of his looks (note γάρ); indeed he is handsome enough to attract many suitors. Who is the subject of λέγοντι, i.e. who has been spreading rumours about Polyphemos' ugliness? Perhaps the other Cyclopes, from whom (at least in Homer) Polyphemos was notoriously somewhat estranged. The whole poem, however, and especially 40, evokes a more varied Sicilian population than we find in Homer – it is not out of the question that Polyphemos is the only Cyclops – and so the vague 'people say' need not be more specific than it would be in more ordinary societies. Moreover, in view of the poem's radical attitude to poetic tradition (above, p. 247), it is tempting to refer 'as they say' to the poetic heritage (? including Idyll 11) which this Cyclops seeks to overturn: 'as I am standardly represented' would catch the flavour.

In seeking to disprove the slur uttered by 'Daphnis', Polyphemos not only challenges our notions of absolute standards of beauty – what, after all, *would* a Cyclops find 'beautiful'? – but of course also provides a perfect demonstration for T.'s readers that 'love can indeed make the ugly seem fair'. Polyphemos is presented as a kind of comic Narkissos, who fell in love with his own reflection in a pond; Hellenistic sources for the Narkissos story are very scarce, cf. Zimmerman (1994), but T. surely knew of this or similar stories. The very insubstantiality of Galateia (is she any more than an εἴδωλον or *imago*?) and the Cyclops' own confident pride make him an apt subject for such delusion. Whereas in Idyll 11 Polyphemos gazed ἐς πόντον in the hope of seeing the beloved Galateia (18), here he looks ἐς πόντον and sees his own beloved self: instead of Γαλατεία, there is γαλάνα (for the etymology cf. Hor. *C.* 3.27.14–20, Eustath. *Hom.*

1131.5), instead of a girl (κώρα, cf. 1.82) there is his eye, κώρα. Plato had observed how the lover sees himself in the beloved 'as in a mirror' (*Phdr.* 255d5–9); as Galateia is, at one level, merely the embodiment of the sea, so Polyphemos truly does look at 'the beloved' to find himself, cf. in general J.-P. Vernant, 'One ... two ... three: *eros*' in D. M. Halperin *et al.* (eds.), *Before sexuality* (Princeton 1990) 465–78. For Polyphemos and Daphnis cf. above, pp. 247–8.

Ovid's Galateia amusingly interprets Polyphemos' looking into the water as making himself beautiful for her, *iam libet hirsutam tibi falce recidere barbam | et spectare feros in aqua et componere uoltus* (*Met.* 13.766–7). T.'s verses are also reworked at Lucian, *Dial. mar.* (78 Macleod) 1.3.

35 ἧς δὲ γαλάνα: the naïvely realistic explanation recalls 11.58–9.

36 καλὰ ... καλά : the Cyclops' fancy suggests the origin of the chimerical Γαλάτεια. **μοι:** Ahrens's μευ may well be right, but the unemphatic dative hardly 'makes ὡς παρ' ἐμὶν κέκριται tautologous' (Gow). **γένεια** 'beard', marking the passage of time since he was sick with love for Galateia, 11.9 ἄρτι γενειάσδων; for the plural cf. Bulloch on Call. *h.* 5.75. The Cyclops' beard will in fact have been as ugly by ordinary Greek standards as his face, cf. 3.8–9n., 11.31–3n. **κώρα:** only here in T. in the sense 'eye' (8.72 σύνοφρυς κόρα may pun on the two senses). Cf. Pl. *Alc.* 1 132e7–3a3, 'And have you observed that the face of someone who looks into another's eye (ὀφθαλμός) is reflected in the seeing area (ὄψις) opposite, as in a mirror, and we call this the pupil (κόρη); it is an image (εἴδωλον) of the person looking'; Polyphemos' choice of word, therefore, both allows the play with the two senses of κώρα, and alludes to how the 'eye' sense was felt to arise.

37–8 'and it [i.e. the sea] reflected the gleam of my teeth whiter than Parian marble'; exact parallels for this use of ὑποφαίνειν are lacking, and this, together with the nearness of κατεφαίνετο and the awkwardness of having to understand πόντος from 35, has led to suspicion about the text. Fritzsche proposed αὐγὰ λευκοτέρα (λ. α. *iam* Meineke). In Idyll 11 whiteness was on the side of 'Miss Milky'; now the Cyclops has it. **ὀδόντων:** any mention of the Cyclops' teeth will evoke the use to which he was to put them in *Odyssey* 9. **Παρίας ... λίθοιο:** Parian marble was regarded as the purest, whitest kind, cf. Pind. *Nem.* 4.81 στάλαν ... Παρίου λίθου λευκοτέραν, *RE* xviii 1791–5, Nisbet–Hubbard on Hor. *C.* 1.19.6. Paros is not mentioned in Homer; the Cyclops evokes marble statuary in yet another 'anachronism' (21–2n.) which distances him from his Homeric model. There is an amusing dissonance between the 'high' image of this verse and the rusticity of 39.

39–40 Polyphemos takes rustic measures to avoid the potentially evil consequences of his pride in his own appearance, cf. the very similar sequence at Men. *Perik.* 302–4 (the clownish Moschion), 'I'm not, so it would seem, unpleasant to look at or meet, in my view (οἴομαι, cf. 37 ὡς παρ' ἐμὶν κέκριται) by Athena, but [rather attractive] to women; but now I should most of all respect Adrasteia [i.e. Nemesis]', Pl. *Phaedo* 95b5–6 'don't boast, lest some evil envy (βασκανία) ruin our discussion'. Others understand that the spitting avoids the possibility that his own reflection will put the 'evil eye' upon him, as in the story of Eutelidas told by Plutarch (*Mor.* 682b = Euphorion fr. 175 Powell, cf. Zimmerman (1994) 39–46, 70–1), or that the spitting protects his beauty from the evil thoughts of others (Schweizer (1937) 7, Gershenson (1969)). The assimilation of the Cyclops to a Narkissos-like figure sits well with all of these explanations. Spitting as a form of apotropaic magic occurs in many situations and many cultures, cf. 7.126–7, Call. fr. 687 (= *Hecale* fr. 176 Hollis), Thphr. *Char.* 16.15, Straton, *Anth. Pal.* 12.229 (spitting to avoid Nemesis), F. W. Nicholson, *HSCP* 8 (1897) 23–40, and three is the most common number in magical contexts of all kinds. That the Cyclops has become not only conventionally pious (21) but a believer who requires instruction in rustic superstition is a clear sign of how far he is adapted to a 'bucolic' context. So too, the presence on his island of 'old women who deal in magic' is a further move towards the stylised 'realism' of the other bucolics.   **δέ:** postponement to the fourth place is not found elsewhere in T., but is very common in Middle and New Comedy (cf. Men. fr. 380.3, *Dysk.* 109, T. W. Allen, *RPh* 11 (1937) 280–1); despite occasional tragic examples (Soph. *Phil.* 618, Eur. *Ba.* 269), this may be a colloquial feature of Polyphemos' speech.   **γραία:** Σ 7.126 claim that this spondaic form is Doric. **Κοτυτταρίς:** Kotys or Kotyto was the name of a Thracian goddess whose cult had spread throughout the Greek world, especially to Corinth and Sicily, cf. *RE* xi 1549–51. Bassos, *Anth. Pal.* 11.72 (= *GP*

1637–42) has a πολύμυθος γραῖα called Κυτώταρις or Κοτυτταρίς, probably in imitation of T.; Kotys is a not uncommon historical name.

[41] = 10.16, where it is obviously in place; here the reference to the reapers would be pointless, and it is perhaps unlikely that an old woman was piping to the workers.

42–6 A five-line closure to match the opening five lines. We must assume that Damoitas stops singing because he has now 'answered' each of the points in Daphnis' song.

42–3 These lines offer a mannered reworking of the opening ones: the boys' names are again together, but in reversed order, and ὁ μὲν ... ὁ δέ repeated (2–3n.). The mutual exchange of gifts marks the contest as a 'draw', cf. 5n. **ἐφίλησε:** there has been much discussion as to whether this kiss is erotic, or merely a mark of friendship. If we accept the reality of this often blurred distinction, then it is obviously true that some kisses in Greek literature are not erotic (cf. *Od.* 16.15, Soph. *OC* 1131 etc.); nevertheless, kissing elsewhere in T. is erotic (cf. Bowie (1996) 92) and sometimes homosexual (5.135, 12.27–37), and within the context of the bucolic corpus and the subject of the songs the boys have just sung, this seems the natural interpretation here. **αὐλόν** 'a [single] pipe', rather than the familiar double pipes of classical times, cf. 5.7, *Il.* 10.13 αὐλῶν συρίγγων τ' ἐνοπήν, *Ecl.* 5.85 *hac te nos fragili donabimus ante cicuta.*

44 Δάφνις ὁ βούτας: a further mark of 'ring composition', cf. 1.

45 Whereas Idylls 1, 3 and 5 contrast animal carnality with unsatisfied human passion, here the heifers respond to the harmonies (both emotional and musical) of Daphnis and Damoitas; we are here not far from the 'pathetic fallacy' (1.71–5n.) or the manner of later pastoral in which 'play' completely takes over from 'realistic' hard work (cf. esp. the musical animals of *Daphnis & Chloe*). As Dover notes, the asyndeton (which caused Fritzsche to delete the verse) should be seen, *inter alia*, as a closural device.

46 The verse structure – punctuation at the caesura separating two phrases of equal meaning – mimics the harmony of the singers. **νίκη:** an unaugmented third-person imperfect, the regular Doric contraction from -αε, cf. 2.155 ἐφοίτη, Buck (1955) 37. **μέν:** lengthened in imitation of a Homeric licence; emphatic μάν may be correct (cf. 1.86–91n.), but here the opposition has point. How a 'victory' could be decided in the absence of a judge is never stated: presumably by mutual agreement, which would be another sign of the boys' unusual harmony.   οὐδάλλος 'neither' (= οὐδέτερος) is not found elsewhere.

VIII Idyll 13

Idyll 13 tells the story of Herakles and Hylas as an example of the universal power of Eros: Herakles loved the beautiful young Hylas, but lost him in Mysia when the boy was dragged by nymphs into a pool while fetching water during the Argonautic expedition. The *Argo* subsequently sailed off without Herakles, who had to travel to Colchis on foot.

The poem is addressed, as is Idyll 11, to T.'s friend, the doctor Nikias (above, p. 215). As Idyll 28 and Epigram 8 depict Nikias living at Miletos, Idyll 13 is often called a 'poetic epistle', and biographical narratives have been designed to explain why T. tells Nikias the story of Hylas (Nikias has told T. to give up paederastic affairs; T. is consoling Nikias for the loss of an *eromenos* etc.). There is, however, no stress upon the act of writing and or sending, or upon the journey which the letter is to undertake, whereas these are standard features of Ovid's poetic epistles. Pindar 'sends' his songs to the victors he celebrates, and in Idyll 28 T. tells 'the distaff', i.e. both the (real or fictional) gift to Nikias' wife and the poem itself, to accompany him on his journey (28.3–5). There is nothing like this in Idyll 13, and indeed the evidence for poetic 'epistles' in Greek at any period is very scanty; nothing is known about the Ἐπιστολαί of Aratus (*SH* 106, 119). The opening section is indeed less stylised than the main body of the poem: whereas well under 10% of the nouns are accompanied by a definite article, a far lower figure than is standard in the bucolics, more than half of the examples occur in 1–15, cf. Rossi (1972) 290–2, Hunter (1996a) 40. Nevertheless, such 'conversation' with an addressee belongs to a much older tradition than 'the poetic epistle' which developed from it. Nikias' rôle is to be compared with that of the addressees of archaic poetry, Hellenistic epigram, and many of Horace's *Odes*: these are friends, often fellow symposiasts, to whom one's hopes, fears and conclusions are entrusted. It is a more natural fiction that Nikias is present as the poem is recited, than that

he is far away; a very similar paraenetic structure informs the post-
Theocritean Idyll 21, addressed to a Diophantos. Interpretations in
terms of the biographies of T. and Nikias have been influenced by
Propertius 1.20 (below, p. 264), where the Hylas story is an explicitly
admonitory tale for the benefit of the addressee Gallus; cf. also
Horace's use of mythic narratives after extended 'personal' introduc-
tions (*C.* 3.11 (Lyde), 3.27 (Galatea)).

In comparison with the bucolic mimes, Idyll 13 stands closer in
technique (e.g. similes), metre and style to the mainstream of Hellenistic hexameter poetry. In particular, the high probability that,
within the space of seventy-five lines, it twice rewrites the first two
books of the *Argonautica* gives it as good a claim as any Theocritean
poem to be 'a little epic' (cf. below, pp. 264–5, 16–24n.). In length
and scope, however, it is well short of what are traditionally
regarded as Hellenistic 'epyllia', poems such as Moschus' *Europa* and
the *Megara*, and – other than Idyll 11 – its nearest analogue in the
Theocritean corpus is 22.1–134 in which another Argonautic narrative is preceded by an introductory hymn. Unlike, say, the *Europa*,
the Hylas narrative is not told 'for its own sake', but to exemplify a
gnomic truth, and though the hexameter associates it formally with
'epic', in structural terms it has clear affinities with sympotic elegy
and lyric. It is an excellent illustration of how Hellenistic poetry
creates analogues of archaic and classical forms, rather than simply
'crossing the genres'. The two dominant influences on the narrative
style of Idyll 13, as on all Hellenistic narrative, are the relatively
short narrative units of the rhapsodic tradition and the lyric narrative of, e.g., Pindar and Bacchylides. From lyric derives the rapidity
of T.'s narrative, in which significant moments are juxtaposed,
rather than mediated by transitional passages.

The dialect of Idyll 13, labelled 'Doric' in the MSS, seems to stand
as close to the most 'Homerising' of the bucolics, such as Idyll 7, as
to the 'epic' Idyll 22. Epic touches there certainly are – ὅτε (not
ὅκα), σφέτερος etc. – but in language, as well as structure, T. has
reshaped his Herakles to fit a broadly un-epic mould.

The story of Hylas' abduction by nymphs may be understood as a
story of a young man's transition from being the *eromenos* of an older
man to a new status as object of female desire (7n.), but it is clearly
also an aetiology for a (real or believed) ritual practice of Mysia,

cf. Strabo 12.4.3 'still to this day a festival is celebrated among the Prusians; it is a mountain festival (ὀρειβασία), in which they march in procession and call Hylas, as though making their expedition to the forests (ἐπὶ τὰς ὕλας) in quest of him'. This aetiology is important at 58–60, and more explicitly at *Arg.* 1.1348–57 and perhaps also in Nicander (below, p. 264), to whom the Hylas narrative in Antoninus Liberalis 26 may go back: 'to this day the inhabitants of the region sacrifice to Hylas beside the stream, and three times the priest calls him by name and three times Echo answers him' (Ant. Lib. 26.5). The Mariandynoi, another local people, were famous as dirge-singers, and one of their heroes, Bormos, is strikingly like Hylas: 'they say that he was the son of an eminent rich man, and that in beauty and youthful flower he far surpassed all others; when super-intending work in his own fields, he went to get water for the work-ers and disappeared. So the people of the countryside sought for him to the strains of a dirge with repeated invocation, which they all continue to use to this day' (Athenaeus 14 620a). Athenaeus' source is Nymphis of Pontic Heraclea (*FGrHist* 432 F5b), a contemporary of T. and Apollonius, and such local chronicles were widely exploited by Hellenistic poets. Callimachus, *Epigr.* 22 (= *HE* 1211–14) concerns a Cretan goatherd called Astakides who was 'snatched by a nymph from the mountain' and became ἱερός (cf. 13.72), thus replacing Daphnis as the subject of shepherds' song. Whether or not this epi-gram alludes to Idyll 1 (above, p. 3 n. 8), it shows how close are nar-ratives of the Hylas type to the canonical bucolic myth; T.'s version of Herakles and Hylas is indeed assimilated to the story of Daphnis, as part of the bucolicisation of epic (cf. 64–71n.).

The earliest writers associated with Hylas' name are the cyclic poet Kinaithon (Σ *Arg.* 1.1355–7c) and the mythographer Hellanicus (*FGrHist* 4 F131a) of the later fifth century; Callimachus' version of Herakles' encounter with Hylas' father Theiodamas (frr. 24–5 = 26–7 Massimilla) and certain features of Apollonius' version, partic-ularly the rôle of Polyphemos, suggest a rich tradition now lost to us (cf. M. G. Palombi, *SCO* 35 (1985) 71–92, Hunter (1993a) 39).We have, however, no good evidence for the association of Hylas with the Argonautic expedition before the Hellenistic period; this may just be chance, but it is suggestive that the rich scholia to Apollonius give no indication of a rôle for Hylas in the otherwise influential treatments of the Argonautic myth in Antimachus of Colophon and Herodorus of Heraclea (both late fifth to early fourth centuries). Moreover, other explanations for Hylas' disappearance were known (cf. Σ *Arg.* 1.1289–91), and Hesiod recounted how Herakles was left behind by the Argonauts when *he* went to search for water on the Magnesian coast (fr. 263 M–W), while Antikleides of Athens (*FGrHist* 140 F2, ?fourth century) told how (presumably on the Argonautic expedition) Herakles' son, Hyllos, went to look for water and did not return. The Hellenistic poetic version, therefore, looks like a fusion of two 'water' tales – an Argonautic one, and a local Mysian legend. Whether that fusion was in fact a creation of the Hellenistic period we cannot say.

Beyond T. and Apollonius, the story of Hylas was treated by Nicander in the *Heteroioumena* ('Metamorphoses') and was at least mentioned by Euphorion (frr. 74–6 Powell); *Hylas puer* is listed among hackneyed poetic themes at Virg. *Georg.* 3.6. Nicander is named as the source of the account in Antoninus Liberalis 26 of how the nymphs metamorphosed Hylas into Echo, so that Herakles could not find him (Ant. Lib. 26.4, cf. 58–60n.); these citations in the MS of Antoninus are, however, of very doubtful value. More interestingly, Σ *Arg.* 1.1207 (= Call. fr. 596, cf. 39n.) reproves Apollonius for giving Hylas a κάλπις, because in Homer this was carried by a girl, and adds: 'it would have been better to use ἀμφορεύς, as Callimachus did'. This does not prove that Callimachus somewhere mentioned (or treated) Hylas' disappearance, but it has some evidential force, and the idea is not at all improbable. It has often been thought that the narrative of Hylas in Propertius 1.20 (among whose sources is Idyll 13) may go back to Callimachus, but there is no positive indication, unless the opening verses, which seem to echo Catullus 65.15–18 introducing a translation from Callimachus, are a signal of Propertius' debt to the Greek poet.

Herakles and Hylas are the subject of a major episode at the end of the first book of Apollonius' *Argonautica* (1.1172–1357). That there is an intertextual relation between T. and Apollonius is obvious on even the most cursory reading, and the question of priority has dominated criticism, even when critics have acknowledged the possibility of an elaborate process of mutual criticism and re-writing. The question cannot be handled in isolation from that of Idyll 22, in which T. tells the story of Polydeukes' boxing-match with Amykos, a story which begins *Arg.* 2. This handling of two Argonautic – and otherwise rather arcane – narratives which are contiguous in Apollonius, and in such a way that the two Idylls must be read together and indeed 'follow' each other to form a kind of narrative (cf. Hunter (1996a) 59–63), makes it more likely that T. knew, and wrote for an audience who knew, some form of *Arg.* 1 and 2, rather than vice versa. This commentary assumes that, and the cumulative gain for the understanding of Idyll 13 which accrues from such an assumption will, it is hoped, carry its own persuasive force.

Title. Ὕλας in Π³ and regularly in MSS, cf. 7, Σ *Arg.* 1.1234–9a.

Modern discussions. Barigazzi (1995); Campbell (1990); Di Marco (1995a); Effe (1992); Fuchs (1969); Griffiths (1996) 103–11; Gutzwiller (1981) 19–29; Köhnken (1965); Köhnken (1996b); Mastronarde (1968); ; Otis (1964) 398–405; Perrotta (1978) 187–204; Pretagostini (1984) 89–103; Rossi (1972); Segal (1981) 54–61; Serrao (1971) 111–50; Stanzel (1995) 229–47; Van Erp Taalman Kip (1994); Wilamowitz (1906) 174–9.

1–4 Two couplets marked by mannered parallelism; the second emphasises mortal ignorance, a theme hinted at already in the dilemma of Eros' parentage in 2.

1–2 'Not for us alone, as we used to think, did [the god], whichever one it was who had this son, beget Eros.' The antecedent of ᾧτινι is 'suppressed'.   οὐχ ἁμῖν: the dative marks the person affected by an action, whether for good or ill (K–G 1 417–20): which it is in this case is one of the questions posed by the poem. Lines 1–2 leave open whether 'we' is 'T. and Nikias' or 'all mortals', and 3–4 refocus the expression to make clear that it is the latter; by the end of the second couplet *every* reader will feel implicated in the assertion. It may be true that 'a man seriously in love is inclined to feel that no one can ever before have been so afflicted' (Dover), but why would anyone ever have thought that Eros was created either specially for them or even just for all mortals? Greek poetry and mythology were full of stories of divine *eros*, both heterosexual and paederastic, and no *topos* was more familiar than Love's control over Zeus. The point may be that this *topos* does indeed usually focus on men and/or gods, rather than heroes (although they too were not, of course, immune from *eros*), and it is Herakles' heroic, rather than divine, status which is emphasised, cf. 5–6, 72nn., Di Marco (1995a) 122–4. 'As we used to think' may be an intertextual signal, i.e. 'before we read *Argonautica* 1'; in his other 'Argonautic' poem T. also marks his version as secondary (22.27, with Hunter (1996a) 149 n. 32). **μόνοις:** a hint at a standard consolatory topic, 'we're not the only ones …', cf. Asclepiades, *Anth. Pal.* 12.50.1–4 (= *HE* 880–3) πῖν', Ἀσκληπιάδη· τί τὰ δάκρυα ταῦτα; τί πάσχεις; | οὐ σὲ μόνον χαλεπὴ Κύπρις ἐληίσατο, | οὐδ' ἐπὶ σοὶ μούνωι κατεθήξατο τόξα καὶ ἰούς | πικρὸς Ἔρως, *Arg.* 4.57–8. Whether Nikias needed consoling we do not know, but we certainly do not have to assume it. **ἔτεχ':** here of the father's rôle, as ᾧτινι makes clear. The parentage of Eros was a notorious puzzle to which poets and mythographers had given widely different solutions, cf. Σ ad loc., Pl. *Symp.* 178b, Antagoras fr. 1 Powell, F. Lasserre, *La figure d' Eros dans la poésie grecque* (Lausanne 1946) 130–49. T. here 'shares a (literary) joke' with Nikias, a fellow poet; in Idyll 11, by contrast, it is Nikias' practice of medicine which influences the opening presentation of *eros* as a disease (cf. 11.1 n.). **ἔγεντο:** this aorist of γίγνεσθαι, both with and without the augment, is widely used in post-Homeric poetry, cf. 9, 14.27, 17.64, Bulloch on Call. *h.* 5.59.

3–4 οὐχ ἁμῖν: the first spondee since the corresponding opening of 1 emphasises the repetition, which Σ 1–2b sees as imitative of the enthusiasm of the lover. 'You seem to me καλός' is a version of our 'I love [or 'fancy'] you' (cf. 6.18–19n.); therefore, 'a καλός seems to me καλός' amounts to 'I love a καλός boy' (as Hylas indeed was, cf. 7). There may be a quotation from Euripides' *Andromeda* (fr. 136.1–4 Nauck) σὺ δ' ὦ θεῶν τύραννε κἀνθρώπων Ἔρως, | ἢ μὴ δίδασκε τὰ καλὰ φαίνεσθαι καλά, | ἢ τοῖς ἐρῶσιν, ὧν σὺ δημιουργὸς εἶ, | μοχθοῦσι μόχθους εὐτυχῶς συνεκπόνει, cf. M. Treu, *PP* 22 (1967) 81–93, Di Marco (1995a) 135–9. Quotation would suit the address of poet to poet, and Herakles was the hero of μόχθοι. **τὸ δ' αὔριον:** usually feminine, but cf. 2.144 τὸ ἐχθές, Palladas, *Anth. Pal.* 5.72.4 τὸ γὰρ αὔριον οὐδενὶ δῆλον. If we knew what was going to happen, we would try to stop ourselves from being affected by *eros*; not only are *we* too weak to do this (cf. 30.31–2) – 'bronze-hearted Herakles' also was to prove too weak – but *eros* also makes us forget 'tomorrow' once it has got hold of us, cf. 67. For a similar gnomic opening, which compares all-knowing and organising Zeus with 'short-sighted' mortals who feed on optimistic hopes, cf. Semonides fr. 1.1–5 West.

5–6 Herakles is 'son of Amphitryon' rather than of Zeus to emphasise the similarity of his experiences to those of T. and Nikias; in this poem it is Hylas who will gain immortality (cf. 1–2, 72nn.). **χαλκεοκάρδιος:** the heart is the seat of many different emotions and virtues (for *eros* cf. 30.9 etc.), including unbending courage and endurance, cf. Archilochus' good military leader who is 'full of heart' (fr. 114.4 West). Someone whose heart was of bronze (cf. *Il.* 2.490, Hor. *C.* 1.3.9–10) or iron (LSJ s.v. σιδήρεος 2) should not fail before the challenge of *eros*; cf. Pind. fr. 123.3–5 Maehler (someone who did not melt at the sight of Theoxenos) ἐξ ἀδάμαντος | ἢ σιδάρου κεχάλκευται μέλαιναν καρδίαν, R. Kirstein, *Hermes* 125 (1997) 380–2.   **τὸν λῖν** 'the famous [Nemean] lion', cf. 7, 16, K–G 1 598, LSJ s.v. ὁ A I. This accusative form (Pfeiffer on Call. fr. 807) occurs elsewhere only at *Il.* 11.480, in a passage which is to become important later (58–60n.); the rare epicism makes the tonal shift of ἤρατο παιδός the more striking.   **τὸν ἄγριον:** Herakles spent his life among beasts 'outside civilisation', but through *eros* even he succumbed to beauty (3) and was civilised (8–9). J. Griffin (in E. M. Craik (ed.), *'Owls to Athens'. Essays ... Dover* (Oxford 1990) 121) proposed Ἀργέον 'Argive', but cf. *Arg.* 1 1243–4.

7 Herakles' unsuccessful love for Hylas is ironically given a status parallel to that of his triumph over the Nemean lion, cf. 66–7n.; the point is made explicitly in a late elegiac poem (*P. Oxy.* 3723) in which Herakles' love for Hylas is 'one labour too far'. Cf. Ovid, *Her.* 9.5–6 *quem numquam Iuno seriesque immensa laborum | fregerit, huic Iolen imposuisse iugum.* τοῦ ... Ὕλα suggests 'the famous Hylas' (cf. previous note), but one of the ironies is that Hylas was rather obscure (contrast the Nemean lion) until Apollonius had brought him into prominence. **χαρίεντος:** a standard adjective for both beloved boys (2.115, 12.20) and women (3.6, 11.30, 14.8). Someone who seems lovely has (in the lover's eyes) been cherished by the Graces, cf. Ibycus, *PMG* 288.1 Εὐρύαλε γλαυκέων Χαρίτων θάλος; in *Arg.*, the nymph sees Hylas κάλλεϊ καί γλυκερῆισιν ἐρευθόμενον χαρίτεσσι (1.1230). Such erotic *charis* was particularly associated with boys on the edge of manhood, cf. *Il.* 24.347–8 (Hermes) κούρωι αἰσυμνητῆρι ἐοικώς, | πρῶτον ὑπηνήτηι, τοῦ περ χαριεστάτη ἥβη; Hylas too is πρωθήβης (*Arg.* 1.132), ready to become the object of female admiration, *quo calet iuuentus | nunc omnis et mox uirgines tepebunt* (Hor. *C.* 1.4.19–20). **πλοκαμῖδα:** Hylas, like the model 'ephebe' Apollo (*Arg.* 2.707), had not yet cut his youthful locks, which is a familar *rite de passage* for both sexes in many cultures, cf. Euphorion, *Anth. Pal.* 6.279 (= *HE* 1801– 4), Hor. *Epod.* 11.28. In Athens the κουρεῶτις ἡμέρα 'hair-cutting day' (the third day of the Apatouria) marked the enrolment of young men in the phratries. πλοκαμίς is more commonly used of (braided) female hair, and this emphasises Hylas' status as an object of desire. There is probably no reference to a specific lock kept long until adulthood (cf. Ath. 11 494f, Eur. *Ba.* 494); nevertheless, φορεῖν is an unexpected verb in this context, and there may be an eroticisation of Apollonius' introduction of Hylas as πρωθήβης <u>ἰῶν τε φορεὺς φύλα- κός τε βιοῖο</u> (1.132).

8–15 These lines form an expanded equivalent of *Arg.* 1.1210–11, where it is stated that Herakles had taught Hylas to carry out his duties in an orderly and careful fashion. Apollonius says nothing explicit about Herakles' ultimate plans for his squire, whereas T. makes it clear that the hero aimed to educate Hylas in the traditional aristocratic mould. An analogy between the paederastic rela- tionship and the parental one is not uncommon, cf. Theognis 1049– 50 σοὶ δ' ἐγὼ οἷά τε παιδὶ πατὴρ ὑποθήσομαι αὐτὸς | ἐσθλά, Pl. *Rep.* 3 403b 4–7, Hunter (1996a) 170, and 'as a father teaches his dear son' may be understood as 'the lover's false conception of his rela- tionship with the boy' (Gutzwiller (1981) 20); for the 'displaced fathering' of Greek, especially 'Dorian', paederasty, cf. P. Cartledge, *PCPS* 26 (1981) 17–36. The traditional picture is, however, here complicated in three ways. The image of the hen and her chicks suggests 'mothering' of a rather different kind (cf. 53–4). Secondly, in some versions at least – and certainly in *Arg.* – Herakles had killed Hylas' real father (Theiodamas), so that 'surrogate fathering' was certainly necessary; Socrates of Argos (later than T., but of uncer- tain date) in fact made Hylas a son of Herakles and *eromenos* of Poly- phemos (*FGrHist* 310 F10, 15), and 8 may allude to such a version. Thirdly, Herakles' treatment of some at least of his real children was notoriously destructive; here the loss of Hylas will lead to madness (71n.), rather than madness leading to the death of his children.

The verses are a striking example of Theocritean structure: three assertions – Herakles loved Hylas (6), he taught him everything (8), he never left him (10a) – are each expanded, but in an ascending sequence of complexity, with the final expansion (10b–15) itself composed of an ascendingly complex set of three parallel units. (Valckenaer transposed 8–9 after 13, but Herakles' constant presence, no less than his teaching, aims at the outcome hoped for in 14–15; Gow suggested moving 14–15 after 9, so that 16ff. (where see n.) are more clearly marked as a specific instance of 10–13. With either change, however, αὐτός (9) would stand very close to αὐτῶι (14).)

8 υἱόν: υἱέα (K) as a dactyl is guaranteed once in Homer (*Il.* 13.350) and not uncommonly in Hellenistic poetry (*Arg.* 2.803, 4.1493, Call. *h.* 6.79, *Epigr.* 10.3). As disyllabic υἷα was also available, it seems unlikely that T. would have used the trisyllabic form in a weak position, cf. 17.33.

9 ἀγαθὸς καὶ ἀοίδιμος: as Theognis (237–54) wanted to make Kyrnos, and cf. the fantasies of the lover at 12.10–11. Herakles teaches not merely 'physical courage and endurance' (Dover) but also the morality of good (i.e. well-born and powerful) men. T. provides a list of Herakles' own teachers at 24.105–34, and Σ7–9e lists Rhadamanthys, Amphitryon's cowherds and Cheiron. ἀοίδιμος (cf. Bulloch on Call. *h.* 5.121) suggests that Herakles' intention was to make Hylas the 'subject of song', as he himself was; Apollonius and T. showed that, in this at least, Herakles was successful, though not in the way he planned. ἀοίδιμος occurs only once in Homer, where Helen tells Hector that Zeus brought evil upon Paris and herself so that they 'would be a subject of song for future men' (*Il.* 6.358); Σ(bT) notes that Homer thus 'subtly glorifies his poem', and the present passage is similarly self-referential.   **ἔγεντο:** cf. 2n.

10 χωρὶς δ' οὐδέποκ' ἦς: cf. Call. *h.* 5.59 (Athena and Chariklo) καὶ οὔποκα χωρὶς ἔγεντο. That poem is also about a young man who comes to a spring for water; like Hylas, Teiresias finds a nymph – his mother – and becomes ἀοίδιμος (121). A connection between these two poems is not unlikely.

10b–13 These lines are an elaborate expansion of 'never', which develops the Homeric division of the day: cf. *Il.* 21.111 ἔσσεται ἢ ἠώς ἢ δείλη ἢ μέσον ἦμαρ κτλ., Call. fr. 260.55 (= *Hecale* fr. 74.14 Hollis) δείελος ἀλλ' ἢ νὺξ ἢ ἔνδιος ἢ ἔσετ' ἠώς. Post-Homeric scholarship explained that ἠώς denoted the morning, 'midday' covered the whole middle section of the day (ὅροιτο here marks the transition between periods, cf. Call. *h.* 5.73 μεσαμβριναὶ ... ὧραι) and δείλη was the time from mid-afternoon until sunset; there was an analogous threefold division of the night, cf. Bühler (1960) 49–50, M. Schmidt, *Die Erklärungen zum Weltbild Homers und zur Kultur der Heroenzeit in den bT-Scholien zur Ilias* (Munich 1976) 198–202. The grand, ascending tricolon gives particular emphasis to the surprising and homely picture of a hen and her chicks, which suggests the lengthy time descriptions familiar from epic, particularly (and perhaps significantly) *Arg.*, cf. Fantuzzi (1988) 121–54. Just as the significance of time descriptions and similes can seep into the surrounding narrative, so the roosting chickens prepare for the camp of the Argonauts (32–5).

The text here is uncertain. Triple οὐδέ would have to mean 'not even', suggesting that these were three times when we might have expected Herakles and Hylas to be apart; triple οὔτε thus seems much more probable, cf. Denniston 193. The transmission points to ὅκχ' ... ἀνατρέχηι in 11 and ὅποκ' in 12, and there is no case for introducing ἀνατρέχοι by emendation (cf. K–G II 549–50).

11 λεύκιππος: cf. Bacchyl. fr. 20c.22 Sn–M; the new day is λευκόπωλος at Aesch. *Pers.* 386 and Soph. *Aj.* 673, and at *Od.* 23.241–6 the horses of Dawn are Λάμπος ('Shiner') and Φαέθων ('Blazer'). At 2.147–8 a similar periphrasis marks the gap between the epic world and the domestic tragedy which Simaitha relates; here the juxtaposition of 11 and 12–13 has generic implications: what sort of 'epic' narration is this going to be?

12 ὀρτάλιχοι 'young chickens', cf. 7.132n., Fraenkel on Aesch. *Ag.* 54.

13 αἰθαλόεντι ... πετεύρωι 'smoke-blackened roost', a typically Theocritean mixture of poetic adjective (Livrea on *Arg.* 4.597) and prosaic noun; the roost was presumably placed high on the wall or in the rafters.

14–15 πεπαναμένος 'fashioned', 'trained', a prosaic word appropriate to the hero of πόνοι; cf. *P. Cair. Zen.* 59378.16 Θέωνα ... πεπονημένον ὑπό μου. πεπλασμένον at 7.44 is closely analogous. **αὐτῶι δ' εὖ ἕλκων** has so far resisted interpretation and emendation; to the commentators add White (1979) 80, and U. Hübner, *Phil.*

136 (1992) 313, who proposed αὐτὸν δ᾽ εὖ ἕλκων in the sense 'exerting himself [physically]', cf. Pl. *Parm.* 135d3, *Euthyphro* 12a6 συντείνειν ἑαυτόν. Σ offer interpretations for αὐτῶι, αὐτῶι and αὐτῶ, and suggest a metaphor from ploughing. If it is corrupt, αὐτῶι may have arisen under the influence of αὐτῶι in 14.   **ἀποβαίη** 'turn out', 'come into the state of', cf. Pl. *Rep.* 4. 425c 4–5 (on the education of young men) καὶ τελευτῶν δὴ οἶμαι φαῖμεν ἂν εἰς ἕν τι τέλεον καὶ νεανικὸν ἀποβαίνειν αὐτὸ ἢ καὶ τοὐναντίον, *Symp.* 192a6.

16–24 These lines take the Argonautic expedition all the way to the Phasis, i.e. they offer one Theocritean sentence to match the whole of *Arg.* 1–2. The remainder of the poem offers a slightly more leisurely version of *Arg.* 1, but also brings us at the end to the Phasis, i.e. it elides the whole of *Arg.* 2 (a 'gap' partly made up by Idyll 22). In view of this structure, the similarity of 16 to *Arg.* 1.4, χρύσειον μετὰ κῶας εὔζυγον ἤλασαν Ἀργώ, is unlikely to be coincidence; T. thus marks the beginning of the 'epic' narrative.

16–18 ἀλλ᾽ marks a transition to a new stage of narrative and need not convey any sense of contrast, cf. 22.103, 141, Denniston 22. The Argonautic expedition is a particular instance of the general proposition that Herakles and Hylas were never apart. For a different interpretation cf. Rossi (1972).

16 τὸ χρύσειον: cf. 6n.

16–17 Ἰάσων | Αἰσονίδας: the combination of name and patronymic is not merely a marker of the heroic age, but perhaps also a humorous allusion to *Arg.* by means of a phrase which Apollonius never actually uses: in *Arg.* Jason is always 'Jason' or 'son of Aison', never both.

18 προλελεγμένοι ὧν ὄφελος τι 'the chosen ones, who had anything useful to offer', a further combination of the poetic (in fact a Homeric *hapax*, *Il.* 13.689) and the prosaic, cf. Pl. *Apol.* 28b7 ἄνδρα ὅτου τι καὶ σμικρὸν ὄφελός ἐστιν, Ar. *Eccl.* 53. The Apollonian equivalent reveals the 'poetic' way to say this: *Arg.* 3.347–8 Παναχαιίδος εἴ τι φέριστον | ἡρώων. In one verse T. 'covers' (and dismisses) the whole Apollonian catalogue, cf. *Ecl.* 4.34–5 *alter erit tum Tiphys et altera quae uehat Argo | delectos heroas.*

19 ταλαεργός: in earlier epic only of mules, so used of Herakles with a certain humour.   **ἀφνειὸν Ἰωλκόν:** the Thessalian city from which the expedition set sail; on the various forms of the name cf. M. L. West, *Glotta* 41 (1963) 278–82, Braswell on Pind. *Pyth.* 4.77 (b). It is usually feminine, and is presumably so here, as ἀφνειός is regularly of two terminations. In Homer Iolkos is ἐϋκτιμένη (*Il.* 2.712), and the legendary eponym of the people of Iolkos, Minyas, possessed great wealth (Pausanias 9.36.4–5); cf. the wealth of Pelias at Pind. *Pyth.* 4.150.

20 The rare form *ssdds* (cf. 7.133, 26.36 Καδμεῖαι πολλαῖς μεμελημέναι ἡρωίναις) gives weight to Herakles' appropriately heroic ancestry.   **Μιδεάτιδος:** Alkmene's father Elektryon is treated as king of Midea in the Argolid, cf. 24.1–2, Pind. *Ol.* 7.29, Pausanias 2.25.9. The learned allusion evokes a distant past of heroic legend.

21 κατέβαινεν: probably 'went down [from the city] to the ship [lying in harbour]', rather than 'embarked' (Campbell on Quint. Smyrn. 12.269) or just 'arrived at'; the progression from Iolkos (19) to the ship argues for the first interpretation. The harbour of Pagasai lay some twenty stades from Iolkos (Strabo 9.5.15), and Apollonius describes Jason's passage to the harbour (1.306–19); Pindar, however, draws no explicit distinction between city and port in a verse which was not far from T.'s mind, *Pyth.* 4.188 ἐς δ' Ἰαολκὸν ἐπεὶ κατέβα ναυτᾶν ἄωτος κτλ. *Arg.* 1.131 may well be the starting-point here, σὺν καί οἱ ῞Υλας κίεν 'Hylas accompanied Herakles'. **εὔεδρον:** a variation of the Homeric εὔσελμος and the less mannered εὔζυγον of *Arg.* 1.4.

22 In *Arg.* the Clashing Rocks, which were believed to guard the entrance to the Black Sea, break the stern-post of the *Argo* (2.601), but everything is easy for T.'s heroes. Pindar calls them συνδρόμοι πέτραι (*Pyth.* 4.208–9); they are often Κυάνεαι or Συμπληγάδες or these two names are combined (Eur. *Med.* 2), though not by Apollonius, for whom the Rocks are Κυάνεαι or Πληγάδες; Συνδρομάδες should be understood as a variation upon these names, and 22.27 πέτρας εἰς ἓν ξυνιούσας itself varies the present line.

23–4 There are three principal problems in these much discussed lines. (i) 'But [the *Argo*] shot through and clear of the Rocks and ran into deep Phasis' omits the journey along the southern coast of the Black Sea; Griffiths's Πόντον for Φᾶσιν (cf. *Arg.* 2.579) would remove this apparent oddity, and βαθύς more obviously suits the Black Sea than the Phasis (εὐρὺ ῥέων at *Arg.* 2.1261). In Pindar too, however, we move directly from the Rocks to the Phasis (*Pyth.* 4.207–13), even if not quite so abruptly, and cf. 16–24n., Hunter (1995) 15–18. (ii) αἰετὸς ὡς μέγα λαῖτμα 'as an eagle [soars] over a vast expanse' most naturally refers to the Pontic voyage rather than to the passage between the Rocks; βαθὺν δ' εἰσέδραμε Φᾶσιν will therefore, if sound, not be parenthetic, but will denote the successful conclusion of the voyage, which is compressed into the first half of 24. The Rocks are here represented as the only serious obstacle to the outward voyage, and this is in keeping with T.'s conception of the heroic ease of the trip, cf. M. Campbell, *Maia* 26 (1974) 331. Gow's view that μέγα λαῖτμα is in apposition to βαθὺν Φᾶσιν is unconvincing. In *Arg.* the safe passage of the *Argo* is preceded by the safe passage of a dove; Philip Hardie points out that T. finds another use for that dove in the Πελειάδες, 'Doves', of 25. (iii) ἀφ' οὗ τότε is very curious Greek (cf. Griffiths (1996) 108), though hiatus at the weak caesura is well attested (22.116, 191, 24.72). Line 24 was deleted by Meineke, and it is easy to see a reason for interpolation: that the successful passage of the *Argo* put an end to the Rocks' movement had to be mentioned, as in the corresponding passages of Pindar (*Pyth.* 4.210–11) and Apollonius (*Arg.* 2.600–6). For further discussion cf. Wilamowitz (1906) 178–9, Rengakos (1994) 107.   διεξάιξε: T. nowhere else uses ἀίσσειν or its compounds, but the verb is very common in *Arg.* (over 30 instances of the simple verb alone), it is tempting to see here an imitation of an Apollonian verbal mannerism, cf. *Arg.* 1.1157 (the *Argo*) διὲξ ἁλὸς ἀίσσουσαν, 2.561 (the dove released 'to dart' through the Rocks).

25–8 T. uses the epic ἆμος ... τᾶμος also in 24.11–13, and Apollonius introduces the Hylas episode in this way (*Arg.* 1.1172–8). Whereas, however, Apollonius marks the time of day at which the Argonauts reached Mysia, T. marks the time of year when the expedition began, cf. Hes. *WD* 414–22, 679–81 (spring sailing), Gutzwiller (1981) 23. The Hesiodic flavour of both form and substance mark this as a very different kind of 'epic narrative'.

The Pleiades (23–4n.) are 'the stars by which men determine the order of their lives' (Ath. 11 489e); when, after their winter disappearance, they become visible again before sunrise (late April / early May), this marks the transition from spring to summer and hence the best time to resume sailing, cf. Hippocr. *De reg.* 3.68, West on Hes. *WD* 383–4. T.'s Argonauts can choose the most propitious time: they are apparently under no pressure from Pelias (who is not even mentioned in the poem). J. K. Newman, *The classical epic tradition* (Wisconsin 1986) 90, calculates that Apollonius' Argonauts, on the other hand, were forced to set out in the autumn.

25 ἐσχατιαί: marginal land away from the farmhouses; the new lambs are already old enough to run free with the flocks.

26 τετραμμένου 'turned [to summer]'.

27–8 θεῖος ἄωτος | ἡρώων 'godlike and foremost heroes', cf. Pind. *Pyth.* 4.188 (21n. above), *Arg.* 2.1091 ἀνδρῶν ἡρώων θεῖον στόλον, Perrotta (1978) 312–13. ἄωτος 'prime [of]', 'perfection [of]' is a high poeticism appropriate to the theme; it is a favourite word of Pindar, cf. R. A. Raman, *Glotta* 53 (1975) 195–207, M. S. Silk, *CQ* 33 (1983) 316–17. 'Godlike' is no empty praise: many of the Argonauts (though not Jason) were 'sons and grandsons of immortals' (*Arg.* 3.366).   **κοίλαν ... Ἀργώ:** the epithet adds a further epic touch. Apollonius has κοίλη ναῦς of the *Argo* (1.1328), but never κοίλη Ἀργώ: here, then, is a further non-Apollonian 'epicism' (cf. 16–18n.).

29 The Argonauts sail (presumably non-stop) in a north-easterly direction; hence the importance of the South Wind (cf. Pind. *Pyth.* 4.203, *Arg.* 1.926). T.'s narrative is even swifter than Pindar's, for the latter's Argonauts (like Apollonius') must first row away from Pagasai (*Pyth.* 4.202). Apollonius' Argonauts reach Mysia after seven sailing days (not counting the activities on land along the way).

30–1 Kios (modern Gemlik) was a Milesian settlement on the southern coast of the Propontis (Sea of Marmara), cf. *RE* xi 486–7. Kios was originally the name of a river, and the city was said to have been founded by the Argonaut Polyphemos (*Arg.* 1.1321–3, 1345–7); 31 is therefore an 'anachronistic' forward reference, as both the present tense and the reference to the principally autumnal activity of ploughing suggest (cf. Hes. *WD* 384, 448–51) – the Argonauts arrive in the early summer. Whereas the arrival of Apollonius' Argonauts is marked by a time-description which emphasises what hard work ploughing is (*Arg.* 1.1172–8), in T.'s Mysia even the cattle seem to find it easy: τρίβοντες perhaps picks up Apollonius' περι-τριβέας ... χεῖρας (1.1175) to make this point.   **αὔλακας εὐ-ρύνοντι** 'cut broad furrows', cf. Arat. *Phaen.* 253 ἴχνια μηκύνει 'he takes long steps'. Strictly speaking it is not the cattle who 'wear away the ploughshares', but the earth itself, cf. *Georg.* 1.45–6 *depresso incipiat iam tum mihi taurus aratro | ingemere et sulco attritus splendescere uomer.*

32–3 A very similar scene is described in 22.30–3, cf. Hunter (1996a) 60–1. Homer too has 'landing scenes', cf. *Od.* 15.495–502, *Il.* 1.432–9, Arend (1933) 79–81, Serrao (1971) 122–9, but T. dwells at greater length than Homer upon the 'bucolic' preparations. The corresponding scene at *Arg.* 1.1179–86 is particularly close, and these passages have been central to the debate about priority, cf. H. Tränkle, *Hermes* 91 (1963) 503–5, Köhnken (1965) 34–9, Serrao (1971) 129–34. Lines 32–3 seem to suggest that the Argonauts intend to spend the night at Kios, as in *Arg.*, cf. 69n.   **ἐκβάντες κτλ.:** the same half-line begins 22.32; this can hardly be a coincidence. **κατὰ ζυγά** 'in pairs', a prosaic expression pointedly juxtaposed to the Homeric δαῖτα πένοντο (*Od.* 2.322, cf. V. J. Matthews, *LCM* 10 (1985) 68–9) and wittily placed after a description of ploughing (and hence 'yoked') bulls. An alternative interpretation, 'by rowing-benches', has obvious attractions, but it makes 38 (which Griffiths (1996) 108–9 deletes) curiously superfluous. In *Arg.* Herakles rows with Ankaios (1.396–400) and in Val. Flacc. with Telamon (1.353–4). **πολλοὶ δὲ μίαν:** the quintessential Argonautic virtues of co-operation and solidarity are here on view, cf. K. J. McKay in *Studi di filologia classica in onore di Giusto Monaco* (Palermo 1991) 377–85.

34–5 Text and interpretation are disputed. Gow construes μέγ' ὄνειαρ with σφιν, 'a great benefit for them because of the bedding it offered', but the traditional punctuation after ἔκειτο, 'a great benefit for their beds' is a striking and convincing variation on a Homeric pattern. ἔκειτο itself is not impossible, but the expected verb is παρά-κειμαι, and either λειμὼν γὰρ παρέκειτο (Hunter) or λειμὼν πάρ σφιν ἔκειτο (A. Griffiths, *CQ* 22 (1972) 108–9) seems possible. With the former, σφιν will have intruded after the loss (presumably by haplography) of γάρ or παρ, or because μέγ' ὄνειαρ was thought to require a personal dative; with the latter, we will have a brief example of the familiar *est in conspectu* type (Austin on *Aen.* 2.21), and ἔνθεν will bear its normal meaning of 'from there'; elsewhere T. always uses ὅθεν for 'whence'.   **βούτομον ὀξύ** 'sharp sedge', cf. Lembach (1970) 42–4. Both ὀξύ and ἐτάμοντο emphasise the etymology of the 'cattle-cut' (or perhaps 'cattle-cutting') plant.   **βαθύν:** possibly 'thick' (cf. 4.51) rather than 'tall'.

36 Ὕλας ὁ ξανθός: the article suggests familiarity with 'the fair-haired one', cf. 6n. Fair or sandy hair is conventional in literature for young men and women, though by no means restricted to them, cf. Lat. *flauus*. Hylas' closest Olympian model, Ganymede, was ξανθός when Zeus carried him off 'because of his beauty' (*h. Aphr.* 202–3). ἐπιδόρπιον: first here and in Lycophron (*Alex.* 609, 661); Apollonius (1.1208–9) repeats the Homeric ποτιδόρπιον (twice in the Cyclops episode, *Od.* 9.234, 249). In *Arg.* the linguistic Homerism points to the 'Cyclopic' nature of Herakles and the presence of a 'Polyphemos' (cf., e.g., J. J. Clauss, *The best of the Argonauts* (Berkeley 1993) 186–9); T. too is not unaware of this literary model cf. 58–6on.

37 Spondaic rhythm marks the unyielding *arete* of Herakles and 'unbending Telamon'. Telamon, Ajax's father and Achilles' uncle, is a constant companion of Herakles in mythology, and in *Arg.* it is he who tries to turn the *Argo* around when the crew discovers that they have left Herakles behind (1.1289–1344). Like ἀστεμφής (Livrea on *Arg.* 4.1375), the epithets associated with him stress martial strength: κραταιός (Pind. *Nem.* 4.25), ἐϋμμελίης (*Arg.* 1.1043), ἀρηίφιλος (*Arg.* 3.1174).

38 μίαν ἄμφω: the juxtaposition emphasises their constant togetherness, cf. 33n. above.   δαίνυντο τράπεζαν: T. has used δαῖς immediately above, and he varies a standard epicism with what seems to be another combination of the prosaic (cf. LSJ s.v. τράπεζα 1 2, Lampe s.v. в) and the poetic: δαίνυσθαι is an epic verb found only here in T.

39 Cf. *Arg.* 1.1207 τόφρα δ᾿ Ὕλας χαλκέηι σὺν κάλπιδι κτλ., 1.1221 αἶψα δ᾿ ὅγε κρήνην μετεκίαθεν κτλ. Both the 'parenthesis' of 39 and the speed with which T.'s Hylas finds a suitable pool, within the same verse in which he sets out, contrasts with Apollonius' epic technique of digression by which Hylas' setting out is separated from his arrival by ten verses relating how he came to be Herakles' squire; Apollonius himself explicitly calls attention to the digression (1.1220), and so τάχα here refers both to Hylas' quick success and to the relative speed of the narrative.   χάλκεον: the heroic–epic world remained in the memory of Greek poets a 'bronze world', i.e. one before the introduction of iron-working, cf. West on Hes. *WD* 150. In *Arg.* this detail becomes functional in the noise which the bucket makes as Hylas dips it into the water (1.1235–6).   ἄγγος: Σ *Arg.*

1.1207 notes that it was ἀπρεπές for Apollonius to give Hylas a κάλπις, which was something which women carried (cf. 5.127, *Od.* 7.20). Although classical practice is not so clear-cut (Gow on line 46, Pfeiffer on Call. fr. 596), T. may have wished to score a stylistic point here and in 46 (κρωσσόν). Whereas ἄγγος is non-specific and perhaps more prosaic than κάλπις, κρωσσός is largely poetic; T.'s variety is in contrast to Apollonius' epic sameness (1.1207, 1234).

40–2 Where Apollonius resisted the temptation for a description of this *locus amoenus* (1.1222–3), though he knows the name of the spring (!), T.'s poetic concerns are very different. The learned, botanical catalogue is highly evocative of the pool's mysterious dangers, cf. Lembach (1970) 90–5, Elliger (1975) 354–5, S. Amigues, *REG* 109 (1996) 474–86. The lushness which covers two verbless lines is further marked by the absence of third-foot caesura in 41, as the plants grow over the normal divisions of the hexameter; for such a rhythm cf. 22.72, Fantuzzi (1995a) 230. Hylas cannot (presumably) see these plants in the darkness, but we here listen to a description by the poet, not an account of what 'Hylas' sees; whereas in 22.34–43 the Dioscuri go sight-seeing in the sunshine (cf. 44), here Hylas wanders into darkness.

The association of lush vegetation (χλωρόν, θάλλοντα) with female 'otherness' and sexuality has a long history. Particularly important is the flourishing of nature around Calypso's cave (*Od.* 5.63–74); Calypso, 'the hider', was a nymph who wished to hide Odysseus away and make him her immortal husband (*Od.* 7.255–7) – a close parallel to Hylas' fate. Relevant too is the flowery *locus amoenus* from which Persephone was carried off by Hades (*h. Dem.* 6–18, cf. Gutzwiller (1981) 25–7, Hunter (1993a) 40. On T.'s use of the mysterious power of water cf. Segal (1981) 47–65.

40 ἡμένωι 'low-lying', with an implication of 'sheltered', 'hidden away'.

41 χελιδόνιον: perhaps 'lesser celandine', which grows in wetlands (Dioscorides 2.181, Lembach (1970) 93). ἀδίαντον 'maidenhair fern', *Adiantum capillus-veneris* L., another plant of wet areas (Thphr. *HP* 7.14.1); the name 'Unwetted' was explained by the fact that moisture does not remain on the surface of the plant.

42 θάλλοντα σέλινα: cf. 3.21–3n., Hor. *C.* 1.36.16 *uiuax apium.* There is probably an echo of *Od.* 5.72–3 (Calypso's cave) ἀμφὶ δὲ

λειμῶνες μαλακοὶ ἴου ἠδὲ σελίνου | θήλεον.   εἰλιτενὴς ἄγρωστις
'creeping dog's-tooth', *Cynodon dactylon* Pers. Σ associate the adjective
with εἰλεῖν, but it does not occur elsewhere, cf. Lindsell (1937) 80.

42–4 These lines are the only example among the poems generally regarded as genuine – 25.29–31 being the only other instance
in the corpus – of three successive *spondeiazontes*; Gow lists 13 examples in all Greek hexameter poetry. Line 44 is a very rare and heavy
verse (*dssds*). This mannered use of metre (continued into the spondaic opening of 45) marks the mystery and challenge of the *locus
amoenus*.

43 χορὸν ἀρτίζοντο: a variation of, and allusion to, Apollonius'
less striking ἄρτι | νυμφάων ἵσταντο χοροί (1.1222–3).

44 ἀκοίμητοι: unlike Argonauts or Homer's Olympians, nymphs
never sleep; they are a constant danger.   **δειναὶ θεαὶ ἀγροιώταις:**
the nymphs resemble Calypso (*Od.* 7.246, 255) or Circe, δεινὴ θεὸς
αὐδήεσσα (*Od.* 10.136). Σ refer to the condition of nympholepsy, but
the experience of 'nympholepts' is usually a heightened sensibility
and religious awareness, cf. W. R. Connor, *CA* 7 (1988) 155–89; a
Hylas or an Astakides (above, p. 263), who disappear completely, are
a different category of those 'taken by' nymphs.

45 A line consisting of three names or nouns, only the third of
which is qualified, is a regular pattern, cf. 4.25, 7.68, 26.1, Hes.
Theog. 902 (the Hours) Εὐνομίην τε Δίκην τε καὶ Εἰρήνην τεθαλυῖαν,
909, *Od.* 2.120, Ovid, *Met.* 12.460 etc. It is not unlikely that T. had
some source for these three names; this piece of learning may be
intended to cap Apollonius' single, nameless nymph. Eunike is the
name of a Nereid at Hes. *Theog.* 246 and of the haughty city girl of
Idyll 20; Malis, 'apple-tree' (8.79), is appropriate to the lushness of
the *locus* and to the presentation of the nymphs (cf. 47n.), and
Nycheia, 'night lady', is the name of a spring nymph also in *Anth.
Pal.* 9.684.   **ἔαρ θ' ὁρόωσα** 'whose look is springtime', cf. Ar.
Wasps 455 βλεπόντων κάρδαμα, K–G 1 309. The eye is traditionally
the site of dangerous bewitchment; the beauty of Nycheia's gaze
conceals the dark powers indicated by her name.

46 The purely dactylic verse, coming after a heavily spondaic
passage, marks the speed with which things now happen.   **ἤτοι**
marks a transition to a new stage of the narrative, cf. Denniston 554;
it occurs only in 'epicising' poems (Idylls 13, 22, 24, 25).   **ἐπεῖχε**

ποτῶι 'held out [the bucket] to the stream'.   πολυχανδέα: a
touch of epicising grandeur, which is lightly ironic in view of Herakles' capacity for food and drink, cf. 58–6on.   κρωσσόν: cf. 39n.

47 The nymphs 'grow upon his hand'; the phrase is a familiar
epicism (LSJ s.v. ἐμφύω II 2), but here T. gives a literal weight to the
verb. Was Hylas really carried off by nymphs, or does his corpse lie
concealed in the vegetation? Are these nymphs divine spirits or
'natural phenomena'? T. evokes 'rationalising' interpretations of the
story, such as that of the otherwise unknown Onasos in which Hylas
simply drowned (*FGrHist* 41); νύμφη is a familiar metonymy for
'water'. Relevant is an etymological play between ῞Υλας and ὕλη, cf.
Prop. 1.20.6–7 where *Hylae* and *siluae* occur at the end of successive
lines, Strabo 12.4.3, *Orph. Arg.* 643–5.

48 The emphatic anaphora of πασάων is of a kind familiar in T.,
but also corrects Apollonius' single nymph. In most accounts Hylas
is indeed taken by a plurality of nymphs; even the account in Apollodorus, which otherwise seems to follow Apollonius, has the plural
(1.9.19). A single nymph is found in Val. Flacc. and Petronius, *Sat.*
83.3 (where there is an obvious contextual motive).   ἔρως κτλ.:
cf. Archilochus fr. 191.3 West (ἔρως) κλέψας ἐκ στηθέων ἀπαλὰς
φρένας. In view of 1–2 it is tempting to print ῎Ερως here, cf. 2.133–8;
at the beginning of the poem, however, there is an explicit concern
with the god's lineage.   ἐξεφόβησεν: cf. 2.137 (ἔρως) νύμφαν
ἐφόβησε, Moschus, *Europa* 89–90 (the Zeus-bull) οὐκ ἐφόβησε φααν-
θεὶς | παρθενικάς, πάσηισι δ' ἔρως κτλ. (presumably an echo of T.).
T.'s verse is a variation on *Il.* 14.294 (Zeus and Hera) ὡς δ' ἴδεν, ὥς
μιν ἔρως πυκινὰς φρένας ἀμφεκάλυψεν, cf. 2.82, 3.40–2n.; the
Homeric verb has in fact replaced ἐξεφόβησεν in most MSS of Idyll
13. ἐξεφόβησεν is less usual than Apollonius' ἐπτοίησεν (1.1232, cf.
Serrao (1971) 140–3), as ἀνεπτοίησαν at *Europa* 23 in turn varies
Apollonius' ἐφόβησαν (3.636). Those affected by *eros* feel a kind of
terror at the loss of control over their emotions, 'Eros is regarded as
a victor over sanity, like panic Phobos in battle' (Dover); cf. further
55n.

49 Ἀργείωι ἐπὶ παιδί '[with desire] for the Argive boy' cf. 2.40,
10.31, Hunter and Campbell on *Arg.* 3.28. The epithet is difficult; in
early epic it means little more than 'Greek', but this is hardly
enough for T. That Amphitryon and Alkmena were both Argives (cf.

24.104) or that there were settlements of Dryopes from Hylas' homeland in the Argolid (Arist. fr. 482 Rose, Call. fr. 25 = 27 Massimilla)
are unsatisfactory explanations, and it seems unlikely that T.
here alludes to an otherwise unknown genealogy for Hylas; Campbell
(1990) 114 suggests a link with Alcaeus fr. 283.3–4 Voigt κ' Ἀλένας ἐν
στήθεσιν ἐπτ[όαισε | θῦμον Ἀργείας, Τροίωι δ' ἐπ' ἄν[δρι | ἐκμά-
νεισα. In view of μέλαν ὕδωρ, the star image which follows, and the
earlier suggestions of Hylas' feminine beauty, ἀργείωι 'gleaming
white' deserves consideration (M. G. Bonanno, L'allusione necessaria
(Rome 1990) 203–6), cf. Prop. 1.20.45 cuius ut accensae Dryades candore
puellae, Petr. Sat. 83.3 candidus Hylas, but the existence of the form
depends upon two very uncertain glosses in Hesychius (α 7017,
7019).   μέλαν: cf. Il. 16.3 κρήνη μελάνυδρος. Black is here not
just the colour of death, for no light reaches this secluded woodland,
cf. M. F. Ferrini, Rudiae 7 (1995) 213–29.

50–1 Hylas' fall is compared to a shooting star: the descent is described in rapid dactyls which fall into the spondaic πόντωι. We are
perhaps to visualise Hylas' long fair hair streaming behind him like
'the tail' of such a star or a κομήτης ('hairy one'), cf. Campbell
(1990) 114–15. Il. 22.318, which compares the gleam of Achilles'
spear to ἕσπερος, ὃς κάλλιστος ἐν οὐρανῶι ἵσταται ἀστήρ, is
immediately preceded by a reference to the 'beautiful golden hair'
on the crest of his helmet. Hylas' disappearance also suggests the
death of a hero in battle, cf. Il. 13.389 ἤριπε δ' ὡς ὅτε τις δρῦς
ἤριπεν ἢ ἀχερωΐς, but the verbal evocation points to difference
rather than similarity.   ἀθρόος 'in a heap', 'with a whoosh'. The
enjambment marks the speed and suddenness of the descent; Virgil
imitated this effect in describing the fall of Palinurus, Aen. 5.859–60
liquidas proiecit in undas | praecipitem ac socios nequiquam saepe uocantem, cf.
Hunter (1993a) 183–4.   ἤριπεν: the simplex verb picks up a previously used compound, as very commonly, cf. R. Renehan, Greek
textual criticism: a reader (Cambridge, Mass. 1969) 77–85. For the regular use of the aorist in similes cf. 63, Goodwin §§158, 547–8.
ναύτας: perhaps 'steersman', rather than just 'sailor', cf. Ovid, Met.
13.419 iubet uti nauita uentis (with Bömer's note). There is a variation
of the device of early epic in which the comments of one (τις) of a
crowd are reported (I. J. F. de Jong, Eranos 85 (1987) 69–84).

52 This line is the only direct speech in the whole narrative told to

Nikias, if we discount the cry of 58. Shooting stars portended winds, and many such stars together were a sign of impending storm, cf. Σ *Il.* 4.75–9, [Thphr.] fr. 6.1.13 Wimmer, Arat. *Phaen.* 926–9, Seneca, *QN* 1.1.12. Here πλευστικὸς οὖρος 'a favourable breeze for sailing' and the subsequent departure of the Argonauts suggest that the omen is a good one (but cf. next note); there is, therefore, point in the simile of a *single* shooting star.   **κουφότερ':** to prepare for bad weather sailors would lessen the strain on the sail by easing the ropes somewhat (perhaps the sense of κοῦφα at Arat. *Phaen.* 421). This may be the point here (cf. Köhnken (1996b) 444), and Hylas' disappearance threatens to delay any sailing. 'A sailing breeze' would, however, be welcome to sailors on a moored or becalmed ship, as in Apollonius' Hylas narrative (*Arg.* 1.1273–5), and if the breeze is a signal for sailing, 'lighter' must mean 'ready' (so Σ), and is perhaps a colloquial nautical term ('ship-shape'). The reason for the Argonauts' sudden departure is thus suggested through the simile, and such a technique would be an example of Hellenistic experimentation with the boundary between simile and narrative, cf. 69n., H. Bernsdorff, *RhM* 137 (1994) 66–72, Hunter (1993a) 129–38. **παῖδες** 'lads', cf. 10.52, Ar. *Knights* 419, Virg. *Ecl.* 1.45 *pascite ut ante boues, pueri; summittite tauros.* The colloquialism is a good instance of T.'s distance from Homer, cf. *Od.* 15.218 (Telemachos to his crew) ἐγκοσμεῖτε τὰ τεύχε', ἑταῖροι, νηὶ μελαίνηι κτλ.

53–4 Herakles' 'mothering' is now replaced by that of the nymphs: κοῦρον suggests 'son' as well as 'boy', cf. *Il.* 21.506 (Artemis and Zeus) δακρυόεσσα δὲ πατρὸς ἐφέζετο γούνασι κούρη. **ἀγανοῖσι παρεψύχοντ' ἐπέεσσιν** 'sought to calm him with soft words'. The verb (Hopkinson on Call. *h.* 6.45) evokes the coolness (ψῦχος) of 'death' in the chill waters of the dark pool, cf. Segal (1981) 55.

55 A remarkable line in which the grand patronymic and participle is set in counterpoint to the closing περὶ παιδί. T.'s rapid narrative does not stop to explain that Herakles' anxiety arose from Hylas' prolonged absence; in *Arg.* Polyphemos acts as the bringer of bad news to the hero. Herakles' distress and subsequent wandering (66) evoke Demeter's frenzy at the news of Persephone's fate (cf. *h. Dem.* 77 ἀχνυμένην περὶ παιδὶ τανυσφύρωι), as Hylas' disappearance evokes the rape of Persephone, cf. 40–2n.   **ταρασσόμενος:**

eros brings 'disturbance', cf. 7.126 (a rejection of *eros*) ἄμμιν δ' ἀσυχία τε μέλοι, Campbell on *Arg.* 3.276. Herakles and the nymphs are
suffering from the same invasive 'fear' (note 49 ἐπὶ παιδί – 55 περὶ
παιδί).

56–7 Herakles arms himself for another 'labour', cf. 7n.; this is
just as well, in fact, because otherwise the famous weapons would
have been left behind on the Mysian shore. Herakles' bow, 'finely
curved in the manner of Lake Maiotis [the Sea of Azov]' is of the
'Scythian' type in which two curves are linked by a straight waist
where the bow is held (in the left hand). These verses are illustrated
by many depictions of Herakles, cf. *LIMC* IV 2 s.v. Herakles 15, 17,
39–40 etc.   ἐχάνδανε: literally 'had room for', 'was able to contain', as at *Il.* 11.462, which was in T.'s mind here (58–60n.): this is
not merely a synonym for 'carried', but suggests the size of Herakles'
club, called χειροπληθής at 25.63. The Cyclops, who is one of the
models for Herakles here (58–60n.), also had a μέγα ῥόπαλον,
which resembled the mast of a ship (*Od.* 9.319–24). Both that passage
and its imitation at *Arg.* 1.1190–1205, in which Herakles uproots a
tree for his new oar like a storm upsetting a ship's mast, hover over
T.'s narrative here. In *Arg.* Herakles is carrying both his club and the
tree when he hears the bad news from Polyphemos.

58–60 These lines provide an aetiology for the thrice-repeated
ritual cry of the Mysians in search of Hylas (Ant. Lib. 26.5, above,
p. 263), and evoke a version attested by Antoninus (and Nicander?),
in which Hylas was metamorphosed into Echo; it is typical of the
Hellenistic manner to allude to more than one version of a myth (cf.
47n.). Although the 'thin voice' which answers Herakles presumably
calls out 'Herakles' rather than 'Hylas', the experience of deceptive
distance suggests the familiar echo effect. Lucretius refers to the
production of echo 'when we are seeking our comrades in the shady
mountains' (4.572–6). The origins of Echo, the extreme case of a
'natural' sound requiring human agency and thus a mythic model
for bucolic poetry, is one of the central bucolic myths, cf. Longus,
D&C 3.21–3, Hunter (1997); for Hylas and Echo cf. further *Ecl.*
6.43–4, Prop. 1.20.49–50 (with Fedeli's note), Val. Flacc. 3.596–7,
P. R. Hardie, *MD* 20/1 (1988) 77–8, A. Barchiesi, *Lexis* 13 (1995)
65–7. Griffiths (1995) 105 deletes 60 as a prosaic explanation of 59.

The Homeric model is *Il.* 11.461–3 (the wounded Odysseus) αὖε δ'

ἑταίρους. | τρὶς μὲν ἔπειτ' ἤυσεν ὅσον κεφαλὴ χάδε φωτός, | τρὶς δ'
ἄιεν ἰάχοντος ἀρηίφιλος Μενέλαος. T.'s verses, like *Arg.* 1.1249 μελέη
δέ οἱ ἔπλετ' ἀυτή, also rework Menelaos' subsequent speech to Ajax,
ἀμφί μ' Ὀδυσσῆος ταλασίφρονος ἵκετο φωνή, and the situation of
Herakles and his *eromenos* stands in ironic counterpoint to the 'heroic'
military pattern. Menelaos and Ajax respond to Odysseus' call and
the Trojans scatter like 'flesh-eating jackals' before a 'raging lion',
cf. 61–2 below. In *Il.* 11.466 Aristarchus read ἵκετ' ἀυτή, in order to
match noun and verb; this textual variation is repeated in the transmission of *Arg.* 1.1249, but in T. noun and verb refer to different
voices.

58 Ὕλαν ἄυσεν: 'Hylas' has been associated with ὑλᾶν, ὑλακτεῖν
(cf. Lat. *ululare*), as a rationalisation of a ritual cry ὕλα, cf. P.
Kretschmer, *Glotta* 14 (1925) 35–6; T. may wish us to feel an affinity
between verb and object here.   **ὅσον βαθὺς ἤρυγε λαιμός:** lit.
'with all the force his deep throat could bellow'. Lexica distinguish
two senses of ἐρεύγεσθαι, 'belch', 'disgorge' and 'bellow', 'roar', but
here both are relevant: Herakles' gluttonous throat was notoriously
deep (Eur. *Alc.* 753–5, Call. *h.* 3.159–61 etc.), and although the verb
is not necessarily coarse in Hellenistic Greek, here it may suggest a
likeness between Herakles and the Cyclops who, after his final meal,
ἐρεύγετο οἰνοβαρείων (*Od.* 9.374), cf. 36n. In 61 Herakles will be
compared to a 'lion who eats raw flesh', again like the Cyclops (*Od.*
9.292). So too, in *Arg.* Polyphemos' shouting is explicitly compared
to the roaring of a lion.

59 ἀραιά 'thin', 'faint'; this word is regularly glossed as λεπτή,
ἀσθενής, ἀδύνατος, cf. *Et. Mag.* 134.21–2 Gaisford, ΣbT *Il.* 16.161.
Chadwick (1996) 53 suggests 'sounding at intervals', but this would
hardly need saying.

61 Presumably an interpolation intended to ease the following
'paratactic simile'; for attempts to save the line cf. E. Magnelli, *MD*
35 (1995) 145 n.47. The corresponding passage in *Arg.* has σχεδόν and
ἀπόπροθεν in close proximity (1.1243–4).

62–3 Cf. 58–60n. This is a 'paratactic simile', i.e. one without
an introductory 'as when …', cf. 14.41–2, Perrotta (1978) 42–3,
Bernsdorff (1995), who sees a stylistic imitation of the rapid movement described in the narrative. The corresponding passage in *Arg.* is
1.1243–9, Polyphemos compared to a hungry lion. Herakles does not

wish (literally) to eat Hylas, but the disturbance caused by *eros* is likened to another uncontrollable appetite, that of hunger (cf. 10.30–1). The image of the lion and the fawn as a way of figuring the *erastes–eromenos* relationship is found at Theognis 949–50 and *PMG* 714, and is common in heterosexual contexts, where the point is often that the young fawn is exposed to danger because it is separated from its mother (cf. Anacreon 408, Hor. *C.* 1.23); so here, Hylas, almost for the first time (cf. 10–13), is separated from his protector (cf. ἑτοιμοτάταν), and the mothering nymphs are no substitute. One irony lies in the fusion of 'protector' and 'predator': Herakles, the human lion (cf. *Megara* 5 etc.), is both, and fulfils both rôles badly – he neither protects nor 'captures' Hylas. Here is a second irony: the 'prey' is so close, yet never so far away.   ἔσπευσεν: cf. 50–1n.

64–71 Herakles' madness (71, cf. 2.51) has close parallels in descriptions of erotic frenzy (the Epicurean οἶστρος, cf. 6.28n.) from both 'high' and 'low' literature, cf. Pl. *Phdr.* 251d–e, ' … the entire soul, stung all over, goes mad with pain … in its madness it can neither sleep at night nor keep still where it is by day, but runs wherever it thinks it will see the possessor of the beauty it longs for …' (trans. Rowe). Less exalted is the frenzy which Simaitha wishes upon Delphis and the *erastai* of the magical papyri seek to arouse in those they desire: cf., e.g., *PGM* xxxvi 149–53 'make [*X*] love me [*Y*] with a love that wrenches her guts (ἔρωτι σπλαγχνίχωι) … if she wants to sleep, put whips of thorns under her (σιττύβας ἀκανθίνας) and spikes on her forehead'. Herakles' rampage through 'untrodden thorns' is thus an emotional, as well as a physical, journey; Posidippus, *Anth. Pal.* 12.98 (= *HE* 3074–7) portrays the poet bound by desire on a bed of thorns and tortured with fire, and κνίζειν is commonly used of erotic desire. Just as there are similarities between the fates of Daphnis and Hylas, so Herakles' crazed search and wandering place him in the rôle, not only of Demeter, but also of ἁ κώρα in Priapos' account of Daphnis' situation at 1.82–5, cf. n. ad loc.; Herakles' story has been assimilated to the archetypal bucolic story. Bion saw the similarity, for he combined the wild searchings of Herakles and the nameless girl for his picture of Aphrodite's search for the wounded Adonis, *EA* 19–24.

In *Arg.*, Herakles' rampage is compared to that of a bull which has been stung by a gadfly (οἶστρος) and 'has no thought for the herdsmen or the herd' (1.1266–7); thus T. has rewritten both of Apollonius' similes: the lion simile becomes the experimental paratactic simile of 62–3, and the bull simile is incorporated into the narrative. That Herakles forgets about the expedition is an extreme manifestation of the traditional idea (10.14, 11.11 etc.) that love drives everything else out of your mind; cf. *PGM* IV 2756–8 'may [X] come with all speed to my doors, crazy (μαινομένη), and forgetting her children, her friends and her parents'.

65 δεδόνητο 'raged out of control'; this unusual passive – Herakles has no 'active' control (70) – combines the whirl of Herakles' emotions with the rapid movement of his legs. The verb is used of the effect of love upon the emotions (Sappho fr. 130.1 Voigt, Bion fr. 9.5), but it is mad lust induced by magic which is again suggested here, cf. 2.31, Pind. *Pyth.* 4.218–19 (Aphrodite's magic working on Medea) ποθεινὰ δ᾽ Ἑλλὰς αὐτάν | ἐν φρασὶ καιομέναν δονέοι μάστιγι Πειθοῦς. Homer compares the panic which Athena induces in the suitors to that of heifers sent rushing off by the attack of a gadfly (ἐδόνησεν, *Od.* 22.300); T.'s verb therefore in part identifies the source of Apollonius' simile.   **ἐπελάμβανε** 'took in', 'covered'.

66–7 'Reckless are lovers, [when you consider] all the sufferings which Herakles endured as he wandered through mountains and thickets ...'. The generalisation now draws Nikias back into the poem, cf. 1–4.   **σχέτλιοι:** T. transfers to lovers a description more usually applied to Eros himself, cf. Theognis 1231 σχέτλι᾽ Ἔρως, Μανίαι σ᾽ ἐτιθηνήσαντο κτλ. (cf. 71), Simonides 575, *Arg.* 4.445–6 σχέτλι᾽ Ἔρως, μέγα πῆμα, μέγα στύγος ἀνθρώποισιν | ἐκ σέθεν οὐλόμενοι τ᾽ ἔριδες στοναχαί τε πόνοι τε.   **ὅσσ᾽ =** ὅτι τόσα, as commonly (K–G II 370–1). The construction would be more regular if the sentence had begun σχέτλιος ὁ Ἡρακλῆς. Most editors prefer to punctuate strongly after φιλέοντες and understand ἀλώμενος ὅσσ᾽ κτλ. as an exclamation; the position of ἀλώμενος, however, seems against this.   **ἐμόγησεν** evokes Herakles' labours, cf. 7n.   **οὔρεα καὶ δρυμώς:** the accusatives follow ἀλώμενος 'roam over/through', cf. Soph. *OC* 1686, K–G I 312–13. 'Thickets' emphasise Herakles' likeness to a lion (3.15–17n.).

68–9 Corrupt and hotly debated lines; to the commentaries add Latte (1968) 535–8, Griffiths (1996) 105–6, G. Santangelo, *RFIC* 99 (1971) 418–20, M. Campbell, *GIF* 4 (1973) 153–4.

As transmitted, ναῦς μὲν ἄρμεν' (68) is metrically faulty; Hermann's γέμεν has been the most popular solution, but the explicit contrast between the other Argonauts and Heracles, which μέν ... δέ (70) provides, has point, if 68 is to be retained. Secondly, τῶν παρεόντων is singularly weak; it may be a gloss or a makeweight for an already defective line. ἄρμενα 'tackle' may, but need not, include the sails (cf. 22.13, Livrea on *Arg.* 4.889); that ἱστία (69) was originally a gloss on ἄρμενα was suggested by Santangelo and Griffiths. The meaning 'supplies' for ἄρμενα perhaps deserves more attention than it has received. Thus, if 68 is by T., the text presents as yet unsolved problems, and deletion of this line is attractive.

It would seem that the Argonauts intend to leave as soon as Herakles returns; T.'s Argonauts, unlike Apollonius', are not silly enough not to notice that Herakles is not on board. Unless μεσονύκτιον is corrupt, this planned departure will be in the middle of the night. It is, however, the 'natural' interpretation of 32–4 that the Argonauts originally intended to sleep on the Mysian shore, and therefore – unless (Serrao (1971) 119–22) we accept that T. sacrificed narrative coherence to his desire for a 'bucolic camping scene' – something has apparently made them change their mind: perhaps a favourable weather sign, as the simile of 50–2 suggests, or because of some traditional detail not known to us and here omitted in T.'s rapid narrative. The alternative, that Mysia was never intended to be more than a brief stop for a meal, has been maintained by some critics.

69 ἐξεκάθαιρον: the meaning is unknown, and corruption has often been suspected (αὖτε καθαίρουν, 'took down again', Wordsworth). The Argonauts may be making ready or checking the sails, a job which would rightly follow the preparation of the ἄρμενα, but it is improbable that they are actually unfurling them (Σ glosses ἐξεκάθαιρον as ἐξήπλουν) before deciding to cast off. Alternatively, they are putting them away again because Herakles' absence has delayed their departure. In the latter case, ἐξεκάθαιρον, if sound, will mean something like 'stow away' (cf. *Arg.* 2.1262–3); in the former, 'prepare', 'make ready' has been proposed (Latte, Barigazzi). **ἡμίθεοι:** cf. 25–8n. The variant ἤιθεοι 'young men' would be an accurate enough description of the Argonauts, as the whole expedition is an ideal *rite de passage*, but in the present context it lacks point.

70 Cf. 14.41–2 (a girl teased about her lover) ἕπτετο ... ἇι πόδες ἆγον. The corresponding *Arg.* passage is particularly close, ἐς δὲ κέλευθον | τὴν θέεν ἧι πόδες αὐτοὶ [αὐτὸν: Fränkel] ὑπέκφερον ἀΐσσοντα (1.1263–4).

71 μαινόμενος: cf. 64–71n. A more famous madness caused Herakles to kill his children (8–15n.). This participle (cf. *Megara* 16) does not, however, appear to become part of the title of Euripides' famous play until much later.　　χαλεπὸς ... θεός: probably Eros, the subject of the poem, rather than Kypris, cf. 3.15 νῦν ἔγνων τὸν Ἔρωτα· βαρὺς θεός.　　ἧπαρ ἄμυσσεν: later philosophic theory, following Plato, identified the liver as the seat of irrational 'epithymetic' drives (cf. 'Timaeus of Locri' 100a2, p.138 Marg), but the poetic tradition had long seen it as the seat of violent emotion, particularly, though not exclusively, desire, cf. 11.16 (with Σ), *Anacreontea* 33.27–8 West (Eros) καί με τύπτει | μέσον ἧπαρ ὥσπερ οἶστρος (which includes the ideas from the corresponding passages of T. and Apollonius), Nisbet–Hubbard on Hor. *C.* 1.13.4. Tityos, who tried to rape Leto, was punished by having his liver constantly devoured (*Od.* 11.576–81) and became an image of the man tormented by unsatisfied sexual passion (cf. Kenney on Lucr. 3.992–4). Although the verb is not uncommonly used of emotional distress (Bacchyl. 17.19, 18.11), it continues the mixture of the emotional and physical introduced by ἀκάνθαις (64).

When T.'s Argonauts arrive at Phasis, Herakles' liver is being tormented. When Apollonius' heroes arrive, it is Prometheus' liver which is being literally torn out (2.1248–59), in a torment to which Herakles will put an end. Thus T. both inverts one of Herakles' great feats of heroism, and acknowledges the end of *Arg.* 2 as we approach Phasis.

72 Hylas, rather than Herakles, becomes one of 'the blessed ones', cf. 75n. The irony is not, however, all one way: 'Hylas is numbered among [partitive genitive] the blessed ones' leaves open whether he *really* is 'blessed'. When we last saw him, he was by no means resigned to his fate.　　οὕτω: cf. 11.80n.

73 Ἡρακλέην: a very rare accusative (Zwicker, *RE* VIII 521–2), found also at *Arg.* 2.767 in a passage referring to the events in Mysia and with a similar word-play to that found here, κάλλιπον ἥρω | Ἡρακλέην, cf. Köhnken (1996b) 461.　　λιποναύταν: the first explicit indication that the Argonauts did indeed leave Mysia without Herakles. λιποναύτιον seems to have been an offence in Attic law, cf. Lysias 12.42, Pollux 8.42, J. H. Lipsius, *Das attische Recht und Rechtsverfahren* (Leipzig 1915) 454. In T. it is Herakles who abandons his companions, not (as in *Arg.*) vice versa.

74 ἡρώησε 'quit', cf. 24.101. The word-play Ἡρακλέην ... ἥρωες ... ἡρώησε seems to 'mock' Herakles, just as the Argonauts did, cf. M. G. Bonanno, *QUCC* 24 (1986) 29–38. **τριακοντάζυγον:** the number of Argonauts is standardly given as fifty, i.e. the crew of much the most common size of 'epic' ship, but far more than fifty Argonaut names were known, cf. *RE* II 751–3, J. F. Carspecken, *YCS* 13 (1952) 42–3. A sixty-oared vessel is otherwise unattested. T. may reflect ancient debate about the matter, or the point may be that it cannot have been shortage of space which caused Herakles to leave the *Argo*; perhaps therefore the other heroes mocked him because he preferred the hard way of getting to Colchis – Herakles was indeed notorious for his treks all over the world (cf. *Arg.* 2.777–8 δι' Ἀσίδος ἠπείροιο | πεζὸς ἔβη).

75 Cf. *Arg.* 2.1277–8 Κολχίδα μὲν δὴ γαῖαν ἱκάνομεν ἠδὲ ῥέεθρα | Φάσιδος. In most extant accounts (though not Pindar's Fourth Pythian) Herakles did not in fact reach Colchis, or did not even go on the expedition at all, cf. Σ *Arg.* 1.1289–91, Hunter (1993a) 26; Σ ascribes the present version to T. himself. Herakles did, however, reach Colchis in the accounts of Dionysius Scytobrachion (*FGrHist* 32 F6b) and Demaretus (*FGrHist* 42 F2b), and in Antoninus Liberalis/Nicander he rejoins the *Argo*, although it is not made explicit whether he reached Colchis; Dionysius and Demaretus are probably later than T., though the matter is uncertain, cf. J. S. Rusten, *Dionysius Scytobrachion* (Cologne 1982) 85–92. Griffiths ((1996) 104, 109–11) deletes the line as an interpolation designed to remove the impropriety of a poem which ends with the mocking of Herakles, and he notes that verse narratives often conclude with a οὕνεκεν clause and that πεζᾶι is (most appropriately) a prosaic form (although this carries liitle weight in T.). Wilamowitz had achieved a similar result by strong punctuation after 74, thus making 75 an observation of the poet rather than part of the mockery of the Argonauts, cf. Di Marco (1995a) 133–4. δέ, however, seems a very weak particle with which to introduce a 'correction' of the previous lines. If 75 is retained, T. may make Herakles reach Colchis because otherwise he would leave him as he is in *Arg.*: on the way to the completion of his labours and a place on Olympos (*Arg.* 1.1317–20). By bringing him to Colchis, T. – through his constant evocation of *Arg.* – denies him the reward of divinity, cf. 1–2n. Such is the destructive power of Eros.   ἄξενον: the Black Sea was originally Ἄξεινος 'the Inhospitable' (cf. Braswell on Pind. *Pyth.* 4.203), and Colchis was to prove truly worthy of the name for the Argonauts; the later euphemism Εὔξεινος is first attested at Pind. *Nem.* 4.49.

BIBLIOGRAPHY

Works listed here are cited in the Introduction and Commentary by author and date only, e.g. Cameron (1995).

Alexiou, M. (1974) *The ritual lament in Greek tradition*. Cambridge.

Alpers, P. (1996) *What is Pastoral?* Chicago.

Arena, R. (1956) 'Studi sulla lingua di Teocrito' *Bollettino, Centro di Studi Filologici e Linguistici Siciliani* 4: 5–27.

Arend, W. (1933) *Die typischen Scenen bei Homer*. Berlin.

Arland, W. (1937) *Nachtheokritische Bukolik bis an die Schwelle der lateinischen Bukolik*. Dissertation Leipzig.

Arnott, W. G. (1984) 'Lycidas and double perspectives: a discussion of Theocritus' Seventh Idyll' *Estudios Clásicos* 26: 333–46.

    (1996) *Alexis: the fragments. A commentary*. Cambridge.

Asper, M. (1997) *Onomata allotria. Zur Genese, Struktur und Funktion poetologischer Metaphern bei Kallimachos*. Stuttgart.

Barigazzi, A. (1974) 'Per l'interpretazione e la datazione del carme IV di Teocrito' *Rivista di Filologia e di Istruzione Classica* 102: 301–11.

    (1975) 'Una presunta aporia nel C. 11 di Teocrito' *Hermes* 103: 179–88.

    (1995) 'Sull'*Ila* di Teocrito' in *Studia classica Iohanni Tarditi oblata* (Milan) I 159–70.

Berger, H. (1984) 'The origins of bucolic representation: disenchantment and revision in Theocritus' Seventh Idyll' *Classical Antiquity* 3: 1–39.

Bernsdorff, H. (1994) 'Polyphem und Daphnis. Zu Theokrits sechstem Idyll' *Philologus* 138: 38–51.

    (1995) 'Parataktische Gleichnisse bei Theokrit' in Harder–Regtuit–Wakker (1996) 71–88.

    (1996) *Die Darstellung von Hirten in der nicht-bukolischen Dichtung des Hellenismus*. Habilitationsschrift Göttingen.

Bing, P. (1988) *The well-read Muse. Present and past in Callimachus and the Hellenistic poets*. Göttingen.

Blech, M. (1982) *Studien zum Kranz bei den Griechen*. Berlin / New York.

Borgeaud, P. (1988) *The cult of Pan in ancient Greece*. Chicago / London.

Bowie, E. (1985) 'Theocritus' Seventh Idyll, Philetas and Longus' *Classical Quarterly* 35: 67–91.

(1996) 'Frame and framed in Theocritus Poems 6 and 7' in Harder–Regtuit–Wakker (1996) 91–100.

Braun, A. (1932) 'Gli "eolismi" a Cirene e nella poesia dorica' *Rivista di Filologia e di Istruzione Classica* 10: 181–93, 309–31.

Brioso Sánchez, M. (1976), (1977) 'Aportaciones al estudio del hexametro de Teocrito' *Habis* 7: 21–56, 8: 57–75.

Brooke, A. (1971) 'Theocritus' Idyll 11: a study in pastoral' *Arethusa* 4: 73–81.

Brown, E. L. (1981) 'The Lycidas of Theocritus' Idyll 7' *Harvard Studies in Classical Philology* 85: 59–100.

Brown, R. D. (1987) *Lucretius on love and sex*. Leiden.

Buck, C. D. (1955) *The Greek dialects*. Chicago.

Bühler, W. (1960) *Die Europa des Moschos*. Wiesbaden.

Burkert, W. (1992) *The orientalizing revolution*. Cambridge, Mass.

(1993) 'Bacchic *teletai* in the Hellenistic age' in T. H. Carpenter and C. A. Faraone, eds. *Masks of Dionysus* (Cornell) 259–75.

Burton, J. B. (1995) *Theocritus's urban mimes. Mobility, gender, and patronage*. Berkeley.

Buxton, R. (1994) *Imaginary Greece*. Cambridge.

Cairns, F. (1970) 'Theocritus Idyll 10' *Hermes* 98: 38–44.

(1972) *Generic composition in Greek and Roman poetry*. Edinburgh.

(1984) 'Theocritus' first idyll: the literary programme' *Wiener Studien* 97: 89–113.

(1992) 'Theocritus, Idyll 26' *Proceedings of the Cambridge Philological Society* 38: 1–38.

Calame, C. (1992) 'Espaces liminaux et voix discursives dans l'Idylle 1 de Théocrite: une civilisation de poète' in *Figures grecques de l'intermédiaire* (Lausanne) 59–85.

Cameron, A. (1995) *Callimachus and his critics*. Princeton.

Cameron, Archibald. (1963) 'The form of the *Thalysia*' in *Miscellanea di studi Alessandrini in memoria di Augusto Rostagni* (Turin) 291–307.

Campbell, M. (1990) 'Theocritus Thirteen' in E. M. Craik, ed. *'Owls to Athens'. Essays on classical subjects presented to Sir Kenneth Dover* (Oxford) 113–19.

Cassio, A. C. (1993) 'Iperdorismi callimachei e testo antico dei lirici

(Call. *Hy.* 5,109; 6,136)' in *Tradizione e innovazione nella cultura greca da Omero all'età ellenistica* (Rome) 903–10.

Chadwick, J. (1996) *Lexicographica Graeca*. Oxford.

Cozzoli, A.-T. (1994) 'Dalla catarsi mimetica aristotelica all'autocatarsi dei poeti ellenistici' *Quaderni Urbinati di Cultura Classica* 48: 95–110.

Dale, A. M. (1952) 'ΚΙΣΣΥΒΙΟΝ' *Classical Review* 2: 129–32.

Damon, C. (1995) 'Narrative and mimesis in the Idylls of Theocritus' *Quaderni Urbinati di Cultura Classica* 51: 101–23.

De Jong, I. J. F. (1987) *Narrators and focalisers: the presentation of the story in the Iliad*. Amsterdam.

Deuse, W. (1990) 'Dichtung als Heilmittel gegen die Liebe. Zum 11. Idyll Theokrits' in Steinmetz (1990) 59–76.

Di Benedetto, V. (1956) 'Omerismi e struttura metrica negli idilli dorici di Teocrito' *Annali della Scuola Normale Superiore di Pisa* 25: 48–60.

Di Gregorio, L. (1984) 'Variae lectiones studio dignae' in V. Pisani, ed. *Teocrito. Gli idilli e gli epigrammi* (2nd ed., Milan) 277–331.

Di Marco, M. (1995a) 'Il proemio dell'*Ila*: Teocrito, Apollonio e l' ἔρως παιδικός' *Eikasmos* 6: 121–39.

   (1995b) 'Lessico agonistico e sconfitta in amore: lo "strozzamento" di Molone (Theocr. *Id.* VII 125)' in *Studia classica Iohanni Tarditi oblata* (Milan) 1 625–38.

Dover, K. J. (1978) *Greek homosexuality*. London.

DuQuesnay, I. M. Le M. (1979) 'From Polyphemus to Corydon. Virgil, *Eclogue* 2 and the Idylls of Theocritus' in D. West and T. Woodman, eds. *Creative imitation and Latin literature* (Cambridge) 35–69, 206–21.

Edquist, H. (1975) 'Aspects of Theocritean otium' *Ramus* 4: 101–14.

Effe, B. ed. (1986) *Theokrit und die griechische Bukolik*. Darmstadt.

   (1989) 'Die griechische Bukolik' in B. Effe and G. Binder, eds. *Die antike Bukolik: eine Einführung* (Munich/Zurich) 11–56.

   (1992) 'Die Hylas-Geschichte bei Theokrit und Apollonios Rhodios' *Hermes* 120: 299–309.

Elliger, W. (1975) *Die Darstellung der Landschaft in der griechischen Dichtung*. Berlin / New York.

Erbse, H. (1965) 'Dichtkunst und Medizin in Theokrits 11. Idyll' *Museum Helveticum* 22: 232–6 [= Effe (1986) 286–92].

Ettin, A. V. (1984) *Literature and the pastoral*. New Haven / London.

Fabiano, G. (1971) 'Fluctuation in Theocritus' style' *Greek, Roman, and Byzantine Studies* 12: 517–37 [= Effe (1986) 13–35].

Fantuzzi, M. (1988) *Ricerche su Apollonio Rodio*. Rome.

(1993a) 'Il sistema letterario della poesia alessandrina nel III sec. A.C.' in G. Cambiano, L. Canfora, D. Lanza, eds. *Lo spazio letterario della Grecia antica* 1.2 (Rome) 31–73.

(1993b) 'Teocrito e la poesia bucolica' in G. Cambiano, L. Canfora, D. Lanza, eds. *Lo spazio letterario della Grecia antica* 1.2 (Rome) 145–95.

(1995a) 'Variazioni sull'esametro in Teocrito' in M. Fantuzzi and R. Pretagostini, eds. *Struttura e storia dell'esametro greco* (Rome) 221–64.

(1995b) 'Mythological paradigms in the bucolic poetry of Theocritus' *Proceedings of the Cambridge Philological Society* 41: 16–35.

(1998a) 'Textual misadventures of Daphnis: the pseudo-Theocritean Id. 8 and the origins of the bucolic "manner"' in Harder–Regtuit–Wakker (1998) 61–79.

(1998b) 'Theocritus and the demythologising of poetry' in M. Depew and D. Obbink, eds. *Matrices of genre*. Cambridge, Mass.

Fellmann, B. (1972) *Die antiken Darstellungen des Polyphemabenteuers*. Munich.

Fraser, P. M. (1972) *Ptolemaic Alexandria*. Oxford.

Fuchs, H. (1969) *Die Hylasgeschichte bei Apollonios Rhodios und Theokrit*. Dissertation Würzburg.

Furusawa, Y. (1980) *Eros und Seelenruhe in den Thalysien Theokrits*. Würzburg.

Gallavotti, C. (1952) *Lingua, tecnica e poesia negli Idilli di Teocrito*. Rome.

(1966) 'Le coppe istoriate di Teocrito e di Virgilio' *Parola del Passato* 21: 421–36.

(1984) 'Nuovi papiri di Teocrito' *Bollettino dei Classici* 5: 3–42.

Gantz, T. (1993) *Early Greek myth. A guide to literary and artistic sources*. Baltimore/London.

Gershenson, D. E. (1969) 'Averting Βασκανία in Theocritus: a compliment' *California Studies in Classical Antiquity* 2: 145–55.

Giangrande, G. (1977) 'Aphrodite and the oak-trees' *Museum Philologum Londiniense* 2: 177–86.

(1980) *Scripta minora Alexandrina* 1. Amsterdam.

(1981) *Scripta minora Alexandrina* 2. Amsterdam.

Goldhill, S. (1991) *The poet's voice.* Cambridge.

(1994) 'The naive and knowing eye: ecphrasis and the culture of viewing in the Hellenistic world' in S. Goldhill and R. Osborne, eds. *Art and text in ancient Greek culture* (Cambridge) 197–223.

Griffin, J. (1992) 'Theocritus, the *Iliad*, and the east' *American Journal of Philology* 113: 189–211.

Griffiths, A. (1996) 'Customising Theocritus: Poems 13 and 24' in Harder–Regtuit–Wakker (1996) 101–18.

Griffiths, F. T. (1979) *Theocritus at court.* Leiden.

Gutzwiller, K. J. (1981) *Studies in the Hellenistic epyllion.* Königstein.

(1991) *Theocritus' pastoral analogies. The formation of a genre.* Madison, Wisc.

(1996) 'The evidence for Theocritean poetry books' in Harder–Regtuit–Wakker (1996) 119–48.

Haber, J. (1994) *Pastoral and the poetics of self-contradiction.* Cambridge.

Halperin, D. M. (1983a) *Before pastoral: Theocritus and the ancient tradition of bucolic poetry.* New Haven / London.

(1983b) 'The forebears of Daphnis' *Transactions of the American Philological Association* 113: 183–200.

Harder, M. A., Regtuit, R. F., Wakker, G. C., eds. (1996) *Theocritus.* Groningen.

(1998) *Genre in Hellenistic poetry.* Groningen.

Hasebroek, J. (1921) *Das Signalelement in den Papyrusurkunden.* Berlin/ Leipzig.

Hatzikosta, S. (1982) *A stylistic commentary on Theocritus' Idyll VII.* Amsterdam.

Henderson, J. (1975) *The maculate Muse.* New Haven / London.

Henrichs, A. 1980. 'Riper than a pear: Parian invective in Theokritos' *Zeitschrift für Papyrologie und Epigraphik* 39: 7–27.

Heubeck, A. (1973) 'Einige Überlegungen zu Theokrits Thalysien' *Ziva Antika* 23: 5–15 [= *Kleine Schriften zur griechischen Sprache und Literatur*, Erlangen 1984, 233–43].

Himmelmann, N. (1980) *Über Hirten-Genre in der antiken Kunst.* Opladen.

Holland, G. R. (1884) 'De Polyphemo et Galatea' *Leipziger Studien zur classischen Philologie* 7: 139–312.

Hopkinson, N. (1984) *Callimachus, Hymn to Demeter.* Cambridge.

(1988) *A Hellenistic anthology.* Cambridge.

Horstmann, A. E.-A. (1976) *Ironie und Humor bei Theokrit*. Meisenheim am Glan.

Hunter, R. L. (1983a) *Eubulus, the fragments*. Cambridge.

(1983b) *A study of Daphnis & Chloe*. Cambridge.

(1985) *The New Comedy of Greece and Rome*. Cambridge.

(1989) *Apollonius of Rhodes, Argonautica Book III*. Cambridge.

(1993a) *The Argonautica of Apollonius. Literary studies*. Cambridge.

(1993b) 'The presentation of Herodas' *Mimiamboi*' *Antichthon* 27: 31–44.

(1995) 'The divine and human map of the *Argonautica*' *Syllecta Classica* 6: 13–27.

(1996a) *Theocritus and the archaeology of Greek poetry*. Cambridge.

(1996b) 'Mime and mimesis: Theocritus, Idyll 15' in Harder–Regtuit–Wakker (1996) 149–69.

(1997) 'Longus and Plato' in M. Picone, B. Zimmermann, eds. *Der antike Roman und seine mittelalterliche Rezeption* (Basel) 15–28.

(1998) 'Before and after epic: Theocritus (?), Idyll 25' in Harder–Regtuit–Wakker (1998).

Hutchinson, G. (1988) *Hellenistic poetry*. Oxford.

Isenberg, C. and Konstan, D. (1984) 'Pastoral desire: the third idyll of Theocritus' *Dalhousie Review* 64: 302–15.

Kelly, S. T. (1983) 'The song of time: Theocritus' Seventh Idyll' *Quaderni Urbinati di Cultura Classica* 44: 103–15.

Knox, P. (1993) 'Philetas and Roman poetry' *Papers of the Leeds International Latin Seminar* 7: 61–83.

Könnecke, O. (1917) 'Zu Theokrit 11' *Philologus* 74: 283–312.

Köhnken, A. (1965) *Apollonios Rhodios und Theokrit*. Göttingen.

(1996a) 'Theokrits Polyphemgedichte' in Harder–Regtuit–Wakker (1996) 171–86.

(1996b) 'Paradoxien in Theokrits Hylasgedicht' *Hermes* 124: 442–62.

Krevans, N. (1983) 'Geography and the literary tradition in Theocritus 7' *Transactions of the American Philological Association* 113: 201–20.

(1993) 'Fighting against Antimachus: the *Lyde* and the *Aetia* reconsidered' in M. A. Harder, R. F. Regtuit, G. C. Wakker, eds. *Callimachus* (Groningen) 149–60.

Kuchenmüller, W. (1928) *Philetae Coi reliquiae*. Dissertation Berlin.

Kühn, J.-H. (1958) 'Die Thalysien Theokrits (id. 7)' *Hermes* 86: 40–79.

Kunst, C. (1887) *De Theocriti versu heroico*. Leipzig.

Latte, K. (1951) Review of Gow's *Theocritus*. *Gnomon* 23: 252–7. (1968) *Kleine Schriften*. Munich.

Lattimore, R. (1962) *Themes in Greek and Latin epitaphs*. Urbana.

Laubscher, H. P. (1982) *Fischer und Landleute. Studien zur hellenistischen Genreplastik*. Mainz.

Lawall, G. (1967) *Theocritus' Coan pastorals*. Washington, D.C.

Legrand, P. E. (1898) *Etude sur Théocrite*. Paris.

Lembach, K. (1970) *Die Pflanzen bei Theokrit*. Heidelberg.

Leutner, W. G. (1907) *The article in Theocritus*. Dissertation Johns Hopkins.

Lindsell, A. (1937) 'Was Theocritus a botanist?' *Greece & Rome* 6: 78–93.

Lissarrague, F. (1990) 'The sexual life of satyrs' in D. M. Halperin *et al.*, eds. *Before sexuality* (Princeton) 53–81.

Macleod, C. (1983) *Collected essays*. Oxford.

Manakidou, F. (1993) *Beschreibung von Kunstwerken in der hellenistischen Dichtung*. Stuttgart.

Manuwald, B. (1990) 'Der Kyklop als Dichter. Bemerkungen zu Theokrit, *Eid.* 11' in Steinmetz (1990) 77–91.

Mastronarde, D. J. (1968) 'Theocritus' Idyll 13: love and the hero' *Transactions of the American Philological Association* 99: 273–90.

Meillier, C. (1982) 'La fonction thérapeutique de la musique et de la poésie dans le recueil des "Bucoliques" de Théocrite' *Bull. Association Guillaume Budé* 1982, 164–86.

(1989) 'Un echo épicurien chez Théocrite et le code de la Φιλαλήθεια' *Kentron* 5: 115–34.

Michaelides, S. (1978) *The music of ancient Greece. An encyclopaedia*. London.

Miles, G. B. (1977) 'Characterization and the ideal of innocence in Theocritus' Idylls' *Ramus* 6: 139–64 [= Effe (1986) 138–67].

Monteil, P. (1968) *Théocrite, Idylles (II, V, VII, XI, XV)*. Paris.

Murley, C. (1940) 'Plato's *Phaedrus* and Theocritean pastoral' *Transactions of the American Philological Association* 71: 281–95.

Nauta, R. R. (1990) 'Gattungsgeschichte als Rezeptionsgeschichte am Beispiel der Entstehung der Bukolik' *Antike und Abendland* 36: 116–37.

Nicosia, S. (1968) *Teocrito e l'arte figurata*. Palermo.

Nöthiger, M. (1971) *Die Sprache des Stesichorus und des Ibycus*. Zürich.

Norden, E. (1913) *Agnostos Theos. Untersuchungen zur Formengeschichte religiöser Rede*. Berlin.

Nussbaum, M. (1994) *The therapy of desire*. Princeton.

O'Neill, E. G. (1942) 'The localization of metrical word-types in the Greek hexameter' *Yale Classical Studies* 8: 105–78.

Onians, R. B. (1954) *The origins of European thought*. 2nd ed., Cambridge.

Otis, B. (1964) *Virgil. A study in civilized poetry*. Oxford.

Ott, U. (1969) *Die Kunst des Gegensatzes in Theokrits Hirtengedichten*. Hildesheim / New York.

(1972) 'Theokrits "Thalysien" und ihre literarischen Vorbilder' *Rheinisches Museum* 115: 134–49.

Page, D. L. (1955) *Sappho and Alcaeus*. Oxford.

Parker, R. (1983) *Miasma*. Oxford.

Paton, W. R. and Hicks, E. L. (1891) *The inscriptions of Cos*. Oxford.

Pearce, T. E. V. (1988) 'The function of the *locus amoenus* in Theocritus' seventh poem' *Rheinisches Museum* 131: 276–304.

Perrotta, G. (1978) *Poesia ellenistica. Scritti minori II*. Rome.

Petroll, R. (1965) *Die Äusserungen Theokrits über seine Person und seine Dichtung*. Dissertation Hamburg.

Petropoulos, J. C. B. (1994) *Heat and lust. Hesiod's midsummer festival scene revisited*. Lanham, Maryland.

Petropoulou, D. A. (1959) 'Θεοκρίτου εἰδύλλια ὑπὸ λαογραφικὴν ἔποψιν ἑρμηνευόμενα' ΛΑΟΓΡΑΦΙΑ 18: 5–93.

Pfeiffer, R. (1968) *History of classical scholarship from the beginnings to the end of the Hellenistic age*. Oxford.

Pickard-Cambridge, A. (1962) *Dithyramb, tragedy, and comedy*. 2nd ed., Oxford.

Pollitt, J. J. (1986) *Art in the Hellenistic age*. Cambridge.

Prescott, H. W. (1899) 'A study of the Daphnis myth' *Harvard Studies in Classical Philology* 10: 121–40.

Pretagostini, R. (1984) *Ricerche sulla poesia alessandria*. Rome.

(1992) 'Tracce di poesia orale nei carmi di Teocrito' *Aevum Antiquum* 5: 67–87.

Puelma, M. (1960) 'Die Dichterbegegnung in Theokrits "Thalysien"' *Museum Helveticum* 17: 144–64 [= *Labor et Lima. Kleine Schriften* (Basel 1995) 217–37].

Radt, S. L. (1971) 'Theocritea' *Mnemosyne* 24: 251–9.

Reed, J. (1997) *Bion of Smyrna. The fragments and the Adonis*. Cambridge.

Reinhardt, T. (1988) *Die Darstellung der Bereiche Stadt und Land bei Theokrit*. Bonn.

Rengakos, A. (1993) *Der Homertext und die hellenistischen Dichter*. Stuttgart.

(1994) *Apollonios Rhodios und die antike Homererklärung*. Munich.

Richardson, S. (1990) *The Homeric narrator*. Nashville.

Ridgway, B. S. (1990) *Hellenistic sculpture* I. *The styles of c. 331–200 BC*. Bristol.

Rosenmeyer, T. G. (1969) *The green cabinet. Theocritus and the European pastoral lyric*. Berkeley.

Rossi, L. E. (1972) 'L'*Ila* di Teocrito: epistola poetica ed epillio' in *Studi classici in onore di Quintino Cataudella* (Catania) II 279–93.

Ruijgh, C. J. (1984) 'Le Dorien de Théocrite: dialecte cyrénien d'Alexandrie et d'Egypte' *Mnemosyne* 37: 56–88.

Sanchez-Wildberger, M. (1955) *Theokrit-Interpretationen*. Dissertation Zurich.

Schmidt, E. A. (1987) *Bukolische Leidenschaft*. Frankfurt / Bern / New York.

Schmiel, R. (1993) 'Structure and meaning in Theocritus 11' *Mnemosyne* 46: 229–34.

Schmitt, A. (1981) 'Ironie und Spiel bei Theokrit?' *Würzburger Jahrbücher für die Altertumswissenschaft* 15: 107–18.

(1997) 'Bukolik bei Theokrit – über den Ursprung einer europäischen Dichtungsgattung' in W. Düsing, ed. *Tradition der Lyrik. Festschrift für Hans-Henrik Krummacher* (Tübingen) 3–13.

Schweizer, H. (1937) *Aberglaube und Zauberei bei Theokrit*. Dissertation Basel.

Schwinge, E.-R. (1974) 'Theokrits "Dichterweihe" (Idyll 7)' *Philologus* 118: 40–58.

Seeck, G. A. (1975a) 'Zu Theokrit Eid. 7' *Hermes* 103: 384.

(1975b) 'Dichterische Technik in Theokrits "Thalysien" und die Theorie der Hirtendichtung' in ΔΩΡΗΜΑ, *Hans Diller zum 70. Geburtstag* (Athens) 195–209.

Segal, C. (1981) *Poetry and myth in ancient pastoral*. Princeton.

Serrao, G. (1971) *Problemi di poesia alessandrina* I. *Studi su Teocrito*. Rome.

(1995) 'All'origine della *recusatio-excusatio*: Teocrito e Callimaco' *Eikasmos* 6: 141–52.

Sherwin-White, S. (1978) *Ancient Cos*. Göttingen.

Sicherl, M. (1972) 'El paraclausithyron en Teócrito' *BIEH* 6: 57–62.

Spofford, E. W. (1969) 'Theocritus and Polyphemus' *American Journal of Philology* 90: 22–35.

Stanzel, K.-H. (1995) *Liebende Hirten. Theokrits Bukolik und die alexandrinische Poesie*. Stuttgart/Leipzig.

Stark, R. (1963) 'Theocritea' *Maia* 15: 359–85.

Steinmetz, P. ed. (1990) *Beiträge zur hellenistischen Literatur und ihrer Rezeption in Rom*. Stuttgart.

Strano, M. (1976) 'Considerazioni sul'idillio x di Teocrito' *Helikon* 15/16: 454–60.

Trencsényi-Waldapfel, I. (1966) 'Werden und Wesen der bukolischen Poesie' *Acta Antiqua* 14: 1–31.

Van Erp Taalman Kip, A. M. (1994) 'Intertextuality and Theocritus 13' in I. J. F. De Jong and J. P. Sullivan, eds. *Modern critical theory and classical literature* (Leiden) 153–69.

Van Groningen, B. A. (1959) 'Quelques problèmes de la poésie bucolique grecque' *Mnemosyne* 12: 24–53.

Van Sickle, J. (1969) 'The fourth pastoral poems of Virgil and Theocritus' *Arcadia. Accademia Letteraria Italiana, Atti e Memorie* 5: 129–48

(1970) 'Poetica teocritea' *Quaderni Urbinati di Cultura Classica* 9: 67–83.

(1975) 'Epic and bucolic (Theocritus, Idyll. vII; Virgil, Ecl. i)' *Quaderni Urbinati di Cultura Classica* 19: 45–72.

(1976) 'Theocritus and the development of the conception of bucolic genre' *Ramus* 5: 18–44.

Vaughn, J. W. (1981) 'Theocritus Vergilianus and Liber Bucolicon' *Aevum* 55: 47–68.

Vox, O. (1985) 'Il contrasto di Batto e Coridone nell'idillio iv di Teocrito' *Materiali e Discussioni per l'analisi dei testi classici* 15: 173–8.

Wackernagel, J. (1953) *Kleine Schriften*. Göttingen.

Wakker, G. C. (1996) 'The discourse function of particles. Some observations on the use of μάν/μήν in Theocritus' in Harder–Regtuit–Wakker (1996) 247–63.

Walker, S. F. (1980) *Theocritus*. Boston.

Walsh, G. B. (1985) 'Seeing and feeling: representation in two poems of Theocritus' *Classical Philology* 80: 1–19.

Waszink, J. H. (1974) *Biene und Honig als Symbol des Dichters und der Dichtung in der griechisch-römischen Antike*. Opladen.

Watson, L. (1991) *Arae. The curse poetry of antiquity*. Leeds.

Weingarth, G. (1967) *Zu Theokrits 7. Idyll*. Dissertation Freiburg.

Wendel, C. (1920) *Überlieferung und Entstehung der Theokrit-Scholien*. Berlin.

West, M. L. (1982) *Greek metre*. Oxford.

(1992) *Ancient Greek music*. Oxford.

White, H. (1979) *Studies in Theocritus and other Hellenistic poets*. Amsterdam.

Whitehorne, J. E. G. (1974) 'The reapers: Theocritus "Idyll" 10' *AUMLA* 41: 30–49.

Wilamowitz-Moellendorff, U. von. (1906) *Die Textgeschichte der griechischen Bukoliker*. Berlin.

(1924) *Hellenistische Dichtung*. Berlin.

Williams, F. (1971) 'A theophany in Theocritus' *Classical Quarterly* 21: 137–45 [= Effe (1986) 271–85].

Winter, D. R. (1974) 'Theocritus' Thalysia'. Dissertation Ohio State.

Wright, J. R. G. (1983) 'Virgil's pastoral programme: Theocritus, Callimachus and *Eclogue* 1' *Proceedings of the Cambridge Philological Society* 29: 107–60.

Zanker, G. (1987) *Realism in Alexandrian poetry: a literature and its audience*. London.

Zeitlin, F. I. (1994) 'Gardens of desire in Longus's *Daphnis and Chloe*: nature, art, and imitation' in J. Tatum, ed. *The search for the ancient novel* (Baltimore/London) 148–70.

(1996) *Playing the other. Gender and society in classical Greek literature*. Chicago/London.

Zimmerman, C. (1994) *The pastoral Narcissus. A study of the First Idyll of Theocritus*. Lanham, Maryland.

INDEXES

Italic numbers refer to pages, non-italic to line-numbers of the Commentary.

1 Subject

There is no entry for 'Homer (imitation of, variation from etc.)'.

2 Greek words

3 Passages discussed